"Original, deftly crafted, as well as an inherently fascinating and fun read from start to finish, *Shift* is an extraordinary and unique contemporary 'alternate world' fantasy that is all the more impressive when considering that it is author J.P. Lee's debut as a novelist and launching her *The Shiftwork Chronicles* series. Especially and unreservedly recommended for high school and community library Science Fiction & Fantasy Fiction collections, Shift is an expert blending of fantasy, suspense, romance, and adventure."

— Jim Cox, Midwest Book Review

"Welcome to a world that is almost familiar and yet filled with magic. J.P. Lee introduces a compelling scene of political intrigue and personal struggle that tugs at your desire to explore its depths and nuances. A true YA tale, it follows Sybil through coming of age experiences, family loyalty struggles, questions of morality, and budding relationships. I would recommend this book to any young adult (or young at heart!) who loves non-occult magic, clean (kissing only) romance, relational and political twists and turns, and all-is-not-as-it-seems! Warning: it leaves you wanting to know what happens next!"

— B.W. Green, author of *Lifeblood*

"*Shift* by J.P. Lee is a propulsive story that will captivate readers with its world building and character development. Lee writes with clarity and intensity, crafting a twisty plot that will make you root for the scrappy Sybil and her kin. Tackling found family, prejudice, ostracization, young love and more, *Shift* is a coming-of-age narrative that will have readers begging to spend more time in the magical world of Americana. A must-read for fans of Suzanne Collins and Rebecca Ross."

— Alexandria Faulkenbury, author of *Somewhere Past the End*

"*Shift* is an unflinching exploration of societal inequality and belonging with a rugged mountain backdrop. A seamless mingling of magic and grit, Lee offers high-stakes, political intrigue, and multifaceted characters that will keep you turning pages late into the night."

— Kimberly Dunham, author of *Betwixt*

"I enjoyed this twist on the typical YA novel. Our protagonist, Sybil, is raised to become a criminal for hire. Not only is her shapeshifting skill highly well developed, but she also has an in with her older brother, who gets her put on an assignment. The political game is just beginning as Sybil steps into the outside world. She is determined, observant, and ready to prove herself. The shapeshifting element continuously drew me in, making me want to keep reading. I was fascinated by the main character and the way she views the world and circumstances she finds herself in. I would love to continue this series and see where this political game is headed."

— Holly D. Morgan, author of the *Disparate Energy* novels

"*Shift* is a dynamic, immersive, and twisty tale where things are not what they appear and intrigue lurks beneath the surface. Lee weaves a masterful story that contemplates morality (or lack thereof) in humanity and blurs the lines between good and bad. Set in a lush, re-imagined America, you can't help but root for the plucky Sybil as she faces the journey laid before her. *Shift's* unique blend of fantasy, history, intrigue and so much more make it an appealing read for not just young adults or historical or fantastical fiction lovers; but quite simply, for anyone who just wants to read a good book."

—Meredith (early reader review)

"It's the kind of writing that makes a story actually stick with you—when you can't quite tell who to trust... is a memorable read."

"Filled with magic, mystery, and political intrigue, *Shift* is an absolute treat for young adult fantasy fans...Fantasy fans will love this series."

"...readers cannot help but turn those pages one after the other...it will leave you thinking about it long after you finish reading. *Shift* ticks all the right boxes with action, adventure, found family, and a little bit of romance.

— 5-Star Reviews, *Reader's Choice*

Shift

Shift

J.P. Lee

ah
Apprentice
House Press
Loyola University Maryland

First Edition

Library of Congress Control Number: 2025948867

Casebound ISBN: 978-1-62720-656-3
Paperback ISBN: 978-1-62720-657-0
Ebook ISBN: 978-1-62720-658-8

Cover by Maria Spada
Internal Design by Ben Turner and Cecelia Durborow
Editorial Development by Ben Turner
Promotional Development by Colleen Bayley

Published by Apprentice House Press

Loyola University Maryland
4501 N. Charles Street, Baltimore, MD 21210
410.617.5265
www.ApprenticeHouse.com
info@ApprenticeHouse.com

To my husband and my son,
You are my inspiration, my dream, and my greatest adventure. I love you always.

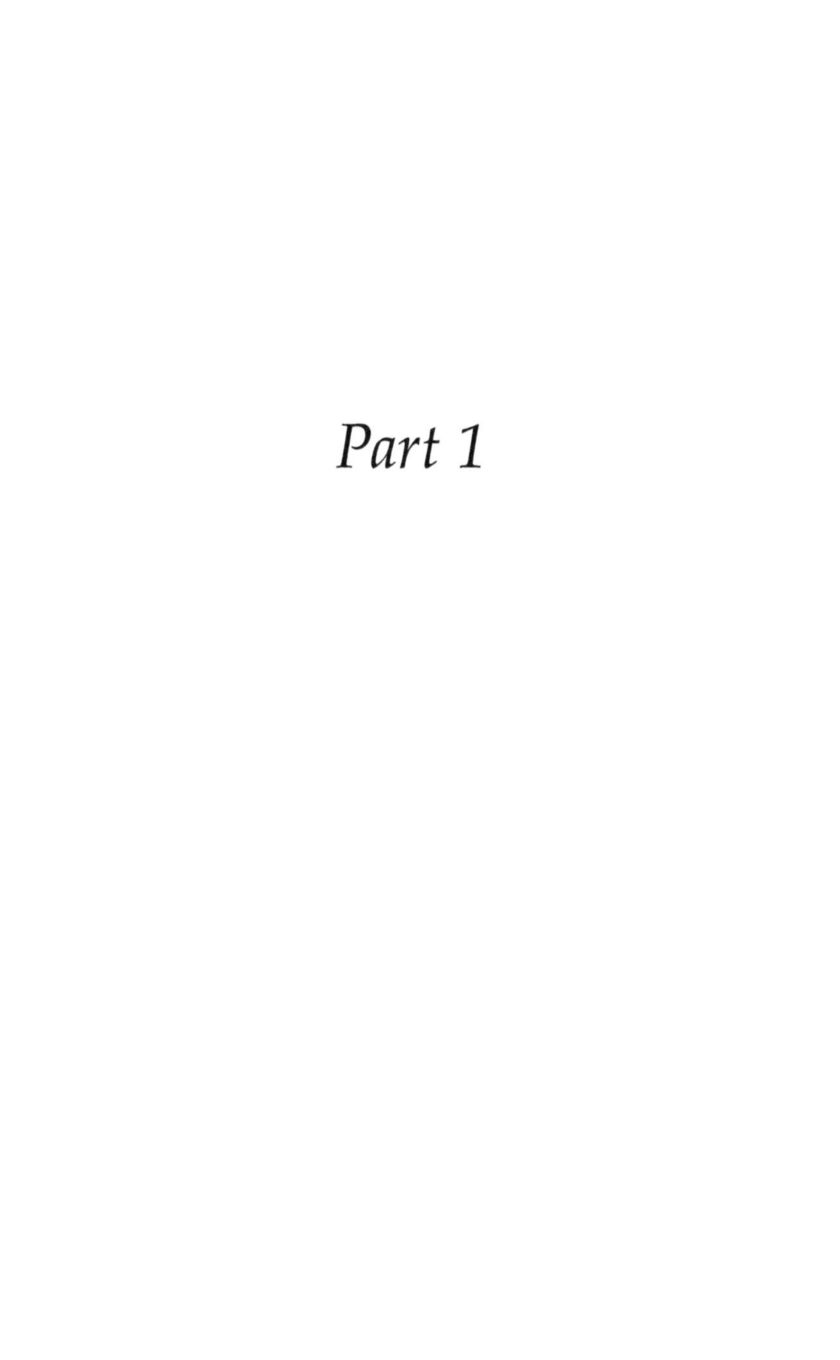

Part 1

1.

The magi of Eastward Americana were a comfortable sort of folk. They valued consistency, predictability, order, and control. Magic in and of itself was considered a rather unrestrained element, but the Eastward magi had spent the last century perfecting what magic could and should be in an era of peace and prosperity. The magi were quite proud of this, of how their skills and strengths fit so neatly into organized categories with strategic purposes.

The Eastward magi—as they referred to themselves, the 20th century wizards of their time—were composed of three branches of magic that encompassed the care of their world and each other. There were the Sages, who, as far as they were concerned, were the eldest branch. As they were the most knowing and the wisest, it was only reasonable they should be the most ancient, though no one knew for sure. Only legends remained of Origin and the Ancient Days, and little fact. But Sages, with their foresight and influence over the mind, slid naturally into roles of leadership and education, although they were the fewest in number.

The Thanes were a powerful force, both in number and capability. Their magic strengthened them, secured them, and destroyed others. They found themselves meeting the needs of Eastward as the militia, the security officers, and the strategists. They were defenders of Eastward until their dying breaths, although this had yet to play out due to the peace the land found itself in.

Next came the *Sylvaar*, who were in truth the most ancient *and* the greatest in number. They came from the forests across the sea not long after Origin and rooted themselves in the expansive, ever beautiful Americana. But now, in Eastward, they humbly lived out their days enjoying all manner of handy work and labor. From farming to healing, weather watching to crafting, the Sylvaar were grounded in their land, which seemingly underwent both change and unchange over hundreds of years.

And so you see, they made Eastward as orderly as they themselves were. Rows of homes painted in pastel colors, sidewalks with not a crack in them, white-washed fences framing blooming gardens, neatly plowed rows of farmland, and organized cities of brick and stone. The magi perhaps took for granted their harmony and prosperity. Some criticized their isolation from the rest of the world and disinterest in its affairs; but none could say they were not thriving. They had found their stride as a young country off the heels of independence. It was a most excellent time to be a magi, as any of them would tell you if you stopped them upon a cobblestone street.

But they had a problem. A small problem, granted—in the larger picture, as many a Sage would insist—but it was still a problem. It dwelt in Appalachia.

No one in Eastward liked to think much at all about what lurked in the Appalachian Highlands. Truly, it'd be more correct to say *who* dwelt in the mountains, but even that seemed too generous an acknowledgment for most. They were too disorderly, too unpredictable, and their magic was much too untidy. They were the only present threat to the magi. They were the topic brought up at every presidential election and every *Haervest* and *Christmaesse* supper.

They're called *Shifts;* a grisly kind of people not quite considered magi but most certainly not devoid of magic. It was just that their magic seemed to have no place in Eastward, and no one knew what to do with them. What value did it add to have a Shift around, constantly changing their appearance? They had joined the other magi around Independence from Westward, but their lives under Westwardian rule were a long-lost memory, even to themselves who were always more concerned about the present than their past.

It wasn't long before the new country of Eastward realized Shifts were volatile. Too volatile for their tastes. They were hot-headed, quick-tempered, passionate, and proud. Their magic reflected this. They relished how unnerved the other residents of Eastward were with their nasty tricks of impersonation and habits of shapeshifting at random. And it was all they could do. There was no other aspect to their magic. What good could magi like that do for Eastward?

The Shifts, though quite bad-tempered, were not stupid. They recognized the problem before any other branch of magi did. Conflict was born. The Sages sought resolution, but even they struggled to agree on how to find the Shifts a proper position in society. The Sylvaar wanted them gone, and the Thanes could not help but emphasize the threats the Shifts posed to Eastward. They could not be contained, nor could they be tracked. They could assume others' identities, and, for all intents and purposes, they could completely *disappear*. How could they be held to the same standard as the rest of the magi? And God knows the Shifts had demonstrated little honor to uphold Eastward's values.

The conflict persisted for nearly a decade until the remaining Shifts were finally rounded up and restricted into small communities, although many magi wanted them eradicated or sent out from Eastward entirely. Only the Sages showed grace and reminded the rest of the magi of the Shifts' crucial participation in their Independence. Unfortunately, nothing is quite so simple as that, and that was far from the end of the Shifts.

They proved, in fact, to be quite problematic. However, they could also be adaptive and tenacious. They knew their magic held power that the others' did not, and, before long, a select few magi came to the same conclusion. It was peculiar, to say the least, but the ability to become another would play a key role in the future of Eastward as leaders came and went and titans of industry rose up and crashed down again.

Behind it all were Shifts—impersonating and manipulating. Thanks to a handful of greedy and power-hungry magi, the Shifts had at long-last found their purpose in Eastward; and Eastward had to come to terms with the fact that their Shift problem was far from over.

It would've been easy to send the Thanes in and be rid of the Shifts once and for all, but the red tape surrounding a government-sanctioned genocide was astronomical and terribly bad for morale. The Sages ran an interesting study not long after the Shifts' new role had been recognized by the public and learned that crime as a whole had gone down in Eastward. No one had any desire to offend those who had the resources and connections to hire a Shift. And you had to have connections to get one.

Thus, the Eastward magi straightened up even more, hoping a blameless life would keep them from drawing the attention of a Shift. And it seemed, the Sages' study revealed, that having a handful of semi-controlled, professional criminals to handle their dirty work within society drew the average citizen away from petty crime.

A subject of great contention, even now, but the Shifts were allowed to stay in their bordered communities until someone had need of their services. It's really quite reasonable then why the magi winced at the thought of Appalachia and the people who resided there. Would their Shift problem ever go away?

Not that the Shifts had much say in the matter. This sentiment was felt acutely by many Shifts but none more than the young who had yet to make it off the mountain for work, including Sybil.

She was an ordinary young woman, as Shifts tended to be, with wavy brown hair, honey-colored eyes, and an angular face. Her only unique features were the freckles that splashed across her cheeks. She was not unlovely. Her wide-set eyes and pretty smile caught the admiration of more than one, but most would still consider her to be average.

Her every memory was of this place, filled with her kin, within its Thaneish borders. It was all she knew, and, at seventeen, it would be another year or more before she would have the chance to know what else was out there.

She sat before a stone fireplace, long gone out, with a worn quilt drawn about her narrow shoulders. Frigid air blew in from cracks in the walls, and the old cabin creaked and groaned. It was the symphony to which she fell asleep most nights in these long winter months. She missed the cacophony of frogs, bugs, and birds that sang her to sleep in the summer.

It could be quite boring being an underage Shift. You had to wait within the confines of the *beorg* (what they themselves called their mountain home) which was only a handful of acres. There was little to explore and little area to hunt or forage—a special tactic, no doubt, by the elites who managed the Shifts. It kept them dependent on their employment to Eastward, forcing a reliance on this employment just to bring food home. Outside of the thirteen roughly hewn, mostly dilapidated wood cabins the seventy or so Shifts shared, there were two outhouses, a storehouse, and a small gathering hall, which had recently been finished. One could only play tag or hide-and-seek in the woods so much as a child before it became very dull.

It could be quite interesting once training began. Aside from perfecting one's shapeshifting capabilities, there was also a variety of other skills that needed mastering, which enabled them to perform crime at a higher level. Practicing with pistols, knives, and daggers, as well as wrestling and boxing with each other, proved entertaining, both to partake in and to observe. Sybil had once spent several hours practicing breaking into a safe that one Shift had smuggled back from a job.

And there were the stories. Stories of operations accomplished, of what life was like outside their borders, of what to expect, and what you needed to know about the magi.

So, it wasn't all boring, and it was far from aimless, at least some of the time. But it was winter now, and no one felt like storytelling. There was little to do in the long dark days but sit around and stoke the meager fires.

Sybil stared into the dying embers. They needed more firewood badly, and she dreaded the task of bundling up to chop more when daylight came about. She'd love to pass the job off onto her brother, but he would be spending the morning at the gathering hall. It was Career Day today, and many magi would soon be arriving with needs to be met.

Perhaps *that* was the unique thing about Sybil. She and her brother Arthur were the only known blood relatives within their beorg. Most Shifts were dropped here between their first and second birthdays (when they typically exhibited signs of this unwanted magic) by the private managing firm of the Shift enterprises. Sybil and Art were dropped together, at six months and three years of age respectively. It caught the attention of the other Shifts at the time, but there was no way to know why or how this came to be. They were a fluke amongst their kin, and that was all there was to it.

Art believed there had to be some reason behind this abnormality, something special about the blood they shared, but neither of them held any specific theories. Sybil was starting to think that this blood relative thing was hurting her. Art was an exceptional

Shift in many ways. He had great endurance in his work, able to full body shift for far longer than the rest of them with ease, atop being extremely adaptable.

Sybil, on the other hand, was not known for her shifting or fighting prowess, much to her dismay. Art reminded her she was three years younger than he and would get there with time and continued training. She could only hope. If she didn't learn and master enough to garner attention from an employer, she'd find herself stuck in the beorg training new recruits, or worse, caring for the new drops.

Sybil shuddered at the thought. She knew it was hypocritical of her, considering someone had to keep her alive as a six-month-old Shift. Her eyes flitted to one of the sleeping figures on the lumpy, old mattress in the corner. Freida had raised both her and Art. She'd been good to them for so long, and Sybil deeply cared for her, even if she preferred not to admit it. But supervising toddlers and making sure they had something to eat was not the future for her. Sybil belonged off the mountain, or so she told herself as she practiced and trained as much as weather and time would allow. When she turned eighteen, she'd ensure there would be no excuse for anyone to not hire her.

"What are you doing awake?" A low voice asked.

Sybil jumped a little, consumed as she had been in her thoughts. She twisted to see her brother's large figure lumbering towards her. Though he was only a shadow in the blackness of their cabin, she could picture his muscular frame, square chin, brown eyes, and close-cropped brown hair. He didn't share her freckled face.

"I couldn't sleep," she answered truthfully.

Art lowered himself on the floor in front of her, mimicking her position by pulling his knees up and draping his arms over them. "Thinking about Career Day?"

"Yeah."

“I know it’s hard on you when I go off for a while,” he said.

It was hard on her, but she didn’t want to admit that to him. Art had always been successful in acquiring jobs, but in the last eight months, he’d been hired every single Career Day and been gone for not just a few days but for two to three weeks at a time. He never spoke about where he went or what he did. There was a code between employee and employer, obviously, but Sybil found his increasing absence more painful than she expected.

Art—and Freida, come to think of it—had been the only steady presences in her life. Art was the primary one who had been training her, and she knew under his tutelage she could excel as well. But, in the last months, they’d barely trained at all. He didn’t have the time to critique her shapeshifting, spar with her, or give her new tips about work away from their beorg. He’d be gone; he’d come back and crash hard, sleeping for several days straight; he’d wake just in time for the next Career Day.

There were others she could train with… Her mind wandered to tall, slim Xavier with his long hair and sharp gray eyes. But most paid her little mind, knowing she was Art’s sister, and steered clear.

“It is what it is,” she replied lamely.

“I wish I could tell you…”

“It’s okay. I know the drill.”

“You’ll be joining me soon. I know it. Before long, you’ll be eighteen, and employers will line up to hire you. I’ll vouch for you. Your resume will be more impressive than mine in no time,” Art said.

Sybil rolled her eyes, “Yeah, right. I don’t exactly want to be hired just because you said I should. I want to be taken seriously because of my own skills.”

“You will be.”

She scoffed. “Don’t lie to me, Art. You’ve never pulled your punches with me before; don’t start pandering to my feelings now.”

"I'm not pandering to your feelings," he said sharply. "And I'm not pulling my punches. You're way more capable than you think you are. If you could just gain some confidence, you'd be a damn good Shift."

"Oy, you two!" hissed a gravelly voice. Freida.

Art and Sybil glanced at her narrow figure, sitting up ominously in the bed.

"Hush up before you wake the rest of them!" Them, of course, referred to the five other kids who lived in their cabin: Joan, Roger, Dean, Nell, and Paul. They were all underage and under the general supervision of Freida, who had been retired from Shiftwork for eighteen years now.

Freida, Nell, and Joan slept on the solitary bed's lumpy mattress, which was pushed into the far right corner. Sybil slept on a straw mat at the foot of the bed, and, on the opposite side of the room, only a few feet away from the girls' bed, were two more pads on the floor. Paul and Roger shared one, and Dean and Art took the other.

"Save your chatter for the sun. I'm old, and I want to sleep."

"Sorry, Freida," Art said. He looked back at Sybil, "Come on. We can talk more in the morning."

Sybil nodded her head, but as she watched him soundlessly make his way through the cabin to his bed, she knew there would be no time to talk at all.

Morning came quickly. It seemed to Sybil that no sooner had she laid her head back down on her pallet that the first rays of sun broke through the single grimy window. She rubbed at her dry eyes and shivered. Art was already up and coaxing a fire back into the dead fireplace. He caught her looking at him.

"You'll have to get some more wood today, Syb," he instructed.

She didn't respond except to tighten her hold on the thin blanket draped over her and pull it over her head.

"Now, now, up, you lot," grunted Freida, nudging the two small, sleeping figures next to her in the bed before clambering out of it. At eighty-one, Freida was easily the oldest living Shift in the beorg. Her hair was iron gray and always tied back in a thick braid that hung down her bent frame with wisps about her wrinkled, weathered face. She was old, but she was a force to be reckoned with, complete with a foul tongue and keen insight. Her experience as a shapeshifter was unparalleled, but Freida was also the closest thing many Shifts had to a guardian. She garnered respect wherever she walked. And despite numerous injuries over the years and an achy back, she walked swiftly and surely.

Sybil felt a kick to her leg and emerged once more from her blanket. Freida had already pulled a worn flannel over her nightdress and was stepping into a brown skirt which she secured around her waist.

"Up now, or you'll have no breakfast," Freida ordered, moving to heat a pot of water over their fire.

"Do we *have* to go today?" Roger asked from his mat.

"*Of course* you'll go today," Freida snapped. "Show some loyalty to your kin, child."

"Besides, you learn a lot observing Career Days," Art volunteered as he buttoned up his best pale jean shirt.

"They're all the same," Roger protested.

"You'll go," Freida said in a tone that confirmed the discussion was over and busied herself opening a can of beans. At her words, they dragged themselves from their beds and began to pull their clothes over their pajamas.

Outside of the beorg, on occasions like Career Day, it would've been right to dress in one's Sunday best. But Shifts had no sacred Sundays and no best dress. Their garments were worn, patched, and frayed. With the winter temperatures, dressing consisted of layering on as many items as possible… and still being cold.

"Sybil, get the bread," Freida ordered as she poured weak but scalding coffee into two tin mugs, one for herself and one for Sybil and Art to share. She drank from her cup immediately, not reacting at all to the steaming liquid reaching her tongue. That was Freida for you. It was as if she had no weakness. And if she did, she had suffered and persisted through it until only hardened scabs were left.

Sybil pulled a sweater over her head and reached under her pillow for the small handheld mirror. It was a cracked and somewhat useless excuse for a mirror, but it was all she had. She combed her hair with her fingers and swiftly swept it into a knot at her neck.

"Stop ogling yourself, Syb. You look the same as the last time you checked," Roger said, chucking a flannel at Dean. Both boys were in the throes of adolescence with gangly limbs, changing voices, and acne-peppered skin.

"I'm not *ogling* myself," Sybil hissed, but she put the mirror back under her pallet.

"The bread," Freida reminded.

With a heavy sigh, Sybil crossed the cabin and rummaged through the solitary cabinet fastened to the cabin wall next to the fireplace. "There's only two pieces left."

"Give 'em to the young'uns," Freida said, without looking up from her warming pot of beans.

Two delighted and dirty faces appeared at Sybil's elbow. Paul and Nell. They greedily snatched the bread from her hands and began stuffing their mouths. Joan, straddling childhood and adolescence at twelve, looked longingly at the bread and dejectedly stuffed a leg into her trousers.

Each member of Sybil's cabin had the same plainness to them that marked all Shifts, but their eyes were bright and their faces eager. As soon as the beans were heated, Freida doled the small portions onto tin plates, and the cabin mates scarfed them down.

Art passed on the coffee and let Sybil have the entire cup. She found this odd but didn't say anything. She'd take what she could get to fill her stomach. Provisions were getting low this winter, and it was showing in the thin faces of Shifts all throughout the beorg.

"All right, let's get to it," said Art before the last bites had been swallowed. He stood by the door, waiting for everyone to line up before opening it to the cold, harsh air outside. Dean shrunk away, trying to slip back to his pallet; but Freida swatted him hard, and he braved the cold with the rest of them.

The sun was nearly high, and its light made the snow glisten. Icicles hung from the naked trees surrounding the beorg, their black shadows and silhouettes looming over them. Every slouchy, crooked cabin was coated in fresh fallen snow, and footprints dotted the ground leading from the cabin doors. Their breaths clouded around them, and their feet made crunching sounds as they crossed from their cabin past their neighbors' cabins to the gathering hall in the center of the beorg.

Even in the most bitter weather, the Highlands were beautiful. While Sybil longed to go and see something—*anything*—else, she couldn't ignore the beauty of the beorg. The weather could be harsh, but the land could also be fruitful and fragrant. Colorful.

The beorg was not large but not too small. There were about seventy Shifts residing at any given time, most between the ages of ten and forty. The cabins were the same—one room, made of log, and complete with a stone chimney. Several had front porches with rickety beams and slouching steps.

A gust of wind blew, and Sybil wrapped her arms around herself and ducked under Art's arm into the gathering hall. A newer build, the hall was one of the few buildings that didn't yet have holes or gaps in the walls for the air to pierce through. The fireplace was also larger and put out a decent amount of heat when lit. There were wooden benches where members sat for meetings and a long, narrow table neglected against a wall.

Some Shifts had beaten them to the hall and were already seated. More filed in behind them. They wore the same hard expressions, their mouths in grim lines and their eyes heavy. No one was very clean; Sybil couldn't recall the last time she'd managed more than a sponge bath since the weather turned.

The exception was a tall man in a dark navy blue suit, a long wool coat draped over his arm.

Caught off guard, Sybil blinked a few times. She had never seen him before. He had neatly trimmed brownish-red hair and a perfectly shaped beard, not like the Shift men whose hair and beards hung long and greasy.

Sybil nudged Art. "Look over there. Who's the suit?"

Art had already noticed him. He glanced sideways at Sybil before seating Joan, Nell, and the boys on a bench in the back of the room where underage Shifts observed Career Days. He took Sybil's elbow and pulled her close. "I've never seen him before," he mumbled.

"Never been at a Career Day?" Repeat employers were very common.

Art answered with a swift shake of his head. "And not only that... Look around. He's the only one here."

He was right. She'd been to many Career Days, and there were *always* multiple employers. The fewest she'd ever seen in one meeting was three. Always dressed well and always with lots of money. Most employers were jumpy and often seemed in a hurry to leave, just in case someone discovered they'd been here. But this man seemed to have an air of authority about him. A powerful confidence that took control of the room. He wasn't reacting in the slightest to the numerous sets of eyes on him or whispers about him.

"I'll see you," Art said, releasing her arm and making his way up front to sit with the other adult Shifts.

"Come sit," Freida said to Sybil, patting the bench next to her. "And don't look so interested."

Sybil detected the slightest apprehension in Freida's voice. It made her sound more cross than usual. "Who do you think he is?" Sybil asked quietly.

"Whoever he is, he's nothing special. He's just another employer, Sybil. Another one ready to take advantage of our skills and misfortune. They're all the same. Best to remember that."

But Sybil thought that he looked quite comfortable, like he had all the time in the world to be in the presence of a bunch of dirty criminals.

2.

"Good morning." No one echoed the man's greeting. "My name is Director Lowell Vox." His voice was deep, unwavering, and commanding. "I'm from the Eastward Bureau of Community Affairs."

"The Bureau of what?" barked one Shift near the front. Sybil craned her neck and spotted a peer of Art's—Bo, a beefy fellow with little common sense.

"Community Affairs," Director Vox repeated, unfazed. "From Washington. My department monitors the activity, history, and development of a number of small people groups across the country, such as yourselves."

"You're with the government?" Someone asked.

"What do you want?" shouted another. Several other exclamations rose up, but Director Vox didn't react. He waited patiently for the noise to die down, and, when it did, the corner of his mouth turned up. Sybil wasn't sure if it was a smile or a sneer.

"I would be more than happy to answer your questions, if you'd allow me a moment to speak," he said politely.

Sybil watched out of the corner of her eye as Freida leaned forward and squinted her eyes, studying the man closely.

Director Vox clasped his hands behind his back. "If I may continue? How many of you were aware there was a presidential election this year?"

A woman—Ethel, Sybil identified by her whiny, high-pitched

voice—piped up, "Considering we don't get a vote, why would we be?"

"A fair point," demurred Vox. "You see, a new administration took office as of this past December. And your newest president, Branson Calloway, has sent me here to both greet you and extend his goodwill, but also to make you aware of some changes that will be taking place to your community." His speech was careful and crisp, not at all like the lilting, lazy dialect of the Shifts.

"Changes?" Freida repeated, mostly to herself.

Heated exclamations rose up from around the room once more: "We don't need changes to the beorg!" "No other president has interfered!" "We've been operating like this for decades!" "Go home!"

A voice boomed above the rest, silencing everyone, "What kind of changes, Director?"

It was Virgil, another senior Shift. At sixty-one, Virgil's experience had elevated him to an as-near-a-leadership position as they had in the beorg. He was old enough to be seasoned but young enough to still have fight in him. The Shifts respected his years of experience, and for the most part, no one crossed him. He could be quite lethal.

Vox's blue eyes traveled the room until he spotted Virgil in the crowd. "Thank you, Mr..."

"Virgil. Just Virgil."

"Virgil," Director Vox nodded in Virgil's direction. "Let me assure you they're quite uncomplicated improvements. It's a simple change in management."

"Management?" Freida mumbled.

"Since the inception of the Shift program, you have been managed by a private firm based out of New York," Vox began. "The Guild of Eorls is a centuries-old collective of businessmen, leaders, and titans of industry. They are the ones you have to thank for your cozy set-up here in the Highlands. They are the ones who have coordinated bringing new Shift children to you and the ones who ensure the boundary around you remains secure. Well, for brevity's sake, the government has acquired the management of the Shifts from the Guild. This was one of the Calloway Administration's first acts. It was very important to the president."

"Friends," Vox continued, though Sybil was getting the distinct impression Vox was not very friendly at all. "I am here to verify the accuracy of the information we obtained from the Guild in order for the Calloway Administration to have precise data regarding you and your kin. This should enable us to best assist in building a better future for you." *Better future?*

"Does this mean we'd be taken off the mountain? Get work in other kinds of places?" Art said. Sybil was surprised he spoke up at all. Art was the sort to listen and observe, not to insert himself into a debate.

"I'm afraid those are questions to be addressed later, once the data is acquired." *Data?* What did that mean? Why did he keep talking about them as if they were numbers on paper? Sybil's brain reeled.

"No one can make any good decisions, and, by extension, any progress, without accurate information. It's likely the records from the Guild are factual, but they appear to be rather limited. We would like to have a better, more holistic understanding."

Sybil knew confusion was plainly written on her face. She couldn't make heads or tails out of the words coming from the director. One glance around the room proved she was not alone in the sentiment.

"These changes..." Virgil began.

"There will be no immediate upheaval to your daily life, except for a temporary suspension in all scheduled operations."

Pandemonium ensued as Shifts jumped to their feet and roared, "What?" "I have a job lined up for the end of the week!"

"You can't do that!"

"Friends, I am sorry, but there is nothing I can do. These orders come straight from Washington. No one will be coming or going through your boundary."

He proceeded evenly, giving little attention to the steaming Shifts around him who had no choice but to settle back down and listen. "I will verify the content received from the Guild of Eorls and ask you a few further questions. I'll take the information to Washington for evaluation. Only then will we proceed with any plans or changes that could impact you. I ask you not to be concerned regarding your future. This is a simple, routine transfer of management from private to federal."

"And we have no say in this," stated Virgil coldly.

"I'm afraid not." Vox did not seem sympathetic. His lip curled upward again. "I have brought with me an assistant to distribute paperwork for you to fill out—"

"Beggin' your pardon, Mr. Director," Virgil drawled, leaning forward to rest his elbows on his legs. "We can't fill out your paperwork."

"And why is that?" Vox asked sharply.

"We can't read or write," Ethel's grating voice replied. The admission sounded worse coming from her.

"None of you?" Vox's careful countenance cracked just a touch.

Everyone shook their heads, mixed expressions on their faces. Everyone but... Art. He stood up, stony-faced, and expelled a breath. "I do, Director."

Sybil's mouth fell open. He could *read*? Why had Art never mentioned this? It was more than a little unusual. In all her life, she had never known of, or heard of, a Shift being literate. Isolated as they were, how would they learn? Who could teach them?

Besides, reading and writing opened the door to knowledge and freedom the magi never wanted them to have, not to mention equipping them further for their operations. It defeated the purpose the magi had determined Shifts to have in Eastward.

Freida's eyes narrowed, and she felt them boring into her, determining if Sybil too harbored this secret alongside her brother. Her face flamed. She tolerated all kinds of secrets from the people in this beorg but never from her own brother. She glared back at Freida and gave a sharp shake of her head. Freida soundlessly tilted her chin in acknowledgment and directed her attention back to the front.

For Vox though, the revelation that at least one member out of the Shift beorg could work with him appeared to help him recover. He cleared his throat, "Excellent. Your name, man?"

"Arthur." Art's voice was steady, but his face was expressionless.

"Excellent. Thank you." He turned his attention back to the group. "Arthur, my assistant, and myself will have to go through the paperwork with you individually."

Sybil wondered where this assistant was he referred to. She hadn't seen anyone on their snowy walk from the cabin to the hall. Then again, she felt a little stupid for assuming a man in Vox's apparent position would arrive at the beorg alone. It'd be unwise for his own safety.

"It may take a bit longer than initially intended, but that shouldn't be a problem." Disdain over their illiteracy was almost imperceptible in his tone. Almost. "Make yourselves comfortable. Once we have concluded, you'll be permitted to return to your cabins for the remainder of the day." *Permitted?*

"Permitted?" Bo voiced next to Art. "What, so we're under lockdown now?"

It was telling that Vox ignored him. "If you'll excuse me for a brief moment, I'll fetch my assistant. She awaits me outside." Vox flashed a genteel but cool smile, revealing even teeth, and strode through the aisle and right out the door, as though he had been here many times before, like it was his home and the Shifts were common visitors.

The instant he disappeared into the cold, further commotion erupted amongst the members. It often felt like Shifts were incapable of uniting even over a common enemy, over someone like Vox coming into the beorg and taking charge. Many a meeting or career day ended with black eyes and fat lips. It was these types of behavior that gave the Eastward magi great concern and hesitation over Shifts being part of their *fyrnship*—what the Shifts called society outside the mountain. They were primal, hot-headed, and frequently out of control.

Sybil, her face quite hot, jumped up to confront her brother, but she felt Freida's viselike grip close upon her thin sweater.

"Sit down, Sybil," Freida instructed in a non-negotiable voice. "This don' concern you."

"It does!" Sybil insisted. "That's my broth—"

"Art'll need to face the consequences of this revelation himself. You can't fight his battles for him," Freida said. When Sybil looked at her, Freida's lined face was strangely calm.

Sybil plunked herself back down on the bench, and it wobbled slightly under her force. Roger shot her a glare from the other side of Freida. She sent him a rude gesture in return. Heated voices recaptured her attention up front. Bo and Ethel were both in Art's face, shouting at him.

"No wonder you've been getting so many jobs, kid," Ethel said from behind the safety of Bo's enormous bulk. "He's a cheater, folks! A cheater and a liar. I've been here for thirty-two long, dirty, stinkin' years. But no one wants *me* for my experience. We're supposed to have a level playing field here! But this one 'ere… he's thrown in his lot with *them*," she said venomously.

"You've stacked your deck," shouted Glen, one of Ethel's cabin mates, rising from his bench.

Art straightened, and a muscle visibly twitched in his neck. "This is between me and my employers." He eyed Bo and then Glen, who glowered at him on his left. "C'mon, man. Get it out of your system now; I know you need to. Hit me!"

Sybil couldn't help but flinch as Bo's meaty fist collided with Art's cheekbone. She heard Roger and Dean exclaim excitedly, while little Nell gave a small cry.

"What is going on here?" Vox bellowed, his voice carrying impressively from the back of the gathering hall. "Good Lord, I underestimated just how *primitive* you people are." Disgust dripped from his words, taking in the sight of the heated crowd and the bruise beginning to color Art's face. "Step apart at once."

"And what are you gonna do if we don't?" asked Glen. "This don't concern you. This is between us and our kin."

An expression flashed across Vox's face, but Sybil couldn't put her finger on what it was. He noticeably squared his shoulders, tilted up his jaw, and said almost pleasantly, "I am here for administrative purposes only, but I cannot very well tolerate you killing each other in my presence. That would cause quite the displeasure with my department. Once I am gone, by all means, you may get back to it." When nothing but silence followed, he added, "Take your seats."

Vox strode past the rows of Shifts, a young woman in his wake. His assistant, undoubtedly. She was dressed in an impeccable wool suit and looked as if she had smelled something detestable upon entering the hall. Her poppy-colored nails clutched a stack of paper. She wobbled slightly as she walked, her heels clicking on the uneven floor.

"This is my assistant Elsa Llewelyn," Vox said. "If you would please make three rows, in front of myself, Ms. Llewelyn, and Arthur here—" This comment appeared to catch Art off guard as he awkwardly looked around him. "We will take your names, verify the information provided from the Guild, and then ask the questions that the Calloway Administration needs answered. Then you will return to your cabins. I know it is not in your nature to be forthcoming, but I will know if you're lying. So will Ms. Llewelyn."

With that, he confirmed for them that they were Sages who would easily be able to detect tricks of the mind and manipulate them for the truth.

"Arthur, up here, please." Vox gestured to a space next to him. Elsa Llewelyn stood on his left, looking more and more disconcerted with her situation. She filed through her paperwork and passed some of it to Vox, whispering "Sir" to him as she did so. Art rose to his feet and took a step to the front and turned around, his bruised face expressionless.

Sybil hated how much he looked like one of *them* as he took papers from Vox and his eyes scanned the content.

"Let's not drag this on for any of our sakes. Stay seated until one of us calls your name and then come up here to verify your information," said Vox. Without looking up from his papers, he added, "The underage as well. They are not exempt."

There was an uncomfortable silence. No one wanted to be the first called. Vox passed a handful of papers to Art, and the rustling exchange seemed magnified by the tension. He called out, "Molly!"

Molly rose boldly from a bench in the middle with her jaw set and strode to Vox with her head high. Her movement broke the trance that had seemingly settled over the space.

Elsa Llewelyn's nervous voice wobbled out, "Roger?"

Roger, seated on the opposite side of Freida, tripped a little on his way to her. He glanced backwards at Freida who gave him a curt nod. He visibly inhaled and walked to Elsa, who grimaced at the sight of the gangly, dirty teenager.

Whispers broke out amongst the waiting Shifts. When Freida

was called, Sybil was left with Paul and Nell next to her. Paul loudly whispered questions, and Sybil woodenly answered, not really paying attention to him.

"I don't understand—why's that man here?" Paul asked.

"He's from the government."

"Where's the government?"

"Washington… I think," she said belatedly.

"Where's Washington?"

"I don't know."

"What's Art doin' up there?" contributed Nell's small voice from Sybil's right. A number of haughty retorts came to her mind, but Sybil bit them back. They'd only lead to more questions from the kids.

"He's… helping," she answered tightly.

"What's he helpin' with?" Paul whispered.

"Paul, for the love of… Please. Just be quiet, and let me pay attention."

Paul pouted, his forehead scrunching and his eyebrows pulling together. "Freida says asking questions is an important part of Shiftwork," he said importantly, his lips puckered.

"Go stand up there with Freida then," Sybil retorted. Paul went silent but kept throwing her dirty looks.

The calling of names persisted, interrupting the low chatter at irregular intervals.

"Bo?" from Elsa.

"Gemma?" from Art.

"Virgil," called Vox. Virgil had a strange smugness in his expression.

Several lewd comments regarding Vox's assistant Elsa Llewelyn reached Sybil's ears. She bit her lip not to laugh as her gaze landed on Elsa on the other side of Vox, looking practically cornered and terribly stressed as more than one Shift crowded around her, eager to stir up trouble. Her face was flushed. Tendrils of blonde hair escaped her fur cap, and she kept dropping her pen.

Vox's voice steadily grew louder and sharper, "For the *third* time, *sir*, just answer the question."

A small streak of delight ran through Sybil that, even if they didn't have a choice in the matter, the Shifts were able to make the overall experience unpleasant for their guests.

"Sybil." Art's lips tightened into a line. When their eyes met, he gestured for Paul and Nell. "I have them too. Bring them up, and we'll take care of their forms first." Art was like a stranger as he gave instructions. Sybil stared blankly but grabbed Paul and Nell's hands and yanked them with her to stand before him.

"I know pretty much all the answers to their questions. For all three of you," Art said.

"Are we just gonna pretend it's not strange that you're *reading* government-issued paperwork?" Sybil asked, releasing Paul and Nell's hands to cross her arms over her chest.

Art glanced at her and said simply, "We'll talk about it later."

"What if I want to talk about it now?"

"I'm not talkin' about it with you now. This is not the place or time. It's too crowded." She hated how bossy he sounded. Well, he had always been a little bossy. He was her impressive big brother, but today, it gnawed at her. It felt like he wasn't on her side. Or their kin's.

"What kinds of questions are these, anyway?" She asked.

"Most of these are about our history and our drop-off dates. And then this second half here is about our work and natural forms."

Sybil's heart fluttered uncomfortably. "Our... history? Like, our parents and family?"

Art met her eyes and said, "'Fraid not."

Sybil sighed, wishing she hadn't asked and embarrassed that

she felt a twinge of disappointment. What good would it do to know her parentage? They hadn't wanted her, Shift as she was. They gave up two children to a beorg of strangers because they were not like them. Because they were ashamed of them. Why should she care about them?

"Are you listening to me?" Art snapped.

"No—sorry. What did you say?"

Exasperated, he held out the paper to her and pointed with his finger. "This is what the Guild collected on us when we were dropped here. It's name, date of birth, sex, state of birth, parents' branch of magic, and date of drop off. Uh, this one is Paul's, and here's Nell's. I've verified both of 'em."

"Where was I born?" Paul asked, bouncing slightly on his toes.

Art smiled. "Georgia."

"Where's that?"

"A few hours from here," Art said.

"What about Nell?" Paul continued.

"Pennsylvania."

"Where's that?"

"North a ways. And, according to the Guild's records, you were both born to Thane magi."

"A Thane..." breathed Paul reverently. "I guess that means I'll be a big and strong fighter."

Sybil and Art exchanged a quick look. Art calmly said, "If you grow to be a big and strong fighter, it will be because you've trained yourself in Shiftwork. Nothing more. Paul, I want you to take Nell and wait at the back of the gathering hall for Sybil. She'll go back with you to the cabin when we're finished."

Sybil placed a hand on Nell's thin shoulder. The child looked up at her with her huge chocolate eyes, dirty strands of hair hanging against her forehead. Sybil offered her a small smile, which Nell did not return, and pushed her gently after Paul. She trailed after Paul without a word.

"This one here is yours. Do you want to know what it says?" Art asked.

"I guess so."

"So, date of birth here—the third of August, nineteen thirty-four. Female, obviously. And then you and I were, apparently, both born in North Carolina."

Sybil felt like Paul as she asked, "Where exactly is that?"

"East of us. Shares our mountains but butts up to the coast. And then here it says we were born to a Sage."

"A Sage? Just one?"

"I suppose that means they only knew the branch of one of our parents and not both. And then drop off date was January the fourteenth, nineteen thirty-five, which does put you at about six months old."

"And you around three years."

"Right."

"What's the next part on here? The part the director said the government added?"

Art nodded. "Here, you'll see a list. It's asking about what particular skills you have in Shiftwork. Things like arson, kidnapping, homicide, manslaughter, burglary, larceny, public indecency, robbery, blackmail, fraud, counterfeiting, trafficking, identity theft… and so on. Here it asks about special skills. And then it asks about what jobs you've had, including noteworthy employers, though I can't imagine any Shift selling any of their employers out like that. It'd only come back to bite 'em in the end."

Art tapped the paper with the pen. "I filled this out for Paul and Nell, since they're underage and it's irrelevant. You also are underage, so we probably don't need to answer any of it." Sybil wasn't sure if she should feel relieved or frustrated. She didn't like being passed over as a full-on Shift because she was only a few months away from being legal.

"*But* because you are so close to eighteen, I wasn't sure if you wanted me to mark any special skills."

"What do they list?" Sybil asked.

"Hand-to-hand, cover-ups, martial arts, shooting, explosives. Poisons, safes and vaults, transports, and undercover."

"Well, you'd probably know better than I what to mark," Sybil said stiffly. "You're the expert on this stuff."

Art arched an eyebrow at her. "Stop being whiny. You're good at lots of these things, especially hand-to-hand and undercover. You've not exactly had a chance to practice a lot of these other skill-sets yet, not up here in the beorg."

"Put what you think is best. Anything else?"

"Yeah, natural forms. Hair color, eye color, height, weight. Identifying marks."

"Brown; brown; I'm not sure, and I'm not sure," Sybil answered robotically.

"Your freckles probably count as identifying marks. And we each have those birthmarks." Art's mark splashed over his right fist, but Sybil's was a smaller tan patch across her left wrist. "Oh, and then your shoe size."

"You're joking."

"I'm dead serious. That's what it's asking right here…" He pointed at the paper like it would help her comprehend.

"What's next on the list? My breast size?" Sybil scoffed.

"Well, that would be relevant to your natural state, if you care to volunteer it."

"I'll pass," she said dryly. "I have no idea how big my bloody feet are. Do they measure all these things in the fyrnship?"

"I suppose they have to because they buy their clothes premade in department stores. They wouldn't know what sizes to buy if they didn't." *Are we really talking about this right now?*

"Arthur!" Vox barked. "Hurry it up." He had noticed how long Sybil had been lingering, and his eyes focused on her for a long moment before moving on. He called from his list, "Laurel?"

Art's eyes darkened.

"Is that it?" Sybil asked.

"Yeah, that's about it. Go take Nell and Paul back home."

"Thanks, Director," she said.

"Quit with the sass," Art growled.

"We're talking about this—*you*—later. I won't forget." Sybil tossed her hair over her shoulder and marched off to get the kids, leaving an exasperated Art in her wake. She heard him say, "Oy, Tanner! You're up."

3.

The rest of Career Day felt like it would drag on forever. Sybil deposited Paul and Nell inside their cabin, where Freida was waiting, having already returned with Roger, Dean, and Joan. The old woman made no attempt to enlist Sybil's assistance but rather encouraged her with a pointed look to go back out. Freida seemed to understand the need to follow what all was occurring, as well as the need for some space from the onslaught of questions no doubt to come.

Sybil ducked back out to sit on their rotting front step and watch the happenings. The winter chill bit straight through her layers of shabby clothing, but the sun was high in the sky and bore down on her.

She wrapped her arms around herself, tucking her feet beneath her to keep them from sinking into the snow. Amidst the naked trees, birds chirped cheerfully, unaware of the strange day the Shifts were having. Time could've stood still, and she wouldn't have known the difference except for the periodic marching of Shifts from the gathering hall back to their cabins. Each stomped out the door with expressions ranging from fury to humiliation to grim resignation. For the most part, none of them spoke with each other and kept their eyes down. Then a tall figure, who had to stoop to fit through the threshold, stepped into the sunlight. Sybil's heart did an eager flip-flop.

Xavier was Art's peer and, perhaps relevant to know, a bit of an enemy. Enemy was a strong word, but the two rarely saw eye-to-eye and competed for many of the same jobs. Art saw Xavier as hot-headed and reckless; Xavier viewed him as too cautious and calculating. Regardless, she knew her brother would quite possibly skin her alive if she went out with Xavier.

Which is why she never told him. They'd only hung together a handful of times, and Sybil felt no guilt keeping that from her brother so far. It wasn't as if they were *together,* but Sybil couldn't deny how much she liked being around him. He was exciting, funny, and carefree in a place lacking in all three.

Xavier, unlike the other Shifts who returned to their cabins, did not appear stressed or bothered by Vox's arrival. His unshaven face had its trademark, relaxed expression. While Art often concealed his emotions and took on a stony persona, Xavier was expressive; his face constantly betrayed what he was thinking or feeling. He was handsome, at least by Shift standards, with long sandy hair typically tied back with a strip of cloth and clear gray eyes.

He must've felt her eyes on him because Xavier's head swiveled her direction, and he smiled brightly. She grinned back and lifted her hand in a small wave. Xavier quickly looked around, making a bit of a show of it for Sybil, craning and leaning, and then did a little hop-skip before walking toward her. In several long strides, he reached her.

"How goes it, Syb?"

"Well, you know, it's been a bit of an unusual day," Sybil said.

Xavier laughed. It was a space-filling, contagious sound. "You could say that again. That director is somethin' else, don't you think?"

Sybil couldn't help but giggle along with him, but then she said, "You did hear his explicit orders to return directly to your cabin, right? No loitering?"

"Were they *really* orders?"

"Uh, yeah, I think they were."

Xavier waved his hand dismissively. "Eh, there are loads of us still in the gathering hall. He'll be occupied for a while. Can I sit?" He gestured to the slouching step Sybil was curled on.

"Be my guest."

Xavier plunked himself next to her. She was surprised the step didn't split under his weight, not because he was a heavy man but because the step was in poor condition and he dropped with some force. He stretched his lanky legs out in the sun. "Lordy, that sun feels good."

Sybil lifted her face to it. "It sure does."

"You look cold. I wouldn't be able to stand straight if I was folded up like that," Xavier said, gesturing to how her feet were tucked underneath her.

She laughed lightly. "Well, it *is* cold."

"I'll see if I can get you a pair of wool socks on my next job." He waggled his feet in his faded work boots. The sole of one was near ready to peel right off. "They make all the difference when your shoes are bad."

"I'll take 'em." She couldn't remember the last time she had new socks.

"Surprised that brother of yours hasn't dressed your cabin better."

"Oh, here we go." Sybil rolled her eyes. "Don't start, Xavier. I have no desire to be part of your stupid rivalry."

"But we have so much fun!"

"I'll pass." She waited a beat, "But I'll still take the new socks." Xavier's peal of laughter made her insides feel like they were melting.

"You think you'll be able to get another job soon, with Director Vox showing up here and all?" Sybil asked, staring out at the field of snow before them. The stream of departing Shifts had slowed to a trickle.

Xavier tilted his head to the side, "Eh, I can't imagine why not. I mean, he didn't make it sound like the government had different intentions for us, right? At least, that's not how I took it. Just a change in management, y'know?"

Sybil grimaced.

"You don't agree?"

She hesitated. "You take the optimistic route."

He shrugged and nodded his head. "Yeah, yeah, that's true. I get that a lot. I just feel like, why worry about things that you don't know for sure are happening? Why bother until you have to? I'd rather not be miserable until I have to be. Why, Sybil—could you be impressed with me?" He said, pointing to her face which had betrayed her.

She swatted his hand away. "I didn't know you could be so..."

"Profound? Philosophical? Wise? *Articulate?*"

"Smart."

"There's a lot you don't know about me," Xavier teased.

"Well, since none of us are goin' anywhere, I'm thinkin' I've got plenty of time to find out."

"What is *he* doing over here?" Art demanded. Several curses quickly ran through Sybil's mind.

She jumped to her feet, feeling unnecessarily guilty, but Xavier just reclined further, his upper back pressing into the front door of the cabin. "Nice to see you too, Arthur."

Art clenched his jaw. "You're supposed to be in your cabin," he said stiffly.

"You're supposed to be illiterate."

Sybil winced. *Ouch, Xavier.*

Two veins popped in Art's neck and forehead simultaneously. "I need a word with Sybil. I'd like you to leave," he said, as diplomatically as he could muster.

"Sybil and I were having a very nice conversation, weren't we,

Syb?"

"*Sybil*," Art said warningly.

She looked at Xavier apologetically. "Another time, Xavier." After all, Art had already been punched in the face once today.

"I can take a hint." Xavier launched himself up with a dramatic grunt of exertion. He stepped past Art, very nearly brushing him with his shoulder, and stuffed his hands in his worn coat pockets.

"Hey, Xavier!" Sybil cried. He turned back. "Don't forget about my socks." A smile broke out on Xavier's face, and he winked at her before continuing on his way, whistling a folky tune.

"What's this about socks?" Art asked irritably.

"Xavier has kindly promised to bring me a new pair on his next job."

"How'd you like to go get your own pair?" An uncharacteristic grin shattered Art's steely expression.

"What?" Sybil exclaimed. "You're joshin' me."

"I swear I'm not."

"I'm underage."

"I'm not."

"*What?*"

"Sit down; I'll tell you everything."

Art explained that, as the number of Shifts inside the gathering hall dwindled, Vox passed his remaining paperwork—as well as Art's—over to Elsa Llewelyn and requested she finish up. Then, he took Art to a corner and privately requested him for an important operation.

"He really seemed to trust me for this op, given I can read and write. But after he explained the basis for the op, I told him I thought a team would be a better fit, rather than a solo Shift. When he asked who I'd be willin' to work with, I named you."

Sybil reminded herself to close her mouth. "But I'm underage," she repeated stupidly.

"It's all taken care of. Vox had the same concerns, but I told him that you were talented, that I helped train you, and that I'd take full responsibility for you outside the beorg. A new Shift would be *far* easier to work with than one who had experience. Experience means you're more set in your ways. You have rhythms and routines for accomplishing your ops.

He waved his finger at her. "But you... You'll go in not only open-minded but receptive to my feedback. I've got an excellent track record, so Vox was amenable." Art paused, "You *will* be receptive to my instructions. Otherwise, I'll pick someone else."

"You said those things about me? That I'm... talented?"

"It's the truth. You're quite competent, a quick learner, and adaptable. That can be just as valuable as years of experience. Vox agreed."

"So..."

"So, if you're up for it, he'd like to meet with you himself. He's waiting in the hall now. If he has no glaring concerns, he'll give you the full details of the op, and we'll head out tomorrow."

"*Tomorrow*?" Sybil's voice cracked. She pressed her hands to her head.

"You're ready, Syb," Art reassured her. "I really think you'll do well on this op, and I think we'll make a good team. We're a unique fit—you and I."

"What's the op?" Chills raced over her body, and she was certain it was not from the winter air.

"I'm not sure I should say. You'll find out once Vox confirms he wants you. Employer confidentiality and all."

"Wow," Sybil breathed. "I can't believe this. Here I was, feelin' a little nervous that his arrival here meant the end of Shiftwork or something."

A shadow passed across Art's face.

"Art? What is it you know? It's not the end of Shiftwork, is it?"

"I… I don't know if that's true."

"But we're about to go on an op?"

"I mean, I don't know for sure. I just get this feeling that there's more here than just a change of management."

"But a director from Washington wanting to hire us seems like a good sign… that he sees value in Shiftwork?"

"Perhaps. Or he knows this is his last chance to act. The nature of the op is rather extreme, which makes me suspicious. Time will tell though." *Extreme?*

"Should we be worried?" Sybil asked, searching Art's plain face. What would the Shifts do if there was to be no Shiftwork?

"Time will tell," Art repeated. "For now, Vox is in the gathering hall waiting on you. Go charm him, and let's do this op together. Talk about a once-in-a-lifetime experience, Syb. Don't blow it."

4.

Art's parting words to Sybil instilled little confidence. When she entered the gathering hall for the second time that day, it was empty except for Director Vox and Elsa Llewelyn, who was stuffing papers into a large yellow folder in the corner. Vox sat on a bench at the front, looking rather tired. He straightened when he saw her and rose to his feet.

"You must be Sybil," he said as she stepped over the threshold. "Shut the door behind you. I don't wish for our conversation to be overheard."

She wordlessly obeyed and approached him with her heart beating rapidly. He held out a hand, and she gave it a firm shake.

"Let's talk," he said. "Your brother had good things to say about you, despite your track record or lack thereof. He is under the impression you are moldable and eager to please, which, in his opinion, makes you an excellent candidate to work alongside him on this important operation."

Sybil wasn't sure if she should respond or simply listen. Vox plowed ahead, "This is a job of a very sensitive nature. I will not tolerate carelessness." His sharp eyes narrowed on her, and she struggled to maintain eye contact with him.

"How many inches can you do?" He asked abruptly.

"Height or width?"

"Both."

"I can vary height by up to eight inches total, grow or shrink. Width anywhere from four to twelve, depending on which part of the body we're talking about."

"Shades? Skin, hair, eyes?"

"All of them."

"Textures? Shaping? Bone structures?"

"Yes—sir," she added belatedly.

Vox pulled a photograph from within his wool coat. Sybil tried to not let the interest show too obviously on her face. It was of a woman with pale hair, a long straight nose, blue deep-set eyes, and a thin mouth. She was fair but not beautiful. He tucked the photo back into his coat pocket.

"Please shift into this woman. Five seconds."

A test. Of course. Her stomach somersaulted, but she steadily responded, "If you wish." She closed her eyes.

Focus.

She fixed her mind on the woman from the photograph. The silver sheen to her soft wavy hair. The length of it, framing her face, barely dusting her shoulders.

Her face... Narrow. Everything was narrow and straight. The chin was pointed. The shoulders, thin. Her nose, sloped.

A buzzing sensation started in the back of her head before radiating down... down... Her body tingled, from her fingers to toes, not painfully but not comfortably either. She felt the tugging sensation in her stomach, the jolt in her chest, the adrenaline coursing through her.

Focus.

The blue of the eyes was light, with some gray to them. They weren't bright or electric. More like the color of sky when it snowed, with the blue mixed in. Although her eyes were closed, Sybil could see rainbow spots against the black of her eyelids.

"Well done. That was only four seconds," Vox said, breaking her trance.

She opened her eyes and met his.

"The likeness is indeed remarkable." He approached Sybil. He slowly circled her. Even though she didn't look like herself, she didn't like the feeling of Vox's severe gaze on her. He was the kind of man who missed nothing. She was being scrutinized. Studied for faults and errors.

"Such a peculiar form of magic." He didn't say it as a compliment.

"Thank you, Director."

"Please, you can change back. I am unnerved having this conversation with you looking like her."

The buzzing, the tingling, the tugging at her navel—it all faded nearly simultaneously as Sybil changed back to her natural form. She sat down on a bench. She suddenly remembered Elsa in the corner. She quickly looked over to her, but she must've been deeply engrossed in her organization. Or...

"Mr. Director, is Ms. Llewelyn well?"

"Ms. Llewelyn is fine. It's a little Sage trick, to stay her mind for a time to give us privacy." *Stay her mind?* "Tell me about your practical skill set," Vox ordered.

Dragging her gaze from Elsa, Sybil answered, "I am skilled in boxing and proficient with both rifles and pistols."

Vox cut in, "Your accuracy?"

"Excellent." *Ish.*

"What else?"

"I am competent in picking basic locks and safes. I can develop poisons out of common elements and ingredients, from household cleaning supplies to plants. I am discreet when I need to be, able to sneak in and out of places without detection; but I am also able to command a room and capture attention. This lends to my capabilities undercover—"

"That's quite enough, thank you," Vox cut her off. He stared off at the wall, clearly engrossed within his own mind. She swallowed and forced her hands into her pockets to keep from fidgeting in the long silence.

Finally, he said, "I think you will do well alongside your brother." A breath she didn't realize she'd been holding escaped her, and tension fled her shoulders. She hoped Vox didn't notice.

"Thank you, sir. If I may, who was the woman?"

"First Lady Calloway," Vox said, coming to sit across from her.

"The new president's wife?"

"One and the same. And a dear friend of mine." *A* dear *friend?*

"Sir, is she the target?" Sybil asked, her brows pulling together.

"No—her husband."

Sybil felt slapped, she was so taken aback. "The *president*? The new president?"

"Yes, Branson Calloway." Vox confirmed, practically spitting the name out, as if it left a bitter taste on his tongue.

"Sir... It's unusual for Shiftwork to extend quite that far... I don't recall many ops targeting newly elected presidents. In fact, the last president to be targeted was President Thorne, five decades ago." Sybil wasn't sure why she was hedging. Art had already agreed to this, and she should too or else she'd lose the opportunity. But her first op targeting the president of Eastward Americana was downright frightening. It was foolish to assign someone so inexperienced to such a task.

"Impressive memory."

"Isn't President Calloway your... boss?" Sybil glanced at Elsa again, but the woman seemed as unperturbed and still-figured as ever.

"For all intents and purposes, yes. And he's a formidable Sage himself. Quite competent at discerning lies," Vox said pointedly. "Will that be a problem?"

"No," she lied firmly. "But I'd like the details of the op now."

A tight cool smile distorted Vox's features. "Certainly. Now's as good a time as any." Vox retrieved a pale yellow folder from within his coat and flipped it open. A photo of a handsome, dark-haired man was pinned to the inside, drawing Sybil's attention.

"Is this him?" She asked.

"Yes. Branson Calloway. Born on the twelfth of April, 1910 to Dale Eugene Calloway and Madeline Anne Calloway. Forty-one years of age. Married Cecelia Ellen Hughes in 1938, with whom he shares two children: Lenora Ellen Calloway, born 1943, age eight, and Donald Eugene Calloway, born 1945, age six," read Vox rapidly.

"Calloway attended Weymouth University in Delaware with a specialization in Intermagical Affairs. Went to graduate school at Weymouth University for Law with an emphasis on Intermagical Relations and International Affairs. Graduated with honors and awards, of course," he mumbled under his breath. "Interned in the governor of Delaware's house before moving into the Delaware General Assembly and then transitioning into federal government. He'd been in the senate for two years before beginning his campaign for the presidency." Vox pierced her with a hard look. "Did you get all that?"

Another test. "Yes."

"When was he born?"

"April the twelfth, 1910."

"His children's names?" He quizzed.

"Lenora Ellen Calloway and Donald Eugene Calloway," Sybil replied, an edge in her own voice now. Vox already selected her. Why was she still on trial?

"Well done. Arthur said you had a good memory." Sybil didn't respond, but her mouth thinned into a line. She could feel her diplomacy beginning to wane, and her stewing temper starting to boil. She didn't like Lowell Vox very much.

"You and Arthur will make your way to Washington, District of Columbia—this is where the president lives," he added, in case she was confused. She was simultaneously appreciative of the clarification and offended by it. "How you get there is on you. And then you will do whatever is necessary and required to kidnap one or both of Calloway's children." He watched her face as he said this, to see if she flinched or balked about such an action, but she didn't let it betray her. It was a big job for one's first, but, beyond that, well within the realm of normalcy for Shiftwork.

When she didn't react, Vox continued, "Hold them for a minimum of twenty-four hours—enough to set off panic and pandemonium for Calloway before you return them."

"Easy enough. Though I admit, I don't see why you need two Shifts to do this."

"Well, I wouldn't, if that was all there was to it. But you see, I would like to add onto this op with a little smear campaign on Calloway directly. This is where it helps to have a woman involved."

Sybil raised her eyebrows questioningly.

"I want some... compromising photos leaked, ideally amidst the kidnapping," Vox said. His voice held an unmistakable measure of thrill. "Calloway, well, he's an aggravating man. He is an all-Eastward sort of man. He comes from good lineage, with a solid upbringing, a well-rounded education. He has a lovely wife, children. He is wealthy. Hard working, yes, and extremely driven. Proactive. Clever. He is a quintessential leader of the people."

Sybil wasn't following what this had to do with the compromising photos, but Vox was on a roll.

"He ran on a platform of family values, of honor, and integrity.

He ran on bringing progress about whilst holding on to the traditional values that have built this country. He emphasized the unity and hard work that formed Eastward from nothingness—that of the three branches of vulnerable magi who fled the West... well, four, if you consider you Shifts," he added sarcastically. "So, you see, by discrediting him, smearing his good name, proving him to be a hypocrite in his personal life—it makes him vulnerable, hitting him in the core of his values. Not to mention drastically affecting his ratings with the public. Vulnerability opens the doors for other leaders to step in and influence him."

"Leaders such as yourself."

"Precisely."

"Seems like somewhat drastic action to take over not liking the man."

Vox's smile was rather chilling. "It's more than that, dear," he said rather condescendingly. "Calloway has an unhealthy interest in the Shifts, hence the government's requisition from the Guild of Eorls. That was all him."

"Why does he care so much? From what you've described, someone like him should be far removed from issues pertaining to Shifts like us."

"One would certainly think. I'll tell you the same as I told your brother Arthur: President Calloway, I believe, is trying to change the system. He wants to bring about reform—reform that is not needed. His plans are all about integration. National cooperation. Are you following me?"

No. "I'd like to hear more."

"I, among others, hold an alternative view—that this integration is a waste of time and resources for everyone involved and is only going to lead to many people getting hurt, including Shifts such as yourself. Calloway is poorly prepared for this kind of overhaul and is blinded by idealistic foolishness. It's all foolishness, and I will not sit idly by watching Eastward flounder and fall in spectacular fashion with Calloway in office."

Movement from the corner caught their eyes as Elsa Llewelyn's head dipped forward and her hat slipped over her eyes.

Vox paid her no mind. "So, Sybil. As you can imagine, I need this done quickly and efficiently. This is the last opportunity to get a Shift out of here unsuspected before the registration process is completed.

"My registration will be delayed?"

"It will be conveniently at the bottom of the pile, as well as Arthur's. You should be home and back in your cabin before it's finalized. Do we have an accord, Sybil?"

Sybil smiled and shook his outstretched hand. "It'll be my pleasure to work for you, sir."

5.

To no one's surprise, no further employers showed that Career Day. Vox and his assistant, freed from the mind staying, briskly acquired their belongings and made their way to the tree line, where the beorg's boundary ran. Upon crossing through it, a hazy ripple momentarily disturbed the air. And then they were gone, leaving no sign of their presence behind. The day that had started so strangely now seemed quite ordinary.

Sybil and Art spent the remainder of the day making the necessary plans for their op, given they would need to leave promptly in the morning. Freida kicked the underaged Shifts from the cabin, exclaiming they were getting on her nerves and insisting that the cold air would do their constitutions some good. Sybil knew Freida made that up because she used the same excuse on her when she was younger.

When Art first told Freida that he had an op and that it needed to stay under wraps, she did not question him. In her eyes, Art was an adult—much younger than she, of course, but adult nonetheless. That meant they were peers, and she would not tell him what to do or pick apart his choices.

When Sybil's name was brought up, however, her eyes narrowed skeptically. She looked between the two of them and said simply, "I hope you know what you're doing. I'm going to Virgil's for a smoke."

Freida disappeared into the snow, leaving the cabin empty for

Sybil and Art to strategize and prepare. Sybil had no doubt that was on purpose.

The siblings spent their private time comparing notes on what Vox told each of them, and they were relieved to find no glaring discrepancies in narrative or expectation.

They determined to leave quite early the following morning before any other Shifts could wake and cause trouble for them. They would most certainly have questions—why Sybil was going despite her age, why they had an op while all other Shiftwork was suspended. They'd be disinclined to accept the vague answers Sybil and Art would be required to give due to employer confidentiality.

They would hike down the mountain, catch the first train at the nearest station in Miltown, and make their way to Washington as swiftly as possible. Once there, it was of utmost importance to find and make connections in order to get to Calloway and his children effectively without wasting time.

They packed their gear in two small rucksacks. There wasn't much to bring. The essentials included Art's set of knives, his handgun, bullets, and rope. They added some spare clothes and a small quantity of food, which is all they felt comfortable taking from the cabin. They'd nick more outside the beorg, Art told her when Sybil questioned how little they had. He even told her to take some back out.

"They'll need it here more than us, at least for the time being. If all ops are suspended, I'm not sure what rations will look like," he admitted.

They didn't talk much in this time, except for the occasional question from Sybil or order from Art. She knew she'd be required to follow his instructions outside the beorg. Her inexperience could *not* hinder the success of the op. For now, with their plan already in place, Art remained characteristically quiet, if not pensive. He was not one to speak unless something needed to be said.

When darkness fell early in the evening and their cabin mates returned, Roger had an armload of firewood and looked thoroughly ticked; Freida looked triumphant.

Art made up a satisfactory fire, and they ate bread and jerky before it. The kids talked and wrestled and argued like any other day. Sybil, however, felt lost in her thoughts as she realized this would be her last night in her cabin before she would leave the boundary for the first time and see what was on the other side. She would experience the fyrnship of the magi, the magic of *their* world, the one that had excluded her kin. The thought lit a flame in her stomach and brought her ever-present temper to a low simmer.

"What do you think, Sybil?" Joan poked Sybil in the knee with her foot. "Hello? I'm talking to you."

"What? Oh, sorry, Joan. I was..."

"Not listening," Joan pouted. "I know. You never listen to what I have to say."

"Oh, come off it, that's not true. I was just a little distracted is all," Sybil said. "Tell me what you said again."

"I want to go squirrel huntin' tomorrow. Can you take me?"

Sybil felt Art's eyes on her. "Tomorrow isn't good for me. Maybe Roger can go with you."

"Oh, *please*, Sybil! Roger yells at me too much."

"I do not!" interjected Roger from where he sat cross-legged, whittling a stick he confiscated from the firewood.

"You do too!" Joan whined. "And then you scare away all the squirrels."

"*You* scare them off with all your stomping around and—"

"That's enough," Freida declared loudly. "There'll be a blizzard tomorrow. No one's goin' squirrel hunting."

"A blizzard? How d'you know?" Dean asked, pushing himself

up onto his elbows. Paul let out a frustrated cry. The boys were shooting marbles, and Dean's movement caused the rotting wood planks underneath him to dip and the marbles to roll. It was far from a fair game as their wood-whittled marbles varied in size, shape, and weight.

"My bad knee, boy," snapped Freida.

"Yeah, Dean, *duh*," inserted Roger while Art mumbled, "Oh, here we go." Sybil caught his eye, and they both suppressed grins. The way Freida talked, she could predict snow with her right knee and rain with her left elbow. And a stretch of hot sunny days was just about unbearable for her arthritic joints.

"I'm tired of snow!" Joan moaned.

"And I'm tired of your whinin', child," said Freida with a severe look. "Go to bed if you got nothin' better to say."

Dean, Paul, and Roger broke out into mocking laughter, and Joan sulked. She got up and aimed a kick at the boys' marbles, but Sybil caught her by the wrist and shook her head. Joan glowered at her and marched off to the bed in the corner, which she climbed upon and crossed her arms and legs tightly.

Little Nell touched Sybil's shoulder and handed her a hairbrush. "I can't get the tangles out," she said quietly. Sybil smiled and brought her around to sit before her. She began brushing the girl's long sheet of caramel-colored hair, starting at the ends and working her way through the knots. Complicated feelings rose up in her as she did so.

She was excited, if not rather scared out of her wits, to have her first job, but she also felt conflicted over the thought of leaving everyone here, not to mention lying to them about it. It put a damper on the eager anticipation she wanted to have and made her feel much unlike a Shift to feel any remorse in the first place. Her hands stilled in Nell's hair.

"I think that's good for tonight," she said, handing the brush back to Nell.

"I think we should all turn in," Freida determined. She shut the protests down swiftly with her eyes and rose to her feet. It took her a moment to straighten all the way up. "Don't look at me like that, boy," she shot at Art. She shook her leg at him. "I'm tellin' you, it'll be a blizzard tomorrow."

Sybil woke before the sun with a headache and her stomach knotted with nerves. Sure enough, howling wind hissed through the cracks in the cabin walls and rattled the window pane. She and Art sprang from their beds and dressed quickly in the dark cabin. Sybil's hands shook from the cold and from her nerves. She missed several buttons on her faded tawny overcoat and had to completely start over in order to right it. While Art poked at the fire, she snatched their rucksacks from under the bed as quietly as she could to not disturb Freida, Joan, and Nell sleeping atop it.

She crept up to Art and whispered, "I'm gonna run to the outhouse, but everything is ready to go."

"I'll meet you out there," he replied, blowing on his hands.

Sybil wrapped her scarf around her head and face. She could barely get the door open against the wind and the new foot of snow that had accumulated overnight. She threw her weight against it, and it budged enough for her to slip through the crack. Snow smacked her in the face as she rushed to the outhouse, and she could barely keep her eyes open against the piercing wind. She ducked her head and tried to shield her face as best she could, inwardly cursing the conditions. Of all the days to hike off the mountain for work...

She collided with a solid figure. "Who's there?" She exclaimed.

"Sybil?" hollered a voice over the wind.

"Xavier?" She cried. "What are you doing out here right now?"

"What are *you* doin' out here?"

"Goin' to the *outhouse*, you idiot, what do you think?"

Even over the wind, she could hear his laugh. "I had to get more firewood for my cabin."

"Shoulda done that yesterday."

"I didn't know a blizzard was gonna hit!"

"You would've if Freida lived with you," Sybil said.

"Look, we'd better not be caught out here long in these conditions. I'll see you later," Xavier said, close to her ear so she could hear him.

"Yeah, later." As long as she didn't freeze to death on the way off the beorg… or get caught and thrown in jail during her op… She wanted to tell him where she was going, that it would be days before he'd see her again. But he was already gone, his tall figure concealed by the whirling snow. She sighed into her scarf.

Sybil hurried through her business, her hands going numb, and rushed back to the front of her cabin. As if he had been waiting by the door, Art pushed it open and came out right on time. When the slanted snow assaulted him, he swore loudly, but the curse was swept away by the wind. He shoved Sybil's rucksack at her.

"We'd better get moving if we don't want to freeze to death," he said over the howling wind.

"Did anyone see you leave?" Sybil asked, hoisting the rucksack over her shoulder. Her gloveless hands ached and throbbed already.

"Nah, I don't think—" Art was interrupted by the cabin door scraping open again.

Freida stood in the crack in her night shirt, her wiry braid swung over her shoulder and her face unflinching in the icy air. Art and Sybil stood rooted, unsure what to do or say. Freida wasn't one for dramatic goodbyes.

The old woman took in their rucksacks and layers of clothing.

She thrust a large pair of black gloves at Art and said, "Make sure you come back." The door slammed shut again.

The siblings shared a look. Art turned the gloves over in his stiffening fingers. "You wear 'em first," he said over the wind and passed them to her. "We gotta get moving."

Sybil didn't argue and shoved her hands into the too-big gloves. She hurried to keep close to Art as they walked toward the tree line.

The tree line on the far side of the beorg, to the right of Sybil and Art's cabin, marked the boundary established by Thanes at the beorg's inception. It was indistinguishable apart from the odd direction the leaves grew. They pointed inward, giving the trees the illusion that they folded into themselves. In winter time, however, when the trees were bare, it was nearly imperceptible from the rest of the wood.

Sybil stayed close to Art, for the visibility was low and it was difficult to hear anything above the noise of the blizzard. Even still, she practically crashed into him when he stopped.

"This is the boundary," he said, cupping his mouth with red hands.

Sybil wasn't sure how he could possibly know with the snow blowing as it was, but she trusted him. He ran his fingers over a knot in an oak tree. Moments later, the air before them rippled slightly, wrinkling and then smoothing out again.

An imposing figure stood six feet away and gestured at them with a jerk of his arm. Art grabbed Sybil's hand and pulled her with him. She wasn't sure what she expected—if she'd *feel* a certain way going through Thaneish magic—but nothing discernible occurred. No tingling like when she shapeshifted. No cold or warmth washed through her. It was entirely ordinary.

The snowfall was heavy on this side of the boundary, but the wind seemed decreased. She could hear better as the man said,

"State your name and business."

"Art and Sybil. We have scheduled Shiftwork for Director Lowell Vox," Art said confidently.

"Confirmed." How he confirmed this was unclear, as he didn't look over or check any documentation.

"I don't recognize you. Where's Sergeant Downs?" Art asked.

"Downs is on temporary leave. My name is Jeremy Woods. Sergeant." The Thane crossed his arms over his muscular chest, apparent even under his thick coat. "Be quick about your business."

They didn't exchange farewells, and Art and Sybil began hiking down the rough trail, leaving the Thane and their beorg behind.

6.

The siblings barely interacted on their trek down the mountain, except for wordlessly exchanging the gloves. The ground was slippery, and rocks, crevices, and roots were hard to spot under the snowfall. Twice, Sybil's foot caught, and she nearly rolled her ankle. It was slow going, and she could focus on nothing about the forest around her except for getting to the road in one piece. She thought it would never end, that perhaps she'd die before even stepping foot off the mountain.

"There it is," Art huffed and pointed to a break in the trees where the edge of a dirt road was barely visible. He tugged off the gloves and passed them to Sybil. "It-t should get-t much easier from-m h-here." His teeth chattered.

Sybil, who had no feeling in her hands anymore, struggled to put the gloves on. "H-how f-far is the nearest-t t-town? We've got-t to get-t warm." To their relief, the blizzard had died down significantly, but they were still frozen through.

They broke through the tree line. The dirt road before them was not wide or particularly smooth, but it was distinctly not a trail and extended straight out of Sybil's sight. It was less dirt and more so a mixture of mud and snow, but there were tire treads on it. Out from the shadow of the trees, the clouds had split, and the sun shone down through their opening.

"H-how long d'you think-k we've been w-walking?" Sybil

asked, not giving Art a chance to answer her prior question.

"P-probably five or six hours. Judging by the sun, it's n-nearly mid-day," Art said, looking up at the sky.

"Art, we've gotta take a break-k. Not eaten anythin..."

Art shook his head, "We need to get to the t-town. Can't make a fire w-with the wood. It's t-too wet. Don't! Don't sit down!" He exclaimed, snatching Sybil by the arm and pulling her up from where she'd begun to sink. "We keep going."

Sybil didn't think she could keep going. Her toes were numb, her legs were tired, and her stomach was so, so empty. Art glanced at her, and she could see the intensity in his eyes. *This* was what it was to be a Shift. You had to persist through horrible things, and you could not be weak, or you would fall. Would fail. And when you did, none would weep for you, and another would replace you. Even through her dry, exhausted eyes, she could tell Art was judging her.

She grit her teeth and yanked her arm from his grasp. "F-fine." She marched off.

"Other way," Art said.

She socked him in the shoulder as she crossed back in front of him. "Screw you." She could've sworn he almost cracked a smile.

As Art had promised, it *did* get easier from that point on. The tire tracks in the road were muddy, but there were no obstacles and it kept their feet out of the deep snow that they'd been sinking in the entire way down the mountain. With the sun shining and a break in the wind, feeling returned to Sybil's extremities and her teeth stopped rattling. Though Art was adamant they eat as little as possible until they were certain they'd have food access on the job, the little bread they did share went a long way in revitalizing them.

"For the record, I've not forgotten about the discussion you promised me we'd have about you knowing how to read and write," Sybil said after a long period of silence. She finally felt warm enough from the exertion of the long walk to unwind her scarf from her face. "I'm sure it'd help us pass the time."

Art grunted.

"You said we'd talk about it later. It's later."

"It's kind of a long story," he returned.

"If you couldn't tell, we happen to have a long trip ahead of us. C'mon, out with it, Art. I've been quite patient, y'know."

Art sighed dramatically. "Fine. What d'you want to know?"

"Oh, I don't know. How'd you learn?"

"On a job."

"Lordy, Art," Sybil rolled her eyes. "I never would've guessed *that*." He shot her a scathing look. "What job? Stop being difficult."

"*Fine*. I had a job back in April up in Virginia. I was staging a number of break-ins for a businessman on his rivals. During one of them, I ran into a Thane who recognized me because he used to guard the boundary. Sergeant Downs."

"The one Sergeant Woods replaced?"

"One and the same." Art shrugged. "He told me he had an employer who had some unique work but wasn't ready to show at Career Day. I thought it was a trap of some kind, and we got in a pretty bloody fistfight."

"I remember that—you came home lookin' terrible."

"Thanks. Well, he's a Thane. He outlasted and overpowered me. Took me to this mystery employer..." He hesitated a moment. "It was the director. Lowell Vox."

"What?" Sybil exploded, stopping in her tracks. "You *knew* Vox before yesterday?"

"Yeah."

"And you just pretended *not* to? You both did? Wait—did you already know about this op?"

"Um, yeah.

Sybil swung her rucksack at him hard. He flinched but didn't budge. "What the hell, Art?"

"Well, let me finish!" Art insisted loudly. "Yeah, I've known Vox since April. Apparently, he had several Thanes tracking Shifts and their Shiftwork, trying to determine who he felt was capable enough to work for him. And willing to see the bigger picture to do so in an unusual capacity. He said he needed an inside man. Told me some about the happenings surrounding the election… This was before Calloway had been elected, of course, but campaigning was in full swing. He set it up that every month, I'd have pre-established work for him. Some were actual jobs he needed doin'. Other times, I'd meet with someone on his team, and they'd work with me on my reading."

"Why did he care so much about you being able to read or write?" Sybil asked.

"C'mon, let's keep walking," Art said, beginning again as if he just realized they'd been standing stationary. "He knew he had a big job coming. This one, in fact. He never told me what it was during our time together, but he kept mentioning the 'big one.'"

Art paused for a moment. "Vox is a real controlling guy, Sybil. He didn't think just any Shift would be able to make it to the president without being able to navigate society a little more expertly. So he made sure I could read and write, so I'd be best equipped."

"So you were just… meetin' with him from April until?"

"Until November, really. All my December jobs were legit. For him, yeah, but legit nonetheless."

"What was he having you do?"

"All manner of things. The work ran the gamut. I did break-ins and a handful of kidnappings, predominantly. Two arsons."

"And this was all to lead up to *this* specific job targeting the president's family?"

"More or less. He told you about wanting to discredit Calloway, right? It was sort of part of that but more so about causing chaos for those who surrounded and supported Calloway. *Support* Calloway," he amended.

Sybil watched him out of the corner of her eye. "Interesting," she said after a long moment.

"So, you see, it's not really a huge deal. It was just preparation for this job. But employer confidentiality, y'know."

"I know." Sybil's mouth twisted. "But it's strange."

"Yeah. It is."

"You trust him?"

"Of course not," Art said. "Never trust an employer, Sybil. There is nothin' trustworthy about any of them. They've got nothin' but their interests in mind. They'll sacrifice you in a heartbeat to keep their hands clean."

"But?" She prompted.

"But Vox is a very competent, strategic man. Can't say I disagree with his concern over the Calloway Administration. And the work has been good. Steady, interesting, and well-supported."

Sybil thought of the extra food they'd had over some of the summer and autumn months. "Okay," she said quietly, fixing her eyes on the road before her.

"This is all *highly* confidential," Art said.

"I'm not stupid, Art. I know that," she clapped back.

They walked quietly after that until the road turned to snow-covered pavement and dipped. At the foot of the hill rested a little town, nestled neatly in a snowy valley, framed by the mountains.

"That's our first stop," said Art. He readjusted his rucksack. "When we get down there, we're going to need to stay out of sight until we reach the train station."

"What about loading up on food?"

"One of us can swipe some once we know how much time we have before the train leaves. We can't afford to miss it."

"This is Miltown?" Sybil asked as the hill began to flatten and she could see distinct buildings before her.

Art pointed to a sign. "Population: 842. Small-town Eastward right here, Syb. Filled to the brim with routine-driven magi who'll be looking for the first sign of trouble to report on. It's important for us to stay out of sight here, much more so than the big cities."

"Can't we just shift into someone?"

"Well, obviously," Art said, exasperated. "But unless you have some nice, freshly laundered and pressed clothes in your rucksack, you'll stand out like a sore thumb."

Sybil couldn't help but brush a hand over her worn trousers and frayed overcoat. "Right," she said tightly. "Any more advice?"

Art laughed rather derisively. "For you, just the most important: you *cannot* look like you've never been off the mountain before. It'll be a dead giveaway you're a Shift. I know everything is new to you, and you'll have questions. That's fine. But you're a Shift first and foremost. You're no tourist. Besides, you've been hearing about the fyrnship your entire life. You know the way most things are supposed to work and generally what to expect. If you go around acting all interested in things you shouldn't think twice about..."

"Dead giveaway," Sybil confirmed.

"That's right. Welcome to Miltown, Sybil. Take a quick look because we're headin' to the sewers." Art made a grand welcoming gesture.

In contrast to the dusty, monochrome shacks and equally plain and dusty Shifts of her beorg, the village of Miltown was colorful, orderly, and clean. It had even sidewalks, shiny wrought-iron benches and lamp posts, buildings painted different colors, and signs with fancy script by shop entrances. The winter snow lay like a soft blanket over it all. The orderly trees, planted in exact rows, were just as naked as those in the beorg, but somehow they looked prettier down here. Artistic and dainty instead of skeletal and imposing.

Art led her off the main road to an alley behind the shops of Main Street. He had been through here many times, given it was the best place to stock up and get direction to wherever your op led you. The residents of Miltown had no understanding that the beorg of Shifts was just up the mountain from them and how many Shifts frequented their small town. If they did, it would certainly send them into an uproar of monumental proportions.

Even the alleyways of Miltown were cleaner than the whole of the beorg. The snow had been shoveled, making paths from the backs of businesses to their waste bins and tools, but the piles were sooty and grimy as opposed to the crisp white snow drifts on the main road. It smelled of chimney smoke, trash, and cigarettes. The buildings blocked the wind and sun simultaneously, and the shadows helped conceal their presence.

Sybil and Art walked quickly and silently, ducking behind waste bins or the brick half-walls that divided the businesses from each other whenever they heard voices or doors opening. It was a conscious effort for Sybil to keep her head down and not study every detail of this place. Art's words echoed in her mind: "You're no tourist." But it *was* hard to pretend she wasn't interested.

Familiar as Art was with Miltown, they made quick progress. Before long, they turned down a new alleyway, and Sybil heard the piercing whistle of a train.

"We're close," mouthed Art. "Stay near me."

The alley twisted, and they had to sneak their way across a sidewalk to get behind another row of shops. Art told Sybil they were lucky it was a weekday because most Miltown magi were at work or school; it made their out-in-the-open crossings less challenging.

"Okay, this is the back of the station," Art explained. Sybil craned her neck and saw they were indeed in the shadow of a long, red-brick building that rose up with a clock tower in the center. "Just need to figure out which train is headin' north," he said mostly to himself.

Sybil watched him, feeling awkward. Art was experienced and comfortable in this world, and she felt like he was holding her hand like a child at every turn. He had to. She didn't know where she was or what to do next. He did. She should be grateful to have the help on her first op, but it made her feel rather annoyed.

An enticing smell wafted on the air, and she realized how hungry she was. It'd been some time since they'd had that bread. That was most certainly not helping her mood.

Art whispered, "Stay here. I'll be back."

"Where are you going?"

"To find the right train!" He hissed. "Stay out of sight."

"Can I come?"

"No! Do what you're told, Sybil." He was gone in a blink.

Sybil stood there, frustrated, hungry, and tired. She inhaled sharply and wanted to cry over how wonderful that food smelled. It was like nothing she'd smelled before. Where was it coming from? Her stomach rumbled loudly. Art had told her to stay put, to stay out of sight. He wouldn't be gone for long, but... it'd save them time if she snagged something for them to eat on their ride. That would be a way she could finally prove useful to her brother.

She checked to the right and left for any sign of life and then crept along the back of the train depot until she reached the end of the building. She could see from here that it was an eatery and market together, with displays of produce outside, as well as small chairs and tables at which patrons could eat. She was just preparing to dart across the way when a middle-aged woman dressed in a wool coat and polished heels came around the corner. Sybil swore and crouched.

An idea struck her as the woman passed by. And, without a second thought, Sybil jumped up and locked her arm around the woman's neck. So surprised as she was, the woman didn't resist or fight back until just before she lost consciousness.

Delighted at her work, Sybil dragged the woman behind the nearest waste bin and peeled the wool overcoat off her. She studied the woman's features closely. A crooked nose, hazel eyes, a lined forehead, fair skin, thick black hair.

Eagerness coursed through Sybil as she shifted into the woman. The buzzing began at her skull before flooding her blood down to her toes. Her fingertips tingled, and a familiar warmth washed over her. She couldn't resist smiling.

When it was over, she made sure to add extra pounds around her hips and rear to mimic the woman's frame. She pulled the woman's overcoat over her clothing, instantly amazed at its effectiveness against the winter temperature. She attempted to pull the cap from the woman's head until she realized it was pinned. She fished around the black hair until she located the pins, extricated them, and promptly fastened the hat atop her matching hair.

Gloves! She snatched them too. And a purse.

Nearly giddy, Sybil checked her work in a back windowpane and could find no faults. She quickly confirmed she was in no danger of the woman waking before straightening and waltzing across the road to the shop like any magi of Miltown would.

7.

"Ah, good morning, Mrs. Atwood," a friendly voice exclaimed.

Sybil had barely entered the cafe and market. She froze with her hand still on the doorknob, her stomach lurching.

"Good morning," she said carefully. It dawned on her that she had no opportunity to listen to Mrs. Atwood or observe the woman's mannerisms, and her own speech could quickly betray her. If she could disguise her drawl at all, it'd help.

"It's a fine day for shopping!" The shopkeeper was speaking to her again. A rather pudgy fellow, he had thinning blonde hair and a sizable nose. His face was kind, and his cheeks were rosy. He was loading shelves with round loaves of bread. *That* was what she had been smelling. Fresh bread. Sybil's stomach rumbled noisily, and she hoped the shopkeeper couldn't hear it.

"Yes, yes, it is," she said in a tight voice, higher than her own. She folded her gloved hands together, the purse strap over her elbow knocking into her widened hip. She tried to appear relaxed, though her heart raced and thoughts of "*What am I doing?*" whipped through her mind.

"Are you looking for anything specific today? Anything I can help you with?" The shopkeeper asked.

"Oh, just looking for now. Thank you—" She searched the man for identification. She spotted a white, oval name plate pinned above his apron but couldn't read it. Flushing stupidly, she repeated, "Thank you," before scurrying off to browse.

Her eyes curiously traced the shelves. She spotted a few things she recognized, like bread, flour, meats, and canned goods. Yet it seemed there were hundreds of things on which she'd never laid eyes. The produce section, in particular, boggled her mind. There was such variety in color, shape, size, and texture, and the only ones she recognized were apples because of the handful of apple trees within the beorg.

A new dilemma struck her. She couldn't read the price tags, nor could she interpret money. Even as she held the woman's purse, she knew she could be betrayed by hesitancy on paying, something Mrs. Atwood would not think twice about. Sybil chewed the inside of her cheek and mentally berated herself for rushing into this.

Art was going to kill her. Worse, he was probably already back and wondering where she was. This had been a huge mistake.

Sybil studied the purse. It was rather large... She glanced over her shoulder. The shopkeeper continued organizing the fresh loaves of bread on the wooden shelf, but then the door swung open with a *ding-ding* of a bell hanging over it. A finely dressed, white-haired woman entered.

"Good morning, Mrs. Simpson!" The shopkeeper cried without pausing his task.

"Good morning to you, Mr. McCormick," she said crisply. Sybil watched from behind the shelves as Mrs. Simpson leaned near to the shopkeeper and said in a false whisper, "Did you hear about the Waltons?"

Mr. McCormick practically threw the last loaf of bread and clasped Mrs. Simpson's hand. "It's such a shame, truly. Mr. Walton should have *never* bet so much of their savings on that race. Any sensible magi would know Barbaro was the dark horse. The animal was never going to be in the money..."

"Well, it's more than *that*, Mr. McCormick!" Mrs. Simpson insisted bossily. "Because of his lapse in judgement and the subsequent dramatic loss of funds, their young Melania may very well have to part ways with her dream to study music at Hallowdale! They sent scouts to the district last quarter, you know. I have *always* said she was a gifted girl who could play for the president himself! And now her lousy gambling father may have ruined her chances!"

"Let's not forget there are scholarships, Mrs. Simpson. She may have her chance yet," said Mr. McCormick.

"Oh—and speaking of the *president*," Mrs. Simpson continued as if Mr. McCormick hadn't spoken a word. "This morning's newspaper said that he sent ambassadors to Southward *and* Westward to invite them to this year's gala. No president has ever included foreign dignitaries at the Veteran's Gala. Everyone knows it is to celebrate the Thanes of Eastward!"

"Why, Mrs. Simpson," chortled Mr. McCormick. "Don't be such a critic. He's barely been in office a full month. Give the man a chance."

"I don't have to give him a chance to know I don't like him!" Mrs. Simpson stuck her nose in the air. "I'll never understand why *anyone* would vote for him. All this change and progress for the sake of progress."

"It wasn't all progression. Have you forgotten his traditional values? That was an integral part of his campaign, if you'll remember," said Mr. McCormick.

"Traditional values, bah! How can you possibly be traditional and *progressive*? And all this nonsense of increasing our involvement with international affairs... Why ever should we want that? How in the heavens will that benefit Eastward? Oh," she moaned dramatically. "Picture one of those Southward *cowboys* at our gala. A sight that will be! Calloway is making a mockery of the event! I can hardly imagine it."

"Tsk tsk, Mrs. Simpson," tutted Mr. McCormick. "You won't have to imagine it. The gala is only a few days away. Sunday, isn't it?" Sunday was the day after tomorrow.

Sybil listened intently for any lull or change in the conversation and quickly began stuffing small items into Mrs. Atwood's purse. Two apples, a wedge of hard white cheese, two cans of corn. What she really wanted was a loaf of that bread, but there was no way it would fit into the purse. She bit her lip as she rummaged through it to find the green paper money. She analyzed it. What had Art told her about recognizing the bills? Her mind was blank. Curse whoever changed the monetary system in Eastward from gold and silver to paper bills!

"Why, Mr. McCormick, you've raised the cost of bread!" Mrs. Simpson's voice shrieked, piercing Sybil's ear.

"Now, now, Mrs. Simpson," the storekeeper said soothingly. "We are both old enough to know how times change. I do my best to keep my prices reasonable, but I myself must also make a living. Prices have risen everywhere."

"It's that blasted Calloway and his new administration. Mark my words—he'll drive the economy into the ground!"

"Mrs. Simpson, really. I *hardly* think a loaf of bread going for twelve cents instead of ten equates to an economic collapse."

Twelve cents. Sybil landed on a bill that had two numbers on it instead of just one. She had to imagine it was larger and hoped she'd be able to fake her way through the exchange. Her stomach cramped painfully, and she felt a little crazed over how badly she wanted that bread.

"Excuse me—I'm sorry to interrupt." She stepped out from behind the shelves.

Mr. McCormick and Mrs. Simpson both looked at her. Mrs.

Simpson's gnarly finger was mid-point.

"Mrs. Atwood? What are you doing here?" Mrs. Simpson's eyebrows shot up.

"Browsing," Sybil said stiffly.

"Did you need help with anything, Mrs. Atwood?" Mr. McCormick asked quickly, even as Mrs. Simpson's mouth prepared a retort.

"No, I was just leaving. Although I think I may take one of these fresh loaves..." Sybil nearly blundered and asked if Mr. McCormick baked them before reminding herself that Mrs. Atwood would absolutely know the answer to that question.

"Certainly, certainly. Follow me." Mr. McCormick handed her a loaf—still warm in its brown paper wrappings—and waddled to the cash register behind a white countertop. "Twelve cents."

Sybil couldn't help herself. "Such a reasonable price given the economy." She could feel Mrs. Simpson's piercing gaze on her. Hoping Mr. McCormick wouldn't notice her hand shaking, she passed him the bill.

He looked at it, and her heartbeat quickened. "Do you have anything smaller, dear?"

"I'm sorry, no. Is it a problem?"

"No, not at all. Just take me a moment to count up your change." Relief flooded Sybil, and her shoulders relaxed. "There you go, Mrs. Atwood. You have a nice day, and tell Mr. Atwood he owes me a game of chess soon."

"I'll be certain to. Thank you, Mr. McCormick." Sybil flashed him a smile and then a cool glance at Mrs. Simpson and walked out the door with the loaf of bread tucked under her arm and the stolen goods in her bag. The bell jingled cheerfully behind her.

She made it back to the alley behind the train depot with no trouble and was pleased to see the real Mrs. Atwood still unconscious. She shifted back into herself and crouched down to begin transferring the items from the purse to her rucksack.

"Where the *hell* have you been?" Art caught her arm and yanked her to her feet. His face was red, the vein in his forehead popping spectacularly. His voice was low but quaked with rage.

"Gettin' us some food!" She sputtered, trying to show him the corn she had just pulled from the purse. He shook her hard.

"I came back here, and you were *gone*, and there's an unconscious woman tucked behind a waste bin, with *your* rucksack next to her. I had no *idea* where you were or if something happened to you. I told you to STAY HERE!" He said, his voice rising now in his fury.

She tried to twist her arm out of his grasp, but Art was stronger than she was. "I was trying to be useful!"

"I don't care what you were doing. I brought you on this op under the agreement that you would do *what I said,* not what you thought would be *useful!*" He spat, shaking her again. "You could've blown this whole thing before it even started!"

"Okay, okay, I'm sorry!"

"I don't know what you were thinking, Sybil. Did that woman see you?"

"No! Of course not."

"You've been a bloody *fool*, Sybil. I've got half a mind to send you straight back up the mountain," Art seethed, wildly flailing his free arm in the vague direction of the beorg.

"Geez, Art, you've made your point. I was an idiot." She nearly apologized but couldn't quite get the words out. "You're hurting me. Let go of my arm before I fight back." Sybil was amazed at the level of restraint in her own voice as she attempted to de-escalate her brother.

Art's chest heaved, and his eyes flared, but he released her and took a step back. She rubbed at the sore spot and flashed him an angry look. "Thanks for the bruises. If you want some fresh bread or an apple, it's in the purse."

"This ain't funny, Sybil. It's really not. I cannot possibly impress upon you the idiocy of what you did." Now he was pacing.

"You're doing a pretty good job of it so far," she retorted hotly, crouching to pack up the remaining food items. He was right; she shouldn't have done it. It was rash. But it did go off without a hitch. They had food now. Mrs. Atwood, Mr. McCormick, and Mrs. Simpson were none the wiser. No harm had been done.

"No harm was done? *No harm was done?*" Art repeated. She didn't realize she had said her last thought out loud.

"Oh, cool it, will you? No harm *was* done. Everything is fine! I'm back, you're back, we've got food, and no one suspects a thing. Be mad all you want about what could've happened, but I actually didn't blow it. I did a good job," she screeched, yanking Mrs. Atwood's cap from her head and pinning it sloppily back atop the unconscious woman's thin hair.

Art kicked a rock, and it shot across the back alley.

Neither of them said anything more as Sybil slipped the warm wool coat off her, revealing her shabby thin clothing again, and draped it over Mrs. Atwood. She shivered as the cold air seeped into her clothes.

"The gloves too," Art said pointedly. Sybil glared at him out of half-lidded eyes as she tugged the gloves off and yanked Mrs. Atwood's cool hands into them. The woman let out a small moan.

"Did you find the right train?" Sybil asked.

"Yeah, it leaves in five. That's why I was so panicked I couldn't find you; we could miss it!" He was heating up again.

She swung her rucksack over her shoulder. "We'll only miss it if you keep yellin' at me. Help me move Mrs. Atwood out of the alley, and we'll go."

"We'd best be quick about it. We gotta sneak aboard," Art said, grabbing Mrs. Atwood from under the armpits. Sybil held her feet, and they brought the woman to the end of the train depot where Sybil had assaulted her. They let her rest against the brick again, mostly out of sight of any passersby, but hopefully close enough to where she'd been strolling that she'd wake thinking she had fallen and hit her head, not wondering why she was in the middle of a back alley.

"This way," Art said, reverting back to business mode. The train let out a long harsh whistle. "We don't have much time."

They snuck around the train depot towards the railroad. At the front, there was a wooden platform with a wide overhang, shielding it and the tracks from snow and rain. Wrought iron benches were secured every few feet on the platform, and they looked as if they'd been freshly polished. The platform was empty. The station, as a whole, was not large, but she assumed it'd be busier. They dodged two train workers, who were consumed with their tasks, but spotted no others.

Sybil's jaw dropped when she took in the sight of the train. It was enormous—quite possibly the largest thing she had ever laid eyes on. It belched black smoke, which plumed above it and filled the sky. Its engine was black with an iron-gray smokestack.

"Follow me. Quickly," Art said by her ear. He pulled her swiftly past numerous train cars until they passed behind the last car, crossed the tracks, and ducked into the surrounding tree line. It was only then that Sybil realized the train station was at the far end of the town of Miltown. She'd passed all the way through and barely seen any of it.

Art gestured to the muted, multi-colored cars. "These are freight cars. This train is headin' to Blacksburg."

"That doesn't sound like Washington," Sybil said.

"Not at all. That's Virginia, but it's just a stopover. It'll switch tracks and head north. As long as weather permits and there are no maintenance delays, it should put us in Washington in about four hours."

"How long to Blacksburg?"

"Three. We won't reach Washington until dark."

Art pointed through the trees, and Sybil followed his finger to a dull mustard-colored car, rusting around the base. It was the first thing she'd seen of the fyrnship that did not appear brand new.

Art explained, "We're gonna get up on that train car there—where the door is half-open—and then pretend we don't exist while the rail police do their final checks. Let's make quick work of it. They'll be comin' around shortly. Train departs at noon."

With one more verifying glance that no one was on this side of the train, the siblings sprinted up to the car that rested idly with its side door slid open. Art grabbed the handle and swung himself up with ease. He reached down and clasped Sybil's arm and pulled her up after him.

"Look around later," he said, as if reading her mind as she took in the metal slatted walls. Art threw his weight against a huge stack of wooden crates and pushed. They budged slightly. "Geez, what's in these?" He grunted. They were two feet tall and two wide and nailed solidly shut. He managed to move it a fraction. "Back here. Can you fit?"

"Probably."

"Shrink yourself if not. I'm not moving it any more," Art panted.

Sybil slimmed herself by a few inches and managed to fit behind them, her back flattened into the wall of the train car. She had to keep her head turned sideways. A sudden, overwhelming sense of claustrophobia settled over her as Art stuffed her rucksack at her feet and pushed the crates closer together again so there was only a few inches of space between the two stacks. "So, uh, what's the plan if these get pushed back into place? I'll be flattened."

"From out here, you can't tell they got moved," came Art's voice from somewhere else in the train car.

"Will they fall when we get moving?"

"Too heavy to tip."

"Where are you?"

"Would you shut up and wait until we get moving? The railway police could come by any moment," he growled.

Sybil clamped her mouth shut and tried to breathe steadily through her nose. The train car felt like an icebox. She couldn't see anything except more crates. The train car had an odd smell of metal, wood, and something else she couldn't determine. Something sharp poked her between her shoulder blades, but there was no room to adjust her position.

That's when two different male voices reached her ears, growing louder by the moment. The train car rocked slightly as one of them climbed aboard. He didn't say anything, but Sybil could hear his heavy footfall as he perused the cargo inside.

"Everything in order?" hollered the one outside.

"Looks like it," said the other. He was far closer to Sybil than she had realized. It sounded as if he stood directly before the crates that concealed her. "Yeah, everything's in order here, Bill."

"Great. Come on down, and we'll seal it up. This is the last one. I know Mike is itching to get going. You know how he is about sticking to the schedule," said Bill.

The car rocked again as the man descended, and Sybil winced as the train car's door slid shut, shrieking and groaning until a solid thud left the interior in stark silence. The door's opening had allowed a ray of sunlight in, like a sheet on the car floor, but now they were lost to a darkness worse than her cabin on a winter's night. Sybil could no longer see the crates to her right, even though she knew they were only inches from her.

She let out a breath she had forgotten she'd been holding.

"Are you okay?" Art asked.

"Yes," she said, her voice sounding small and disconnected from her body.

"Don't move until the train does, just in case."

To Sybil's relief, the train began moving shortly after. With a jolt, a loud hiss of steam, and a long whistle, it pulled out from the station, slowly at first and then quickly gaining speed.

"I could use some of that fresh bread right about now," Art said. He sounded closer to her again.

Sybil struggled to find her way out of her narrow hiding space. She scraped the back of her hand against one of the crates and felt blood trickle down her knuckles. Her sense of panic heightened as she kept getting stuck, virtually blind. When Art's hand closed over her forearm and helped her the rest of the way out, she was fighting back tears. At least Art couldn't see her bloodless face in the dark.

"How did you manage to get stuck?" He asked, his tone humorous.

"I wasn't stuck," she mumbled defensively. "I was blind."

"Sure." Art passed her rucksack to her and sat down, leaning his back against the crates. She joined him, back to her natural size, and fished around in her rucksack for the loaf of bread. The brown paper wrapping crinkled under her fingers. She felt around to open it, broke a piece off, and held it in Art's general direction.

"Here," she said shortly.

"What's your problem? Everything went off without a hitch," Art said, his mouth full of bread. She wanted to retort that *he* had been the one with the problem less than twenty minutes ago and was now reaping the rewards of her efforts.

But instead, she said, “Nothing,” and bit into her own hunk of bread, hoping its taste would wash away some of her sullenness. It was going to be a long trip.

8.

Between the restlessness of the past two nights and the physical exertion of trekking off the beorg, Sybil's exhaustion overtook her quickly. She tucked her rucksack under her head, curled onto her side, and was soon lulled to sleep by the chuffing engine and swaying train car.

She slept dreamlessly and, when she finally awoke, was momentarily disoriented. Her fingers and toes numb, she forced herself upright. She was brushing sleep from her eyes with her frozen hand when it dawned on her they were no longer moving.

Sybil reached over and roughly shook her brother awake, who had also fallen into a deep sleep after eating.

"Wha'?" He mumbled, not even cracking an eye.

"We've stopped," Sybil whispered anxiously.

Art was up in a flash. He grabbed the interior handle of the train car and wrenched it. To both of their surprise—and relief—it was unlocked and creaked open a few inches. He peered out, and Sybil crawled over on all fours to peek out the bottom. Another snowy scene greeted them, but, besides that, she was uncertain as to what she was looking at.

Another train chugged by them, churning up snow and blasting it on the wind with its force. Sybil flung herself away from the opening.

"Are we at another station? Is this Blacksburg?" she asked.

"I can't tell. Step back a bit; I'm going to open this wider." The door creaked loudly, and Sybil winced at how the sound echoed and wailed. Art gripped the side of the car and stuck his head out. "No, this definitely ain't a station. We're stopped on the tracks."

"But where? Did we miss Blacksburg? Are we on the wrong train?" Sybil wasn't tempering her anxiety very well. She never would've expected to feel so suffocated outside the beorg, but the vast unfamiliarity of the fyrnship pressed in at her from all sides. She wondered if it'd bury her before the op even started.

"Hold your horses," Art said evenly. "You see that sign over there?"

Scrambling back to the opening, Sybil poked her head out enough for her eyes to reach where Art was pointing. There was a large green sign, pale under the cloudy sky.

"That says Culpeppr, four miles." At her questioning look, Art explained, "Culpeppr is en route to Washington. We must've stopped for maintenance or because of the weather conditions. I guess Freida's blizzard moved north."

Sybil retreated back to her spot as Art slid the door mostly closed again, leaving them a sliver of light. She propped her rucksack against a crate to cushion her back. "I can't believe you just know all of that. How do other Shifts get around if they can't read?"

Art, still standing, stretched. "Practice. You learn the land. You pay attention. After a few ops, you get your bearings. As much as I hate to admit it, I do have a leg up now. I've been able to read and study maps since Vox contracted me. Maps are invaluable."

"Maybe you can teach me," Sybil said, unable to keep hopefulness from her tone.

"We'll see. Not sure we'll have time for that," Art said dismissively. Sybil flushed, with embarrassment or anger, she wasn't quite sure. He was being so bossy and snobby, as if he really thought he was special because Vox had chosen him to be his representative and equip him with additional skills the other Shifts had no way of acquiring.

You're not special, Art. You're good at what you do, but so are the rest of us, she thought angrily. She'd bite her tongue for now; their op had only just begun. But if he kept up this attitude, she wasn't sure she'd be able to restrain herself.

Ethel's words from Career Day circled in her mind. "*We're supposed to have a level playing field here! But this one 'ere... he's thrown his lot in with* them."

Sybil unconsciously pressed a hand to her stomach, as if she could stay the knots from forming.

"If we're near Culpeppr, we should hit Washington in about an hour, give or take. Once they get movin' again," Art was saying. "Once we get to Washington, we'll want to get off the train before hitting Union Station. There's almost no way to get off undetected in Union Station. From there, our priority is to get connected to Calloway. Every kidnapping is easier if you can make connection with the family and not be seen as a threat before making your move..."

"The ball." The words fell from her lips before she registered fully what she was suggesting.

"What?"

"There's a ball. I overheard someone talking about it when I went to the market for the food." Mrs. Simpson had said it was a gala for the Thanes, a traditional event. And Mr. McCormick said it was Sunday. She relayed this to her brother.

Art was quiet for a long moment. "That's not a bad idea. If we can find someone attending, we can go in their place. I bet the president has to greet the attendees, so you may be able to speak with him and, if you make a big enough impression—"

"*You*? You're meanin' to send *me* to do this?"

"Yeah. It makes the most sense. Can't exactly catch Calloway in a compromising situation with *me*. That was part of this too, remember? That's why we needed you."

"B-but..."

"Are you a Shift or not? I brought you on this op because I knew you were capable." *And because you knew I'd have to defer to you on everything.* "I didn't bring you so I could do it all myself."

When Sybil said nothing, Art forged ahead with his plan, "So, we'll want to get ourselves somewhere affluent so we can find a gala attendee. We'll have you take her identity... Easy enough. You'll go to the gala in her stead, and I'll use the time to stake out the president's mansion and see if I can figure out the best way to access his kids."

"That doesn't seem like the most foolproof plan," Sybil said dryly.

He shrugged. "That's Shiftwork. There's never a foolproof plan."

A couple of hours later, Sybil and her brother skulked in the shadows of yet another alley, this time staring at an enormous, elaborate hotel located on one of the main streets of Washington. It was dark now, but the city of Washington was wide awake under the golden glow of street lights.

Sybil had seen little of the historic city since they leapt from their train car and trudged in sludgy snow to its outskirts, which was when they ducked back into alleyways like the rats they were. Art was far less concerned with someone spotting them now, but he claimed their clothing would still draw attention. From what she could see, smell, and hear, it was clear Washington was a place unlike any other—at least in her world.

"The Alistaire Beck Grande Hotel. We should try to get inside there," Art said lowly. "It's only three blocks from the White House. Gala guests are in there, I'd lay money on it."

"We can't walk inside like this."

"No kidding." Art rolled his eyes. "We need to catch someone comin' out and then send you in."

Fatigue from the day settled into Sybil's body as they waited, and her head repeatedly dropped to her chest as she'd nod off, only to shake herself awake and the cycle to begin again. There was no way to tell how much time passed. Even Art appeared to be fading, the way he slouched against the back of the building, taking refuge in its great shadow. The temperature plummeted with night, and Sybil distantly wondered if she had ever been warm before or would be warm again.

"Let's move around back. This is useless. No one is leaving this late in the day," Art said wearily.

Night on their side, they briskly crossed the road and slipped around back of the Alistaire Beck unseen.

"You're looking for an employee?" Sybil asked.

"Just to get inside. I was hoping for a guest, but—"

"What would you have done with the body?" Sybil finished.

"Exactly."

"There, Art!" Sybil whispered, grabbing his arm. "Someone's coming out."

They both waited, their bodies tense, their breaths held. Sybil felt a bit like a cougar preparing to pounce on its unsuspecting prey. A kitchen boy exited the hotel through a small white door, carrying two large bags of trash. He set them down and lifted the lid of the large brown waste bin. Art nudged her hard.

When the boy turned to pick up the trash to deposit in the bin, Sybil was there. He dropped the trash with a cry that was quickly silenced. He was small in stature, but the weight of his limp body caused Sybil to stagger.

Art sprinted over, and they carried the boy to the opposite

side of the trash bin, where he was completely obscured by it but wouldn't draw suspicion if someone came across him. Sybil moved the trash bags he'd dropped to the ground around him. If anyone saw him, they'd think he'd fallen asleep on the job and picked an unappealing place for a rest.

"It's too bad you can't shift into him," Art said, staring down at the boy and analyzing his features.

"Why?"

"Well, you look more like him than I do. It'd be less work." At her glare, he added, gesturing somewhat helplessly to her figure, "You know, because he's like an eleven year old boy!"

"I know! And he's more than eleven. He has the beginnings of a mustache there," she said, crossing her arms.

Art sighed, and Sybil watched as he shapeshifted into the young boy. His figure became watery, as if she peered through weeping eyes even though hers were dry, before solidifying into a new form. It was a unique sensation to feel as if your whole body was alive, warm and tingling, every sense and cell heating up, but, on the outside, to appear only as if you were a reflection against a waterfall.

Art was a good six inches shorter now and his build far narrower, from his shoulders to the width of his arms and legs. His hair was strawberry-blonde and longer than his close-cropped brown.

"Grab his coat," Art said, peeling off his top layers and shivering in the process.

Sybil knelt and confiscated the boy's jacket. It didn't appear to be a uniform or to have much warmth to it, but it was nicer than what Art had. She passed it to her brother, and he quickly slipped it on over his hole-filled thermal, which his new figure swam in.

As he buttoned it up, Art instructed, "Follow me, but if anyone shows, make yourself scarce. We'll get inside, and I'll check the hotel records to see if there are any female guests staying alone. That's what we really need. Someone you can impersonate with no strings attached."

"And getting into the gala?"

"Eh, we'll have no way of knowing that. You'll just have to use your womanly guiles to make that happen." Coming from the boy's mouth made this statement funny to her, and she bit the inside of her cheek to contain a chuckle.

The plan to get inside the Alistaire Beck went smoothly, except for a few wrong turns making their way out from the underbelly of the hotel and into the guest area. Sybil wasn't sure exactly what time of night it was, but there was little stirring inside the hotel, even from employees, making it easy for them to take the time to figure out where they needed to go. Art being able to read the directions on gold nameplates definitely helped. The hotel itself was a labyrinth—the biggest building Sybil had ever seen, much less stepped foot in.

When they found the lobby with its expansive concierge desk, she kept watch as Art sifted through keys and guest records. It was clear to Sybil now why Vox needed his Shift to be able to read, whether she agreed with it or not. This Shiftwork would be virtually impossible otherwise. Her eyes roamed the lobby of the Alistaire, watching for movement but also absorbing the beautiful space.

The atrium was cavernous with painted ceilings, arched entryways, and marble columns. Ornate tapestries, glass chandeliers, and dark furniture with upholstery of various rich colors like gold, ivory, rust, and navy decorated the space. It was breathtaking. It was something out of a fairytale.

"Got it." Art stood up from behind the desk. "Roxana Bloodknight."

"Excuse me?"

"Suite 366. Roxana Bloodknight. She arrived today by herself from Beaufort, South Carolina. Her father is joining her in four days time to attend the grand opening of the Stānwyrta Chamber of Craftes—"

"What on earth is *that*?"

Art finished, "—which he is apparently a sponsor for. It looks like it's a museum."

"How do you know all that?"

"There's a note," he answered, holding it up and waving it before her like a white flag. He quickly put everything back the way he found it. "Let's go."

They avoided the automatic lifts and took the stairwell to the third floor, being careful not to make any noise. When they found Suite 366, Art offered, "Want to do the honors?"

Suppressing a grin, Sybil whipped out a hairpin she had stolen from Mrs. Atwood and went to work on the door.

They found Roxana Bloodknight asleep in an enormous bed. Art quietly pulled out a flask from his rucksack and pressed a cloth to its opening. He crept up to Roxana's sleeping figure and swiftly pressed it into her face. She jolted before going limp again.

"Chloroform," he mouthed to Sybil.

"You just happened to have a stash of chloroform at the beorg?" She asked incredulously.

"Of course."

"Does Vox supply you?"

"Don't sound so accusatory. I always make sure I have some for any and every op. If I'm low, I get more before I come home. I'd encourage you to learn to do the same," he said bossily, returning to himself, stretching the boy's jacket to a near breaking point. He tore it off.

Sybil didn't know what to take in first: the expensive suite or the unconscious woman on the bed she'd need to become for the foreseeable future. Nervousness swelled inside her at the latter thought, so she did a quick intake of the room in which they stood.

It was as extravagant as the lobby of the Alistaire with a plush rug, a large bed with a curved wooden headboard and a white billowing comforter, and dark-washed side tables with white lamps. There was a stiff-backed chair next to a small writing desk where a pad of paper with the Alistaire Beck logo at the top rested on the desk, a fountain pen next to it.

"Open that door, would ya?" Art grunted. She turned to see he held Roxana Bloodknight in his arms. Even draped and unconscious as she was, she was a beautiful woman. Her nightdress did little to conceal her willowy form. Her hair was a sunny blonde with a golden red hue, and her braid swung as Art moved around. Her skin was the color of fresh cream, devoid of any blemish or freckle. Art had already blindfolded her. They lucked out selecting such a stunning young woman.

Sybil quickly swung open the closet door he had indicated, and he lowered Roxana to the floor. Together, they positioned her where she was lying down again and then bound her hands and feet. They pulled everything out of the closet, including two small valises, a jewelry case, and a number of gowns and coats on velvet hangers.

Sybil deposited the belongings at the foot of the bed, and Art fastened the closet closed.

"How long will she be out?" Sybil asked.

"Hopefully a few hours. Enough for us to get some sleep and start fresh tomorrow." He was already peeling off his travel-worn clothing.

"I'm gonna take advantage of that bathroom over there first," Sybil said.

Art mumbled, "Whatever."

Sybil explored the ensuite bathroom, her mouth falling open

as she entered. It was washed in light and gold hardware, from the faucets to the mirror. A magnificent claw-foot tub stood in the corner, and there was a separate door to the water closet.

That sure beats a hole in the ground, Sybil thought. There was something quite... electric about the space. Goosebumps pricked at her skin, and, when she traced a finger along the gold-framed mirror, the hairs on her neck stood straight.

Suddenly, she felt very timid, realizing that in all her seventeen years, she'd only seen herself in a dull handheld mirror with jagged cracks breaking up her reflection. She'd never seen her body in anything but a window reflecting back at her when the light was right.

Sybil closed the bathroom door and locked herself in. Her hand rested on the knob for a long moment as her heart beat faster and faster. She swallowed and peeled off her clothes until she stood naked, goosebumps spreading across her skin. She kept her eyes on her feet and chewed the inside of her cheek. Dirt lined the creases of her feet and nail beds. She padded back to the mirror.

What was this? What was wrong with her? She had never lacked confidence before. Never felt insecure about her body or nakedness. She bathed in the stream at home with no fear. Xavier certainly seemed attracted to her. But this was different. It was just her and the mirror. No hiding her flaws behind layers of old clothes, dirty windows, cracked displays, Shifted attributes, or the veil of darkness. It was all of her all at once for only her to see.

Sybil breathed in. Breathed out. And looked up.

Frozen, she stared into the mirror. The girl in the mirror couldn't be her. For one, she hardly looked like a girl at all. Her face held no youthful glow or fullness. It was thin, and her skin was rough from harsh weather. Her eyes were a light yellow-ish brown, like the color of raw honey. There was a dullness to them, a lifelessness, an exhaustion. Her long hair was an unimpressive shade of brown and stringy from weeks without a wash.

Freckles splashed across her face and down her neck and arms. She was perhaps a bit taller than she thought she was. She slowly circled, craning her neck to see behind her. She found freckles on her back that she never knew were there.

Lost in her own fascination, she began shapeshifting. For the first time, as her head buzzed and warmth spread through her veins, she watched her own reflection shift. Her figure became watery before solidifying into a new form.

Now, she was Elsa Llewelyn. That pretty employee of Vox's.

She shifted again, watching closely as she turned into the woman Vox had shown her in the photograph, the First Lady. And then back to herself. She let out a laugh of disbelief. Shifts were a wonder. Their magic was a wonder. How could no one else see it in them?

Sybil frowned and leaned forward to inspect the grime coating every part of her. Her lip curled in disgust. No wonder everyone thought Shifts were filthy and diseased. She was gross.

She turned from the mirror to the claw-footed tub. She reached for the knob, but the tub began to fill on its own as soon as her hand passed over it. It was as if the Alistaire knew exactly what she needed and what she wanted.

She didn't know how long she stayed in the hot water. She meticulously washed every part of herself, from her fingernails to between her toes. Twice. She used up the entire bar of soap, lathering, rinsing, and re-lathering her hair and scrubbing her skin raw.

When she got out, there was a fluffy white robe with the Alistaire Beck emblem on it waiting for her. She wrapped herself in it and combed her hair with the golden wide-toothed comb sitting in a porcelain dish on the marble countertop.

Art was dead asleep when she came back to the suite. Roxana Bloodknight, too, remained silent. Sybil padded over to the big bed where Art lay on his back, one arm resting above his head, the other over his chest.

She climbed in next to him and curled onto her side, feeling as if the mattress and pillows would swallow her whole. She only had time to think about how life-changing this one day had been, how she'd been asleep in a crowded one-room cabin less than twenty-four hours ago, how many worlds away that seemed, before sleep overtook her.

9.

The siblings slept hard and late. Art was surprisingly unperturbed by this when they woke, but he quickly got to business. Roxana Bloodknight was making a banging noise in the closet with her fists and feet, and he decidedly pressed more chloroform to her face without a second thought.

"She'll need to eat," Sybil said, still buried under the comforter.

"She will. We're orderin' room service," he said with a mischievous glint in his eyes. He told Sybil what to order and showed her how to dial and use the rotary phone. She called down, pretending to be Roxana, for several plates of food. Neither of them cared that one woman would never eat so much. Art said hotel staff was notoriously good at keeping their clientele's secrets and would think little of the excessive order.

Art took a bath, while Sybil dragged herself from the bed to take inventory of Roxana's belongings, which she had left strewn across the floor. There were party dresses, day dresses, and two coats (one casual, one formal) on the hangers. The valises were empty, but she found the garments—including appropriate underwear, stockings, gloves, scarves, and hats—neatly put away on the shelves of an armoire to the right of the large window.

The jewelry case consisted of three smaller, velvet cases. Tentatively, she ran her fingers over them and popped the latch of the one on top. The suite lights glinted off the diamonds inside.

Wide-eyed, she perused its contents. The stones were cold to her touch. One gold ring caught her attention. It looked like it could be four rings stacked and fused together, but, upon further inspection, it was actually strings of beads layered atop each other. Each string alternated between dainty beads and bolder ones.

Sybil's hand shook a little as she slid the ring onto her middle finger on her right hand and examined it. It was a little loose but not loose enough to accidentally slip off. The metal was cool, but it quickly grew warm once on and seemed to mold to fit her finger. She kept the ring on as she went through the rest of the jewelry—bulky necklaces, dangling earrings, diamond bracelets.

"Stop pawin' at that stuff. Get dressed and ready so when the food arrives, nothing will look amiss," came Art's scolding voice. He stood in the entrance of the bathroom with a towel wrapped around his waist.

"I was cleaning everything up for that very reason, thank you very much," Sybil said hotly. *You get temporarily sidetracked, and that's all he notices.*

Sybil snagged undergarments, stockings, and a modest day dress. She shifted into Roxana in the bathroom, making sure every curve of her body and color hue were correct. Their food arrived shortly after, and she sweetly greeted the bellboy. Art hid in the closet with Roxana while the bellboy laid food trays on the circular table underneath a centerpiece of flowers, which he also replaced with a fresh bouquet.

"Will you be needing anything else, Miss Bloodknight?"

"No. Thank you," Sybil said, trying to minimize her twang and speak as a socialite might.

The siblings feasted on buttered toast, boiled eggs, slabs of crisp bacon, and fresh fruit. Sybil didn't know what any of the fruit was, though she recognized some of it from Mr. McCormick's store, but the flavors exploded in her mouth upon each bite. It was heavenly.

Art made quick work of his plate and then swiped his mouth with the cloth napkin. "Your priority, Syb, is to find a way into that gala to connect with Calloway. The lounge would be a good place to start. We only have four days before Roxana's dad shows up, and the gala is tomorrow."

"What are you gonna do?"

"Make sure she's quiet for the day and then do some reconnaissance."

"You need clean clothes, so you don't have to skulk around in shadows all day."

"I'll nick some from the laundry downstairs."

"The hotel lounge, you say?" Sybil repeated.

And that is where she found herself less than an hour later. Before leaving the suite, she had changed into a prettier dress, fastened pearls around her neck and ears, and styled Roxana's honey hair in a sleek knot. Even Art had the decency to look impressed at her work. She was grateful for the overly polite hotel employees stationed throughout who kindly assisted her in reaching the hotel lounge without getting lost in the Alistaire's enormity. It looked different in daylight.

When she reached the lounge, Sybil quickly took inventory of everyone in the room: mostly older couples and single men. All were well-dressed. A few ladies were adorned with expensive jewelry, much like what she had unearthed in Roxana's luggage. Her eyes scanned left to right.

In the corner, two women were seated in lounge chairs. They were probably in their fifties and wore fashionable dresses made of costly materials. One had white blonde hair piled atop her head with a bejeweled butterfly comb tucked into the knot. The other had darker hair streaked with silver and a massive brooch at her neck. There was a silver tray with a porcelain tea set on the table between them.

A man in a tailored suit with an impressive mustache rested his hand on the back of the dark-haired lady's chair. A silver band was on his ring finger, so it was safe to presume they were husband and wife.

Over to their right were three middle-aged men. Their balding hair and increasing guts suggested middle age, but their faces still held some youth. They wore black suits with plain ties. Two had wedding bands, but the third did not. A thirty-something bartender was behind the counter speaking with two Alistaire butlers.

Only two men struck Sybil as loners. The first had to be at least sixty with a closely trimmed white beard. He held a newspaper in one hand and a teacup in the other. He seemed to have no interest in the happenings around him.

The second was much younger. Upper twenties? He wasn't overly handsome but had a pleasant round face and warm brown eyes framed with rectangular glasses. He stood at the bar, watching the people around him with wistful curiosity. His fingers tapped rhythmically against his pant leg.

Bingo.

A tight-lipped smile slowly spread across Sybil's face. She smoothed a hand over the bodice of her dress and waltzed her way over to him. She couldn't go straight to him; that would be too direct. She perched herself two stools down at the bar, carefully arranged her skirt, crossed her ankles daintily, and waited for the bartender to turn his attention to her.

Immediately, she felt the round-faced man's eyes on her. She looked at him from under heavy lashes and offered a shy but encouraging smile before turning her gaze back to the bartender walking towards her.

"What'll it be, ma'am?" the bartender asked.

"Tea, please," she said demurely. Internally, she wished for something stronger.

"Some for me too," interjected the round-faced man. The bartender nodded and waved to the butlers, one of whom went to work preparing a tray for them.

The homely man extended a hand to her. "Where are my manners? Richard Worth."

Sybil gently put her hand in his and returned, "Roxana Bloodknight." He lifted her hand to his lips instead of shaking it and planted a chaste kiss upon her knuckles. She allowed a rosy blush to creep into her cheeks.

"What brings you to Washington, Miss Bloodknight?" Richard lowered himself to the stool next to hers. "May I?" He gestured to the seat he had already taken.

Sybil nodded before explaining, "I'm visiting from South Carolina. My father is one of the sponsors for the Stānwyrta Chamber of Craftes and will be arriving shortly to join me. I came early to do some shopping."

Richard showed no signs of suspicion as she spoke. Rather, he leaned an elbow on the counter and listened with rapt attention, his eyes never leaving her face except to dart down to her white neck. Or a little lower. But he caught himself and brought his gaze back to her eyes as he responded, "And have you enjoyed your shopping?"

"Oh, yes!" Sybil breathed. "There is so much more here than at home. And we have no hotels so fine as this! I think the Alistaire is quite possibly the grandest place I've ever stayed."

"It likely is."

"Is this your first time here?" Sybil asked, pausing to thank a butler as he set the tea tray before her and Richard.

"Oh, no. My father is a Congressman. I often stay here when I come into town to visit from Richmond." She wondered why he didn't stay with his parents. "The, uh, the Thanes' Gala is this upcoming Sunday."

Sybil took a sip from her painted teacup. "A gala. That sounds simply divine. The last good party I went to was last Labor Day. My daddy threw a soiree on our estate, but I'm sure it was nothing like a gala at the White House."

Richard's mouth quirked up in the corner. "I mean no offense to your father, but I can almost guarantee it doesn't compare. The Thanes' Gala isn't the most ostentatious of balls the president throws, but it is nevertheless a top-notch affair. Everyone who is anyone in Washington is there. It's an elegant and intimate evening." Sybil thought back to Mrs. Simpson's criticisms about inviting foreign dignitaries. "In fact, this is the first major event of President Calloway's presidency." Richard put his cup to his lips.

"Is that right? How divine," Sybil repeated with a dreamy sigh.

They sat in silence for a moment before Richard cleared his throat and said, "You know, if you're growing lonely waiting for your father's arrival, I could really use a date."

"Mr. Worth!" Sybil gasped, setting her teacup down with a startle. It clattered on the saucer. "Don't tell me you're inviting me—a total stranger—to the first high society party of the year!"

Richard's round cheeks reddened. "Forgive me! That was entirely too forward."

A giggle exploded from Sybil. "I would love to accompany you!" She clapped her hands together and then pressed them to her lap. "Oh, Mr. Worth, do you really mean it? You would take me?"

Her rapid acceptance was clearly not what Richard expected, as his eyebrows remained high on his face. This was not a man who was used to ladies saying "yes" so easily. His shock melted into glee. "Why, yes, of course I mean it! Miss Bloodknight, I would be honored if you would accompany me."

"Well, then, yes, Mr. Worth. Yes! Oh, but I'll have to acquire a gown and…"

"Not to worry. I'll take care of it."

"Oh, Mr. Worth, that is too much of you. I can't ask you to do that."

"Not at all. You're saving me from an embarrassing solo entrance at an exclusive event *and* from my mother's increasing concern regarding my bachelor status," Richard said with a wink.

Sybil placed a slender hand on Richard's forearm. "Thank you, Mr. Worth. My mother will be so pleased to hear gentlemen do exist north of the Carolinas."

Clueless as he may be, there was a sweetness about Richard Worth. Like a loyal, goofy dog. It was easy to play alongside him.

"And *I* am pleased to hear you consider me worthy enough to tell your mother about me."

Sybil let out a small, breathy laugh, "My dear Mr. Worth, you are quite the flirt." This statement appeared to impress Richard Worth, and he puffed his chest out.

Sybil was astonished at how smoothly things were going. She wondered if fyrnship magi were trusting—or gullible—by nature. That had to be it because she had Richard Worth eating out of the palm of her hand before her tea cooled.

He didn't question a word from her mouth. He was humble, if not a little bumbling. She learned he worked in an administration for wildlife and forestry for the state of Virginia, and she put two and two together to identify that he was a Sage-born Sylvaar. He inquired immediately about her branch of magi, and she identified herself as Sylvaar also. She wasn't sure what Roxana was, but it seemed a good fit considering she was an heiress to a tobacco tycoon in the deep south. He bought it without a second thought.

Despite his father's apparent status in Washington, Richard himself had never been to a gala like the one on Sunday. He went on and on about what it was like before Sybil stopped and asked him how many of these parties he had been to. He sheepishly admitted this was his first time. His father declined acquiring him a ticket before now. When Sybil prompted him further, he explained how his father had been displeased with Richard's work in wildlife and forestry and felt it beneath the Worth family name. Only now, as Richard had changed positions and would start alongside his father in Washington next month, was it justified for him to attend. This was noteworthy to Sybil because, although he was her ticket inside, she wouldn't be able to rely on him all the way. He was too green in Washington. But he'd do.

After finishing their tea, Richard promptly ordered himself and Roxana a pair of Bloody Marys. She accepted but took small sips. Or faked them entirely. Getting drunk or even tipsy was a surefire way to lose control and drift back into herself. She reprimanded herself for thinking too much like Art.

When Richard was halfway through his glass, Sybil finally felt comfortable broaching a new subject. She hoped she wouldn't regret it.

"Mr. Worth, could I ask for your *professional* opinion on something?"

"Anything, my dear Miss Bloodknight." He suppressed a belch.

She leaned forward and whispered conspiratorially, "My daddy, you see, he didn't vote for our new President Calloway. He had a lot of concern about some of his policies. Especially concerning the Shifts."

Richard let out a loud guffaw, drawing the attention from others in the lounge. "Oh, Miss Bloodknight. Neither you nor your father need have concern about Shifts. President Calloway's proposed legislation is really quite inventive. A modern solution for our modern times! No more cowering and questioning every strange face we come across. This is the 20th century, for land's sakes!" he exclaimed, slamming his glass down on the counter dramatically. His drink sloshed onto the counter, drawing the attention of the bartender, who sighed and went to find a rag.

"That is comforting, I suppose," Sybil agreed primly. "I… I have overheard some criticisms of President Calloway's choice to include dignitaries from other countries at this gala."

"Ah, yes. Southward and Westward both. A strange choice indeed. Westward was quite eager to participate, despite the tense history between our lands."

"Is there reason to be concerned about these decisions?"

"Oh, I don't think so, Miss Bloodknight. President Calloway knows what he is doing. There is no need to worry. This will be a night to enjoy and celebrate only."

"You don't think we'll meet the president on Sunday, do you? I would feel so embarrassed if my family's… lack of support, if you will, of his administration came to light at his own party."

Richard shook his head. "On the contrary, Miss Bloodknight. It is quite likely we'll meet the president and his wife at the gala. It is tradition that they greet their guests. But I will be more than happy to keep your little secret. Never fear though. No politician expects his ideas to be met without opposition. Politics is a cutthroat world, my dear."

"My gracious. I don't know how anyone could survive in such a place."

"Ah, but it must exist," Richard said, lifting his glass toward her as he spoke. "For if it did not, how would any change be brought about?"

"I think that sounds like a lonely way to be. Who can one trust?"

"My father always told me that if there wasn't opposition—if ideas and people were not challenged—then our leaders and our country would be mediocre at best. Push the people. Test the policies. *That's* how greatness comes around."

Sybil internalized this, while she, as Roxana, outwardly agreed, "I suppose you're correct there, Mr. Worth. What is it they say? 'Out of the fire,' no?"

"Quite right, quite right. And please, call me Richard."

Before Richard could order another beverage, Sybil gently proposed she do her shopping for the gala. He suggested a dress shop down the road and offered to take her there himself. He accompanied her to her suite and waited outside the door as she fetched a coat and matching accessories.

Sybil quickly brought Art, who had ducked into the bathroom when she re-entered, up to speed as she dressed in her winter things. He seemed very pleased, and pride swelled in her chest. He told her as soon as she left, he'd be going off himself and not to worry about his whereabouts. They'd reconvene tonight.

As Sybil and Richard walked arm-in-arm on the crowded streets of Washington, Richard chattered quite animatedly. It seemed Roxana's attention boosted his confidence. He talked about his upbringing, his new job, his family, his education. The more he talked, the more Sybil learned, and the less opportunity she had to slip up undercover as Roxana. She was extremely attentive to him, and, while she thought him a bit foolish, Sybil had to admit he was a nice man. In another life, maybe he'd be a friend.

She did eventually tune out his ceaseless talk and enjoyed studying Washington. She was astonished by the architecture, the quantity of colorful motorcars lining the streets, the beautifully manicured lawns and parks. There were so many people, not to mention dozens of shops and stalls in every direction. Some buildings looked new, but others had plainly been there for generations. There was such history here—history she had no part in.

The dress shop Richard took her to wasn't large but was clearly high-end. The sign was painted with gold swirly letters, and exquisite gowns were on display in the tall, arched windows. Richard announced the store as "Baker's" upon arrival.

A middle-aged woman approached them before the door fully closed behind them. She had severe eyebrows, but the rest of her face was pleasant. She wore a perfectly tailored black dress suit, shiny black pumps, and a string of pearls around her neck.

"May I help you?" She asked.

Richard spoke for Sybil. "Yes, I hope you can. This lovely young lady is in need of a gown appropriate for the Thanes' Gala."

The sharp eyebrows pinched, and the woman frowned. "That's Sunday. I'm afraid that doesn't leave us much time, sir."

"Something off the rack would surely do," Sybil amended, hoping the suggestion of wearing a sample dress wasn't a major social faux pas and a giveaway that she knew nothing about fashion or shopping.

"Certainly, with a small incentive, the tailoring could be completed in time, no?" Richard added.

The shop woman hesitated before nodding, "Of course. Our options may be somewhat limited, ma'am, but we will certainly do everything we can to find the perfect evening gown for you. We also carry accessories," she tagged on, gesturing for Sybil to follow her further into the store.

"I'll wait here, Roxana. Pick out anything you like," Richard called after them. Sybil flashed him a dazzling smile over her shoulder.

The shop woman introduced herself to Sybil as they walked. Her name was Ms. Gertrude Popper, and she proudly announced she'd already dressed thirteen different attendees of the Thanes'

Gala. She complimented Roxana's hair color and figure and announced she had the perfect dress in mind. Sybil told her she was open to anything suggested and that she trusted her completely.

Ms. Popper went straight to a rack and pulled off a violet strapless number with yards of fabric in the skirt. "This color, I think, would really bring out the violet flecks in those periwinkle eyes of yours. What do you think?"

Sybil beamed and reached a hand out to graze the silky fabric, "It is elegant, Ms. Popper."

"This overlay of silk organza is beaded with crystals, so every time you move, you will look like you're simply shimmering. Oh, and when the light hits? Breathtaking! Shall we try it on you?"

Sybil was about to agree when a dress over Ms. Popper's shoulder caught her eye. It was the color of rust, strapless, with a curved neckline and layers and layers of thick tulle from the waist down. Some of it gathered in the front, with more layers falling underneath the gathering. It smoothed into a ruched bodice. It was immense, but it somehow looked ethereal as well. Sybil didn't know anything about dresses, but she gravitated towards it.

"Ms. Popper," she whispered reverently. "I've never seen a more beautiful gown."

Ms. Popper followed her eyes to the rust tulle ball gown. "Oh, yes. Vulcan Designs did that one. Unique, is it not?"

"Could I try it?" Sybil knew she should just go with what Ms. Popper had already selected and be an easy customer. But this was likely the only chance she'd ever have to wear a ball gown, and the rebellious Shift in her wanted to wear what she wanted to wear.

"I suppose, but you know Vulcan is quite a sophisticated brand. It's a pretty penny, and the alterations due to all these layers here—" she knelt down and showed them to Sybil, "—will not be easy. I would be concerned about completing it in time."

Be Roxana. "Well… I'll try it anyways. If I have to have it, I have to have it."

Ms. Popper capitulated without another word, delighted at the possibility of selling such an expensive dress, and took Sybil to a dressing room to lace her into it. When she stepped back, she exclaimed, "My goodness, you are a picture, Miss Bloodknight. You have excellent taste."

Sybil turned to examine herself in the mirror and gasped. She had never looked so beautiful, and she wasn't even herself. A tiny part of her yearned to shift back to her natural state and see what *she* looked like in it, but that wasn't her reality. She was Roxana, and this was temporary. She'd never wear or touch something so fine again in her lifetime. Besides, Roxana was far more beautiful than Sybil was. Roxana was a sight to behold.

"Would you be a dear and kindly go fetch Mr. Worth? I'd like his opinion," Sybil said as they exited the dressing room and she stepped on the little pedestal for Ms. Popper to examine the gown for alterations.

"Certainly."

Richard, of course, could not hide his complete pleasure and infatuation with Roxana's beauty in this gown. "Oh, my dear, you *must* have this one."

Ms. Popper paused arranging the voluminous skirt and cautioned, "I told Miss Bloodknight this already, but it's a complicated dress to tailor."

"We can pay whatever is necessary—as long as it's done in time," Richard promptly declared. Ms. Popper's lips turned upward, and she rushed off to find pins to start tailoring.

"Oh, Roxana," Richard sighed, stepping in front of her and taking both of her hands in his. His eyes were sincere behind the rectangular frames of his glasses. "I am so honored you are attending with me. Not one man at that gala will be able to take their eyes from you."

Sybil wasn't sure if that was a good or bad thing, considering the goal of her op. The tiniest pang of sympathy shot through her as she met Richard's gaze, knowing the news would probably devastate him once leaked.

That's life, buddy. You don't get everything you want, and people hurt you.

She'd be doing him a favor. It was an important lesson for everyone to learn at some point; Shifts just learned it real early.

10.

When she finally escaped Richard Worth's presence after their shopping trip and subsequent luncheon, Sybil was near ready to collapse. She closed and locked the suite door, shutting out Richard's fawning farewell, and rested her forehead against it.

She shifted back to her natural state with a weary exhale. That was the longest stretch she'd ever stayed in an alternate appearance, not to mention a full body one. Fatigue washed through her from head to toe, and an ache settled into her head.

Art wasn't back yet, so she took another bath. Soaking in the hot water eased her soreness, though the exhaustion remained. Then, she pulled on one of Roxana's long cotton nightdresses and curled up in the bed. When Art returned after dark, he found her asleep.

He rudely woke her by turning the lights on. "Oy! Get up. Time to reconvene."

She flung her arms over her head and groaned, "Do we have to?"

"*Yes!*" He hissed. He looked no worse for wear. Sybil's head still hurt.

She forced herself upright and grumpily recounted her time with Richard, struggling to remember pertinent details. When she finished, Art launched into a very thorough account of his time scoping out the White House. He told her about how he successfully stalked a White House Thane and found a service entrance to the mansion, or at least its general whereabouts.

"What exactly are you gonna do while I'm at the ball?" She asked.

"I'm hopin' to get in as that Thane and get the interior layout."

"Seems risky."

"Shiftwork is risky."

The steady flame of her temper flared in her chest, but she bit her lip.

"What time will you be leaving?" Art asked.

"Mr. Worth is picking me up at 7:30 downstairs in the lobby."

"Does he have his own driver, or is he using a White House chauffeur?"

"I don't know... Why? Are you hopin' to catch a ride in?"

"Security will be tight. It wouldn't hurt for me to fill in as chauffeur or even be in the trunk," he said.

"I could try to find out. Although it seems like an odd question for someone like Roxana to ask..."

"No, you're right. There's no reason why you should care about that. Leave it to me." A moan interrupted their conversation. "Speaking of..." Art said.

Sybil slid off the bed and pulled open the closet door. The real Roxana Bloodknight lay curled on her side, blindfolded and bound.

"Roxana?" Sybil asked.

"Who's there?" The woman's voice shook. She instinctively curled into herself, as if that would protect her.

"Who do you think?"

"Are you a Shift?" She whimpered.

"Very good," Sybil smirked.

"What d-do you w-want with me? I have money!"

"Just your silence for a few days. And then we will be out of your hair," Sybil said.

"My fath—"

Art interjected, "Yes, we know all about him." Roxana startled at this new voice. "He'll never know we were here. As long as you cooperate, no one will get hurt." Art picked up a piece of hard toast from their breakfast tray and threw it to Sybil. Sybil squatted down and pressed the toast into Roxana's bound hands.

The woman seemed unsure what to do with it.

"It's toast," Sybil said plainly. "Eat it now before we gag you for the night."

Roxana wept openly now, and Sybil glanced back at Art who rolled his eyes.

"Honey," Sybil said sardonically, patting Roxana's shoulder. "Settle down. This really doesn't concern you. We just need you to be quiet. Do that, and everything will be over soon."

Still crying, Roxana nibbled the toast under Art and Sybil's supervision. When she finished, they passed her a glass of water. "Have a good sleep," Sybil said, before gagging her and closing the closet door again.

She hated the twinge of guilt she felt. "She'll be okay, right?"

"Sure," Art said. "Careful, Sybil. Don't start caring now. We have a lot ahead of us still. Don't put faces and personalities to your targets. You're a criminal for hire. You gotta separate yourself, do the crime, and not think twice about it. It's our way of life. It's what Shifts have done for years. You're made for this. The minute you crack—the second those people mean something to you or the luxury of the outside lures you in—that's when you get caught. And once they've got you, they won't let you go."

Sufficiently reprimanded, Sybil crawled back in the bed and rolled to her side, ready to feign sleep and not talk to her brother anymore. She decided she didn't like who he was on the job. Where was the boy who helped her learn Shiftwork? Who picked her up when she fell and motivated her to be better? To be like him.

The memories brought her back to the beorg, and she suddenly wondered how her kin were getting on. Selfishly, she wondered if they missed her. If Xavier was thinking about her. Then she told herself she was being dumb and to go to bed. Despite her catnap, her body was still recovering from the multiple hours of full-body Shiftwork. Sleep came easily.

Sunday morning dawned with freezing temperatures and a loud wind that made the hotel windows rattle, but the sun was bright. When Sybil woke, she bundled a blanket around her and peeked out from behind the heavy drapes to watch the sun rise above the skyline. She wanted to fling the drapes wide open and let sunlight pour into the room, but she decided against it. She didn't want to risk anyone seeing her in her natural state, even if she was on an upper floor. Art would certainly criticize her if she did it, so she watched from behind the curtain for several minutes, absorbing the environment.

It surprised her that, even on a Sunday morning, the city was hustling. Shops opened, and families bustled to and fro in their Sunday best. She would not miss the people here when she went back home, not only the sheer quantity of them but also their politeness and formalities. She had barely been out in Washington and was already tired of the people on the street, always smiling at her. Men tipped their hats; old ladies said, "Good morning" as they walked slowly with their annoying, yapping dogs; and children dodged about with sweets sticking out of their pockets.

She didn't want to go back to an empty stomach, but she found herself missing the roughness of the Shifts. The kindness and politeness of these strangers was stifling. When no one really cared, it was freeing.

Sybil let the curtains fall back into place and left the window. Art was up now too. He grinned at her as he tugged a shirt over his head.

"Big day today! How you feelin'?"

"Fine," she lied.

They ordered breakfast to their room again, and Art wolfed his down. Sybil, however, struggled to eat, preoccupied with thoughts of the ball she would attend before the day was out. More than once, she thought to herself, "What am I doing?"

How could she possibly go into a high society gala and fake her way through it? She didn't know the rituals. Shifts were so far removed from the other magi; they didn't share the same history or culture, at least not anymore. She didn't know how to *dance*.

"I don't know how to dance," she blurted after the notion hit her.

Art started laughing. "You don't need to know how. Just follow your partner."

"*Just follow my partner?*" Sybil shrieked. "I'm sure that's *exactly* what Roxana Bloodknight would need to do. She'd know every dance!" Where was this in her Shiftwork training?

"We can always get her up and have her teach you," Art deadpanned.

Sybil stared at him, her eyes flashing. "You're not funny."

She refused to talk to him any more than she had to after that. He left before she did and claimed he was going to find his way into that service entrance before security tightened up for the guests, apparently having abandoned his earlier notion of catching a ride with her and Richard. She didn't reply, and he didn't seem to care. She found it unfair he was going about his business so secretly on their *shared* op, while he required every detail from her.

She didn't have long to stew about this because, somewhere in the distance, a bell chimed four times, and a knock sounded promptly at her door.

"Just a minute!" Sybil called as she rapidly tried to morph into Roxana. She swung by the bathroom mirror to make sure everything was as it should be before pulling her robe tight and opening the door a crack. "Yes?"

It was a bellboy, holding a black bag nearly as big as he was. "Miss Bloodknight? Delivery." Her dress.

"Thank you. You can hang it in the armoire." Sybil opened the door wider. She handed him a tip, and he disappeared from sight.

Sybil ensured she was downstairs and waiting in the atrium for Richard at 7:30, adorned in her rust gown with gold jewelry, including the heavy beaded ring that had captured her attention earlier. When she spotted it again in the case as she got ready, she felt drawn towards it, and when it slid onto her finger, she felt strengthened. Emboldened. As if it somehow siphoned the weariness and nervousness away.

Sybil received many compliments as Roxana from various Alistaire guests, with questions of where she got her gown and if she was attending the gala often following. When Richard stepped into the hotel in a perfectly tailored black tux, his hair slicked back, his jaw dropped.

"Miss Bloodknight," he gasped. "You are the most beautiful creature I've ever laid eyes upon."

Sybil took his outstretched hand and did a little twirl, concentrating on not slipping in the high-heeled shoes. "Do you really think so, Richard? It's not too much? You know I've never been to such a party before."

"No, no, my dear. You are exquisite. How will I ever be able to repay you for gracing me as my date?"

"Oh, Richard," Sybil giggled. "You are too modest. You underestimate how pleasant your company is." *Ugh.* She straightened his tie. "And you look mighty dapper in your tux."

Richard beamed. "Shall we?" She took his outstretched arm and allowed him to escort her to the waiting silver motorcar.

The Alistaire Beck was near enough to the White House, they could've walked. In fact, they likely would've made better time if they *had* walked. Instead, they rode in a heated car and joined a slow-moving line of expensive vehicles that packed the roads of Washington, bound for the White House. Soon, the mansion came into view, and all thoughts fled her mind. She couldn't help but lean forward to stare out the window.

It was astonishing. Exquisite. She couldn't make out all the details in the darkness of the winter's night, but she identified marble pillars, a domed roof that seemed to glitter under the moonlight, and innumerable windows. Armed Thanes in emerald green winter uniforms lined the driveway and immaculate grounds.

"Beautiful, isn't it?" Richard said. Sybil mumbled an agreement without taking her eyes from her surroundings. Their car pulled around to the front, and a footman opened her door.

He took her hand and helped her out, saying with genuineness, "Welcome, miss, to the White House."

He had to be in his seventies with gray hair and a face full of wrinkles, but he smiled warmly at her, as though she wasn't the hundredth person he'd greeted this night alone. The gentleness with which he helped her out—the kindness of his face and voice—left her uncomfortable.

"Thank you." Her own tone was sharper than she meant it to be, but the old footman didn't react. He was probably used to snobby rich people looking down their noses at him. This bothered Sybil too, because she knew *she* wasn't a snobby rich person.

Richard came around from his side and took her arm from the footman. They exchanged polite smiles, and he guided Sybil up the enormous marble staircase.

Footmen, or butlers, or whoever they were—Sybil had no clue who all these people could be and why so many of them were needed—waited at the door to take wraps, coats, and gloves. Then she and Richard joined the stream of guests filing through the grand foyer into the ballroom.

The ballroom featured a vaulted ceiling, painted in shades of blue, white, and gold, depicting scenes Sybil knew had to be significant to magi culture and history but that she didn't understand. Crystal chandeliers dripped down like icicles.

The room was filled with custom tuxedos, sparkling evening gowns, and snow white floral arrangements. Sybil felt a little lightheaded from the smells, the noise, the colors. Perfume, cologne, alcohol, flowers, violins, chatter, and polite laughter.

Was this real life? Was she—an underage Shift—truly *here,* in the White House? She swayed on her feet.

"Are you well, Roxana?" Richard asked, concerned. "You appear pale."

Focus. "It's so much to take in, Mr. Worth," Sybil responded, swallowing her shock away.

"Richard, please. Remember? Just Richard."

"Oh, you are not 'Just Richard' to me," she purred, finding much-needed focus in her exchange with him. "You are a dear friend and my charming date!"

Richard blushed and attempted to conceal his pleasure from her praise. He squeaked out, "Punch?"

Sybil readily concurred and let him lead her through the crowd to where servers poured cranberry-colored liquid into crystal glasses.

The next half an hour passed slowly and quickly simultaneously. Nothing of consequence occurred as guests filtered into the ballroom and mingled, drinking champagne and punch, while a violin quartet played classical music from a raised platform at the side of the room. Yet, there was so much attracting Sybil's attention she didn't have the capacity to think about her next move.

Richard found his father and mother and cheerfully introduced Sybil. Mr. Worth Senior was a gruff person who did not smile or speak much, even as Mrs. Worth ooh'ed and aah'ed over Sybil and the lovely pair she and Richard made. Sybil decided she liked Mr. Worth Senior for the sole reason that he wasn't friendly. How refreshing.

"Ah! Director Vox!" exclaimed the elder Mr. Worth, throwing up a hand. "Good to see you, good to see you!"

Sybil's throat constricted as Lowell Vox, as stoic as ever, approached them from the crowd. *Breathe, Sybil.*

"And you, Congressman Worth. How do you and Mrs. Worth find yourselves this night?" He shook Mr. Worth's hand and kissed Mrs. Worth's.

"As well as you can imagine," Mr. Worth growled. "This is my son," he added belatedly when Vox's blue eyes flitted to Richard and Sybil.

"Greetings," Vox said coolly. "And who is this lovely young woman on your arm?"

Richard smiled fondly at Sybil. "Miss Roxana Bloodknight."

"Charmed," Sybil said shortly, immediately worried Vox might recognize her voice. She offered her hand. He kissed the finger next to the gold ring. When he saw it, he lingered for a moment.

"What an interesting piece," he said lowly before straightening.

"Thank you," Sybil replied, holding his stare. He released her hand, and she hoped he didn't notice how sweaty it was.

Suddenly, a booming voice cut through the noise of the ballroom and announced the president's arrival. Sybil's heart quickened when Vox mumbled, "And here we go."

Here we go.

11.

Breathless anticipation blanketed the room. Large doors were pulled open, revealing the man himself: Branson Calloway, striding into the expansive ballroom with confidence, exuberance, and ownership.

From shoes to hair, everything about him was impeccable. Though not a physically imposing figure, his warm complexion, rich brown hair, and bright green eyes made him striking. His smile to the crowd was magnetizing, and Sybil could've sworn the crowd leaned toward him, just a little bit. His teeth were straight and white, his jaw firm and square.

Sybil laughed inwardly. *At least he's not short and hairy.*

His wife, First Lady Cecelia Hughes Calloway, the narrow woman whose picture Vox had dangled in front of her, stood next to him, her bony bejeweled hand tucked in the crook of his elbow. She looked smaller and more angular here than Sybil remembered from the photo.

In contrast to Calloway, there seemed to be nothing poised or bold about her. Her face and body screamed discomfort. Even her delicate, close-lipped smile seemed to be hiding gritted teeth and the words: "I don't want to be here." Her amethyst gown fit her like a glove, but between the stiff structure of the sleeves and the pleats in the skirt, the dress looked like it was in competition to be as angular as she was.

Sybil's eyes darted between the two, taking in as much as she could from physical details and body language. Calloway exhibited impressive tenderness and care towards his wife, despite being the host at such a public event. He appeared undaunted by the thousands of stares on them as he placed his hand on Cecelia's back and guided her gently forward, whispering something in her ear. Sybil watched as Cecelia's shoulders dropped slightly, as if the tension had been physically drawn away from them. She smiled a little brighter up at her husband. Sybil's stomach twisted.

Don't start feeling guilty, she ordered. *It's a job.*

The couple made their way toward the center of the room, and the president welcomed his guests in a captivating, deep voice. He started with a few words about being glad everyone was there and some stuff about honoring the Thanes and the veterans who kept the country safe, et cetera. Sybil was no expert in presidential addresses, but she could tell he had command of the room, though everything he said sounded fairly generic to her.

Next, Calloway invited a general up to say a few words, and Sybil tried to conceal her smile when Mr. Worth Senior rolled his eyes in blatant dismay at the man. He grumbled a few unkind words under his breath, and Sybil liked him even more.

Richard softly scolded, "Father. Show some respect." Mrs. Worth put her hand on Richard's shoulder to quiet him and shook her head.

"Who is he?" Sybil murmured to Richard.

"General Yeo," Richard whispered back. "He's working with the Department of Defense on some policy changes regarding the Shifts. That's why my father dislikes him so."

Sybil resisted the urge to scoff and forced both ignorance and innocence into her next question, "Why on earth does the Department of Defense need to be involved with Shifts? They can't pose such a great threat. There can't be what, more than eighty of them!"

"They're a dangerous bunch, Roxana," Richard said gravely. "They can't be trusted. The D.o.D. annually reviews and evaluates appropriate security measures." Sybil knew the Calloway Administration had acquired the management of Shifts from the Guild and was surprised Richard didn't mention it. Unless he didn't know...

Calloway's voice broke through: "I'd also like to thank Madame Ambassador Georgiana Graceland of Westward and Mr. Ambassador Jonathan Yancey from Southward for taking the time and effort to be here with us and partake in this cherished Eastward tradition."

Sybil blended with the crowd to twist around to see the two individuals toward whom President Calloway gestured.

The first was a very tall, very pale woman. She towered over Calloway and wore a black evening gown. She had a long, sloping nose, sharp light-colored eyes, and silvery hair swept up from her neck. A glittering diamond necklace encircled her throat. Aside from her height, Sybil wasn't sure why she looked so different from the other magi in the room, but she did. She looked *other.* Was there something special about the magi of Westward? Something different? She had no one to ask, so she filed the question away.

Mr. Jonathan Yancey appeared to be a far more ordinary magi, at an average height and build with rather unkempt sandy hair and deeply tanned skin. He looked a bit younger than Georgiana Graceland, though not by much. What had Mrs. Simpson called the Southward magi? Cowboys?

Calloway was saying, "As we celebrate those who have protected Eastward since its inception, it is a good reminder for us that, though we come from different places and have diverse backgrounds, we are all Americana magi and should ultimately strive for unity and peace."

"Poppycock," said Mr. Worth Senior.

"Thank you again for being here—each and every one of you," President Calloway said. "For your support for our Thanes, our veterans, their families, and for your generous donations. Please make your way through those doors to enjoy a performance by the renowned Eastward Opera Ballet, accompanied by musicians from the Eastward Classical Symphony Orchestra. Let this be a night to enjoy!" He spread his arms wide.

On cue, double doors swung open on the left side of the ballroom. The violin quartet resumed playing, and sound once more enveloped the ballroom. The guests shuffled through slowly, for this was apparently where President Calloway and the First Lady greeted each individually. They stood at the threshold, shaking hands and smiling.

Richard tucked Sybil's hand into the crook of his arm and said quietly, "Don't be nervous. They won't bite." She was glad he assumed that's why she was nervous. In reality, her brain was abuzz with the fact that she had to get compromising footage of some caliber with Calloway before Mr. Bloodknight showed up in Washington. And that her brother was somewhere on the premises doing God knows what.

They filed in behind the elder Mr. and Mrs. Worth and waited their turn to be greeted by the Calloways.

Branson Calloway was more handsome and lively up close, and his wife less so. She smiled when she was supposed to, but it never reached her eyes. Sybil thought it looked as if it pained her. For someone at the top of the world like the Calloways, she would've expected a much happier woman.

"Good evening. Thank you for being here tonight," Calloway said in his warm baritone. The corners of his eyes crinkled as he firmly shook Richard's hand. "My wife, Cecelia."

"How do you do, ma'am? Thank you for having us, Mr.

President," Richard replied respectfully. "May I present my guest, Miss Roxana Bloodknight. She's visiting us from South Carolina."

"Welcome, Miss Bloodknight. It's a pleasure to meet you. What do you think of our country's capital so far?" Calloway turned his attention to Sybil. Could he see straight through her facade? Her heart thumped wildly.

She internally steeled herself and said, "It's a beautiful city, Mr. President. I've had a very enjoyable time. Your gala certainly makes it a most memorable trip."

"Thank you, Miss Bloodknight. It is our pleasure to have you here." They moved to the next couple in line. It was such a quick exchange. Too quick. What was she to do with that?

The next room was more of a theatre than a ballroom, lined with stiff-backed, upholstered chairs rapidly filling with guests. There was a stage at the front and another group of musicians to its right. Sybil allowed Richard to lead in every way, following him dutifully and unquestioningly. They sat beside the senior Worths. Another more elderly couple followed behind them. The man proudly wore a Thane dress uniform, his head held high.

Once everyone was seated and a respectful silence blanketed the room, music struck up, music the likes of which Sybil had never heard before. Lilting notes that leapt, connected, scaled, dropped, and swelled. Sybil's buzzing mind seemed to freeze, and she became fully consumed by it. Her entire body alive in a way she didn't know was possible. In a way different from Shiftwork when her blood hummed with magic. More *connected*. Connected to something other than herself.

When the dancers waltzed onto the stage and began their variation, something cracked inside Sybil. The careful shell of cynicism and hatred towards the fyrnship and the magi in it split, leaving her with a realization: she was moved by beautiful things.

And *this*—this was so beautiful.

Wide-eyed, lips parted, she was enraptured by the dancers and their leaps, turns, extensions. By the way their dresses floated around their knees and tiaras sparkled in their sleek hair. They moved effortlessly to the music, hitting each beat and note perfectly.

When the performance ended and applause broke out, Sybil felt as if she'd been rudely snapped out of a trance. Richard seemed pleased at her enjoyment and handed her a crisp handkerchief. "Moving, is it not?" He whispered in her ear.

She accepted it and dabbed at the tears on her cheeks she hadn't realized had fallen. For a brief moment, she thought about how mortified she'd be if Art—or any in the beorg—found out about this. About how much something in the fyrnship touched her. But she was still so overwhelmed with the grace and beauty she experienced that she decided she didn't care. Not right now.

She wanted more. Didn't want it to stop. She even had the foolish thought of how much she wanted to do it herself—play such music or dance to it. What would that be like? She could hardly imagine it.

Richard helped her to her feet with a gentle hand, and she realized dimly they'd been advised to re-enter the ballroom for the Calloways to begin the night with the first waltz. *To dance.* There she'd been—daydreaming of it. But tonight was no daydream. This was a job, and her abhorrent dance skills could blow her cover instantaneously. Butterflies took flight in her stomach.

"You appear rather pale, Miss Bloodknight. Are you well?" Richard asked as they walked behind the older couple.

"Yes, Richard, thank you. I think I may take a moment in the powder room before the dancing gets underway though."

"Certainly. Do you require any assistance?"

"No, no," she waved him off. "Enjoy the first dance. I'll find a staff member if I need anything."

Richard masked his disappointment with a genteel nod. "Of course."

She gave him a sweet smile before quickly weaving through the crowd to get to the opposite side of the ballroom before the dance began. That's when she spotted a quite unusual sight: two young children—a boy and a girl—peeking from beyond the doorway, watching the gleaming ballroom with enormous eyes.

Vox's words at their hiring meeting entered her mind: *Married Cecelia Ellen Hughes in 1938, with whom he shares two children: Lenora Ellen Calloway, born 1943, age eight, and Donald Eugene Calloway, born 1945, age six.*

Momentarily stunned at her luck, Sybil quickly recovered and gathered her skirts. What a perfect opportunity. *Just you wait until you hear about* this, *Art.*

12.

"Now, why aren't you two out on the dance floor?" Sybil asked with a warm smile, trying to be as approachable as possible as she stepped past them into the foyer.

The children looked up at her with equally startled expressions. The girl recovered first, rising to her feet and tilting her chin, her sky blue eyes boldly making eye contact.

"We're only watching. The party is for grown-ups, you know." The girl spoke intelligently. Her soft hair was braided down her back and tied with a pink ribbon to match her dark green dress with light pink ruffles.

Sybil peered back into the ballroom before coming around and kneeling down behind the door, her gown settling around her in a wide circle. She pressed her hands into her lap, trying to look as though she was relaxing and planning to be there a while. "I've never been one for parties myself. They're exciting but can be quite overwhelming." She aimed this statement at the boy, who hadn't said anything but hadn't taken his gaze from her either. He tucked his chin into his hands.

Sybil continued, "There's so much to look at. Lots of food to eat too. Have you tried the caviar? It's delicious!"

Talk of food caught the boy's attention. "I haven't," he confessed. "But I don't like caviar."

"You don't?" Sybil asked, feigning shock. "Lucky for you, there are some other options. What do you like to eat?"

"Biscuits," he whispered.

"Oh, Donald, your tastes are simply unrefined," sniffed the girl.

"Where are my manners?" Sybil interjected. "My name is Roxana." She shook hands with both children, a grown-up gesture that made each of them puff up. She couldn't help but notice how smooth and clean their hands were, how full and healthy their faces looked. What a far cry these children were from her cabin mates—grimy, rude, rough children who bickered and talked back and needed more to eat.

"I'm Lenora Calloway, and he's Donald. I'm eight, but he's only six," she said very importantly.

"Well, may I say it is a pleasure to meet both of you. Say... Calloway. You're President Calloway's children."

"That's right," Lenora said.

Sybil asked, "Do you mind if I sit here with you two for a bit? It's quite noisy out there in the crowd, and I confess I'm getting a bit of a headache. Can I tell you a secret? This is the first gala I've been to."

Donald immediately moved to sit down near her. Lenora remained standing to watch the happenings in the ballroom, though she was more than happy to participate with Sybil and Donald. "*I've* been to many parties," she said. "Our daddy is very important, and we get invited to lots of places."

"I bet you do," Sybil said. "It must be very special to have your daddy be such an important man."

"Sometimes," Donald muttered. Sybil cocked her head at him, silently encouraging him to go on. He shrugged his thin shoulders. "Dad travels a lot. And works lots too."

"That's because he has very *important* business to attend to," snapped Lenora.

"I liked it when he was less important," Donald said sullenly. "And Mother is always sad."

"She is not."

"Is too!" Donald retorted, his face growing pink.

"Oh, dear me. No need to argue," Sybil interrupted, holding up a hand. "Why ever is she sad, Donald? You have such a beautiful home here in Washington. Pretty clothes. Servants. I'm sure the *best* toys as well."

"That's exactly right," Lenora said. "Gran says Mother is ungrateful."

"Dad says she's scared," Donald disagreed.

"Scared?" Sybil said incredulously. "Don't you have loads of Thanes to keep you safe? More than anyone else in the country, I bet!"

Lenora gave a huff. "She thinks because Daddy is very powerful now that everyone is out to get us. She never wants to leave the house or let us leave either. We've barely seen any of our new city."

"My, my. Who would hurt innocent children such as yourselves?"

Donald mumbled something very quietly. She had an inkling as to what he said, but she leaned forward and asked softly, "What was that, dear?"

"Don't listen to him; he's being a baby."

Sybil tsked cheerily, "Now, Lenora. That's not very kind, is it? We are all of us afraid of something."

"Not me," she declared.

"No? *I'm* afraid of a few things myself," Sybil told the children. "Snakes, for one. Horrified of them. And frogs too." She shivered dramatically. "Positively hate the way they move. All that sudden jumping and springing. It's dreadful!" This had the children giggling, but then she lowered her voice and said gravely, "But there's something even more frightening to *me* than both of those put together."

"What?" Donald breathed.

"Shapeshifters," Sybil whispered before pressing a finger to her lips. She wasn't sure what possessed her to begin this narrative with them, and she hoped it wasn't a mistake. Part of her wished she could just grab one—or both—and take them back to the Alistaire. The kidnapping would begin, and it would save so much time.

Unfortunately, it would be far too messy. Sloppy work. Poorly planned. Art would possibly dismember her. For now, she'd try to keep them talking, and maybe they could not only connect her to Calloway but give her useful information to share with her brother for the kidnapping.

"Me too!" Donald instantly exclaimed, breaking the trance Sybil had put them in. The words began pouring out. "And Mother also! Dad says they're just people and that we shouldn't let them have power over us and that fear is powerful and so we shouldn't be afraid, or we'll give them all the power."

"*I'm* not afraid of Shifts," volunteered Lenora.

"Your father must be a very brave man to not fear such people," Sybil said, ignoring Lenora. "Has he ever... met one?" The children exchanged glances and shook their heads. "Well, I have." Not a lie.

"You have?" Donald shrieked in both horror and fascination.

"Shhh!" Both Lenora and Sybil put fingers to their lips. She continued, "Yes, yes, I have. It was terrifying."

"What happened?" Lenora asked, trying not to look too interested.

"Did they get you?" questioned Donald.

It would be all too easy to fact-check the real Roxana's family and spoil the entire operation based on her storytelling alone. Then again, she could be long gone before anyone went to verify that information.

And thus, Sybil launched into an elaborate fictional story, drawing upon all her experience as a Shift and playing into everything that frightens people about them.

"I was twelve when it happened, but I remember it as though it was only yesterday. You see, my father is an influential man in the tobacco industry in South Carolina. That's what our family fortune is rooted in, but he has business ventures all over the state, from farming to politics. Much like your family, I would bet.

"Well, not long after I turned twelve, Daddy was preparing for a big company merger with another businessman in North Carolina. It was to be a huge expansion and even more recognition for the Bloodknight family. My mama was a little like yours—nervous about the acclaim and the increased attention. But my daddy insisted this was the right move.

"On the eve of the merger, my brother..." She let her voice trail off for a moment for dramatic effect. "My brother Ewyn went missing. He was seven." Donald's face drained of color.

It was more than a little cruel to make Roxana's fake brother so close in age to these children. She almost made him fifteen, but she thought the younger age would make the story scarier to the children—more relatable—which would hopefully mean they'd not forget it. Which increased the chances it would come up in conversation with their family. All she needed was to get these children to connect her somehow to their father. They couldn't forget her after this night.

"We waited for two whole days for the ransom call. The Shift demanded one hundred *thousand* dollars and for my father to call off the merger. Well, you see, that was over a decade ago, and that was a very significant amount of money! My father scrambled to pull it all together and to cancel his business plans to save my brother."

"Why didn't he call the Thanes? They're really strong! I bet they could've taken one Shift!" Lenora said.

Sybil smiled sadly. "They told us if we involved anyone, they'd kill Ewyn. It wasn't a risk my parents were willing to take."

"Did you get Ewyn back?" Donald asked. He was sitting cross-legged on the skirt of her gown, as close to her as he could get.

"Oh, yes, eventually. My father had to deliver the money in twenty-four hours to a secret location he didn't tell anyone about, not even me or Mother. Ewyn wasn't there. Another twenty-four hours or so later, he appeared at our door at sunrise. It was a difficult time," she said wearily.

"Was Ewyn okay?" asked Lenora.

"Physically, yes. But he was... not the same. He wouldn't talk, wouldn't eat. It was a year before he spoke again. He had nightmares for months. Nightmares about the person made of water," she added, her voice distant, as though she had forgotten the children were listening.

"Made of water? What does *that* mean?" Lenora questioned.

Sybil leaned her head against the door frame. "Ewyn learned Shifts couldn't stay shapeshifted permanently. After a period of time, their whole body would blur as it started to go back to their natural-born state. He said it was like looking through tears though your eyes were dry."

Sybil forced tears into her own eyes and then hastily swiped them away, ending her story with, "Ewyn was never the same. And neither was I. I still wonder about what he must have gone through. What it must have been like to be alone with those shapeshifters, unable to trust your own eyes."

Donald let out a tiny whimper.

"Oh! Oh, honey, I'm so sorry," Sybil snapped dramatically out of her reverie and reached to give him a little hug, rubbing his bony back. "I shouldn't have told you that. I didn't mean to scare you at all." *I absolutely meant to scare you, you little tyke.*

"I… I just can see why your own mama may be a little scared. She may need some extra comfort from you both. Maybe some extra good behaviors," she added with a wink, smoothing down Donald's light hair. Calloway's children nodded dutifully.

"And it's okay to be afraid yourself too," Sybil said. "We're all only human."

Donald gave her a little smile; Lenora pondered her words, staring at the floor.

After a moment, Sybil steadied Donald on his feet and said, "Well. I must be getting going, or my date will be wondering if I've abandoned him! I'm supposed to be in the powder room!" She said, wiggling her eyebrows. They giggled.

Sybil rose with great effort, despite her attempts to be graceful, and shook out her dress. She touched a hand to her hair to tidy it before extending it and shaking each child's hand in turn, "It was an honor to meet you, Lenora and Donald Calloway. Better get one of those waiters to bring you some of that caviar," she teased. She turned and tossed back over her shoulder, "It's better than you think!"

And then she slammed into President Calloway.

The president's hands gripped Sybil's shoulders to steady her, and she gazed directly into bright green eyes framed by thick dark eyelashes. She wavered a moment, thoughts going a million miles. His cologne was intoxicating; his body was solid and well-built. While he was much older than Sybil with laugh lines and wrinkles about his eyes and mouth to match, she found him terribly handsome.

Her next thought was that she couldn't believe she had just fallen into the arms of the target she needed to seduce. In front of his children she had hopefully just hooked on her line. It was all too easy. Was it too easy? What was she missing?

A coldness developed at her scalp, signifying the threat of her appearance fading. *FOCUS*, she all but screamed at herself.

"Oh my goodness," she gasped, clinging to Calloway's arms. "Sir, I am so sorry. Oh, I'm mortified!"

"It's all right. All right," he soothed with his deep voice. "I shouldn't have snuck up behind you. Are you well?"

Sybil needed to think fast. "I think so..." She let go of him and pretended to gingerly test her limbs and balance. She needed to not be well, so he'd not disappear on her. Gritting her teeth, she put her weight on her left foot and let her ankle roll out from under her in the privacy of her voluminous evening gown. She let out a pained whimper. "Oh, oh dear. I think I... I must have twisted my ankle." She balanced a hand against the wall, tucking her left foot in and pressing her other hand to her exposed chest.

"Please, allow me." The president swooped Sybil into his arms, being mindful of her ankle. He said calmly to his children, "Donald, Lenora. Follow me." Relief surged through Sybil for getting away with injuring her own ankle on command, just as it started to ache.

As he carried her out into the foyer, Sybil noted that Calloway kept his hands in appropriate places, not letting his fingers wander from her back or her knees. He didn't even glance down at her neck and cleavage.

The foyer was significantly cooler than the ballroom, and, as the president set her on a long velvet bench pressed beneath an enormous window, a chill went through her, goosebumps climbing up her bare arms. A footman noticed them and came rushing over.

"Mr. President! What happened?" Something about the man's voice struck Sybil as odd, long enough for her to glance up. Her eyes widened.

It was Art. Without a doubt, she knew it was her brother.

She blinked rapidly, trying to determine if her eyes deceived her in some way. He was shapeshifted, yes, as a spindly footman with trim black hair. But she could also clearly see a watery outline around the figure, and there was an occasional flicker where she could nearly make out some of Art's features. Could anyone else see it?

She picked up her jaw and tried to mask her confusion as Calloway said, "Ah, Gerald. Would you be so kind as to fetch Dr. Jameson? He was at the bar last I saw him. This young lady and I had an unfortunate collision, and it appears she's sustained an injury to her ankle," he explained.

"Yes, Mr. President." Gerald—Art—disappeared as quickly as he had appeared.

"Oh, that is not necessary!" Sybil protested, trying to regain control of herself and the situation. "Mr. President, I feel like such a fool. Please, I will be fine. You must get back to your party."

"Nonsense. We can't have guests being disposed of at our own party, can we? What kind of a gentleman would I be, eh, Donald?" Calloway set a hand on his son's tiny shoulder. The boy shook his head aggressively, clearly elated to be looped into manhood with his father. "We met tonight, did we not? Your name... Roxana Bloodknight? Of South Carolina?"

"Yes, sir," she dipped her chin, genuinely impressed he remembered. Then again, he was a Sage.

"I see you've met my children."

"She's been telling us stories!" Donald announced.

"Oh, please—your children have been the ones keeping *me* company."

"This is her first party, and she doesn't like it very much," Lenora explained, very matter-of-factly.

Sybil's mortification escalated. She jumped in to defend herself, "Th-that isn't true at all, sir. I mean, it *is* my first party of this...

caliber, but I am enjoying it very much. It is an incredible event, the most exquisite I've ever attended. I was just needing a little bit of air, a break from the crowd."

Calloway smiled. "No need to be embarrassed, Miss Bloodknight. I completely understand. Galas like these are not my wife's preferred scene either. They can be quite intimidating, not to mention exhausting."

Sybil shyly agreed. "Yes, I suppose so." A grimace replaced her smile as her ankle throbbed. She did a quality job of self-imposing injury.

"I do apologize for hurting you."

"It's nothing, really. It's these shoes!" Sybil lifted her good foot out from under her dress to reveal Roxana's thin, creamy ankle and foot arched attractively in the sleek, gold-colored pumps. "I don't know why I let the dressmaker talk me into them. I just knew I would take a tumble. They're practically stilts!" She giggled. "The things we ladies do for a party, no, Lenora?"

Lenora nodded knowingly and perched herself next to Sybil on the velvet bench. To her dismay, Calloway didn't visibly react to Sybil's performance. Her frustration increased when Art reappeared with Doctor Jameson in tow. A doctor's examination could be most unattractive and would undoubtedly mark the end of her time with Calloway.

"Ah, Dr. Jameson. Thank you for coming so quickly." President Calloway rose and shook the doctor's hand.

Jameson looked less than thrilled to be taken away from his alcohol, but he plastered a pleasant expression on as he said, "Not a problem, Mr. President. What seems to be the issue here?"

Calloway explained again what happened, and the doctor knelt down to check Sybil's ankle. The president politely stepped aside and looked away as Jameson moved aside the skirt of her dress.

Sybil brainstormed about how she could touch him again and get him near her once more when Doctor Jameson's fingers palpated on her sore ankle, and she let out a less than feminine yelp.

Calloway turned and was by her side quickly, concerned. She blushed furiously and apologized.

The doctor stood. "Sorry about that. Nothing more than a small sprain, I'd wager. Where's my bag?"

"Here, sir," said Art, and he extended a black leather bag to him.

"Thank you." Doctor Jameson unlatched it and rummaged around for a moment before retrieving a glass jar the size of a child's fist. "This is arnica. Apply a pea-size amount to your ankle and rub it in until it's been absorbed. It will ease the soreness."

Sybil took the jar from his outstretched hand.

"And rest. No dancing," Dr. Jameson tilted his head toward the ballroom.

She sighed, "Well, I suppose there goes the rest of my evening. I'm so sorry for the trouble."

Doctor Jameson shrugged. "A not uncommon casualty of an evening of dancing and drinking, I'd wager."

"And stilts!" Lenora teased. Sybil winked at her.

Calloway smiled before turning to the doctor. "Thank you, Doctor. Gerald, would you escort the doctor back to the party and make sure he gets a full glass of champagne for his troubles? After that, would you please get a car pulled around to take Miss Bloodknight home?"

"Certainly, sir."

Art and Sybil exchanged a brief look. Her eyes traced the watery outline. It was so bizarre. Did he see it in her also? Was it some Thane magical warning signal the fyrnship had established? Could *everyone* see it?

That couldn't be true, or she'd never have gotten this far into the evening, she reprimanded herself. Not to mention Calloway would've immediately noticed Art wasn't Gerald. *Stop being stupid.*

"That is absolutely unnecessary, Mr. President," Sybil protested as Art left with Dr. Jameson. "I can make my way back to the hotel on my own. You've done enough."

"Nonsense. Lenora, Donald, would you please follow after Gerald and get your mother? I'll wait here with Miss Bloodknight."

"I can wait with her, Dad!" Donald exclaimed. "That's what a gentleman would do."

Calloway patted his son on the back. "You are most certainly that, Donald. But I need you to escort your sister. Gentlemen do that as well, you know."

Donald appeared to be far less inclined to spend time with Lenora rather than Roxana but did as he was asked without argument. His feet pattered on the marble flooring as he ran to catch up with Lenora, Gerald, and the doctor.

The silence between Sybil and Calloway felt thick, but not as thick as the pressure building in Sybil. Her heart pounded against her chest. She had a chance. She couldn't waste it.

She gazed up at him and then bashfully looked away when his eyes met hers. She traced the lid of the arnica cream. "You really don't have to do all of this, sir. You are an incredibly busy and important man. Far too important to even be seen with someone like me."

"I needed a break from the crowd. Bumping into you gave me an excuse. Once you're safely on your way, I'll return to my social duties."

"It's a splendid party."

"I can't take credit for it. I didn't plan a single detail," Calloway chuckled. "I go where people tell me to go when they tell me to go and read what they want me to read."

Sybil looked at him again. "You're the most powerful man in the country, and yet you talk as though you're a puppet."

"No, not quite," Calloway said, folding his hands in his lap and relaxing his posture. He leaned against the wall, his shoulder grazing Sybil's bare one. "But there are a lot more players at work than just me, that's for sure. Tell me, Miss Bloodknight, do you have interest in politics?"

She demurred, "Oh, no, not really. My father had some dealings in, and experience with, local politics for a few years, but he..." She faltered, and her voice trailed off.

"What?"

Sybil swallowed and took a breath, "He immediately withdrew from his involvements after the kidnapping of my younger brother. After that, he was too... weary, I suppose, to go back into the fray."

She was almost afraid to meet Calloway's intense stare. In the short amount of time she'd spoken with him, she noticed he had an intentionality about him that she wasn't accustomed to. When he spoke or asked a question, he did not hesitate to make eye contact and listened as though what you were about to say was the most interesting thing in the world to him at that time. It was unnerving. Intimate.

If he stared at her long enough, would he know she lied? Could she adequately conceal her deception from a Sage like him?

With great sincerity, Calloway placed a warm hand on hers and said, "That must have been incredibly trying and frightening for you and for your family."

"It was," she choked out, flicking a fake tear away. "I'm so sorry. I am making such a fool of myself tonight. In front of *you,* of all people."

An amused, close-lipped smile spread across the president's face, and he handed her a handkerchief from the inside of his tux jacket,

"You apologize a great deal for a socialite." This made Sybil giggle a watery laugh as she blotted her cheek. Even his handkerchief smelled nice.

"Is it too on the nose to say 'sorry' in response to that?" This time, she made the president laugh.

Calloway looked towards the direction of the ballroom, checking to see if his wife and the footman were returning, and then he said, "May I be a little forward?"

Yes. Let's do this, so I can go home. "Certainly."

"I presume Shifts were behind your brother's kidnapping?"

Okay then. That wasn't the direction Sybil wanted to go, but if it kept them talking... "You presume correctly, sir."

"So, it would be appropriate for me to assume you've had some firsthand experience with these people?" he confirmed.

"Y-yes."

"Tell me the first words that come to your mind when the Shifts are mentioned."

"Sir, I am most certainly not suited to give any kind of... advice to *you*."

"How can I be a good leader if I don't listen to the people? I don't only want to hear what my advisors and the experts are feeding me. I want to hear from the people of my country. You can be honest with me; I won't hold anything against you."

Roxana took a moment to ponder the president's words. But Sybil as herself was thinking of something entirely different: she had an opportunity here. Her job was to get the president in trouble with the media, plain and simple. But to try to influence him and hear from his own lips what he was thinking for her kin... She couldn't pass that up either. She had to be very careful what she said.

As she opened her mouth to answer, a young voice cried, "Father, we're back!" Sybil could've sworn disappointment darted across Calloway's face before he stood and scooped his son into his arms and took the hand of his bony First Lady.

"Miss Bloodknight, you remember my wife, Cecelia. My love, this is Roxana Bloodknight. We were introduced earlier this evening. And I'm afraid I have spoiled hers entirely by breaking her ankle in my own clumsiness."

"Not even quite. It's only a sprain, and it was entirely my fault," Sybil said quickly.

The First Lady's voice was so quiet and soft Sybil had to strain to hear her. "It's a shame about your injury on this occasion."

"There will be no lasting effects. I'll be up and dancing in no time." Sybil grinned at Lenora, who stood at her mother's side. "Your children are absolutely charming, by the way."

"Thank you," Cecelia whispered.

"Gerald, bring that motorcar around now," Calloway instructed.

"I really should speak with my date before I leave. I would hate for Richard to worry. Richard Worth?"

"We'll make sure he's notified as quickly as possible. I'll send a footman over momentarily," Cecelia said, kindly but stiffly.

"Thank you so much," Sybil smiled. Internally, she cringed at the awkwardness of the First Lady. *This couple makes no sense,* Sybil thought, her eyes moving back to the president.

Calloway motioned for another man, who was standing sentinel by the entrance to the grand home, to come over.

He moved quickly and fluidly. "Sir?"

"Regis, help Miss Bloodknight up. Her ankle has been injured; be mindful. Gerald is bringing the car 'round, and I'd like you to escort her back to her hotel." Sybil found it interesting that the president knew and remembered the names of so many of his staff.

"Really, an escort back is *not* necessary, sir!" Sybil objected again.

"Of course it is," Cecelia said quietly. "We'd be remiss if anything further transpired to spoil this night for you."

"Precisely," Calloway confirmed. "No more protests, Miss Bloodknight. Regis has been a butler here for many years, and I trust him with my own children. You are in capable hands."

Regis came by and offered an arm to Sybil. She took it, and he helped her to her feet. He bore the brunt of her weight as she tested her ankle. It really wasn't that bad, but she had committed at this point.

"Can you walk, Miss Bloodknight?" Regis asked.

"Oh, I think so. Let's just go slowly." They turned to leave. Sybil paused and twisted back around to say, "I really cannot compliment the success of this gala enough," even though she didn't participate in it at all. "And I am deeply appreciative of your kindness to me this evening." She directed this last bit at Calloway, peering at him from under Roxana's thick lashes.

Donald and Lenora waved, and Cecelia placed her wiry arms around them. She offered Sybil a weak smile. Branson Calloway stepped forward and reached out to shake her hand. "I'm sorry it ends this way for you, but hopefully we'll see you again some time."

Sybil's mind ached on the short drive back to the Alistaire. Regis said nothing, and neither did Art, who drove the motorcar as Gerald. *When did he learn to drive?* She wondered dimly. They had so much to talk about.

She wasn't sure if she should consider the evening a success or not.

On the one hand, she got to the White House, met the president, and hopefully made an impression. She all but fell into his arms. Not to mention spending the evening with his children, who would ideally talk about her to their father. Perhaps keep her name alive.

On the other hand, she was now on her way back to her hotel room by herself. Her ankle hurt. Everything could be utterly ruined if her fabricated story got out or was fact-checked with the Bloodknight family. Not to mention... Would she see President Calloway again? She had to. Tonight wasn't enough for Vox. She needed to humiliate him, and they needed one of the children. There was much still to be done.

By the time they pulled up to the Alistaire, she thought she would go crazy. She thanked Regis politely when he helped her to her suite and waited until he disappeared down the hotel corridor before closing her bedroom door and locking it. Who knew when and how Art would make his way back?

Immediately, all traces of Roxana fled her body in one wave-like *swoosh*. Her ordinary brown hair spilled over her shoulders and into her eyes. She wasn't as thin as Roxana and quickly felt suffocated in the dress tailored to Roxana's measurements and not her own. She clawed at her back to loosen the laces well enough to breathe and kicked off her shoes. She peeled off the jewelry that seemed to weigh three times more than it should.

As soon as the beaded gold ring left her finger, it felt like a hive of bees took up residence. Her bones began to ache, and her eyes burned. All adrenaline and strength escaped her. She wrestled with the lid of the arnica cream jar until it popped open, its grassy, earthy scent reaching her nose, and she liberally applied it to her ankle. And then to her temples. And the base of her neck and into her shoulders, craving relief from the weariness that had only just set in.

She heard the real Roxana whimper in the closet but ignored her. She collapsed onto the bed, face in the pillowy comforter, the gown spread around her, her back open to the air. She didn't have the energy to change or take a bath. Her stomach grumbled, and she realized she hadn't eaten anything of substance in hours. Sleep consumed her before she could do anything about it.

13.

Sybil stirred. A moan escaped her as she attempted to push herself upright. Her eyes were gritty and burned as she blinked them open, only to be met with an intense ray of sun piercing through the half-closed drapes. She squeezed her eyes shut again and lay back down slowly, her head swimming.

It took several minutes before she forced herself into a sitting position again and a couple more before she swung her legs over the side and stood up. Her bones ached, and her muscles felt sore and tender with every move she made.

The fyrnship had no idea the effect long-lasting Shiftwork had on a Shift. There was a price to pay for turning yourself inside out. A few hours here and there were nothing, but an extended operation put the body into a state of exhaustion. The fyrnship didn't realize how this vulnerability acted as a built-in safety for them, as no Shift would be able to stay transformed permanently or even long enough for certain criminal acts.

If Sybil had been more alert, she might have noticed how unusual it was for her to stay shifted as long as she had for two days in a row with as little experience as she had. She might've remembered Art could Shift longer than average as well. She might've attributed it to their shared blood.

But right now, she thought of nothing but how her body was paying the price. It was different from full-fledged pain, hurting instead like every muscle had been bruised. Stretched beyond its typical purpose and use. She belatedly noticed Art asleep next to her and had no recollection of his return to the suite yesterday.

Her face felt sticky from not washing her makeup off the night before. She shoved the ball gown off her, which was now quite wrinkled, and it fell into a heap on the floor. She gingerly took a step out of it and tested her ankle. It didn't hurt to walk on anymore, so that arnica cream had done its job.

But now where was it?

She staggered around the room, searching for it, before finally discovering the jar discarded on the floor. She snatched it up and dragged herself to the bathroom. She had just turned the water on to wash her face when a knock sounded at her door.

She swore under her breath. It took several tries for her to shift into Roxana, surely a result of her weariness. The knocking persisted as she ran around the room searching for a robe to pull over her burning body, calling, "Just a minute!" Her voice was hoarse, and she coughed to clear her throat.

"Wha's goin' on?" Art muttered, rolling over on the bed.

"Be quiet and hide under the blanket!" She hissed. She tied the robe at the waist as she threw the door open.

"What?" She snapped breathlessly. She fought to keep her eyes open as black spots danced in her vision. Her arm shot out to grab the doorframe to steady herself. *I must look so hungover. I* feel *so hungover.*

The bellboy visibly shrank back at her sharp voice but held out an envelope with a pretty golden seal. "For you, ma'am."

"Thank you," she said shortly, snatching the letter. She closed the door in his face.

"What is it?" Art asked. He was sitting up now and looked, quite honestly, as bad as Sybil felt. That made her feel a touch better.

"A letter," she replied, dissolving back into herself.

"Bring it here," Art said. She tripped her way to the bed and gave it to him. She collapsed on the end, willing her head to stop pulsing.

He tore it open and scanned it, wincing a little. "Well, well, well... What d'you know?" He recited: "President Branson Calloway invites Miss Roxana Bloodknight to dine with him and his family this evening, Monday the sixteenth of January, at seven o'clock at his home, the White House."

"Read that again," she said weakly, lifting her head. He did.

"Says evening attire required. A car will pick you up at six forty p.m. Damn. Good job," he said. "Good job."

She laughed in disbelief. "I don't know what to make of that."

"Looks to me like you got exactly what we hoped for out of that gala. This may be your last chance with Calloway though, so we need to get the footage tonight."

"I can't speak for you, but my head is killin' me... I can't do this right now," Sybil moaned.

"Fair enough. I don't feel so great myself," he said, leaning back against the headboard. "We won't get anything accomplished while we're like this."

"This is normal, right?" She asked, dropping her head back to the mattress.

"Unfortunately, yeah. You, in particular... You were full-body shifted for a long time. It takes a toll. You'll need to rest up for tonight. No more shifting 'till then." He perked up. "Hey, that doctor last night, he gave you the arnica."

Sybil nodded.

"Use that. It'll help."

They ordered food to the room and, while they waited for its delivery, took turns in the bath. Sybil liberally applied the arnica cream to her entire body and crossed her fingers it'd take effect quickly. A tiny, mean part of her wanted to keep the arnica to herself, but she couldn't figure out a way to manage that when Art already expected to use it.

After washing up, Art checked on their hostage, gave her a chance to use the bathroom, and offered her some toast and water. Roxana was a pitiful sight, shaking terribly in her rumpled nightdress.

Over black coffee, which soothed the racket in their heads, the siblings recounted their respective nights. Art was refreshingly pleased with Sybil's work, at least compared to how critical he'd been of her thus far. She told him about how she made contact with Calloway's children and with him. He expressed skepticism about the narrative she spun regarding Roxana's fictional brother and the Shifts and made several comments about it being reckless and what she could've done instead. But he ultimately acknowledged it was likely the only reason Calloway wanted to meet with her again.

"Which kid do you think would be best to target?" He asked. "I'd really like to avoid snatching 'em both."

"Donald. More vulnerable," Sybil heard herself saying. She hated herself for it too. She felt guilty every time Roxana made her presence known from the closet; she felt guilty thinking of Calloway's children and his wife... She was careful to not breathe a word of any of these feelings to her brother. She was too sensitive. Too green. That was it: she needed to be desensitized, and that would, of course, take time and experience.

"What did you get up to last night?" She asked, ready to turn the focus onto his Shiftwork.

"I staked out the servants' entrance for most of the afternoon. Found a worker leaving and used him and his badge to get inside."

"You just left his body? Someone will launch an inquiry when—"

"Of course not," Art snapped. "*He* had been drinking. I easily staged him as having passed out drunk, right there in the open.

He couldn't have made it easier for me. He had a flask on him, so I used that to soak the front of his clothes. Used his badge to get in and then quickly switched into Gerald when I found him. The other guy was on his way out, so it'd make no sense for him to be back at the White House for the gala."

"And where did Gerald's body go?"

"Well, aren't we critical about everyone's work now?" Art scoffed, though he sounded a smidge proud. "A supply closet. Much too easy to accidentally get locked in there. It only opens from the outside."

"He didn't see you?"

"Nope. Grabbed a uniform from the laundry and blended in with ease." He began drawing with his finger on the table. He may have known what he was tracing, but it was not clear to Sybil. She stared blankly at him.

He explained, "The staff quarters are underneath the White House, almost entirely underground. It's a complete labyrinth. It would take me days to figure out the layout. I made my way to the reception space with the rest of the staff for the gala, so that part was easy. There are hallways that run up to Calloway's private quarters over here in the back; I know that much. There was also a large layout on the wall. I didn't get much of a chance to study it, but I think that the kids' rooms are in this vicinity." He continued to circle his finger around.

Sybil silently sipped her coffee. The bitter taste burned her tongue.

"Here's what I'm thinking. I'll shift into the driver who picks you up today for your dinner. Then I'll make my way inside to staff quarters and wait in the boy's room until he's back after the meal."

"You think it'll be that easy?"

"No, but it's doable. I heard yesterday a lot of staff have today off because of the work put in for the gala. Nice of Calloway, huh?" He smirked. "I take that to mean there'll be fewer people to dodge around and less bodies that have to fall."

"I hope you're right."

"I am." Art put his mug to his lips.

Sybil hesitated. She didn't know why she was nervous to tell him.

That wasn't true; she did know why.

It was because, outside the beorg, he wasn't the same. He was arrogant and proud and bossy, and she wasn't sure what would happen if she popped that bubble with the news that his shapeshifting was so evident to her. Would he be offended? Angry *at* her?

"I need to tell you something, Ar—"

"Don't use my name!" He said sharply.

"What, why?" She was taken aback. Was this actually the first time she'd said his name aloud since they'd been here? Had he not used hers? That was hard to believe.

"*She* could be listening," Art nodded his head toward the closet.

"Roxana?"

"Yes, Roxana!"

"So what?"

"If she knows who we are—who held her hostage and impersonated her—she could go straight to the authorities. I don't know how it'll work with the government, but when the Guild managed us, if we were caught fair and square, it was instant prison. You know that. I can't imagine the government bein' more lenient."

"But Vox said he'd delay our registration." She felt very small.

"They still have records from the Guild. They'll be able to pick us out if Roxana identifies us. Besides, it wouldn't take much bribery for them to fish out from our kin who was missing during this time."

Their kin wouldn't really sell them out, would they? Sybil

thought of how angry Ethel, Bo, and Glen were when they discovered Art was literate. She imagined how furious everyone would be that, while the government cancelled their ops, Sybil and Art were sent on a high profile job. That Sybil had been hired underage.

"Oh. Yeah, that makes sense." She was starting to feel less small and more angry. She tried to be patient with him and to defer to his leadership. But he didn't have to be so nasty about it.

"That was careless," he declared, reaching for a piece of toast.

This statement was the last thing she needed to lose control. She knocked the toast from his hand.

"Why are you being so mean?" She cried, nostrils flaring.

His eyes snapped open at her outburst.

"You are the one who recommended *me* to Vox. To do this with you! I have tried to do what you asked. I don't offer opinions. But at every turn, you put me down and make me feel *stupid*. You talk to me like I'm... like I'm Joan! Or Paul! I'm your *sister,* and I'm not that much younger. I'm not a child. You could at least try to treat me like an equal."

Now that she started, she had a difficult time stopping. She wasn't even sure she was stringing together coherent sentences. "Is that why you really brought me? To lord your experience and skills over me?"

"Woah, woah, you're way out of line! I'm not *lording* my experience over you! I'm trying to teach you and keep you from making crucial mistakes!"

"If you haven't noticed, I haven't *been* making crucial mistakes. I'm doing a good job. I've been shapeshifted for practically two days straight. I'm exhausted, but I got us into the gala *and* I've got an in with the bloody president of Eastward tonight!"

"I told you well done earlier!"

"Yes, and then you promptly told me all the things I did wrong during my op." She mimicked him, "'It probably wasn't wise to make up a story like that.' 'That's really easily fact-checked.'"

"I also said it's probably the only reason Calloway is inviting you to dinner tonight. I didn't think you were such a baby needing affirmation and back-pats the whole way through," he sneered.

Sybil stiffened. She said crisply. "I don't need my back patted or my hand held. I wanted to work as a team, not as your subordinate. I thought that's what you wanted too. Or maybe you're too wrapped up with Vox and making your new boss happy that you don't care how you treat others along the way."

"That's ridiculous."

"Is it?" Her eyes flashed. "Maybe you really do think you're better than the rest of us because he singled you out. Better than me."

"Maybe I *am* better than you. Have you thought about that?" Art hit the table with his fist.

Sybil sat back. "There it is. At least you're being honest now." She rose from her chair, trying to mask the soreness of her tight muscles.

"I'm always honest."

She stared at him. "Oh, so those six months of lying about where you've been and who you're working for... We're not counting that?"

"I explained that. You know what? I don't have to defend myself to you," Art growled. He threw his cloth napkin across the table in frustration. "You should be grateful. You wouldn't be here if it weren't for me."

"And we wouldn't be meeting with the president if it weren't for me," she shot back. "I'm going to take a walk."

"You can't. We have to plan for tonight."

"Later."

Art jumped to his feet and grabbed her by the arm. "No. I mean it, Sy—" he caught himself. "*No*. We need to plan tonight. We've got to make sure someone can get shots of you and Calloway.

I won't be able to because I've got to make my way to the kid's room." Just like that he was moving back to the op. Always the op.

Sybil wrenched her arm from his. "Fine. I'm taking a bath then."

"You already took one."

"I'm taking another," she hissed vehemently.

And she did. She stewed the entire time she was in the tub. When the water began to cool and she could no longer justify her absence, she crawled out and threw her day dress back on. When she came back out of the bathroom, she was still upset and did not feel like facing her brother. She had thrown a tantrum and hadn't accomplished anything. He was probably going to treat her worse now. Perhaps he'd send her home. Maybe he called Vox and told him to send someone else.

Art was sitting in the same upholstered chair with his elbows pressing into the little round table. His head rested in his hands, fingers absentmindedly running over his short hair.

Sybil sat across from him and wordlessly fished his discarded napkin from where it landed in the jam jar. She wasn't ready to apologize, but she did have news to tell him. What she meant to tell him before their fight.

"When I saw you yesterday—as Gerald, I mean—I could tell it was you."

Art slowly lifted his head. Sybil was a little satisfied he appeared as miserable as she felt. "What d'you mean?"

"When I saw you in the foyer, comin' at Calloway's call, I saw Gerald first. But then... It was like a ripple in your reflection, and suddenly I could see *you*. And then it flickered back and forth sporadically whenever I looked at you. A little like the beorg's boundary."

Art looked positively alarmed. "That doesn't make sense," he said in a tight voice.

Sybil shrugged. "I'm just tellin' you what I saw. No one else reacted, so I don't think anyone but me noticed."

"Are you making this up because you're mad at me?" He asked, narrowing his eyes suspiciously.

"I'm not quite *that* mad. Besides, I've always believed you were an excellent shapeshifter. If I wanted to hurt you, that's not the area I'd go about tearing apart."

"Thanks," he said dryly. He rubbed the back of his neck. "That's… strange."

"I thought so too. Just thought you should know."

"You've never noticed that before? Up on the beorg or anything?" She shook her head.

Art pursed his lips, thinking for a long moment. "I didn't detect anything when I looked at you." Was that a touch of envy she heard?

"Maybe it was a one-off thing," Sybil offered.

"Maybe."

"You wanted to plan for tonight?" She tried to change the subject.

"Oh. Yeah. Yeah, we should."

Over the next thirty minutes, the siblings outlined a plan, though their dialogue was far from friendly. Art had a contact here in Washington who was the editor of a rather scathing magazine that delighted in humiliating public figures. They decided to reach out to him about having someone available to photograph tonight's dinner.

Art told her she needed to go by herself because he was going to scope out places to hold Donald, as there was no reasonable way to sneak the president's son into Roxana's suite. Sybil resisted the idea of meeting Hank Lawrenson on her own—he was *Art's* contact, after all—but Art insisted and made sure to get in a few jabs about how she wanted to be treated as his equal.

He called Hank and set up an appointment for eleven a.m.

sharp at the bar on 2nd Street. Sybil hoped there would only be one bar on 2nd Street. Art set the phone back on the receiver. "There you go. Your first big girl meeting with Hank Lawrenson, editor of *The Outcrier*. Good luck."

Sybil said nothing but pulled out a red scarf from the armoire. She tied it over her hair and slid a coat over her dress.

"It's only ten; I don't know if you need to leave this early," Art said.

"I told you I wanted to take a walk today."

"Are you goin' out as you?" He meant not shifted.

"You said no shifting today. Doesn't leave me many options," she retorted. "Look, I'll go out of the hotel as Roxana, but then I'll shift back to me. I can't use up all my strength before tonight."

"Be careful," Art said in a tone that sounded as if he regretted saying anything at all.

"I will be. Any tips for meeting with Hank?"

"Don't let him fluster you. He loves women."

She sighed. "So that's why you're sending me."

Art shrugged.

She rolled her eyes and shifted into Roxana. At the door, she added, "Good luck on your search. Give Roxana something to eat before you leave."

14.

Crisp, dry air hit Sybil in the face as soon as she stepped foot outside, causing tears to sting her eyes. She inhaled deeply, and a myriad of smells greeted her. Cigarettes, baked goods from the cafe next door, and smoke from the chimneys of nearby homes and businesses, puffing black clouds into the air. Longing for the clean air of the beorg—the scent of dirt, pine, sunshine, and rain—gripped her, and she sighed wistfully. She'd be home soon.

She hadn't thought she'd miss it so quickly. She had spent her whole life dreaming of getting away from the beorg and experiencing the fyrnship. Now she just wanted to be back where it was beautiful and simple. Where there was no *pretense* and far less pressure.

She, as Roxana, slipped into an alleyway to shift back into herself and went out the opposite side. This went unnoticed, and she blended easily into the bustle of Washington.

There was so much to look at and to absorb as she walked. Unlike the sluggish Alistaire this morning, whose guests were sleeping off the excitement of last night's gala, the businesses were lively. Shop employees were in and out of their stores, getting their wares in order, speaking with customers. Businessmen walked with intentional strides in long, brass-buttoned coats and wool caps, leather briefcases in hand. As she strolled the streets of the capital, she found it noisy and exhausting.

On her short walk already, she passed many different types of people. It was true no Shift looked the same, but they were, more or less, the same. Somewhat ordinary features and bland colors. The diversity was greater here. Sizes, shapes, colors. Sybil took careful note of the shades. She had heard of these things, but seeing first-hand would definitely improve the quality of her shapeshifting in the future. She identified strands of gold, caramel, and red in dark hair. Blonde, white, and silver in graying hair. Even bluish hues in black hair. Some skin was perfectly smooth; others full of bumps. Freckles, moles, facial hair. Light skin could be almost translucent in the right lighting or bright red from the cold. The variations in everything from eye shapes to nose lengths to jawlines—she drank it all in. It gave her something to think about other than how overwhelming and unpleasant the city was to her.

Even speech was different here. In the beorg, they shared a lazy way of speaking, where words blended together and vowels rolled into each other. In the fyrnship, they spoke more respectfully, purposefully, and neatly, with each word and letter assigned its due place. Just like the magi themselves… Everyone and everything in its proper place.

Sybil reached the end of a street and noticed the buildings on the corner looked familiar. She paused to think. If she recalled correctly, they had turned off here to go to the White House last night.

A solid force collided with her elbow, knocking her sideways and nearly into the road. An arm snagged her around the waist and righted her.

"Are you okay, ma'am? I am so, so sorry," a bass voice said.

"I'm fine. I'm fine," Sybil said, waving him off and adjusting her scarf. This was twice now she had collided with strangers in less than twenty-four hours. Her ankle twinged at the memory. She glanced at her assailant.

The young man was perhaps in his early twenties and had the

most beautiful shade of skin she'd ever seen. It was a touch lighter than coffee and smooth as melted chocolate. His eyes were nearly black, round, with long lashes framing them and thick eyebrows above. She couldn't see his hair under a formal stiff cap that matched the emerald green uniform he wore, but nothing poked out from under the cap, so she suspected it was cropped close to his head. *Thane. A good looking Thane...*

He flashed a smile, displaying a row of white teeth. "I do apologize. That could've ended badly."

"Nonsense. It was an accident." She sounded rude, even to her own ears.

"Are you sure? I feel terrible. Always in a rush and never paying enough attention," he said with a deep, rumbling laugh.

"Positively. I'm afraid I was in a bit of a daydream myself, stopping like that on the sidewalk." Sybil tried to soften her tone. She felt self-conscious talking to a stranger in her natural state like this. Would he realize she's a Shift? *Maybe we have some inherent smell I don't know about*. If he noticed anything off about her, he didn't let on.

"Where were you headed? Can I walk you the rest of the way?"

What is with these people and escorting you everywhere you go? Sybil thought, exasperated. At home, she went wherever she pleased whenever she pleased in her woods. Well, at least within their boundary. It was the only way she and Xavier could have any amount of privacy.

"That's not necessary, sir," she denied as diplomatically as she could muster. "I'm on a short walk and nearly there."

"It's Killian, by the way. Killian James. No need to call me 'sir.'" He grinned again. "Makes me feel like my old man."

Sybil resisted pinching the bridge of her nose and laced her gloved fingers together instead. She wanted to be on her way. "Mr.

James, then."

"And you are?"

She hesitated inwardly. She couldn't use Roxana's identity, and she certainly wouldn't use her real name. Giving him a sly wink, she said, "Needing to be on my way."

Killian chuckled. "I can take a hint." His laugh was such a warm sound; Sybil was caught off guard when she smiled back.

"Ah, she smiles!" Killian jested.

Sybil felt somewhat stunned by this quick-witted man and couldn't determine what to say next. At her hesitation, Killian grinned more broadly and said, "I'm kidding."

Sybil cleared her throat and said, "It was nice to meet you." She gave him a polite nod and tried to walk away as fast as possible.

"This is awkward," his voice came from behind her a second later, and this time she did roll her eyes. "But I'm headed this direction too. Mind if we walk together until we need to split ways?"

If we must. "We may as well." Sybil hoped Killian wouldn't hear the tension in her voice. He took a couple long strides to catch up to her.

"Where are you headed to?"

"2nd Street, though I could use a point in the right direction," she admitted.

"I can do that. You're visiting?"

"Yes. You?"

"Born and raised here. Working here now, just like my Pop did."

"How nice. Where do you work?" Sybil hoped to keep him talking about himself to avoid any personal questions directed to her.

"Security at the White House, actually."

Is that right? A streak of delight hit Sybil at her good fortune. She slowed her gait and fought to keep the thrill from her face. She'd impress Art if she came back with worthwhile information.

"Oh, really? What an interesting job."

"It has its moments!"

"How long have you been working there?"

"Couple of years. Started during President Burke's administration."

"What kinds of things do you do?"

"Nothing too dangerous, don't you worry," he quipped. Sybil gave him a sideways glance that she hoped he'd interpret as encouragement to continue. "Really just basic security functions, like manning the perimeter of the building or entrances. Sometimes working events. Making sure no one goes in who isn't supposed to. I hope to move up the ranks soon though. Personal security detail, for one."

"I bet you meet many interesting people."

"Now that you'd be right on. I've definitely gotten my fair share of interactions with important people, albeit usually briefly, but I get to see them. I got to meet the representatives from Westward and Southward this past weekend. Interesting folks. President Calloway even knows my name. I'm often stationed by their private entrance."

"How flattering." Sybil was suddenly quite glad she didn't throw out a fake name when Killian asked because the only one that had popped into her head was Lenora Donald, a combination of the president's children's names. Killian would've undoubtedly caught the connection since he knew them personally. "So, you've been inside the White House? What's it like?" *Give me something to work with here, pal.*

"It's an impressive piece of architecture, that's for certain. I've not been everywhere inside, but the ballrooms and Great Dining Hall are phenomenal."

"I can only imagine," Sybil returned kindly. "Is it like that everywhere? So elaborate?"

"Well, I mean, it's home to those people. It has more personal touches elsewhere." Killian met her eyes, "You're awfully curious about a building."

"Tourist," she conceded. "I'm from a pretty small town in South—"

"Ahh, so that's the accent."

She flushed slightly. She hadn't thought to disguise it. "Yes, and we don't have anything like these buildings here. They just fascinate me. They're like palaces."

"Are you visiting the city alone?"

Sybil suddenly felt torn. She either wove in another lie to potentially get caught in, or her curiosity and independence as a young single woman traveling in the capital from somewhere far away would lead to suspicion. Or admiration. Neither of which she needed or wanted.

If he were in security, he'd know all about trying to catch and read Shifts. *Tread carefully, Sybil.*

"For now. My father is joining me in a couple of days."

"Pleasure or business?"

"Pleasure for me, business for him."

"I work the rest of the day, but, if you want a tour guide, I'm off tomorrow."

"That's quite kind of you, Mr. James, but—"

"Killian."

"Killian. But I'm afraid we already have commitments."

"A shame. I don't get to enjoy a fine young woman's company all that often," Killian said. He was smiling again, but Sybil could tell in the intensity of his eyes he was serious. Genuine. She blushed.

"I've embarrassed you. I'm sorry."

Before Sybil could stammer something out, he added, "To be honest, it's been a long few weeks for me. I haven't really had anyone to spend time with outside of my job, much less someone as fascinating as you. I didn't mean to overstep. I've been known to be far more forward and candid than I should be, especially for someone in my line of work."

"You don't even know me. Why would you think I'm fascinating?"

"I know you're not from around here. You have a curiosity with the world around you. You're clever. Independent, it seems. And incredibly beautiful, if you don't mind me saying so."

"You've gathered all that from the few minutes we've spent walking together?"

He tilted his head down to whisper playfully, "Well, I'm a Thane. I read people. Try to determine if they're a threat."

"Am I one?" Sybil met his onyx eyes.

Without faltering, Killian replied, "Not in the slightest."

15.

Sybil conceded to walk with Killian, but the longer she spent with him, the more stressed and conflicted she felt. He was a bold personality. He had an unnerving amount of focus, it seemed, on everything at all times. He was attentive to her but also seemed to have his head on a swivel, absorbing his surroundings.

She was only half-listening to him when the mansion came into view. *The White House.*

"Didn't I tell you you'd pass it on your way to 2nd Street?" Killian said, noticing her stalled steps. "Isn't it magnificent?"

"You certainly did."

"See? I'm a man of my word."

"Is this all it takes to prove one's integrity?" Sybil teased.

"You are awfully skeptical for a woman." Sybil bristled. "Typically my status as a Thane guard at the White House garners some trust and respect!" He faked indignation, but his eyes twinkled.

"That seems to be the kind of thing someone untrustworthy would say," Sybil replied coyly.

"If I prove my trustworthiness to you, then will you let me take you out to dinner tonight?"

Warning lights flashed in her head. Sybil faltered, "Oh, Killian, please, you're being too forward. I'm… I'm not sure I'm comfortable with that." Belatedly, she added, "I don't think my father would like it."

Sincerity saturated his expression. "Geez, I'm sorry. I've been told I can be too much too quickly. My mama would be horrified… I get things in my head, and they come right out of my mouth. Forgive me."

"You're forgiven. But I'm not going to go to dinner with you. I'm sorry."

"And I completely understand. I will accept this walk as a nice, friendly chance encounter and wish you farewell when we get there. Agreed?"

"Agreed." Then, realizing she had yet to get anything useful out of the White House guard, she asked, "Guess you wouldn't want to be a White House tour guide for me though, would you? Let me see some behind-the-scenes things the real tours don't show?"

Killian spread his hands with a grin, "Sorry. No can do."

"Ah, figures. It was worth a shot." Sybil returned a little smile.

They walked in silence until they came up to the towering iron fence and faced the White House. In the light of day, the president's mansion stood more impressively and more grand. She could make out every detail she hadn't been able to the night before. A multitude of large windows, framed in white brick, gleamed. The marble columns shone as though they'd been polished from top to bottom, and she could see intricate carvings where the columns met the roof of the expansive portico.

Beautifully trimmed evergreen trees lined the smooth driveway. They stood out against the white snow covering the expansive lawn. It looked as pristine as the snow at home did, not dirty and full of smoke like the snow shoveled to the side of the streets did. The massive dome on the roof was bigger than she perceived it to be last night, and sunlight glinted off it as if it were made of gold. It was like a small castle in the center of a modern world.

"Breathtaking, don't you think?" Killian asked, wrapping

his fingers around an iron fencepost. "I never get used to it. The grounds out back make me feel like I'm walking through a fairytale. I love it when they entertain out there. It feels like no one can see in. The Sylvaar workers truly do remarkable work on the landscaping."

Out back?

"Can we walk around to see it?"

"Oh, heavens, no. They have massive hedges and walls that you can technically walk *next* to, but you'll never be able to see past them into the grounds. It goes way further back than you would think it does. Same with the house itself. It looks big from the front, but it just continues in the back further than you'd expect."

Sybil pursed her lips in thought. The fence was a tall iron that'd be impossible to scale, though it enabled a full view of the mansion. She wasn't sure if she'd be driven through the front like at the gala or if they would take her to a more private entrance. Killian had confirmed for her those did indeed exist. And if the house was far greater and deeper than the front implied with extensive grounds one couldn't even see from the street... Her confidence in finding a good spot to sneak the president to for photos waned.

This op is doomed.

"I'd love to see that," she breathed, trying not to look like she was analyzing the building too much. "But I suppose it's important for the family to have privacy. And their guests."

"Precisely. Can you even imagine living such a publicized life?" Killian plunged forward before Sybil could respond. "The Calloways are a really kind family. I hate to see all the lies and gossip printed about them in the news by their enemies. I don't know how they stand it." Killian tugged back his coat sleeve to check his wristwatch. "Well, I have to be off to clock in. It was really nice to meet you. And sorry again for knocking you into the road."

"It was nice meeting you too. Thanks for the walk."

"Oh, and 2nd Street…" He extended his arm and pointed to the left. "Take a left up there at the corner, walk down past the House, and then a right on the sidewalk at the end of it. Three more blocks, and you're there."

"Left, right, and straight three more blocks," Sybil repeated. "Thank you, Killian. You saved me time walking in circles."

"I still don't know your name."

"Do you need to? What are the odds we'll ever see each other again?"

"I like to bet against the odds." There was that intensity in his face again.

Sybil bit her lip and then offered her twelve year old cabin mate's name, "It's Joan."

Killian reached out to shake her hand, his eyes locked on hers. "I'll see you around, Joan."

"Goodbye, Killian." Sybil tucked her gloved hands into her pockets, feeling a little bit like a schoolgirl fresh off her first date, and watched his impressive frame stroll down the sidewalk. After a few long strides, he turned left where the fence ended, as he instructed her to do, and disappeared.

As badly as she wanted to see exactly where he went, Sybil forced herself to stay rooted and not to chase after Killian until several minutes had passed. She had to ensure they not only avoided another interaction but that he did not get the notion she was following him.

Sybil inhaled deeply to clear her mind from the bizarre encounter with Killian and began the path he had instructed her. She maintained a casual pace and made sure to look around and smile at things as a tourist might, hoping anyone who might notice her would simply see an unhurried, curious young woman.

When she reached the corner Killian disappeared around, she observed that the fence continued down the entire depth of the front yard, past the house, and continued into the rear gardens. At the house, a massive, impenetrable hedge began, which ran the length of the fence. All as he said. The hedge gave the house a mythical, romantic appearance to it, as if it were a woodland fortress. *Like out of a fairytale*, Killian had said.

From behind the hedge wall, she could see the top of the mansion rising high, but it eventually noticeably dipped down out of view, and she figured this had to be where the lesser known back end of the house began. The hedge and fence continued for what seemed like an eternity.

Sybil never did find the entrance Killian had to have used to get into work, and this bugged her. Art had been able to find it; why couldn't she? She was tempted to retrace her steps and look again when she heard a bell chime. Only once. It wasn't eleven yet, but it would be soon.

She hastened her walk. A right when the sidewalk and mansion's hedge ended. Across the street three more blocks. The faint scent of beer drew her to a bar wedged between two larger restaurants. The entrance was tucked into the brick with three narrow steps leading inside. Sybil glanced around her. The street was empty. It was rather strange a bar would be open at eleven in the morning on a Monday. Wasn't it?

A chill ran down Sybil's spine, and it was not from the cold. Something was off about this place. She swallowed and climbed the steps. The door swung open easily, and the smell of cigarettes and stale beer engulfed her. She instinctively threw her hand over her mouth and nose but resisted coughing. She cautiously surveyed the space.

It was a traditional bar, all things considered, but extremely run-down. In the light of two low-hanging dim fixtures, dust visibly floated in the air. Under a thick, even blanket of grime, the bar counter was scuffed, chipped, and stained. There were only three bar stools, though there was room for triple that. The stools' leather seats were ripped and split in places. It was a long room, probably going back at least thirty or forty feet, but it couldn't be even eight feet wide in the entire building. Between the bar counter, bar stools, and three rickety tables with equally unstable chairs, it would be impossible to maneuver through the space easily.

The shelves behind the bar were void of liquor, except for one shelf that had a poor selection. Anything that had been hanging on the walls, which were covered in a peeling, faded yellow wallpaper, was long gone, with only nails or empty frames in their places.

Disgust wrinkled Sybil's nose. She dropped her hand to her side and muttered, "What a dump."

"Why, thank you," a garbled voice said as a figure rose from behind the bar.

"I didn't think you were open," Sybil attempted to recover, her heart suddenly in her throat. "The place is empty."

"That's how I like it," the figure responded.

Sybil remained stationary and attempted to size him up. She couldn't see his face, but he was very tall, very skinny, and very bald. Long porcelain-colored fingers came into the light as he presented a mug which clinked loudly on the countertop, causing her to jump a little. The man smiled then, his lips pulling back to reveal sharp teeth.

Is he human?

"I think I may be in the wrong place," Sybil said carefully, taking a small step back.

"I don't think you are," said a male voice behind her, breath ghosting the back of her neck. Sybil jumped away with a gasp and stumbled into the wall to her left. The men's cold laughter echoed in the narrow hall, and dread pooled in Sybil's stomach. *This can't be right. This can't be right.*

"You're punctual, baby," said the second man. *Art's editor.*

He stood in front of her now—an enormous bear of a man with a bad comb-over of reddish brown hair, a scraggly beard of the same shade, and beady eyes. Crooked, small stained teeth pinned a cigarette in place. "Hank Lawrenson, editor of *The Outcrier.*" He extended a fleshy hand.

Sybil's heart hammered against her ribs, and her hands shook at her sides. She swallowed hard and tried to gain control of herself. Her arm felt like lead as she lifted it to put her hand in Hank's.

"I know, I know," he interjected. "No names. I know how this goes. Nice scarf." His gaze roamed her frame. Appreciatively? Interested? She wasn't sure.

She grimaced and retrieved her hand, feeling the sudden urge to wash it. Maybe her entire arm as well.

"Let's talk." Hank swept his arm into the empty space before them. "Confidential, of course. Rodney there won't be a problem." He walked ahead of her deeper into the bar and dropped into an unstable chair.

Sybil followed and sat across from him. She hoped she looked stoic and unreadable instead of as frightened and anxious as she felt inside. *Get it together, Sybil. You're* not *a scared little girl.* "Thank you for meeting me, Mr. Lawrenson."

"Call me Hank, sweetheart."

"Mr. Lawrenson," Sybil repeated firmly, all the while clenching her shaking hands together in her lap.

"I was surprised Arthur sent you in his stead. He and I have had a good working relationship for a good while now."

"He sends his regards."

Hank's eyebrows rose lazily. "Sure he does. Alrighty, little miss, what have you got for me?"

"I have been invited to dine with President Calloway and his family tonight at seven o'clock."

"How big is this dinner supposed to be? How many guests?"

"I can't confirm, but I am suspicious it's just me. With his family. There's no event. I had an… interaction with Calloway yesterday at the Thanes' gala. While the invitation didn't explicitly say, the implication is that our dinner is to be some type of a follow-up from that."

"Interesting." Hank pulled the cigarette from between his teeth and rolled it between his fingers. It remained unlit.

"Here is why I need your help." Gaining momentum, Sybil leaned forward in her seat and tapped the dusty table with her palm. "I have limited knowledge of the grounds. I don't know much about the family's private quarters. I suspect *you* do. And I suspect you have methods to smuggle at least one camera in to capture the… moment."

"The moment," Hank mused. He wedged his cigarette back in his mouth and drummed his fingers against his chin. "I like the content, Shift, I do. We could use a good scandal on the Calloways. My primary concern, however, is how likely it is you'll get him in a compromising position amidst a family dinner."

Sybil bit her lip for a moment as she thought. "A fair question, Mr. Lawrenson. I wish I had a foolproof answer for you, but that's simply not how these ops work. I have a few thoughts… It's become rather obvious that the First Lady does not care to partake in political discussions. I would guess at some point in our evening she would excuse herself, and that would provide opportunity."

"And where is Arthur supposed to be throughout this night?"

"Another op," Sybil answered.

Hank thought for a long minute. Only the occasional phlegmy cough from Rodney behind the counter broke the quiet. Finally, Hank reached into his faded coat's inner pocket and retrieved a fat envelope. He pulled a packet of papers out, unfolded them, and smoothed them onto the table in front of Sybil. His beady eyes met hers. "These are the floor plans of the White House."

She reached a hand out to turn the papers toward her but wasn't really sure what she was looking at. There were lines and shapes and lots of small written notes. *Art should be here. He could make sense of this.*

"They're bloody convoluted, aren't they?" Hank said. He reached out a thick finger and traced a portion. "See here? This is the North Wing, or where the president's private living quarters are. If you're right about the dinner tonight, this is likely where you'll be. I'd wager you'd dine in one of these three dining rooms." Sybil followed his finger, her brow knit together. It sort of made sense as Hank explained it, but she wasn't sure she'd ever have connected these rough plans to a physical space on her own.

"How'd you come about these?" she asked.

"I have my sources."

"So a Shift got them for you," Sybil said, matter-of-factly.

Hank chuckled, "Your kin is good for a lot of things, baby. We work well together, the Shifts and me. I won't apologize for that."

"I wouldn't expect you to." Sybil turned her attention back to the plans. "Let's say dinner ends. Where do we go next? A living room or a parlor?"

Hank nodded and set his unlit cigarette on the table. He shifted his seat closer to Sybil's so they could both see the plans. He smelled as stale as he looked, but she no longer felt afraid. "See this room over here? That's a parlor they use for entertaining. The living rooms they'd use as a family would be over on this side, and I don't think there's any way you make it over there."

"Bedrooms?"

"Yeah, four of them off this hall by the living room."

"The family's rooms? Or are those guest rooms?"

"That's the family's rooms. Guest suites are over on this side."

Sybil pursed her lips as she thought. "What's this one?"

Hank squinted and leaned closer to where her gloved finger rested. "Ah—Calloway's office."

The chair creaked loudly as she leaned back into it. She had the sudden, fleeting fear that it might break under her weight and send her to the floor. "If dinner happens in one of those dining rooms, my best bets are to get him alone in either that parlor or the office. The bedrooms are too far away. It'd be too easy to be spotted by a member of staff. Or his family."

"Yeah, I'm with you."

"Do those double lines indicate something?" Sybil asked.

"Yeah. Windows."

She swore and tilted her head back. "The parlor didn't have any. What kind of parlor doesn't have windows?"

"No, no, it has three small ones and then a skylight. Right there."

"You don't say that like it's an option though."

Hank spread his hands. "If you're wanting me to get a camera in, then that room will be one of the hardest to get shots in."

"But the office..." Her voice trailed off as her eyes roamed the plans.

"Big windows there. But even better would be if you could get him outside on the grounds. See if you can get him to show you around or something."

"What about security? Staff out there? Surely your people would be seen. And if they weren't, we would be. If I can't get him to cooperate and be a willing participant, then I have to make it at least *appear* like something happened. And I most certainly can't weave a story together with eyewitnesses ready and willing to prove it was all a lie."

Hank waved his hand in front of her. "Baby, baby, calm down.

There's no need to be excitable."

Sybil pulled her shoulders back. "I'm not *excitable*, Mr. Lawrenson. I am pointing out obvious concerns. A successful op is only successful if it is well planned." *I sound like Art.*

"Whoever thinks Shifts just come out swinging clearly hasn't worked with one," Hank mumbled. "Oy, Rodney! I'm needing a whiskey over here right about now."

Rodney snorted, and Sybil heard the clinking of glass. She kept her gaze fixed on Hank and attempted to mask her irritation with him. She didn't have to like him for them to work together.

"Want anything, darlin'?" Rodney asked as he set the glass down for Hank. He definitely was not human, and Sybil resisted looking at him. Then it dawned on her he reminded her vaguely of the ambassador from Westward… Great height and practically luminescent skin.

"No."

"Can't hold your liquor? *That* is very unlike a Shift," Hank said before taking a sip and exhaling loudly. He smacked his lips.

"I'm going to get us back on topic here, Mr. Lawrenson, because I do not have all day. Will you have someone located where they can see Calloway's office or where they can see if we come out to the grounds? We need compromising photos at the very least."

Another swig and *clank*. Hank swiped the back of his mouth with his coat sleeve. He shuffled the papers in front of her and put a new one over top the original. It looked like a layout of the gardens. *A maze.*

He tapped twice with two fingers. "Right there. My person will be there with a camera."

Sybil nodded curtly. "Good. I guess we're done here."

Hank eyed her. "Not so fast, babydoll. You owe me if this doesn't pan out."

"Owe you what?" If she had hackles, they'd be raised.

"I have a few jobs I could use a Shift for," he replied.

"That's cryptic."

"Need-to-know basis." Hank held her stare.

Sybil wished she had time to run through every possible scenario. Were these ops for Hank, or were they personal favors? At this point, would it even matter? She had to do this for Vox, or her reputation as a Shift would be ruined. Or he'd send her to jail. How much worse could blackmail from Hank be?

Although, technically, he had no way to hold her to it *if* she agreed. She could get out of town before he could cash in on any of these jobs...

Except she couldn't. Because he'd go public about her and Calloway.

And *he* wouldn't be implicated because there'd be no photos. No affair, no scandal for the paper, if she failed.

"The clock is ticking," Hank's voice broke into her thoughts. She looked back at him. He was smirking, a hand stroking his reddish beard.

Commit. You have to, Sybil. "Fine. If, and only if, you don't get your article."

"It's a deal." Hank spat into his palm and reached out his meaty hand.

Sybil tugged off her leather glove, spat into her palm, and clamped it together with his.

"It's been a pleasure doing business with you, Shift."

"Mm, likewise," Sybil said as she jammed her hand back into the glove. "I'll see myself out."

"Don't let me down tonight."

Hank's words—and Rodney's alarming bulging eyes—followed her frame as she stalked through the narrow, dank bar, pulled the door open, and stepped into the light.

Nerves shot, mentally spent, and her stomach grumbling, Sybil made quick work getting back to the Alistaire, shifting into Roxana before approaching the hotel premises. She rode the lift wearily to her floor. The door opened with a cheery chime of a bell.

You have got to be kidding me.

A forlorn Richard Worth stood outside her suite. Cursing under her breath, she exited the lift and exclaimed, "Richard! What a pleasant surprise!"

At her voice, Richard jumped to attention. The way his face immediately flushed, he looked a bit like a child caught stealing from a candy store. He yanked his hat off. "Miss Bloodknight! I've been so worried about you."

"And why on earth would you be so worried about me?"

"Well, you disappeared last night, and I found out you'd been injured, and..."

"Injured? Nonsense! It was only a sore ankle. I would've preferred to stay, but they insisted," Sybil sniffed. She struck out a leg and wiggled her ankle. "See? Right as rain."

"I felt rather stranded without you," Richard said, dejectedly. He twisted his hat in his hands.

"Now, Richard, you know I would've preferred to stay and dance the night away with you!" Sybil laid it on thick as she draped her hands on Richard's arm. "But I couldn't say no to the president," she added in a dramatic whisper. "Can't you understand that?"

Richard sighed and covered her hands with his. "Aw, Roxana. I can't be mad at you. Dine with me this evening." Evidently, there were a lot of requests for Sybil's company for dinner tonight.

"I'm sorry, Richard. I have a prior engagement."

"Tomorrow then," he stated rather than asked.

"My father arrives. I have commitments with him."

Richard looked crestfallen. “Perhaps with your father... I’d like to meet him.”

“I’m sorry, Richard. Perhaps another visit. It truly was a pleasure meeting you and spending the weekend with you. I enjoyed every minute. I just can’t afford more time now. My father needs me.”

“Of course,” Richard replied sadly. “Perhaps I’ll call on you in South Carolina some time. We’ll meet again, I hope.”

“Now wouldn’t that be simply lovely!” Sybil rose on her toes to kiss his cheek. “Goodbye, Richard Worth. I won’t forget you.” And she flounced into her bedroom, giving him one last flutter of her lashes as she closed the door. And locked it.

There.

Two men fended off in one day, but neither was the one she needed under her spell.

16.

Back in the hotel suite, Sybil waited for several hours for Art to return. She checked on Roxana once, but it made her uncomfortable so she stayed away from their hostage as much as possible.

When Art arrived, the siblings exchanged notes, particularly about Calloway's children's bedrooms on the far side of the North Wing. He didn't applaud her efforts, but his typical criticisms were noticeably absent. However, he was rather perturbed about the interaction with Killian and peppered her with questions about him.

"I'm really quite sure he was only bein' friendly," Sybil insisted.

"It's just peculiar he was so interested in you."

"Just because you haven't noticed I'm more than your little sister yet doesn't mean other men haven't," she retorted. Xavier's narrow, scruffy face and mischievous eyes came to mind. Art would *lose* it when he found out they'd gone out. Multiple times. It gave her a sense of rebellious pleasure to think about it.

Art ignored her snide remark and proceeded to tell her about the abandoned warehouse he had discovered off the Potomac River. It was where he intended to hide out with the child for the duration of the kidnapping. When Sybil asked for more details, he shut her down and explained, "You'll be needed here, in case Calloway reaches back out. *Roxana* can't be occupied with this part of the op." Although she was disappointed, she knew it was the sensible, necessary plan.

About an hour before she expected the White House car, Sybil prepared for her night.

She took her time pampering herself, hoping every crevice of her would evoke irresistibility. She wore a backless dress of royal blue satin that hit her mid-calf. She paired it with a gold jewelry set, which included the beaded ring she was fond of. She remembered the way Vox paused when he saw it; maybe Calloway would do the same.

The matching necklace rested against Roxana's sharp collarbones and highlighted her long white neck. Sybil curled and swept Roxana's hair to the side, pinning it with a gold clip that sparkled in the light. Sleek black pumps with a pointed toe elongated her legs and gave her a distinct swaying stride when she walked. Art gave her a nod of approval when she exited the bathroom.

He left before she did to wait outside the Alistaire, planning to catch the White House chauffeur upon his arrival. Per the letter, the driver promptly showed at a quarter to seven, and both siblings were ready. While he was distracted assisting Sybil into the back of the heated motorcar, Art clambered into the front seat. The winter night's darkness provided welcome coverage, and, when the chauffeur sat back in the driver's seat, Art swiftly knocked him out.

He and Sybil awkwardly pushed his body to the back where he fit surprisingly well under the bench seat. She snagged his suit jacket with its White House emblem for Art to slip over his clothes, which were stolen from the Alistaire's laundromat. Whenever the motorcar started or stopped on their way, the unconscious driver's frame would roll and knock into Sybil's calves.

"We're here," Art said, as they pulled through the private entrance, directed by Thanes. "I'll see you later. Make it count."

His parting words gave her the distinct sense of entering the lion's den.

Art climbed out of the car, his arm tucked behind his back

like the chauffeur had done, and he opened her door. She noticed the flicker in his Shiftwork again but tried not to dwell on it. He extended his other hand, and she took it, taking in her surroundings as the car door swung shut behind her.

This was definitely a private entrance. They were within the massive hedge wall, facing the back of the mansion. The gardens were to her left, with an elaborate outdoor entertaining space that led into it. A butler in a gray suit approached the car, offered his arm, and guided her away from Art to a very solid-looking double door under an awning to her right. Ivy crawled up the door frame, obscuring it slightly. It looked ethereal in here, like Killian said. Very different from the grandeur of the front exterior of the House.

"After you, miss," said the butler, gesturing her through the door and into the private residential wing of the president.

As the butler took her white coat and gloves, Sybil looked around the foyer. It was still quite grand with expensive furnishings but on a much smaller scale than the public portion of the mansion. It was warm and more home-like, with lower ceilings, darker wood, and intricate, plush rugs. Cushioned chairs with a small side table sat tucked under a window facing the gardens. A wide stairwell was directly before her with two huge white and green floral arrangements gracing the railings. Doors led off from the entrance on both the left and the right, but the butler took her up the stairwell and down a hall to their right.

Sybil studied the paintings, tapestries, and other art pieces along the hall. It was like a home museum. One caught her eye, and she paused. It was somber, painted in varying shades of gray, black, and brown. It depicted the aftermath of a battle, broken bodies strewn about, but there were four men standing together, their faces obscured, looking towards something far outside the periphery of the painting. Sybil didn't know what this moment of history was, but it was horrifying, haunting, and made her stomach flip.

"That particular piece is one of my favorites as well."

Calloway.

Sybil startled, whirling to look in the direction his voice came from. The butler had wordlessly removed himself, and Calloway's handsome figure stood in the hall, outlined by warm light.

"Mr. President," she exhaled, her hand to her fast-beating heart. "You frightened me."

"Were you expecting someone else?" He smiled.

She flushed. "Not at all, sir. I hope you are well this evening."

"Quite. And how is your ankle?"

"I hardly notice it."

"Excellent."

"Can you tell me about this painting, sir? What does it mean?" Sybil asked.

Calloway nodded and stared at it admiringly. "It's a rather fantastical depiction of the conclusion of Independence Days."

Sybil didn't know what that meant. She wasn't sure if she could ask as Roxana and play it off as an airy heiress, or if that part of Eastward's history was something everyone would know. She stayed silent and gave it an appraising look.

"Such a dark time," Calloway mused. "So much loss due to a hunger for power… And yet, such hope. See how the light breaks through there but doesn't quite reach these magi's faces?" He lifted a hand to point it out but did not touch the painting. "That's hope for a better future. There was suffering yet to come. Difficulty and toil. But hope," he said.

Feeling awkward, Sybil said softly, "That's very… poignant."

Calloway glanced at her, the spell the painting cast over him broken. "I believe our meal is ready."

"Oh, dear. Have I delayed us?" Sybil took his offered arm.

"Have I kept everyone waiting?"

Calloway smiled tightly but didn't look her way. "Dinner party for two tonight." *For two?*

"Your family..." Sybil started.

"Otherwise engaged, I'm afraid. I do hope you will find my company moderately tolerable—at least enough to get through dessert."

"I didn't mean to imply I didn't. I'm surprised is all. I wrongly assumed you took your meals with your wife and children."

"That is typically our habit, yes. But tonight, well, I thought it best if it were only you and myself."

It couldn't be this easy—this *perfect*. The photos might not be staged at all. Just what did Calloway want with her?

Sybil mentally steeled herself. There was no room for nerves, for second-guessing, or for cheating. She was going to do it and do it right. She imagined how impressive it would appear to her kin when she returned to the beorg. Underage with a high-profile, *successful* op under her belt. She'd gain respect and status instantly. Being Art's little sister would be a far off thought for anyone. Her brother's bossy voice entered her thoughts, "*Employer confidentiality,*" and she internally waved him off.

"You have a remarkable home," Sybil commented as they walked the halls. "I suppose I shouldn't be surprised. You *are* the president."

"It is fairly remarkable. My wife has done her best to make it home, but I think we all miss our Delaware house."

"I imagine it was a drastic move for your children especially. A culture shock, if you will."

"Yes, I think so. I find, however, that children are often far more resilient than we give them credit for. Wouldn't you agree?"

"Yes, sir."

"The children have done exceptionally. There is a lot to

explore here in this grand old house. It is unique. Ever-changing. History has played out in this place. The home feels alive, sharing itself with us, sharing its stories with us every day."

"How magical," Sybil said shyly.

Calloway looked at her with his startling eyes, somehow piercing and warm at the same time, "Yes. Yes, it certainly seems to be."

"I would love to see more of it, if possible. Would you be able to show me around after dinner?"

"Perhaps," Calloway replied as he ushered her into an intimate dining setting.

Although the dining room was on the smaller side, it boasted a table capable of seating ten. Calloway passed Sybil off to a butler who guided her to a place setting at one end of the table; Calloway's was at the other. The room was circular, and candles graced the center of the table, casting an orange, dancing glow onto the walls. Sybil had been distracted by Calloway and his smooth conversation as he escorted her here, but she was fairly certain she could pinpoint which dining room they were in based on Hank's floor plans.

Two impeccably dressed servers poured blood red wine into crystal glasses and brought out appetizers, which they transferred to Sybil's plate with silver spoons and tongs.

"Thank you," she said. Looking at her plate, she couldn't identify any of the food on it. It didn't even *look* like food. She wasn't sure how to properly eat it or what utensils to use, so she calmly folded her hands in her lap and looked past the centerpiece to study the president.

Calloway appeared completely at ease, as though Sybil was family rather than a stranger he'd encountered only once before. She studied him as he cut into his meal and sipped from his wine glass, paying her no mind. He wore a black suit and tie and appeared to not have even a single strand of hair out of place.

After a few minutes of silence, he met her eyes and said, "Is the food not to your liking, Miss Bloodknight?"

Sybil glanced down at her untouched plate and back at him. "Not at all, Mr. President. I'm afraid I'm distracted. And perhaps a little ill at ease."

"Oh?"

She let out a breathy laugh, "You may be surprised to hear this, but I've never dined with a president before."

"There must be a first time for everything," Calloway mused, his eyes crinkling at the corners.

"Indeed." Sybil hesitated. "And… I… I must confess, I really did expect your wife to be here," she added, dropping her voice to a near whisper and glancing nervously at the servers.

Sybil wasn't sure if this was the angle to play or not. She had a couple she could pursue: She could dive straight into being an outrageously flirtatious, irresistible tramp, pull out all the tools of temptation, and pray he'd bite. Or she could play up innocence, pretend to misread his signals, and blame him entirely for leading her on. So far, she was leaning towards a combination of the two: naivety with just the right amount of flirtatiousness and tension. If he didn't fall into her arms by the end of the night, she needed to have enough innocence to accuse him of seducing *her*. Or, even better, taking advantage of her.

Both would be problematic if the true Roxana Bloodknight came forward professing it to be a lie. If Calloway also insisted it was false, the story would fall apart. However, if the press was bad enough, Roxana would hopefully feel soiled and deeply ashamed. A true Southern elite, she'd have the resources to flee from the limelight and blend into obscurity, where she could move on and let things die down. Maybe she'd prefer that to coming forward with the truth. It only needed to be seen as a legitimate scandal for as long as possible to cause as much damage as possible in the moment, not permanently.

How delicious it would be printed in *The Outcrier.* The headlines! They'd probably capture more attention than the kidnapping of Calloway's kid… She distantly hoped Art was managing all right.

"Are you questioning my morals, Miss Bloodknight?" Calloway asked evenly, his words drawing Sybil back to their conversation. His tone held no hint of anger at her subtle accusation. He could've been asking her if she preferred eggs or bacon for breakfast, he said it so nonchalantly.

"If questioning is judging, then, no. Not at all. If it's merely curiosity, then perhaps," she replied. "You must admit it is a curious situation I find myself in."

Calloway chuckled at this and dabbed at his mouth with a cloth napkin. "Fair enough." He rose and took his plate in one hand and his wine in the other. The servers by the door both started at this but froze and blended back into the wall when he gestured dismissively at them. He walked the length of the table and set his dishes down at the place closest to Sybil.

She watched him closely, her eyes large and intent. Calloway touched her shoulder lightly before lowering himself and taking another sip of wine. He propped an arm on the table and leaned towards Sybil slightly.

"I, occasionally, have business I prefer to… spare my wife from, if you will. Cecelia is a delicate woman, and the realities of my job tend to be far from that. Delicate, I mean. Surely a lady like yourself would understand my desire to protect her."

Not really. "Of course."

"Last night, you told me your brother had been kidnapped by Shifts."

Err. "Yes. Many years ago." This was not the direction Sybil expected the conversation to go. She fought to keep her face neutral.

"I want to talk about that."

Sybil twisted the ring on her finger. "Sir, I'm not exactly sure what you think I can tell you. I was quite young. A child myself."

"I'm only asking for your experience and your opinion. More information perhaps on what actually went down with your family and brother—that is, if it's not too difficult for you to talk about," he tacked on genially.

Suddenly, she realized how fierce his gaze was on her. Her brain began to feel muddled as his eyes bore into her. It couldn't have been the wine; it'd barely touched her lips. It was as though a heavy gray fog rolled in and absorbed all capabilities of clear or quick thinking. Her mind went monochrome as thoughts and images began to blend into a blank slate.

The fog faded, and awareness settled over her as she identified what had happened.

She leaned forward, closing the space between them. "Mr. President," she murmured. "I don't know how your dinner parties usually go, but I would prefer it if you would not spend the evening attempting to read my mind."

His eyebrows rose.

"I am an open book to you." She angled her shoulders slightly to show off the curve of her neck into her chest. "Anything you want to know, you need only ask. But I expect the common decency of privacy within my own mind."

Calloway sat back in his seat, his finger tracing the curve of his chin absentmindedly and a tight-lipped smile curving his lips. "You picked up on that much faster than most."

"So, it was a test?"

He shrugged and took a bite. "It's a nasty habit."

"And a useful tool for someone such as yourself. Are other

Sages quite as eager to practice magic on their peers?"

Calloway appeared amused. "Definitely not. There's less reason to use magic than there used to be, which I rather think is a shame. It seems only the Shifts have found a place to use their magic whilst the rest of the magi have let theirs grow cold with disuse. Needless to say, I've made waves with my disposition on the use of magic."

Sybil thought of Vox and the way he stayed his assistant's mind back at the beorg. Were Vox and Calloway not so different from one another?

She frowned. "You Sages must walk a finer line with magic than the rest of us."

"If you mean our magic is less tangible and perceivable than other branches, then yes, I suppose we do. But you… You perceived I was reading you. I've encountered that rarely, even amongst other Sages. And you noticed so quickly…" His voice faded.

Sybil did not have enough understanding of the magic in the fyrnship to know what the implications of this were. Her heartbeat quickened, and she felt a bead of sweat forming at her navel.

Trying to remain collected, she asked, "You wanted to know about my brother." She stabbed a vegetable with a fork and hoped it was the correct utensil to use.

"More so about the Shifts."

She arched an eyebrow critically.

"Forgive me—that was callous," Calloway said.

"Forgiven."

"Mr. President?" The interruption broke their terse exchange, and Sybil and Calloway both twisted to see a butler stepping close to Calloway's chair. It was the same man who had escorted Sybil out the night of the gala. Regis, she thought his name was. He was probably sixty-something with white hair and a smooth shaven face.

"Good evening, Regis. Is all well?" Calloway dabbed his mouth with a cloth napkin.

Regis handed a slip of paper to the president. "A message, sir."

Calloway set his napkin next to his plate and accepted the note from him. Sybil tried to look less interested than she was and sipped from the water glass next to her wine. Calloway was expressionless as he folded it back up and addressed Sybil.

"Miss Bloodknight, I offer sincere apologies. I must attend to this." He exhaled and rubbed his bottom lip with the pad of his thumb.

Sybil's face fell, and it wasn't much of a farce. She needed *him* this evening. He couldn't run off without her. What about Hank and the photographer? She couldn't fail Vox, much less be in debt to Hank.

Was this about Donald? Had Art been caught?

Her mind raced as she struggled to come up with some excuse to stay him, but she heard herself saying, "I understand."

Calloway glanced at Regis and then back at her. "Perhaps... Well, this really shouldn't take too long. Perhaps you'd like to finish your meal and wait for my return." *It's not Donald.* Relief swept over her so quickly she felt dizzy.

"I'd... prefer not to dine alone," Sybil said, her voice high with nerves.

Regis interjected, "Sir, might I suggest escorting Miss Bloodknight to the parlor to wait for you? The kitchen can keep dinner warm and bring something up later when you're finished."

"A fine plan, Regis, thank you." Calloway pushed his seat back and stood, clapping a hand on the older man's shoulder. He turned to Sybil, sitting tensely in her seat. "Miss Bloodknight, please. Make yourself comfortable, and I should return post-haste. I'd like to continue our discussion."

"As you wish, sir," she answered.

Calloway smiled, reached for her hand, and kissed it, his lips warm against the cool ring on her finger. "Back in a jif, then. Thank you, Regis."

"Sir." Regis bowed his head.

Calloway was gone like a whirlwind, leaving a somewhat stunned Sybil in his wake.

Regis directed the waiters to clear the table and came around to collect her. "Ma'am. If you'll come with me."

"Thank you," Sybil said.

They walked from the dining room and down the dim halls of Calloway's mansion, and Sybil became grateful for Regis's steady arm and gait. Fatigue was starting to wash over her again, and her empty stomach wasn't helping. She tried to take note of what direction they were going and mentally place them with Hank's floor plans, but a wave of dizziness hit her and she stumbled.

"Miss Bloodknight?" Regis stabilized her and held her by both elbows. "Miss, what is it?"

"I… I'm feeling faint, Regis."

"The parlor is right up here, ma'am. I'll get you some water straight away. Perhaps something to eat to tide you over until the president returns."

"Yes, thank you. I'm sorry to be a bother." Sybil leaned on him a little heavier as they turned a corner and entered a windowless parlor. *No, not windowless.* Moonlight poured in from three small windows and a skylight. This was the room she didn't want to end up in… But Calloway wasn't here. There was still time.

Regis led her to a silk-covered chaise lounge with round pillows. "Rest here, Miss Bloodknight. I'll personally get you something to drink and eat."

"Thank you, Regis. I don't know what's come over me."

She knew exactly what had come over her. After days of full-body

Shiftwork, Sybil's capabilities were waning drastically, her body depleted. An ache set deep into her bones as she sank to the chaise. She couldn't help but relax into it. She pressed a hand to her forehead.

Regis patted her on the arm. It was such a genuine fatherly gesture that Sybil flinched and stared at him. Emotion lodged in her throat. Confusion passed over his face at her jumpiness before he offered a reassuring smile and exited the parlor.

When the door shut behind him, Sybil couldn't help but dissolve into herself. She was feeling feverish. Clammy. She closed her eyes and took several steadying breaths, trying to slow her fast-beating heart. She had to endure. Her body had to last.

She didn't know how long she'd have before Regis returned. It was a risk to rest as long as she was, but she just couldn't force herself back into Roxana quite yet. The gold ring on her finger suddenly felt quite tight and heavy. She yanked it off and clutched it in her fist.

She wanted to study the room—to absorb potential information that could be useful at some point, like a good, thorough Shift would—but her eyes kept fluttering shut. Her stomach cramped. She'd experienced pain before. She'd broken bones on the mountain. Fought off sickness before, with none of the comforts of this place. But this was different. She felt like her body was rejecting her very essence as a shapeshifter. Like it was ready to throw in the towel.

But she wasn't. No surrendering yet.

Sybil inhaled. Exhaled. And tried to shift back into Roxana. It took two tries to get her body to lengthen into Roxana's willowy stature. She was shaking from head to toe, but she had managed it. She stuffed the ring back on her finger and found that the shaking eased a little.

When she opened her eyes, ready to resume her ploy, Regis stood before her with his jaw hanging. The tray in his gloved hands crashed to the ground.

❧

Time stood still as Sybil and Regis stared at one another. Only the rhythmic ticking of a wall clock filled the space between them. The water Regis had brought for her soaked into the rug, the glass shards at his feet. The tray lay discarded a foot away from him with the snack of crackers and cheese scattered about it.

Regis closed his mouth and retreated a step. Without thinking, Sybil rose to her feet, adrenaline coursing through her. Weakness felt far from her now.

He took another step backward, one of his hands absently brushing his suit coat. It was such an out-of-place gesture for the moment, and Sybil knew he was panicking. Then again, so was she.

The next moments were a blur. A flurry of activity. Regis whirled to flee the room, and Sybil attacked. Primal Shift instinct overtook her, and she launched herself at him. With her many years of fight training with her kin, she took the older man down easily.

Her arm locked around his neck in a choke hold, and she held him. Tightly. Tighter. Squeezing him, pressing her forearm to his head to lock it in place. Her heart pounded wildly, and blood rushed in her ears. Regis' legs kicked, then twitched, then stopped. He went limp in her grip.

She didn't let go. She felt frozen, his life draining away in her arms, but still, she could not let go.

Instantly, like a light switching on, her sense returned to her. It nudged her to release the man. He fell to the floor.

She collapsed, slumping against one of the chaise lounges, panting. Sweat dripped down her face as she took in what she had done. With shaky breaths and trembling hands, she crawled on her hands and knees back to Regis's still body and checked for a pulse.

He was definitely dead.

Sybil rocked back onto her heels and pressed her hands to her face. What had she done? This wasn't part of the plan. No one was supposed to get hurt… No one was going to *die*. Nausea rolled through her, and her vision swirled.

Get a grip. You have to get a grip, Sybil!

Her kin's voices went through her head. Freida reminding her repeatedly that the fyrnship had rejected them. Had brought this upon themselves. Art telling her to never hold back. To not see the faces of the op. *Don't hold back*. And she hadn't. She did what she had to do to protect the op.

What she had *to do*.

The words circulated as Sybil unsteadily rose to her feet. *I am a Shift. This is what I do. You can't panic, Sybil. Finish well.*

She rushed to the parlor door and locked it, just to be safe. She didn't know how long she had been holding her breath, but she finally exhaled as she turned and began to assess her situation.

Roxana was long gone once more, and strands of Sybil's dark hair fell into her face. The strap of her slinky dress had slipped from her shoulder, tugging the dress low on her body. She had lost one of her pumps. She subconsciously adjusted the dress as her eyes dragged over to Regis.

He lay flat on his back, his suit rumpled but otherwise no worse for wear. He could be sleeping. *Except he's dead.*

Grimacing, she hobbled back over to him and examined him more closely. She didn't suspect blood based on how she had eliminated him. She gently turned his head. Bruising hadn't begun to color his neck yet, but it would soon.

The clock ticked loudly in time with her heartbeat. Sybil had no way of knowing how much time was passing. Would Calloway's business be finished soon? Was he already on his way back to her?

Swiping a hand over her face, Sybil began to stage the room. Her best shot was to make Regis's death look like an accident—a heart attack, maybe. She needed to delay suspicion long enough for her to get out of Washington. She rolled him over so he lay face down on the expensive rug, near where the tray had fallen. She arranged his arms and legs and smoothed his wispy white hair.

When she stepped back, it certainly looked to her that he had simply collapsed, the tray he had been carrying clattering to the floor and spilling its contents nearby. His appearance did not indicate he'd been attacked or that he had struggled.

Yes, this was good. At the least, it would do. She couldn't very well hide his body in a room of dainty chaises and antique tables. Nothing was bulky enough to disguise a fully grown dead man.

Sybil made sure the room was spotless—aside from Regis's accident, of course—and then shifted back into Roxana. She used an ornate mirror on one of the walls to re-pin her hair and ensure everything was shifted exactly as it should be. After her ordeal, she couldn't be too careful.

She slipped her foot back into the stray shoe and went to unlock the door, stopping to grab a discarded cracker from the floor. After all, she still hadn't eaten. She stuffed it into her mouth and pressed an ear to the door. Nothing but silence. And the ticking clock. She twisted the lock and turned the knob. A feeling of dread—of regret—struck her, and she glanced over her shoulder at the scene she was leaving behind.

The pain she felt unnerved her. Hot tears pricked her eyes. She did not know this man. Was he married? Did he have children or grandchildren? Anyone waiting for him to come home? She shouldn't have killed him. She should've just left him unconscious.

Sybil pressed her forehead into the door as guilt ravaged her. He'd done nothing but be in the wrong place at the wrong time.

An accident… It was an accident.

“I’m sorry, Regis,” she whispered. “I’m so sorry.” She yanked the door open and fled down the empty, dark corridor.

17.

Sybil walked and walked, completely disoriented to where she was in the president's mansion. She thought this was the direction of the dining room, but she was certain she would've come across it by now if it was. She kept expecting to come across a footman or a cleaning lady or *somebody* who could give her direction and update her on the whereabouts of Calloway, but no one showed.

She was about to retrace her steps when she turned a corner and bumped into a solid figure.

"We keep meeting like this." *Speak of the devil.*

"Mr. President, I'm so sorry. I wasn't looking where I was going."

Calloway released her arms and peered around her. "Where's Regis? I was coming to find you. Why are you wandering the halls alone?" His tone wasn't exactly accusatory, but it was skeptical.

"Well, I was in the parlor, and Regis had gone to get me some refreshments while I waited for you. But then he didn't come back, and it seemed to be taking an awfully long time. So... I... Oh, it seems so foolish and impatient of me to say it now. I just thought I'd see if I could find someone who could find him for me. I think I got lost though." *Please, please don't ask questions.* Her heart pounded against her ribcage.

Sybil hoped that, once someone found Regis, she could make the case that she had left due to his excessive delay and was gone long before he arrived, had his heart attack, and fell down dead.

"Seems unlike Regis to take so long at a task, but perhaps he was waylaid. Can I get you something now? We could finish our dinner. I do apologize for the interruption earlier."

"To be perfectly honest, I think I've lost my appetite. While you were gone, I kept thinking about what you asked to discuss—the Shifts."

"Ah."

"I'm ready and willing to talk about our experience, but I'd really like it to stay between us. It's very personal. Is there somewhere quiet we could go?" *Not the parlor, not the parlor, not the parlor.* Walking into a room and finding a dead body would kill any opportunity she had to seduce the president tonight. It would signify immediate failure for her op.

Calloway thought a moment. "The parlor, perhaps? Regis may be back by now."

Sybil laughed a little. "At the risk of sounding entitled, I *was* hoping to see more of the mansion?"

Calloway gave a small shrug of his shoulders, more so to himself, as if thinking "What's the harm?" He held out his arm to her. "As you wish. Take a walk with me."

"You have a strong mind," Calloway said casually, guiding her through the hallways.

"That's a rather random observation," Sybil replied.

"It's a compliment. Most individuals do not resist as well as you did to mind-reading. I was very impressed. At dinner, I mean."

"It was a nice party trick," she said.

At this, a burst of genuine laughter came from Calloway. It echoed in the empty hall. "I've never heard it described that way before, but yes, I suppose it is."

"How would you describe it?"

"It's my magic. It's who I am."

"A mind-reader."

"In simplistic terms, yes. Though I prefer the traditional term of a mind-*keeper.* There's more to it than breaking into someone's head. It's a shepherding of the mind. Tending to it, understanding it."

Sybil didn't know quite how to respond, so she kept her mouth shut and nodded. She focused on the paintings on the walls they passed. They came upon a heavy door.

"Here we are. Wait until you see this... Beautiful in a whole different way." He pushed the door, and it swung open to reveal a room filled with books. More books than Sybil could have imagined existing.

"My private study," Calloway said reverently, closing the door behind them.

Very private, Sybil thought.

"It's wonderful," she said. She let go of Calloway's arm and explored the shelves. She ran her fingers over the bindings—some worn and frayed with faded titles, others new and crisp with gold and silver scripts. Small items also decorated the shelves. Many of them looked foreign, and Sybil wondered if they were from other countries. Probably places she'd never heard of, that she could never imagine.

From the moment they stepped into the room, with its dark wood-paneled walls and bookshelves and its expansive arched window, she felt the tension. The magic. It was similar to the Alistaire Beck in that she could feel it in her core, in every fiber of her being. The tangible energy. It made the hairs on her arms and neck stand straight. But yet, it was different here.

The Alistaire had an aura of regality, of luxury, of elevation and power. Calloway's study was like stepping back in time. Stepping into both home and memory at once. It smelled of wood and paper and coffee and, oddly enough, freshly laundered clothes. The room itself seemed to be telling Sybil to lower her defenses, to open up, to be comforted, and to be vulnerable.

It was a frightening feeling.

Sybil made her way to the solitary window, passing a wall of graphite portraits—she assumed they were of prior presidents—and peered out curiously. The glass was icy against her hand. She tried to keep thoughts of a photographer out of her mind, just in case Calloway wormed back in, but all she wanted was to know if someone was there, capturing President Branson Calloway locked in his dim, personal study with a young woman who was most definitely not his wife.

That's when Sybil spotted it. A glint. Barely noticeable and gone in an instant. Her breath caught. A camera lens pointed in this direction; it had to be. *Please,* please *be Hank.*

She pivoted to find Calloway lowering himself into his leather armchair behind the mammoth walnut desk, as far away from the window as he could possibly be. Naturally.

"So, you wish to know about my brother's kidnapping," she said, approaching him, feigning calm even as her insides roiled.

"Yes, Miss Bloodknight. I need every bit of truth I can glean from those who have had personal experiences with Shifts," Calloway replied. *Why does he care?*

"Well... What do you want to know?"

"Walk me through it."

Sybil knew she had to be thorough and accurate because Calloway would see right through any inconsistencies. Any hesitation. "As I told you at the party last night, I was only twelve.

My seven year old brother Ewyn got kidnapped, and a ransom call came later to my father."

Calloway interrupted, "Do you remember anything about Ewyn's disappearance? Was it at night, or the middle of the day? Was he home?"

"It was at night."

"And you didn't hear anything?"

"Nothing. It was as if a ghost had taken him. There was no trace. Not even a footprint."

"Your family—did they involve the local Thane authorities?"

"At first, yes. They tried to find some leads at the house when Ewyn first went missing, but there was nothing. When the ransom call came, the Shift made it very clear no Thanes were to be further involved. So they weren't."

"How was Ewyn returned to you?"

"On our doorstep when the sun came up, forty-eight hours later."

"Did he identify the Shift at all?"

"It was a man, but he was blindfolded the whole time. Except once... His blindfold slid down, and he watched the man shift."

"What was that like?"

"Ewyn said it was like looking at someone underwater or with rain streaming down your glasses. But he was seven, sir. And it was months and months before he spoke about it. I'm not sure if you can go off of that as an accurate representation."

"Did he get a sense for how old the Shift was?"

"No, sir, I don't believe so."

"Did the Shift speak another language at any point?" He thought they had their own language? Sybil had never heard something so absurd. Her brows knit together in confusion.

"I don't believe so," she repeated. "At least, Ewyn never

mentioned it."

"What about religion? Did he ever mention..."

"Mr. President!" Sybil interjected. "I am more than happy to tell you what happened to my family. But I was not there. My brother was *seven*. He didn't interrogate his captor or hold conversations with him. He was... traumatized. If you want cultural information on the Shifts, then you might consider going to their rundown mountain village to find it out for yourself!"

Calloway's left eyebrow lifted.

Sybil gulped, and her heart pounded so hard she reflexively pressed a hand to it in an attempt to steady it. "I... sir..." she stuttered, struggling to recover from her outburst. Roxana would be mortified, but Sybil's temper had started to simmer. She was growing dangerously close to not caring. This evening was going slowly and inefficiently—*Regis*—and she wanted to get things over with and get home. But she had to get control. Regain control. *You're Roxana, Sybil. Roxana.*

"Sir, please. Accept my sincerest apologies. I shouldn't have... You make me feel like I can speak my mind, and, well, you see..."

"It's okay, Miss Bloodknight." Calloway closed his eyes for a moment. "I was insensitive for pressuring you to remember such a painful time in your life, something so traumatic for your family. And you were just a child yourself. I am the one to ask forgiveness."

Sybil stuttered, "Um, apology accepted, sir."

"May I ask a final question? And then we shall table this unsavory talk."

Sybil nodded slowly. Her skin felt very hot.

"Did your family ever discover who hired him? Were they able to access the records from the Guild of Eorls?"

"What is this guild?" Sybil knew about it, but Roxana might not.

"The Guild of Eorls," Calloway repeated. "It was the private firm that managed the Shifts once they were ostracized from society after the Inweard Conflicts." *The what?* "Shifts could only be contacted through the Guild, and they managed the Shifts' boundaries."

"I didn't realize we had been so well protected from Shifts this whole time," Sybil sniffed. "A boundary..."

"The public prefers to neglect some of those pertinent details in preference for the negative. It's more exciting that way. However, the Shifts being managed by the Guild did not guarantee people were safe from them. Frankly, they organized crime for Eastward."

"You speak of the Guild in the past. What has become of them?"

"Yes, I do. A keen observation. My administration has taken over its responsibilities and subsequently dissolved the Guild."

Putting on shock, Sybil said, "*You* manage the Shifts now? The government is organizing the crime?"

"Now, now, don't panic, Miss Bloodknight. I have very different intentions with the Shifts than the Guild had. This is why I seek information from you, someone who had firsthand experience with them."

Calloway rose from his chair and began to stroll the length of his office, his hands clasped behind his back. Sybil fought the urge to slump against the desk while he wasn't looking. She was growing tired.

"Miss Bloodknight, my fascination with the Shift people began many, many years ago. I have never been one to be content, let's say, with the status quo. When I was in university, the Shift situation piqued my interest. To say the least," he added under his breath.

"It struck me how isolated they've been, how ignored. It seemed wrong to abuse their... unique skill set. To limit them in such a way when the rest of the magical classes have been able to develop and secure their place in society, especially when the Shifts played a crucial role in Independence Days. They were, for a time, one of us magi. Don't you find it all peculiar, if not wrong?"

Roxana. Not Sybil. "Peculiar, perhaps," she agreed. "But, if you don't mind me saying, it's for the best."

"I've certainly heard that before."

Sybil stood and stalked to the window, not meeting Calloway's eyes as he paused his pacing. "Mr. President, the damage done to my family… Irrevocable. All because of a Shift."

"I'd like to challenge you there," Calloway said. "All because someone *hired* a Shift. No?"

"Well, yes, but…"

"If we take away that option, imagine how society could change."

"Do you not think someone else would take their place? Whether in committing crime or in finding a way to exploit the Shifts once more? You'll never have a crime-free society. Man is not like that."

"I couldn't say for certain. I'd like to think, if there were no middleman to hide behind, that perhaps the people would be a little bit more concerned about getting caught performing such crimes themselves. About facing the consequences themselves."

"But what of the Shifts, sir? You seem to think that you could stop the Shifts from being criminals. But that's who they are, Mr. President. They know nothing else. They're ignorant, uncultured, aggressive, and hot-tempered. You don't know what they will do, what they're capable of. And you want to give them the freedom to explore that?"

Calloway smiled. "You should join Congress, Miss Bloodknight."

Sybil flushed. "I've overstepped again."

"Not at all. I appreciate your candor. It's nothing I haven't heard before. Or considered myself. There is obviously much to consider. Regulations, restrictions. As someone who has been impacted directly, I must ask you: What would you do if the Shifts were brought down from their mountain?"

Sybil deadpanned, "I'd buy a shotgun and lock my doors, Mr. President."

The corner of Calloway's mouth quirked, and he came to stand by her in front of his study window. "You can't see it on a black night like tonight, but this is one of the most beautiful views from the mansion. You can see the entire length of the gardens. Even in winter, it's captivating."

Mental fatigue set in for Sybil as Calloway rapidly changed the conversation and she tried to keep up. Was this a Sage trick designed to wear people down until they just agreed with you? To exhaust her mind so he could break into it?

"Is our talk over?"

"Should it be?"

"I don't feel I was particularly helpful. In fact, we argued."

"I'm not afraid of argument. An appreciation of discord and debate is healthy, in my opinion. Where would the world be if everyone agreed on everything? Or worse, if we didn't get to speak our mind?"

"I suppose it would be very different."

"Yes, I imagine so." Calloway rested a forearm against the window pane and leaned to peer out. "Would you like to see the grounds?" *Yes, yes, yes. Please take me to see the grounds.*

"If you wish." Sybil glanced up at him. She envisioned their silhouettes in a photograph, the way she gazed at him and he stared down at her, his body looming over. She swallowed. "Then perhaps after we could return and finish our dinner."

18.

Calloway led Sybil down the stairwell, through the foyer, and out the door by which she arrived. The same butler who initially welcomed her inside helped both of them into their coats and held the door for them.

Pale light from perfectly spaced lamp posts outlined the pathway and the statues and foliage that framed it. Sybil asked polite questions about what the statues represented, who sculpted them, what the president loved most about his garden, and the like.

She asked if they could walk along the water, which, if she was correct, would lead them towards the camera she had seen earlier. She desperately hoped it was still there. And that it was indeed a camera and not some trick her desperate mind had played on her.

"Are you not cold, Miss Bloodknight?" he replied.

"I find the winter weather exhilarating and refreshing," she said. "Besides, this is a very warm coat."

"That surprises me, considering your southern roots. I would've thought it would be far too wet and freezing for your taste."

Sybil laughed, "Well, when you're used to the humidity of the Carolinas, anything is tolerable. At least for a short amount of time. I'm not sure I could live here."

"I assume you haven't been farther north then. The winters up the coast are even worse."

"I don't have much of a desire to go any further than right here,

Mr. President." A glint caught her eye again. They were still there! Now was the time to act.

"We should head back for our meal," Calloway said. "It's getting rather late." He turned to start walking back, but Sybil stopped him, grabbing his arm.

"Wait, please. I... I have to ask you something."

"And what might that be, Miss Bloodknight?" Calloway's eyes flickered to her hands on his arm but didn't linger.

"Did you *really* only ask me here because of my brother? Because of the Shifts? Or... or was there something more to your invitation?"

"Did you not believe me the first time I answered this?"

"It feels like there was something more," she repeated. "Something between us."

"Something more? Miss Bloodknight, I assure you I don't know what you're talking about."

Sybil tightened her grip on him and pulled him closer. She could feel his muscles tense under her fingers. "You don't know? Branson, you invited me here for a private dinner in your home. You invited me into your private study."

"Branson?" Calloway sputtered, finally looking caught off guard for the first time in Sybil's interactions with him. His eyebrows rose, his eyes widening. "Miss Bloodknight, I..."

Sybil broke in again, "I know you feel the tension between us. The pull. You can't deny it." Calloway began to gently try to break from her grasp. She persisted, "No one would ever know. Nor even suspect. I won't say a word. You find me attractive, don't you?"

"Miss Bloodknight, you are a very lovely woman, but I don't believe this is appropr..."

Sybil kissed him, clinging to him tightly, refusing to let go. His body was taut, clearly trying to determine what to do. She kissed him and kissed him, running a hand up his back and into his hair;

and then he kissed her back.

For only a second.

The president broke away abruptly and, in his effort to escape, shoved her. It was a far harder push than he intended, and it sent her spiraling backwards before collapsing on the stone pathway. Both of them were panting, and he seemed as stunned as Sybil.

Snow melted into her clothes, chilling her. Bits of rock cut into her hands and legs where her dress had left her legs exposed. A button from the collar of her coat had popped off and lay a few feet from her.

Sybil shakily sat up, looking at her hands in dazed silence. She began trying to cover her legs conservatively. The ankle she twisted the night before throbbed. Her hands trembled, and she struggled to get to her feet. Once upright, she looked at the president, betrayal and hurt in every crevice of her face, her chest heaving.

Calloway, too, was panting, his face a bright shade of red. He looked disheveled and mortified. When their eyes locked, he forced out, "M-Miss Bloodknight. I didn't mean to... Are you well?"

Sybil forced tears to her eyes and let them begin rolling. "You led me on," she whispered.

"What? No, no, Miss Bloodknight. I had no intenti..."

"You led me on!" She repeated louder. "Y-you kissed me!"

"I was confused. I didn't mean... I was caught off guard, Miss Bloodknight. *You* kissed me. I didn't mean to hurt you." Calloway reached out to her, and she slapped his hands away.

"Don't touch me!" she snapped, her voice shrill. "From the first moment we met, you made me think you desired me. You yourself carried me in your arms, sat with me, invited me to your home to dine with you *alone*. You *really* think I believed you had asked me here for... for research opportunities on those damn Shifts? Your family—absent! You take me out here in the dark for a walk in one of your favorite places *alone*, and you think it's *my* fault I kissed you?"

"Miss Bloodknight, those were not my intentions in the slightest!" Calloway protested, distraught. He ran a hand roughly over his face and up into his hair, as if he could erase from his own brain what transpired. "I didn't… I didn't mean to lead you on in any way. Sincerely, I didn't. You misunderstand! Please, let's get out of this cold and get you checked out by a physician. And we'll talk. We'll work this all out."

"No! Don't touch me. I want to go home," she cried. "Just get me a car and take me back to my hotel."

They walked in a brutally awkward silence—Sybil limping slightly because her ankle actually hurt now—back to the driveway. Calloway did not touch her.

He called for the butler, who came out and wordlessly assessed the situation. He looked alarmed. "A motorcar for Miss Bloodknight, please, Mr. Bridget." Calloway's voice cracked a little on her name.

"Yes, sir." Mr. Bridget made quick arrangements, and the same car that had brought Sybil to the house pulled up shortly to take her away. After the driver assisted Sybil into the car, Calloway knelt at her open door.

"Miss Bloodknight, I don't know what happened tonight. I cannot begin to express my apologies for the confusion, for your injuries, or for your feelings. It was never my intent to hurt you in any way or for you to interpret my actions in that manner."

Sybil, who let tears flow freely down her face, hastily rubbed at her cheeks. "You say that, Mr. President. You say it wasn't your intention, that you didn't mean any of it. But we both know you did."

"No, Miss Bloodknight. I would nev…" His voice dropped to barely a whisper. "Please, d-don't talk to anyone about this. Not yet."

She stiffened. "You wish to buy my silence?"

"Not at all! I simply want the appropriate parties to be involved with dealing with this unfortunate circumstance. I still would like to get you checked by a doctor. It was a… hard fall. We'll cover the cost."

"Perhaps, sir, Miss Bloodknight should remain with us…" Mr. Bridget added from behind.

"Absolutely not!" Sybil shrieked. "I don't want you wasting your breath, time, or money, President Calloway. I know you don't really care," she said sharply. "Driver, I'm ready to go now."

She took one last look at Calloway. A wave of something—empathy, perhaps?—washed through her at the sorry sight. His handsome face was grave, his green eyes dull and his lids heavy, as if he was too exhausted to keep them open. His coifed hair was mussed. He looked so dejected, so embarrassed, and so uncertain that Sybil had to remind herself again he was only a target before she could feel badly about what she'd done.

He was simply another target.

And, as long as the moment was actually photographed, it would be a job well done.

If it hadn't, then she'd just blown her op for good.

19.

"Seems like we both had a successful evening," said the driver in a familiar voice. Sybil met Art's eyes in the rearview mirror. He was shifted into the same chauffeur as before, but his body possessed the same strange rippling quality that revealed to her it was him.

Feeling faint from the ordeal, Sybil slumped in the backseat. She couldn't yet shift back into herself in case someone saw inside the car. Closing her eyes, she mumbled, "How did things go for you?"

"Great," Art replied. He sounded uncharacteristically chipper, which soured Sybil's mood further. "As soon as I got the car parked in the garages, I slipped into the staff quarters as the chauffeur and used those plans Hank gave you to get straight up to the family's quarters. There was hardly anyone there—everyone being off after the gala—so it was the perfect night for it."

"Was he in his bed?"

"He had just gotten tucked in. Off without a hitch."

"Is he in the trunk?" Art nodded. "Is he okay?"

"He's not hurt, if that's what you're really asking," he answered. "He's unconscious right now from a small dose of chloroform. He'll wake soon though."

"What's your plan to get him to the warehouse?" Sybil asked wearily, resting her head against the window and not bothering to open her eyes.

"Well, I have to drop you off. Roxana can't be away in case

someone from the White House comes knockin.'"

"And you have to return the government car."

"Nah, I'm gonna ditch it somewhere to throw 'em off the scent."

"And what? Walk with Donald to the warehouse you found?" Sybil sat up slightly and frowned.

"It's dark. No one will see."

"That's stupid."

"You got a better idea?"

"At least wrap him up in something."

"There's a spare suit jacket in the trunk."

"Better than nothing." The Alistaire came into view. "How am I supposed to get in contact with you?" Sybil asked.

"I dunno if you should. Stay here and play your part. Donny Boy and I will hang out. I'll handle the ransom call."

"I was hopin' to be part of it."

"We talked about this. I wasn't part of your stint with Calloway. Part of being a good Shift is knowin' when to trade off. You can't be everywhere and have your hands in everything. This is just fine. It's why I wanted two of us for this op," Art said.

"Do you have any food or anything to keep Donald comfortable?"

"It's only twenty-four hours, Syb," Art said with a raise of his eyebrows. "Comfort isn't exactly a Shift's priority."

Sybil twisted the ring on her finger. "He's just so young. If I can get away tomorrow, I'll bring some and check in on you."

Art narrowed his eyes. "Only if it makes sense. Don't blow your part of the op because of this kid."

"I won't blow it. Just trying to be useful," Sybil said through gritted teeth as Art parked the car in front of the Alistaire. "Good luck."

They smoothly played their parts as chauffeur and heiress once more before parting ways. Sybil ensured several Alistaire staff and guests saw Roxana's disheveled appearance on her way to her suite. She closed and locked the hotel room for the night, quite ready to sleep for days.

That's when she noticed a hulking shadow in the corner. Frozen at the door, she looked around for any object to use as a weapon. As if reading her thoughts, a gravelly voice came from the shadow.

"Not here to hurt you, Shift." *Hank.*

"What are you doing here?" She tilted her chin up, hoping to exude confidence she didn't feel in the slightest. She was mentally, emotionally, and physically drained from her encounter with Calloway barely even twenty minutes ago. Her muscles ached, and a stabbing pain pulsed in her temple and her ankle. She wanted—*needed*—to shift out of Roxana.

"Here to chat. Compare notes."

"How'd you get in my room?"

"I have my ways. Come in, come in. Turn the light on," Hank said. He came into view as he left the chair in the corner he'd been lounging in and came to recline on the bed. She'd sleep on the floor tonight.

His button-down was rumpled, unwashed, and looked more yellow than white. It hung half-tucked out of his belt. Although purple moons encircled his eyes, they were sharp and alert.

"Cigarette?" He reached into his pocket and extended his pack towards her.

"I'll pass."

He put it away and stared at her. "So. Roxana Bloodknight. What a pretty little thing she is."

Sybil gripped the front of her coat. "That was certainly what I was going for."

Hank stretched an arm above his head. "Well, go and get yourself comfortable. We've got things to talk about."

"Fine." Sybil stepped into the bathroom and transformed back into herself. She slid the satin gown off and pulled the day dress she'd worn earlier over her head. She hastily rubbed some of the earthy smelling arnica cream into her skin. It didn't eradicate the fatigue, but it took the edge off. When she came back out, Hank smiled in her direction.

"That's better. Come sit, my dear. I'm pleased to report we had *complete* success tonight. That photographer of mine got some pretty juicy photos of you and our good president."

"That's good news."

"Indeed it is." Hank rubbed his hands together. "Babydoll, I haven't had something this sweet in months."

"Happy to help," she said.

"I gotta get these to print as soon as possible, so let's finish this thing, hey?" Hank pulled out a pad and pen from his frayed overcoat. Uncapping the pen with his teeth and then replacing the cap with his unlit cigarette again, Hank started, "Roxana Bloodknight. From South Carolina, right?"

"Correct. Beaufort."

"What were you doing in Washington, Miss Bloodknight?" He emphasized the last name and winked at her.

Playing along, Sybil sweetly said, "I came ahead of my father, Mr. Lawrenson. He's a sponsor for the Stānwyrta Chamber of Craftes which opens this week. I wanted to do some shopping."

Hank's eyes crinkled. He was perhaps more in his element than she was. He began rapid-firing questions at her: "How long have you been in Washington?"

"Since Friday night."

"And you went to the gala?"

"Yes. With a Mr. Richard Worth, whom I met here at the Alistaire lounge."

"And you met the president that night?"

"Yes, we quite literally bumped into each other, and he carried me to where a doctor could tend me and waited with me. Alone," she added.

"Isn't that nice," Hank said, jotting down on his pad of paper.

Sybil continued, "He sent me home in a car, and an invitation arrived this morning for Roxana to dine with him. I thought it would be a dinner party, and it turned out to be a private meal."

"Excellent," Hank said. "Into his study and then out for a walk..." He said this to himself more so than to Sybil.

"I do hope you got pictures of both."

"You bet." Hank studied Sybil. "As Miss Bloodknight, of course, did you feel the president led you on?"

"Undoubtedly, Mr. Lawrenson."

"And he made a move on you?"

"Sure."

"What did you do when he tried to kiss you?"

"Well, I fought against him, of course. He knocked me down. I got scrapes on my hands and knees to prove it."

Hank laughed again. "This is divine."

Sybil pressed her lips together to subdue her own delight. Together, the story they fabricated and its accompanying photographs would go out in the news tomorrow, and it would be the most scandalous thing to hit the pages in a long while. She could feel the success in her bones. Remorse over what she had done to Calloway—and likely to his marriage—dissipated into glee.

Regis.

Well, it was a shame about Regis, for sure. But what was a Shift to do? If she hadn't killed him, he would've ruined everything.

"Anything else you need, Mr. Lawrenson?"

"I think that covers it." Hank swung his legs over the side of the bed and tucked his pad of paper back into his coat. "Look for tomorrow's *Outcrier*. It'll be one spicy feature."

"Front page, I hope."

"Above the fold. Guaranteed."

Sybil extended a hand as he lumbered toward her. "Pleasure doing business with you, Mr. Lawrenson."

"And you, Shift. I'll let myself out." Hank shook her hand and left the hotel room.

As soon as the door shut behind him, Sybil rushed to lock the door. Exhaustion hit in full force. She stumbled back towards the bed but fell to her knees before reaching it. She fell asleep right there on the floor.

Bu-ringggg. Bu-ringggg.

Sybil's eyes fluttered open at the noise. *Curse that phone.* A sliver of light slipped in from between the drapes. It had to be morning. She slept all night on the floor without hardly moving. As she attempted to rise, she was pleased to discover she was not in pain from the Shiftwork, but her muscles were tender, as if her entire body were bruised.

She swore as her groping hand knocked the phone onto the floor. Fetching it, she slammed it to her ear and snapped, "What?"

"Well done." It was Vox.

"Director," she gasped, immediately wide awake.

"I assume you haven't read the exposé."

"Th-that'd be correct."

"I've taken the liberty of having the paper delivered to your room. I thought you may like to see the quality of your work."

"I take that to mean you are pleased."

"Extremely. Clever of you to make it appear as though

Calloway hadn't fallen prey to your seductions but the other way around. Your brother was quite right when he suggested you'd be the right Shift for the job."

"Thank you." Somewhat stunned, she fell to the chair and clutched the phone cord tightly in her fingers.

"You will be in Washington until Arthur wraps with his part of the operation, correct?"

"Yes, sir, that was our plan."

"This means the job is not finished. Roxana is about to become the most popular woman in Washington. Stay on your game, or it will all be for nothing. Are we clear?"

"Very."

"Oh, and such a shame about Regis." Sybil froze. "He was such a nice man."

"Director, it was..."

"Have a good day. And do check out the paper at your door." Sybil heard the *click* of the line disconnecting, and she tiredly lowered the phone back into its cradle. Her face dropped into her hands, and she didn't know how long she sat there.

Regis was an unexpected casualty of the crime. She felt dreadful about it; she truly did. The image of him lying on the floor was burned into her memory. A first kill always stuck with a person. But she'd be lying if she said she wasn't more concerned with getting caught, with Vox or Hank throwing her under the bus.

Sybil sighed and forced herself to sit up, smoothing her hair out of her face as she did so. She had to rally. The press was likely already camped outside the Alistaire waiting for Roxana. Roxana's father could accelerate his arrival here at the news.

Before she did anything though, she snatched open her hotel door and picked up the rolled-up newspaper at the threshold. Disappearing back into her room, she unfurled it. Right there—above the fold as

Hank had promised—was a smattering of black-and-white photos of her and Calloway under a bold-printed headline she couldn't read.

One was of the two of them standing in front of Calloway's office window. In the moment, she hadn't realized how close he had been to her. To an outsider, with the angle of the camera, it looked as though Calloway's chest pressed into Sybil's back, and you couldn't see his hands. Sybil knew they were by his sides, but no one else did.

The second photo was of the kiss in the garden—a perfect shot of the moment Calloway kissed her back, hesitantly touching Roxana's slim waist in his confusion. But her personal favorite was the one of her on the ground, the skirt of her dress skewed, highlighting Roxana's beautiful legs. Again, she knew Calloway stood in horror a few steps away from her, mortified to have knocked her down in his effort to escape. But no one else knew that. That's all that mattered.

There were several more shots, including one of Roxana as she had gotten back to her feet. She was staring down at the gravel on her hands, and you could just make out the damage to her coat. It was all perfectly compromising in every way, and pride surged through Sybil, energizing her and making her briefly forget the continued work ahead of her.

She quickly flipped through the pages of the paper to see if anything about Regis had been printed but couldn't discern anything. He definitely would've been found by now. Perhaps his death was under investigation, and no information would be released until results came back. There was nothing regarding Donald as well, that she could tell. She knew it was unlikely Calloway would go to the press so quickly after the kidnapping of his son. He wouldn't risk Donald's life that way. Either way, things were escalating.

A thump came from the closet. Sybil whirled around and ran to open the door. The real Roxana was on her side, and the bindings at her feet were nearly unravelled.

"Not so fast, honey," Sybil said, quickly moving to redo the bindings. At the sight of Roxana, she paused. Roxana looked rough. Her face was blotchy and pale; her honey hair, a nest of tangles. Guilt pricked her conscience again. She sighed. "Do you need to use the bathroom?"

Roxana nodded tearfully. Sybil reached forward, helped her up, and moved the blindfolded woman to the bathroom. She stood guard as Roxana did her business and quickly guided her back to the closet. She fastened the bindings better. Roxana shook and jumped at every touch.

After a moment's hesitation, Sybil pressed her hand to Roxana's and whispered, "I know you're scared. It won't be much longer."

She mumbled something against her gag. Against her better judgement, Sybil loosened it, threatening, "You scream, you won't live to regret it." When the gag fell around Roxana's neck, Sybil noticed aggravated red marks all around the woman's mouth from where the cloth cut in.

"W-why is this happening?" Roxana wept.

"Things beyond you, I'm afraid," Sybil answered unsatisfactorily. "When does your father arrive?

"Tuesday," she whimpered.

Sybil swore. "Is he sharing this suite with you?"

"No, he always gets his own room," Roxana replied, a note of incredulity in her voice, clearly perplexed as to why Sybil asked her this.

"What would he expect upon his arrival?"

"He... W-we go to dinner. The museum opens tomorrow at eleven in the morning... He'll be there with the other sponsors at nine for breakfast and networking."

"What does he expect of you?"

"Only to be at the museum grand opening. And our dinner reservation."

Sybil went to the table and grabbed some of the food that had been sitting out from their meal yesterday. She brought it to Roxana. "Here. Eat."

Roxana did, eagerly.

Sybil thought for a moment, sitting cross-legged at the closet threshold, and only the sounds of Roxana chewing and sniffling filled the space. "Would you be required to go to those events if somethin' had happened to you?"

Roxana stilled, mid-bite. "Wh-what do you mean?"

"If there were negative press or some conflicting stories about you, would your father force you to go or keep you from the limelight?"

"I... I can't say. I don't know. What have you done?" Roxana asked. "What's happened?"

"Nothing," Sybil snapped. "Keep your voice down. What time is your father supposed to be gettin' in?"

"On the five o'clock train." Roxana reluctantly resumed chewing.

Five o'clock. That gave her most of the day to check in with her brother and determine what she should do.

"What's his name?"

"Father's?"

"*Yes!*"

"Horace Bloodknight."

"Thank you. We'll be out of your hair real soon." Sybil gave Roxana a drink of water before securing the gag over the young woman's mouth again. The poor socialite would gain her freedom only to realize her reputation had been ruined. Even if she and Calloway could convince the fyrnship that it was all a farce—that they'd never met and it was the work of a Shift—the damage was done.

Sybil ordered a simple meal to the room for herself and, while she waited, bathed and swept her hair up. She dressed in a practical day dress that buttoned to her neck, cinched at her waist, and flowed easily around her knees. She hoped to look as traditional and modest as possible to drive home the notion that Calloway took advantage of her, rather than the other way around. No one could look at Roxana today and think she was bold enough to do any such things.

As she ate, she peered out the window to see if any members of the press lurked. Surely enough, there were several loitering about. She watched with amusement as Alistaire Beck workers went out and argued with them enthusiastically about leaving. At the end of the interaction, the Alistaire could not force the press to leave, since they were outside the building. If Sybil wanted to find Art and Donald, she'd need to leave through the back.

A quarter of an hour later, she bundled up and slid out through the back of the Alistaire, the same way she and Art had arrived—a lifetime ago, it seemed. She dodged employees and guests, and, as soon as she was out of sight of the hotel, she ducked into the alley and shifted back to herself. She clutched a small bag loaded with bread and sausages from her breakfast to bring to her brother and the child, as well as a copy of the newspaper, tucked safely under her arm.

Art told her the warehouse he found was neglected near the Potomac. She should've asked for more directions. She wandered around through Washington blindly. She found the river eventually and strolled alongside it, looking as innocent as possible, while scanning the area for abandoned buildings.

One single-story warehouse with several blown out windows caught her attention, and she made her way toward it, her head on a swivel for anyone watching her. She cautiously cracked the door and slipped inside. It was deserted, dark, and dank, reeking of fish.

"Hello?" She whispered.

A shadow moved in a corner. "Did anyone follow you?"

"No."

"Are you sure?"

"Yes, I'm alone. Where's the boy?" She passed Art her bag, and he began rifling through for something to eat.

"Over there, restin' on some old burlap bags. Wait—" he caught her by the arm. "You can't go to him."

"Why not?"

"He knows your voice," Art said plainly. Sybil's shoulders drooped, and he released her. "Sorry, Syb. This isn't a time to be maternal."

"I'm not maternal," she retorted. She was never maternal with the kids at home. She was seventeen for crying out loud, a lifetime away from anything even resembling motherhood. But she wasn't heartless, and her heart betrayed her when she heard Donald's small voice cry out. It reminded her of a wounded animal.

"You really should go," Art said, watching her face closely. "I'll give him the food. I promise he's safe."

"I brought you a copy of the newspaper," Sybil said, handing it to him. "Thought you may be interested."

Art scanned it, squinting in the poor light. "Nice job. This is *great*. Better get back before someone sees you're gone."

"I know," she sighed. "Roxana's father is supposed to arrive tonight. We have to wrap this up fast. I know twenty-four hours is the norm, but this is the president's kid. Surely Thanes are scouring the city already."

"Tonight?" Art cursed. "Okay, okay. That throws a wrench into things. Let's shoot for the morning. Can you play through today?"

"I… I guess so, but… he's Roxana's *dad*. He'll see straight through me!"

"I doubt it. He's a busy man. There's a good chance he rarely spends time with his daughter. You faked it with the president of Eastward; you can do it one more time with this ol' man." Art clasped her hand. "You did your part of the op really well. I just need you to hold on long enough for me to do the same."

Sybil shook her head even as she said, "I'll do my best." *I'm just not sure it'll be enough.*

"Be ready to leave at six in the mornin' tomorrow. Meet me in the alley across from the Alistaire."

"Six in the mornin' across from the Alistaire," she repeated.

Art gave her a long look and let go of her hand. "Stay safe."

"You too."

20.

Sybil made it back to the Alistaire without complication. She re-entered through the back; the press was still comfortably camped out front. She shifted into Roxana out of an abundance of caution. Before she reached the elevator, she heard:

"Miss Bloodknight!"

Crap.

Sybil reined in her aggravation and turned to greet Richard Worth, flying towards her with a newspaper in his hand. "Mr. Worth."

"This, th-this… *this*!" He sputtered, shaking it out to show her. "What a disgrace! My dear Miss Bloodknight, how do you fare after such an ordeal? I can't believe this happened to you!"

Richard looked terribly disheveled, his shirt untucked, his tie askew, mud on his shoes. As he flurried closer to her, she smelled whiskey on him. He didn't strike her as one to get drunk, but she heard the slur in his voice. She wondered if he had gone drinking after she rebuffed him yesterday.

"It's nothing, Mr. Worth, truly. A misunderstanding."

"Says the victim of a heinous act!" Richard exclaimed. "You are far too generous and forgiving, my dear. I am simply mortified knowing of my part in this."

"Your part?" Sybil asked, puzzled.

"Oh, yes! If I hadn't taken you to that gala, you wouldn't

have even *met* that cow Calloway. I am so deeply sorry, Miss Bloodknight. Do forgive me!"

This was so ridiculous she nearly rolled her eyes. "An apology is not necessary, Mr. Worth. This had nothing to do with you. If you'll please excuse me..."

Sybil began to make her way to the door, but Richard grabbed onto her arm. "Richard, what are you doing? Please—I'd like to be left alone."

"Miss Bloodknight, I insist on escorting you *myself* for your safety."

"Mr. Worth, that is *entirely* unnecessary. I am perfectly capable of riding the lift to my floor and walking down a hallway," Sybil said, feeling thoroughly vexed.

"Roxana," he said her name almost reverently as he gripped her wrist more tightly. "Roxana, my dear. You've been through a shock. A *trauma*. I must do my duty as a gentleman to take care of you." His words blended together.

You fool, Richard. I don't need anyone to take care of me, Sybil seethed. She'd been taking care of herself all her life. She never needed a man's permission or protection. Not once. She appreciated Art's support and Xavier's attention... But she didn't *need* them. She didn't need anyone. And no one needed her.

"Stay here with me. Just a day or two longer, and I'll make arrangements to bring you home."

"I have arrangements, Mr. Worth. My father arrives post-haste. If you'd please release my arm, I'll be on my way."

"Tsk, Miss Bloodknight. What if someone were to see this," he waved the paper at her again, "and think you a *loose* woman?" He whispered aggressively. "And take advantage of you *again*? We cannot have that. I'll deliver you to your father personally."

The urge to cause Richard bodily harm was growing; Sybil

knew it would only take her seconds to send her knee to his groin and get away from him. He wouldn't know what hit him. Roxana, however, would never do that, which put her in a bind.

"Please, Mr. Worth. Release my arm. I assure you I will be fine. If anyone needs assistance, I think it may be you. You're drunk, Richard."

"I'm not drunk!"

Firmly and clearly, Sybil said, "Yes, you are. Mr. Worth, I am going to ask you once more and only once more. Let go of my arm."

"You heard the lady," a bass voice broke in. "Step away from her."

Killian James strode toward them with long, confident strides.

"Who are you?" Richard asked, fumbling but releasing Sybil. His bloodshot eyes narrowed as he analyzed the imposing figure before him. As nice as Richard was, he looked like a child standing in front of tall, muscular Killian in his handsome Thane uniform.

"My name is Killian James. I'm the lady's guard, provided by the White House directly." *No.* "She is in perfectly safe hands." Killian smoothly positioned himself between Sybil and Richard. Sybil held her small purse to her chest nervously.

"I've never seen you before." Richard lifted his chin in a challenge and wobbled slightly on his feet. Poor, poor Richard.

"Are you acquainted with every employee of the White House?" Killian asked pointedly.

"W-well, no," Richard faltered.

"What reason would you have for encountering me before now?" Killian remained steady, little intonation in his voice or expression on his face.

Richard's thick brows pinched.

"I'll take Miss Bloodknight's safety from here, Mr. Worth, was it? Excuse us, please." Killian placed a hand between Sybil's shoulder blades and propelled her into the lift before Richard could make any further moves.

"Goodbye, Richard," she called softly, trying to act as Roxana would in this situation. She was ready to be rid of the man, useful as he'd been. Everything—everyone—grew useless eventually. Richard watched them disappear from sight as the lift jerked upwards.

"Thank you," Sybil said to Killian.

"You're welcome. Did he hurt you?"

"No. No, I'm fine." Out of her periphery, Killian nodded sharply and pressed his lips together. He appeared upset. Reminding herself that Killian had met *Sybil* and not Roxana before, Sybil asked, "Did the White House really send you?"

"Yes," Killian replied. The bell dinged as the lift came to an abrupt stop, and the gate opened.

"You sound less than pleased about your assignment," Sybil said coldly, stepping out of the lift and stalking away from him towards her suite.

"All assignments are equal in merit and worth; I approach and complete each one with integrity and intentionality," Killian recited.

"That from the Thane handbook, is it?" Sybil stopped in the hall and spun to look at him.

"It is. And it's what I hold as true. Pleased or not about where I am or to whom I am assigned, you will be treated with the same level of integrity and intentionality as I would give to the president of Eastward."

"Ah, so you *don't* want to be here," Sybil said tersely.

"It is irrelevant."

"I suppose you think I made this all up!" She cried.

"It is irrelevant," he repeated in a tight voice. He tilted his chiseled jaw up and stared over her head.

Sybil crossed her arms. "You believe Calloway."

"It is—"

"Oh, *shut up!* You men are all the same. I don't want or *need* you here. Go home and tell Calloway he doesn't need to *spy* on me. I'm not talking to the press. I'm waiting for my father to arrive, and then I am getting out of his horrible city as quickly as possible."

"I was not sent to spy on you," Killian clarified, realizing he was losing control of his detail.

"No? Not to take care of a liability? Make sure I don't speak to anyone about your good president?"

Killian's eyes narrowed slightly, but his tone remained the same when he spoke, "No. Listen, I don't pretend to know what all went down yesterday, but regardless, you deserve peace and privacy and a safe trip home. President Calloway said the same, and that's why he assigned me here. Believe what you will, but I am truly only fulfilling my orders, as I would for any other detail. I have no stakes in this game. You could be lying about everything, and I'd still be here doing my job," he said bluntly.

She forced tears into her eyes and whispered, "You weren't there, Mr. James."

"I apologize for my sharp tongue."

"You may stay outside my room until my father arrives," Sybil said. "I don't want to talk any further."

"As you wish, Miss Bloodknight."

21.

Killian camped outside Roxana's suite the entire day. With nothing to do but wait, Sybil found herself dozing on and off, mentally and physically exhausted from the last few days. Part of her was disappointed and frustrated there was nothing for her to do while Art spearheaded the kidnapping. The other part of her was grateful for the respite, knowing there'd be no room for mistakes once Horace Bloodknight showed.

Her thoughts frequently drifted not to Art and his status with Donald but to the beorg. She wondered what was happening there, how Freida was holding up with the kids by herself, if they were warm enough. She was feeling quite spoiled lounging in this beautiful hotel on her op; it was not typical for jobs to play out in such a way. She'd been well fed, properly clothed, and warm and comfortable for the better part of a week.

How hard it was to imagine returning to the beorg. Its beauty was untouched, raw, which she loved and missed. But going back to a one-room cabin that let all the cold air inside, chopping firewood, sleeping on a thin mat, eating stale bread... She ran a hand over the linens of the enormous bed. Well, it may be more difficult to return to than she thought.

She felt rather embarrassed when she wondered if Freida would be proud of her and was grateful no one could see inside her mind in that moment. Freida wouldn't care. None of the Shifts would be *proud* of her. That was foolishness. But she'd gain their respect, and that was just as good.

She'd nod off with this cycle of thoughts, and then, just as quickly, she'd wake again, imagining a sound, thinking it was Roxana in the closet, and panicking that Killian might've heard. Killian stayed silent himself, and, each time she checked the peephole, he stood stationary next to her door with his arms crossed in front of him.

Shortly before Horace Bloodknight—whom she actively tried not to think about—arrived, Sybil washed her face and touched up her hair. She liberally applied the arnica lotion over her arms and legs... Anything to strengthen her for tonight. She changed from the simple day dress to a more appropriate dress for a dinner out. It was black, belted at her waist, and came to her neck, though it was sleeveless. She fastened a pearl choker, which lay neatly over the neckline of the gown, and slipped white silk gloves over her hands. If she didn't fool Horace at first glance, she'd have no chance.

A heated exchange with Killian alerted Sybil to Horace Bloodknight's prompt arrival at her suite. Sybil peeked through the peephole. He was a large man, both in height and girth, with a bulbous nose and round apple cheeks. He shared Roxana's fair skin and blonde hair, though his was considerably thinned.

"What are you doing outside my daughter's suite?" He demanded. His voice held the same lilt as Roxana's, though it was less severe than the Shifts' accents.

"I've been assigned here as a precaution only, Mr. Bloodknight, I presume?"

"Yes, yes, where is my daughter? Who assigned you?"

"The Calloway Administration. Your daughter is safely inside," Killian answered steadily.

"The Calloway Administration," Horace spat. He whipped a newspaper out from under his arm and shook it at Killian. "The same Calloway who assaulted *my* daughter? That's right—I've seen the papers, and don't you think this will be the end of it. I will not let him get away with this. I've said from the beginning: he should never be in office!"

"Sir, that is quite enough. This is not the time nor the place. I am simply doing my job. Now that you are here to assist your daughter, I shall gladly step aside," Killian said coolly. "Good day."

Horace watched Killian's back until he vanished into the lift before rapping on the suite door three times, hard. "Roxana? Roxana, my love? It's Father."

Sybil took a deep breath and opened it. "Father," she whispered.

"Oh, my dear Roxana." Horace pulled Sybil into his arms and held her close. He stroked her soft hair and cradled the back of her head, as if she were a child to be soothed after a scraped knee. "How... how did this all transpire?" he asked, shutting the door and settling her at the table.

Sybil was thankful to go straight to Calloway; she was far less likely to reveal her fake identity on this topic compared to others. She relayed everything that occurred, from meeting the president at the ball to their disastrous meal, with as much drama and emotion as she could muster.

By the end, Horace had his head in his hands. "An outrage. It's just an outrage."

"It's okay, Father," Sybil said meekly. "I simply want to return to Beaufort and let things die down on their own."

"No! Absolutely not! We must pursue justice for you, Roxana, my love."

"Father, I insist we don't! It is my word against the president of Eastward's! What good will it do? No one will believe me."

"He cannot get away with this. He should have *never* gotten into office!" Horace roared again.

Sybil reached out and took Horace's hand in hers. Horace looked truly pained when he lifted his eyes to hers. "Father, I beg you. Please let it lie. I would like to go home. Do I have to stay for the grand opening of the museum?"

Horace hesitated. "I... No, of course not, love. The first train home in the morning. I promise."

"Thank you, Father." Sybil wondered if she should kiss his cheek or hug him. Was Roxana affectionate with her father? She acquiesced to squeezing his hand and releasing him. She swiped at an invisible tear under her eye. "Where is dinner tonight?"

"You still wish to dine out?" *There was an option not to?*

"Uh..."

"I presumed, if you wished to avoid the grand opening, you'd also want to eat in your room and avoid the press," Horace said, sitting back in his seat. *Yes, yes, I would.* "But we can certainly dine out, if you prefer. It would be a great display of your strength."

Sybil wasn't sure how to respond, and Horace was studying her intently. She pictured how it would appear to the press: *Heiress Claims Assault, Goes for Formal Dinner Hours Later. Heiress Holds Head High after Alleged Assault.* Which was better for the story? She couldn't help but think a display of strength and pride would downplay the narrative she was attempting to curate.

"Love?"

"I... I would much prefer to stay in tonight, Father, but if you wish me to go out with you, I will do as you ask." She felt most comfortable putting the ultimate decision in Horace's hands.

He smiled weakly at her. "Stay in, my dear. Rest. I'll order a meal to your room. No need to even go to the dining room downstairs."

"And what about you, Father?"

"My love, I'm afraid I must leave you again. A colleague plans to join us—me—tonight at The Gilded. A Mr. Dupont. Do you recall him from Mother's garden party last spring?"

"Oh... Mr. Dupont, yes, of course."

"I'm afraid I cannot leave him hanging at this late hour. Will you be all right here on your own?"

"Yes, Father. Enjoy your meal."

A loud thump sounded in the closet. And then another one. *Curse you, Roxana.*

Horace glanced around the room. "Did you hear that?"

"My luggage must've toppled over," Sybil said. She quickly forced tears to her eyes. "I'm sorry to be such a burden, Father. I feel I've brought such shame to you. To Mother," she said dramatically.

Suspicion promptly dismissed, Horace rose and pulled Sybil into his arms. The tender gesture unnerved her, reminding her of Regis and his fatherly demeanor. She tensed.

Horace noticed and loosened his grip on her. His mouth thinned into a pitying line. He let go. "I'm sorry, daughter. I'm so sorry. I'll... I'll call room service for you from my suite. I'm down the hall three rooms." His voice cracked a little, and, as he turned away from Sybil, she could've sworn tears were in his eyes. He was brokenhearted for what his daughter supposedly endured last night, and it made Sybil feel sick.

"I'll check in on you after my meal with Dupont," Horace said as he closed the door to Sybil's suite.

Sybil secured the door and then checked on Roxana in the closet, who stared at her with red, dry eyes. The two women glared at one another. That was too close, but she couldn't fault her for trying.

After that, she watched out the window to pass the time. When the members of the press suddenly picked up their heavy cameras and began rushing from the Alistaire, she knew they had caught wind of Donald's disappearance at last. The sinking feeling in her stomach sank a little deeper.

She picked at the dinner delivered to her room and ultimately gave most of it to Roxana. Feeling hopeless and desperate to hear the news reports about Donald, she scoured the hotel suite until she found a little radio in the coat closet. She stood there with her back pressed into the closet door, messing with buttons and dials she did not understand, trying to get some semblance of clear sound from it. Eventually, static faded into a man's booming voice:

"If you are tuning in once more to hear an update on President Calloway's son, Donald Calloway, I'm sorry to share he is still missing. White House Thanes and Washington Thanes are working together tirelessly to secure him and apprehend his captor. Although there is no proof, all signs—and I think we all know—point to a Shift behind this. President Calloway has been unavailable to make a statement.

"Meanwhile, some magi have questioned if Donald Calloway's disappearance could be related to the visitation of representatives from both Southward and Westward. From Southward, Mr. Ambassador Jonathan Yancey, and from Westward, Madame Ambassador Georgiana Graceland. Both Graceland and Yancey departed Eastward earlier this morning. The question at hand, then, is if one of them could've contacted a Shift to accomplish this criminal act. With long-lasting tensions between Westward and Eastward, many magi expressed concern at Graceland's presence at the Veterans' Gala, which was held this past Sunday night.

"It has also been reported to Channel One News through anonymous sources that the management of the Shifts for decades has changed, and they've been recently acquired by the Calloway Administration. Why this has been withheld from the general public is unclear. We have reached out to the White House for comment on this verified tip and will report back to you."

The man paused and sighed dramatically. “Regardless of the circumstances surrounding Donald Calloway’s disappearance, we at Channel One express our sincerest sympathies to the Calloway family and wish to see Donald safely returned to them as soon as possible. This is Theodore Benedict. Goodbye for now.” A merry musical tune played, signaling the end of the broadcast.

Sybil turned the dial, and the tune cut off. It was good news. Mostly. Donald hadn’t been returned yet, and Art hadn’t been caught. Hopefully, the next broadcast would announce his arrival back at the White House, and Sybil and Art would be on a train home in the morning.

All this time, she hadn’t realized the White House’s acquisition of Shift management from the Guild of Eorls had been such a close-kept secret. Calloway had talked about the Shifts during his campaign; it was obvious he wanted to change things. He admitted it to Roxana over their dinner. Why keep it quiet? Vox hadn’t implied it was a secret when he showed up on the mountain. Was it just until the registration was completed, so they could present to the fyrnship an orderly picture with all the relevant information to assuage any fears at one time?

Sybil fell onto the bed and rubbed her temples. She was so weary and so ready to go home. She couldn’t reconcile how Shiftwork could be such a thrill and such a headache at the same time.

22.

Sybil's last day in Washington did not go according to plan whatsoever. It started out acceptably. Horace Bloodknight indeed checked in after his meal, tenderly kissing her forehead and again encouraging her to rest. Wishing her to sleep well, as if she had a choice in the matter.

Before she had gone to bed, she packed a small valise with her belongings. She slipped the newspaper Vox had provided her, as well as their knives and rope from her old rucksack, which had been stowed away in the bottom of the armoire since they arrived at the Alistaire. She also set aside the beaded ring, planning to keep it on her person when she and Art left in the morning. After all, there was no rule against collecting a keepsake from one's first op.

She worried she wouldn't sleep, her mind so abuzz, but she slept deeply and woke feeling surprisingly refreshed. But unfortunately, just as she was rising and preparing to slip away to the alley to meet Art, Horace showed again. He had her train ticket in hand and an Alistaire Beck porter at his side to pack up her things.

Sybil hovered around anxiously, supervising and ensuring the porter did not approach the real Roxana's hiding place. After the porter stacked her trunks onto a trolley and headed to the lift, Horace persuaded Roxana into sharing a light breakfast with him in the dining room. It was the first time during her stay that she dined there. It would've been a pleasant experience being waited on in the warm room with its roaring fireplace if she weren't so stressed. It smelled richly of coffee, fried potatoes, fresh bread, and grilled meats.

Horace spoke about his time with Mr. Dupont and the sculptors whose work he was most eager to host in the Stānwyrta Chamber. Halfway through their meal, Sybil spotted Richard Worth behind a large newspaper. He appeared no worse for wear. If he saw her, he made no move to acknowledge or approach her. That was a small relief.

Horace made it impossible for Sybil to slip out on him. The moment she asked to be excused from the meal, he rose with her and tucked her hand into his elbow. He walked her to the hotel concierge and promptly employed an Alistaire Beck driver to take her to Union Station. Sybil had no choice but to go along with it. She tried to excuse herself to a bathroom, but Horace pointed out it was nearly seven-thirty already and she really needed to get going if she didn't want to miss her train. She could use the water closet on the train, he told her.

She rode in the backseat of the hotel motorcar, anxiously picking at her fingernails. She'd left far too many loose ends. She had no way to release Roxana, to threaten her into silence or cooperation, which meant she could blow everything wide open the moment Alistaire housekeeping found her.

Then there was Art. And Donald. Horace made a few comments about the boy still missing as he perused the paper over breakfast, but nothing more. Sybil thought the plan was for Art to be back at the Alistaire first thing, so how could the boy not be back yet? What happened if she left Washington without her brother? He'd kill her.

If he had been waiting for her in the alley as promised, he would've seen her climbing into the hotel car and driving off. Perhaps he was following her? He'd meet her at the train.

Before she knew it, she was on the train platform. There were two photographers snapping photos of Roxana. She played her part, dropping her head and her eyes. A defeated heiress, homeward bound in shame.

And then the train was chugging out of the station, and she was sitting in a first class compartment, leaving Washington, her brother, and a trail of damage in her wake.

The train puffed south down the coast, belching black smoke into cement-colored skies. Snow flurried down and mixed with the black. Sybil focused on the scenery, trying to steady her mind. It was fascinating to watch it fly by. She imagined it was like the moving pictures she'd heard the fyrnship had. The ever-changing landscape flashed in sequence so quickly it blended together into an illusion that it was what moved, rather than she.

She found solace in the clicking of the train on the tracks, the hissing of steam being released, the occasional squeal when the train turned on a sharp corner. It reminded her of the orchestra of sounds nature played back home—an industrial version.

The trip went quickly, more quickly than the train ride up to Washington. Sybil was distracted not only by the scenery but by people-watching the others in her train car. She made a game up of trying to guess what branch of magic each person was based on their mannerisms. It was all about what someone did and could do, rather than what they looked like.

She had always been told how predictable fyrnship magi were. How easy they were to prey upon. Notoriously boring and unchanging, they were. They didn't share the wildness of the Shifts—their volatility.

Thanes were quiet, observational, analytical people. *Killian*

James seemed to break the quiet part of that mold, Sybil thought sourly. Sages were talkative, animated, engaging. They talked more than they listened, but they never babbled. They spoke with intentionality and purpose. They reeled their audience in, often involving them and making them feel important. The Sylvaar fell somewhere in between on the communication scale, but they often talked with their hands—and worked with their hands, holding more blue collar jobs than the other two classes. They were driven, consistent, and honest.

At least, that's what she'd been told all her life. So she passed the time taking in the others in her first class train car and deciding for herself if that was true.

Over the course of the trip, Sybil determined the two women in front of her—one older, one younger, perhaps a grandmother and granddaughter—had to be Thanes. They sat in stoic silence, their clothes starched and buttoned up. To her right, Sybil knew it was a family of Sylvaar, primarily because there was a young boy who kept throwing tantrums, and the parents ignored him, engaged in conversation about a new building going up at home. They also had jovial faces, and the wife wore a bright floral dress, which seemed an odd choice for wintertime.

Out of the nineteen people in her car, Sybil concluded there were four Thanes, nine Sylvaar, and six Sages. The six Sages seemed to be the only ones giving her a second thought, probably because they were the only ones who bothered to read the morning's paper. She felt eyes on her oftentimes, but no one spoke a word to her.

The first class train attendant brought her a cup of coffee on his round and told her it would be one more hour. She savored its richness, the velvet texture, knowing it would be the last time she got to taste something so smooth. By tomorrow, she'd be back to the thin, watery coffee and hard, salty jerky that sustained the Shifts through winter. She sighed. The glory of the Alistaire Beck was never intended to last. At least she'd be free of the stifling fyrnship society and its expectations. No more escorts, no more niceties.

When the train pulled into the station in Charleston, Sybil was one of the first to disembark. Horace had told her a Bloodknight chauffeur, Mr. Avery, would be waiting to take her the remainder of the way to their estate in Beaufort. Unfortunately, Sybil had no earthly idea who Mr. Avery was or what he looked like.

Lights and noise exploded in her face before her feet hit the platform.

"Roxana! Roxana!"

"Over here, Roxana!"

"What happened with the president?"

"Did he force himself on you?"

"Have you seen the White House's statement?"

"The people need to hear your story!"

"Tell the truth!"

Sybil was not prepared for this onslaught. It had not been like this in Washington. Strangers in her face, shouting at her, shoving their cameras and recorders to catch her every word and reaction. Panic exploded in her chest.

She quickly turned and ducked, trying to shield her face with her hands and locking her eyes to the ground. She couldn't count how many pairs of shoes were crammed around her, stepping on each other, nearly stepping on her.

Repeatedly, she mumbled, "Excuse me," as if that would get them to back off.

She never would have guessed she'd be one to feel claustrophobic or to fall prey to panic, but her present circumstances made her question that. The crowd, the noise, their body heat, their scents—perfume, sweat, cologne, tobacco. Her heart raced. Sweat beaded on her forehead. Her vision blurred.

"I can't breathe," she gasped, stopping and pressing a hand to her chest, as if she could force her lungs to work again. "Please, I can't breathe!"

The paparazzi heard nothing and crowded around her even tighter: "Roxana! Just a moment!"

"Have you seen the president's statement? How do you respond?"

"Roxana!"

"Please!" She pleaded. "I… I need…" Her knees weakened. She was going to faint. Her anxiety increased tenfold at the thought, knowing she wouldn't remain Roxana if she went unconscious. Everything would be ruined. She'd be ruined. She swayed on her feet, and her stomach roiled. She stumbled.

"ENOUGH!" A man's voice roared above the rest. A hand snagged Sybil's elbow, and an arm slid around her waist. She couldn't focus well enough to tell who it was. Perhaps Mr. Avery, the driver, come to her rescue?

"Back away now. You lot should be ashamed of yourselves. Back!" He shouted again. "Give the woman some space. She has nothing to say to you. You got your footage. Now get out of here."

There was some pushback, but the man held firm. "Don't you have something better to do? Go make up some more stories to ruin somebody else's life."

Sybil swayed again, and the man lifted her into his solid arms. Her swirling vision began to settle. The black spots lessened. Her heart yet raced, and her chest hurt. Though she could still hear the crowd, they were growing more distant. The contrast, however, felt like pure silence. Their smells lingered, but she was finally catching whiffs of cleaner air.

In her daze, she slowly realized she was being carried to a wooden bench at the end of the platform, away from disembarking passengers and passersby who had paused to observe the paparazzi.

The man seated her and said, "Put your head between your knees. I'll get you some water." This voice sounded vaguely familiar, she realized dimly, even as she obeyed and planted her clammy face in her skirt. She caught a glimpse of a chocolate hand.

It was Killian.

She cursed into her knees. And cursed again. Had he followed her here? She was glad her face was buried in her own lap as she wrapped her head around this news. *Get it together.* Keep *it together*.

When Killian's hand touched her shoulder, it broke into her trance and scared her out of her wits. *Roxana!* She screamed to herself as her exhaustion, stress, and surprise threatened to dissolve her back into her natural state.

"Hey, hey," Killian soothed. "I didn't mean to scare you. I brought some water. Sit up slowly. Are you feeling better?"

Sybil obeyed and lifted her head. He set her valise by her feet.

"I don't think I've ever seen someone so pale," he said.

Sybil silently took the small cup from him and sipped at the water.

"It was wrong how the paparazzi ambushed you. Right off the train like that. I apologize," he said sincerely.

"Just doing their jobs, I suppose," Sybil muttered.

"That's one way of looking at it."

She said curtly, "I suppose Calloway sent you to continue spying on me."

Killian lowered himself to sit next to her on the bench and stretched out his legs. "If that's how you wish to see it, I can't stop you. He just wanted to make sure you got home safely. We have no need to rehash our prior conversation."

"Once again, your presence is not necessary. I am waiting for my driver and then will be on my way."

"Where is your driver?"

"He's... getting my bags," she lied.

"I'll wait until he arrives." *No. No, no, no. What will it take to get rid of you*? "I'm simply fulfilling orders, Miss Bloodknight, which were to see you back to your home, not to a train station."

Sybil sat with her hands wrapped tightly around the little cup of water in quite a foul mood. She didn't talk to Killian, didn't look at him. She was thoroughly peeved. She was supposed to be on her way back to the beorg with her brother. Instead, she was having to keep up the charade first with Roxana's father and now with Killian and eventually with the driver Mr. Avery.

Killian appeared no more happy to be there than she was, but he maintained greater external decorum.

"Miss Bloodknight?"

Both Killian and Sybil jumped at the unexpected guest. It was a middle aged man in a plain suit. Killian spoke first, "You are?"

"Elliot Avery, sir. I work for Miss Bloodknight," he said. He had a gentlemanly manner about him.

"Yes, it's good to see you, Mr. Avery. Mr. James here was just... keeping me company." Sybil shot Killian an angry look.

"She was practically assaulted by paparazzi when she disembarked," Killian explained. "May I ask where you've been?"

Mr. Avery eyed Killian suspiciously. "I was acquiring Miss Bloodknight's luggage. I didn't know she had already disembarked. I'll take it from here, Mr. James."

Killian shrugged and spread his hands. "If you insist. I've done my best, Calloway," he said to himself.

"Yes, you may tell President Calloway your assignment is complete. I hope not to see either of you ever again," Sybil said theatrically. "Come along, Mr. Avery."

Sybil and Mr. Avery left Killian at the little bench on the train platform, and Mr. Avery guided her to the car. She waited, every nerve of her body electric, until they had pulled away from the station. Then, she whipped out a knife, slipped from the valise at her side, and held it to his throat.

"Careful, Mr. Avery. Don't make any sudden moves, and you won't get hurt."

"Miss Bloodknight," he whispered in horror, eyes not leaving the road before them.

"I'm not Miss Bloodknight, though I think you've gathered that. Turn around and drive to Miltown. Do what I say, and we won't have any issues."

"Miltown?" He choked.

"North Carolina. Go. *Now.*"

Mr. Avery whipped the car around and sped back down the road. Sybil vaulted herself from the backseat of the luxurious vehicle to the front, where she could better control Mr. Avery. She stayed as Roxana in an effort to protect her Shift identity. Avery would know she was a Shift, but he didn't have to know her face.

Right or wrong as this play was, she was out of ideas on how to get back to the beorg. By this point, someone had certainly discovered Roxana at the Alistaire. All Sybil needed to do was to get safely within the boundary of the beorg. The job would be done, and she could wash her hands of Roxana Bloodknight, Killian James, and Branson Calloway.

Art… Well, he was on his own now. There was nothing she could do for him. He'd say the same if their roles were reversed.

Mr. Avery drove at top speeds. They careened around turns and flew through traffic signs. Sweat dripped down his panicked face. Sybil, on the other hand, grew increasingly calm the closer they got to Miltown. She was almost home.

Eventually, they arrived in Miltown, and Sybil directed him

through the town and onto the road that she and Art had walked down. When she spotted the trail coming down through the snowy woods, she ordered him to stop.

She pushed open the stiff car door and hopped out, her heeled boots crunching into freshly fallen snow. Avery glanced at her with wide eyes, hands glued to the steering wheel. Sybil held the knife out toward him with one hand while she retrieved Roxana's small valise from the backseat. Her knives, a copy of her newspaper, some extra food, and the stolen ring were safely packed inside; she had no interest in parting from them. She came back around to Mr. Avery.

"Well, Mr. Avery, I can't say I'm particularly sorry about all this... You've been most helpful. Safe travels home," she said sardonically.

Mr. Avery put the car in reverse and flew back down the trail without a word.

In the absence of the rumbling car engine, Sybil remained stationary for a moment, absorbing the complete silence and untainted winter air. She closed her eyes and breathed in and out, savoring it. Remembering it.

When her eyes fluttered open again, she admired the trees rising up higher and blacker than anything she saw in the city, their limbs stark as they stretched heavenward. It was quiet. So quiet. Nothing but the occasional chirp of a bird or snap of a twig.

There wasn't much good about the beorg, but it was home.

She was home.

Clinging to her valise, Sybil dissolved blessedly back into herself and began the long trek up the trail before her muscles stiffened.

Part 2

23.

Sybil hadn't exactly been expecting a "Welcome Home" banner, but she never anticipated being attacked by two Thanes at the boundary.

Blindsiding her, they roughly blocked her from going any further and held her immobile as they demanded answers as to where she had been, who she worked for, how long she'd been gone, which cabin she lived in, who her cabin mates were, and her age.

Hiking up the mountain had temporarily warmed her, but, locked stationary between these two men, her sweat dried in the cold air. Her fancy heeled boots from Roxana's closet had not been practical to walk miles in, and her stockings were soaked through, her toes numb. She knew from the sharp pain that blisters had formed at her heels. She shook as she stood there with the guards, both from the temperature and from frustration.

"I was on assignment! I was working! For Director Lowell Vox!" She insisted breathlessly, trying to tug free. Their holds tightened on her, and one of them rolled his eyes at her.

A squat guard approached them, a huge file in his hands. He asked one of the guards holding her arms, "Who does she say she is, Williams?"

Sybil's face flushed. "I'm standing right here," she hissed. "My name is Sybil. I was on assignment for Director Vox."

The guard rifled through his papers, seemingly searching for her registration paperwork to prove she was who she said she was and that her answers matched up. But then she remembered. She wasn't in the registration paperwork. Vox had said she and Art would be delayed...

All three guards wore the same forest green uniforms as Sergeant Woods had, but she didn't recognize any of their faces. *Sergeant Woods!*

"Where's Sergeant Woods? He can vouch for me," she said. They ignored her.

"I can't find her," he said eventually, without looking up. "Name again?"

"*Sybil*," she growled.

"Any chance Vox would've removed her for some reason, Smith?" Williams, the guard on her right, asked.

"Not that he told me. I'm going to have to call Washington," Smith said with a burdened sigh, closing his folder of papers. "Williams, Burns, better take her to the Hold to wait."

The Hold? Sybil's eyes widened, and she protested vehemently as the guards dragged her the rest of the way up the hill into the beorg. She was so distracted resisting them and cursing them that all her previous thoughts of being glad to be home and soaking in the beauty of her snow-covered, silent mountain were cast far away.

"This is ridiculous. Who else *but* a Shift would be trying to get *back* here of all places? Check my bag! My bag, check it! The newspaper... That's my work! Call Director Vo..." Her words died in her throat as she was wrestled through the boundary and her home came into view.

Out of the thirteen scattered cabins, only four had smoke coming from their chimneys. There were hardly any footprints in the snow, aside from the tracks she and the guards were making. And guards... They were stationed everywhere. There wasn't a Shift in sight.

The beorg was dead. Far more dead than usual.

"Where is everyone?" She gasped. "It's a ghost town. What has been going on here? What have you done?"

"You ask a lot of questions," Burns—the guard on her left—muttered.

"I've been gone not even a week, and the whole place is different. *What have you done?*" Her voice rose, but she wasn't sure if it was fear or anger that caused it.

"*We* have followed our orders. Nothing more."

"I don't believe a word out of your mouth." She wrenched her arm free. "I'm going to *my* cabin and finding my family." Family? Where did that come from? She'd never considered them family before, except for Art.

When Burns went to snatch her, she threw a punch, but he ducked and his fist collided with her cheekbone before she could block it. She stumbled backwards, her hand flying to her face.

"Get her in there," Burns snarled, and Williams grabbed her harshly and forcibly hauled her away. She wanted to kick and scream, but she was distracted by the pain radiating through her cheek.

The Hold was their meeting hall. Their prized building was now their jail. Williams opened the door and shoved her inside.

"Don't think about trying to get out of here. We've prepared for you dirty escape artists and your tricks. Once everything is cleared up with Washington, you can go. As long as you behave." He slammed the door.

Sybil stood in the hall, stunned. Before her were ten other Shifts in varying states of disarray. Some had visible injuries—bruises, gashes. One had his wrist in a makeshift sling. After being off the mountain in affluent social circles all week, the dirt and grime soaking into their pores seemed worse than she remembered. The stench of unwashed bodies was *definitely* worse than she remembered.

Her eyes roamed everything in horror, her breath coming out in short gasps. The building was ice. The fireplace had clearly not been lit since she left. The roughly hewn benches had been pushed against the walls, making a sort of platform that several people slept upon. Her entrance captured the attention of most of the Shifts in the room, but some only watched her with indifference or, perhaps, resignation. She identified Virgil and Glen before her eyes fell on Xavier.

His back was to her, but she knew it was him from the long wavy hair hanging limply against his shoulders. He always stood tall, confidently, his chest up and his broad shoulders back, but here, he sat hunched over, appearing quite small. Defeated.

As if touched by her eyes, he twisted to face her. He had a black eye and a bruised jaw. His lip was split. But seeing her, his battered face lit up.

"Sybil!" He rushed to her and embraced her, lifting her off her feet to his height. He held her tightly, like he would never let her go, his scratchy beard pressing into her hair. When he set her down, he gave her a once-over. "Oh, wow, you look great. You're so clean. And this dress. What is this? Cashmere?"

"You wouldn't know cashmere if it stood up and introduced itself to you," Glen said from his position reclining against the wall. His head was tilted back, and his eyes closed, clearly too weary to be impressed at her unceremonious arrival.

"I wish I could say the same for you," Sybil replied. "You look like hell. You all do."

"Where's your brother?" Virgil rasped.

"He fell behind."

"Pity," Glen spat. "The traitor."

"Enough, Glen," Xavier said.

Sybil's eyes flitted between the two of them and decided it was as good a time as any to forge ahead with questions. "What is goin' on? Why are you all in here? Where is everyone else?"

Xavier exchanged glances with the others and took her hand. He led her to a corner and sat down. The other Shifts in the room sat back, not exactly wanting to participate but nosy enough to watch the conversation unfold. They seemed content to let Xavier take the lead. She settled next to him, tucking her feet underneath her.

"It's been a mess, Sybil." He rubbed the back of his neck.

"Clearly."

"After you and Art left, things got really weird. Really weird," he added more to himself than to her. Sybil's heart hammered. Xavier was simultaneously very much himself and very much a stranger. He looked like Xavier, and he sounded like Xavier. But his eyes, his smile, his body language... It was all different. It was like he wasn't really there.

"Xavier," she murmured, her brow furrowing in worry. "Are you okay? What happened to your face?" She touched his lip gingerly. He grimaced, covering her hand with his and guiding it away.

"The guards here... We had a disagreement."

"Start at the beginning," she ordered.

"After you left, a bunch of Thanes came in. They put up some extra magical boundary on top of ours that keeps us from being able to shift. It stops all magic, we think, because they stay completely armed at all times. They took over the food rations. None of us can access a thing without going through them. And they immediately cut the rations. They confiscated all our weapons—knives, guns, even slingshots and ropes. Really, they took anything that could be considered valuable to us. They won't let anyone in or out of their cabins unless strictly necessary. And then, people started disappearing."

"Disappearing?"

"Yeah. But I don't think it was accidental. None of us do," he nodded to the others in the room, who bobbed their heads in agreement. "No one saw 'em go, and they had to be in cahoots with the guards because there was no other way out."

"How do you know they were in cahoots and not taken? Captured?"

"I mean, we don't. Not for sure. That's definitely a possibility. Either way, when we brought up people missing, the guards didn't act concerned, didn't check their precious new records, and were very clear the conversation was over." He gestured to his busted face.

"Who was taken? Or… left?" She asked, incredulous.

"Ethel. Bo, Dan, Laurel, and Tanner."

"And you have no clue why or how?"

"None."

Virgil interrupted from the other side of the room, "Well, we have theories. Those who left had nothin' in common. Different ages, genders, skill types. It only makes sense they could get out if they were working for someone like Vox. Like you were. They have to be. Just dunno what for."

"You really don't think they were taken?" Sybil asked, feeling hope die in her chest and betrayal rise to replace it.

"Maybe. Maybe not," Virgil said unhelpfully. "What I do know is Dan's lucky hat, which is not valuable to anyone but him, is gone. Ain't no way on earth a guard woulda snagged that. Dan's only ever taken that with him on an op."

A pit formed in Sybil's stomach. Xavier tilted his head back against the wall and exhaled. She copied his position, her shoulder brushing against his. "And you're all in here because?"

"They wouldn't let us out to hunt. Restricted us goin' out to use the outhouses. This group confronted them, and this was the result."

Sybil rubbed her forehead, a sharp ache developing at her temples. "This is unbelievable."

"You're tellin' me. They've kept us in here for two straight days now."

"Have you eaten?"

"A little. We're all a little worried about the kids. A lot of them have been left on their own. We don't know if they're being fed or not."

Glen piped up, "The guards kicked a number of us out of our cabins so they'd have a place to sleep. Sixteen Shifts were in my cabin before they threw me in here. Who knows how many more in the others..."

"I don't... I don't even know what to say. I wish I had known; I wouldn't have left," Sybil said.

"Sure you would've. Shifts go with the work," Glen said wryly.

"Well, what happens now?" She asked.

"Beats me," said Xavier. "We're not sure where to go from here. We can hold our own in a fistfight, but we're no Thanes. They've taken everything. They're armed. Fed, healthy, and prepared for anything that comes their way. It's a completely unfair advantage."

"We're in trouble," Sybil said.

"Yeah," Xavier sighed. He absentmindedly fingered the hem of Roxana's expensive coat. Sybil watched him before placing her hand overtop his. He smiled at her when she did, although it looked more like a grimace with his beat-up face. "Your op... How'd it go?"

She couldn't keep her own smile from her face. "Really well. Maybe... maybe it'll be enough to stop whatever is happenin' here."

"Did you bring me back those wool socks?"

"What?"

"You promised me a pair of new socks."

"No, I didn't." Realization dawned on her. "*You* promised me."

"Yes, but *my* op got cancelled. Yours did not. Sybil, I'm wounded."

"I'll try to make up for it."

"I'll be countin' on it."

24.

Storm clouds rolled in with night, covering the moonlight and slamming sheets of cold rain into the sides of the cabin. Inside, without a fire going, it was utter blackness. Though the Shifts sat near each other in a haphazard circle, it was nearly impossible to see each other's faces or movements.

Two guards came in with a portion of dried meat and a pail of water. The Shifts passed the pail around, taking turns drinking from it. Unable to see her hand in front of her, the water sloshed onto Sybil's coat, bringing about a string of profanities from the others for the wasted water. The water froze and numbed her hands.

When the guards left, Virgil explained to Sybil they'd not be back until morning, so they had plenty of time to talk. They spoke in hushed tones, not wanting to risk being overheard. Everyone wanted every piece of information on Calloway. Of the group, only Virgil had experienced such a high profile operation, and it had been decades. She told them what the White House was like, what Calloway's family was like, and what Art had been doing last she saw him. Sybil saw no sense in respecting client confidentiality now.

She said, "Something is off about Calloway. He acts like he's the savior of the Shifts. He wanted to know everything about us, from our religion to if we speak our own language. It was ridiculous. Obsessive. It freaked me out."

"What I want to know is why on earth it matters to him. And

to Washington. Why do they need answers to questions like that?" Xavier asked.

"Well, if they're askin' questions, it means they're at least not planning to wipe us all out," Glen said.

"No, I don't think they are. Calloway implied he had a reason for acquiring us from the Guild of Eorls."

"Is it possible—" Virgil interjected, "—they're planning on selling us?"

"Come again?" Sybil asked, as Xavier and Glen both exclaimed, "What?"

Marnie, a woman in her early twenties whom Sybil wasn't used to interacting with, actually laughed, "You're crazy, Virgil. That is the most absurd thing I've ever heard."

"What she said," said another.

"You can't sell a people group." Sybil could practically envision Glen throwing his hands up at the bizarre notion.

"Can't you?" Virgil growled. "People deal in people all the time. They pretend they don't, but they do. We've been accessible to anyone in this country for the Guild's price and our land and rations. They come along to get us to do the dirty work, they keep their hands clean, and so on and so forth.

"They come here on Career Day to do their shopping on which Shift will do the best job for them. They pick us based on skills, gender, age. How is that *not* dealin' in people? And who's to stop another country or private agency of some kind from joining in? They could come here, pick which of us they want, and take us back to their domain. If Washington gets a good enough price, who's to say they wouldn't jump at the chance to be rid of us?"

"Oh no, what if they want to experiment on us?" Marnie gasped.

"No one is experimenting on anyone," Sybil stated firmly. "Calloway kept mentioning bringing us off the mountain and not doing criminal work anymore. He was really clear on that. He thinks we're... better than we are. More than criminals."

"No crime?" Marnie repeated. "What would they do with us? What's the alternative?"

"Experimentation," teased Glen. Marnie tossed him an angry look.

"Stop it, Glen. I don't know what it would look like or how they'd do it. I'm not even sure what kind of power Calloway has to make that come true, but I don't think it can be quite that nefarious." Sybil shook her head. "Calloway is obsessed with us. As long as it's up to him, he won't be rid of us."

"Well, there's nothin' we can do about Calloway right now anyways," Glen said. "More pressing is the Thanes here."

"I disagree," Xavier said. "We're on little food, hardly any sleep, and we're missin' some of the best Shifts. We're outnumbered and outmatched. What are we gonna do about a bunch of Thanes?"

"It doesn't matter. We need a plan. For as many scenarios as we can think of! You may want to sit around here and do nothing, Xavier, but I'm not. I'm not going to let someone come in and take us away. Not my freedom, no way," exclaimed Glen. Sybil heard the brushing of fabric and steps as Glen got to his feet.

Xavier's voice rose as he did, "When have you *ever* seen me sit around and do nothing? I have no intention of losing my freedom either, but we gotta think this one through, man. I got my face tore up for rushin' in without thinking. I have no desire to repeat that."

"Then let's think it through *quickly* and get our acts together before we get any weaker and they get any stronger." Glen faced off with Xavier.

"This may not be an 'Us versus Them' scenario, guys," Sybil said, jumping up as well. The tension hung over them like a heavy, wet blanket, and she knew if they didn't get tempers under control soon, they'd all be in trouble. "Don't forget, we have *someone* on our side. Peculiar as he may be, Vox is working against Calloway."

"I don't know, Syb," Marnie said from the floor. "I agree this isn't a 'wait and see' scenario. This could be life or death. How are we to know? We're sitting ducks like this."

"Hear, hear!" Glen slapped his hands on his legs in agreement, drowning out Sybil's protest that she was sure it wasn't as dire as life and death.

"Quiet down!" Xavier said harshly. "You may as well hold up a sign that says 'Hey, we're planning a revolt!' to the Thanes!"

Glen ignored Xavier. "Virgil, what do you think?"

There was a long pause before Virgil spoke in his irritatingly slow drawl, "I think there's nothin' more to be done tonight."

Glen let out a growl of frustration. "Seriously, man? You're the one thinking they're *selling* us! Are you losin' your nerve? I guess that's what happens when you get old and no one hires you anymore."

"They're *not* selling us!" Sybil insisted, as Xavier lifted a hand towards Glen: "Hey, that's enough."

Glen put his finger in Xavier's face. "You wanna go at it, Xavier? I'm sick of your high and mighty ass attitude."

Xavier stepped closer and grit out, "Kiss off."

Sybil couldn't see what happened next, but she felt Xavier's body get knocked away from her and knew Glen had tackled him. She rolled her eyes and sighed defeatedly. Why did every disagreement they had include their fists? She heard Marnie shouting at them to stop, and she could make out silhouettes of other Shifts gathering around. Everyone was hesitating, knowing that if they got involved in Glen and Xavier's squabble, they'd end up covered in bruises too.

Virgil finally bellowed, "Enough. No more." Boldly, he ventured into the fray and pulled Glen off Xavier. He thrust him backwards, and several Shifts caught and restrained him.

Xavier staggered to his feet just as the door burst open and four Thane guards marched in, armed. In the light of their lanterns, Sybil could see blood pouring from Xavier's nose. He had his hand to it, and the red liquid streamed over it and dripped down his arms to the floor. Glen's lip was swelling, but it was clear he had gotten more good punches in than Xavier had.

"What is going on here? Come now, be quick about it," one guard ordered. He had a hulking frame and cruel eyes. By the subtle shrinking back of those around her, Sybil knew at once that this guard was not a new face to the others. They knew him, and they feared him.

"Just a quarrel," Marnie volunteered quickly.

"A quarrel, eh?" The guard gave the disheveled group a once over. "What was this one over? Did someone get an extra sip of water?" He mocked. The guards with him laughed.

"Somethin' like that," Xavier coughed out and spat to the side. He had pulled his shirt over his head and was holding it to his nose. In the lantern light, Sybil could see bruising across Xavier's stomach. She swallowed tightly.

Virgil stepped forward. "We don't need you in here, Sergeant Gable. We've got this under control."

"Oh, do you now?" The sergeant chuckled condescendingly. "Sure looks that way."

"We deal in our own way," Virgil said. "And it does not involve you."

Swiftly, Gable brought the brunt of his gun down on Virgil. Sybil gasped, but hers was the only exclamation she heard as the old man crumpled to his knees.

Gable bent at the waist and eyed Virgil. "While I'm here, *everything* involves me." Then he straightened and declared to the group,

"Consider this a warning. Next time, there'll be consequences."

"Consider us warned," Virgil grunted. The other Shifts stood silently in their semi-circle, watching the exchange between Virgil and Gable, with his guards behind him. Sybil was surprised by the fear in her fellow Shifts' eyes. She had never seen so many Shifts so wary, so concerned, all at the same time. Whatever was going on here was messing with her kin, and it was starting to mess with her.

With a curt nod, Gable said, "As you were," and disappeared back out into the night, taking his guards and the light with him, leaving in his wake darkness and cold air. And Virgil on the floor.

There was a collective exhale when the door slammed shut. Marnie and two others swiftly went to Virgil's side and assessed the damage. He waved them off and, groaning and wincing, made it to his feet on his own.

His eyes roamed the inky space, and he spoke into the silence, "I reckon this has been dealt with for tonight. Get some sleep." His tone offered no room for questioning, and the group dispersed to various corners to curl up in or benches to lie down on.

Sybil cautiously made her way to Xavier. She reached out. "Are you okay?"

"I think so. May have bruised a rib."

"I'm okay too, Sybil, thanks," Glen called from a few feet away.

"You're an idiot, you know that? Both of you." She helped ease Xavier down to lean against the planks of the wall.

"I know."

"Your nose still bleeding?"

"It's slowed, I think," he replied, pulling the shirt away from his face and handing the damp, filthy garment to her. Unfazed, she took it and rang it out. The blood warmed her hands slightly.

"You're gonna be cold," she said, holding out the shirt.

The white of Xavier's teeth flashed in the darkness. "Nah,

baby. Not if you're next to me tonight."

"In your dreams," she laughed. Only someone as full of life as Xavier could flirt in such circumstances.

She took one last look around the meeting hall before she felt Xavier's hand close around her wrist. He pulled her down next to him. Washington felt very far away, indeed, but so was home. This was not the beorg she knew.

25.

Sybil slept soundly, despite the cold and the hard surface of the meeting hall floor. This was what she was accustomed to, and she was surprised how easy it was to adjust back to it. She stirred against Xavier's chest.

The morning light streamed in through the window, illuminating the dust caught in the air and dried mud—and blood—layered on the floors. It also revealed the new damage to Xavier's face. Adding to the split lip and black eye he had when she arrived yesterday was a broken nose and bruising across his forehead. She rubbed a hand over her face and moaned. The last thing they needed to do was beat each other up. But if there was anything more true of a Shift than their hot tempers, it was their abhorrence of change. If force worked to solve a dilemma in the past, there was no reason to use words in the future.

"I look that good, eh?" Xavier said, his voice heavy with sleep. She met his gray eyes. He forced a smile, but it was apparent his face was stiff and sore. "Can't take your eyes off me. What would Art say?"

"I didn't know you were awake."

"You can look at me anytime, Syb. Although, it's more fun for me if I'm awake when you do." He paused before pointing to her cheek. "Where'd that come from?"

"A welcome home gift from the guards." She touched two fingers to the tender spot.

The door to the meeting hall swung open with a loud bang. Gable and several other guards filed in. "Rise and shine. C'mon, look alive. Which one of you is Sybil?" Her name sounded disgusting coming from his lips.

Tentatively, Sybil rose to her feet and said, "I am."

Gable gave her a once-over that lingered longer than necessary. She clenched her jaw. "You're free to go. That mix-up with your registration paperwork has been taken care of."

Her eyes darted around the room. The other Shifts watched her grimly. She felt torn between staying with them, being part of the decisions they made, and wanting to get out of here.

Before she had the chance to make a decision, a guard snatched her by the arm. She resisted, trying to reach back for Xavier, and protesting, "Wait, stop. Just give me a minute. I only need a minute!"

But he was stronger than she was and quickly had her out in the snow. After the hours in the dim cabin, she had to throw her hands up to shield her eyes from the brightness of the sun reflecting on the snow. Her heart seized painfully at the swift separation from Xavier. They'd just been reunited, and she wasn't even able to say goodbye. The awful shape he was in… Their situation… When would she see him again? Would he be okay?

The guard marched her straight to her cabin and said, "I'd suggest staying put here, Shift." His tone was surprisingly kind, as if he genuinely didn't want her in further trouble. He pushed her inside and shut the door behind her.

Her young cabin mates flooded her, her name echoing around the room. Shift children were notorious for their resilience, both physically and emotionally. They were resourceful, clever, and always disrespectful. To see the fear so blatant on their thin faces reinforced even further how badly things had been going here.

Sybil threw her arms around them as an unfamiliar wave of

protectiveness surged through her. Roger passed little Nell to her. Tears and snot streamed down Nell's face as she locked her arms and legs around Sybil's frame.

"It's okay. I'm back now," she tried to be soothing, but her voice sounded hollow. Relief washed through her that they hadn't yet been forced to share their cabin with displaced Shifts and that they still had Freida with them throughout this time.

Freida hobbled from the bed. She seemed far more frail than she did a week ago. "Sybil," she said softly. She placed a weathered hand on Sybil's cheek. "It's good to see you."

"You too, Freida." Sybil turned her face into Freida's hand.

"Where's Art?" Roger asked.

Sybil held Nell tightly, and, strangely, it seemed like the child was comforting her more than the other way around. She drew in a breath and tried to figure out what to say as she met their gazes.

They were all so close in age. Roger, Dean, and Joan were each separated by only a year, as were Nell and Paul, only several years younger. Roger was close to working and had mastered a multitude of Shiftwork skills. He was a good shot and an excellent thief. His ability to get in and out of tight situations, both literally and metaphorically, was unparalleled by his peers.

Dean and Joan both had an aptitude for poisons. Joan was able to rattle off what most of the local plants could be used for. She could scale a tree better than anyone. All three were improving on their shapeshifting abilities every day. They were already working and waiting for their first Career Day, even though it was years away.

Now Sybil had to wonder. Would they ever experience one? Would they experience the thrill of being chosen to be part of an important op? Would they have the opportunity to see life outside their beorg, as she had at long last?

And Nell and Paul were little sponges, absorbing their way of life and surprising themselves with a minor shift here and there. It was sporadic, uncontrolled. But for all young Shifts, those things took time. Would they never experience changing their entire physical being and becoming someone else? The freedom that gave a person? The power? Or would they be relegated to a magical boundary that took away what they were born for?

"Sybil, are you okay?" Joan's high voice broke into her thoughts. Sybil nodded.

"Of course. It's just good to be home."

"While it's still home," Roger said bitterly.

"We're dyin' to know what's going on!" Joan exclaimed.

"Now, now, you lot, she's only just returned. Let her get in the door here, and we'll talk," Freida commanded.

The children parted, and Sybil made her way to the lumpy old bed. Nell rested her head on her shoulder and clung to her tightly, but her tears ceased flowing. Sybil collapsed on the mattress, and the urge to go straight back to sleep overwhelmed her. Expectant faces crowded around her once more, so she rallied herself and said, "Okay, what do you want to know?"

An onslaught of questions answered her, so she quickly held up a hand and said, "Okay, okay, stop. Art and I got separated. And I don't know when he'll be back. I'm not sure when we'll be able to get back out like normal either."

"So those guards are still out there?" Joan asked nervously.

"Yes. The guards are still there. We don't know how long they'll be staying."

"What are we gonna do about it?"

"We're workin' on that, Dean."

"Who is 'we?' Who is still here?" Freida asked.

Sybil rubbed her temple again with her free hand. "Uh, I've seen Virgil, Glen, Xavier, Marnie, Susan, Penn. I think I spotted

Pete, Carl, and Lawson too. It was pretty dark, but they were all in the meeting hall with me."

"Why were they in there?" Roger asked.

"Because they asked questions." Her words were far sharper than she intended them to be. She softened, "They caused trouble."

"What does this mean for us?" Roger asked.

Freida interjected, "It means we keep our heads down, and we wait. Wait and see."

"I'm goin' crazy in here. We haven't been able to get out except to use the outhouse since you left!" Roger exclaimed.

"And they even control how often we can do *that!*" Joan whined. "Nell wet the bed last night."

"Joan," chastised Freida sternly.

"I get it, guys. This sucks—" Sybil began.

"Do you? Because while you've been gone traipsing around the fyrnship, we've been freezin' our butts off and starving!" Roger yelled.

Sybil shouted back, "*I* am not the bad guy here! I don't know why Art and I were chosen to go, and I certainly didn't know what was gonna happen after we left. Back off, all right?" Nell whimpered against Sybil's chest. "Oh, great, now she's cryin' again."

Roger's face turned red. "Don't be stupid. We all know Art got to go because he can read. He cheated, and then *you* got special treatment because you're his *sister*."

"Quiet!" Freida shouted. "No more. No more."

Roger probably would've stormed off if he could have, but it was pretty hard to do that in a one-room cabin. Instead, he went to the dead fireplace, squatted down, and stared into the ashes, his narrow back toward them.

Joan and Dean stared at Sybil. She slowly breathed out, trying to regain control of her temper.

Suddenly, Paul asked, "You won't leave again now, will you, Sybil?" She had forgotten he was sitting next to her, he'd been so quiet.

"No, Paul. I'll stay here with you from now on. I promise."

The days and weeks that followed Sybil's return home bled together in spectacularly dull fashion. Each morning, she woke on her mat with Nell next to her. Joan stayed in the bed with Freida, but Nell had a very hard time parting from Sybil.

Before she even dragged herself from the bed, she began dreading the long hours of sitting in the log cabin doing nothing. Dreading the guards showing up to deliver never-enough bland food. Dreading the children's bickering.

She despised the feeling of being a prisoner in her own home. Every day, she had to find permission to go to the outhouse or to get firewood. It depended on the guard she spoke to. Some were nice enough, others indifferent, and more were quite cruel.

She hated the darkness and the stuffiness of the cabin. Their candles burned out not long after she returned home, and the blackness grew overwhelming and suffocating. Once, on a sunny day, she tried to open the front door and let some fresh air and sunshine in. Her eyes burned at the brightness, and tears streamed from them. By the time she adjusted to the light, three guards were firmly reprimanding her to not do so again. They didn't buy her excuse that she was just letting the light in and gave her a swift backhand to the face. They shoved her and the kids back inside and yanked the door shut.

The children complained from sunup to sundown. They complained about rumbling stomachs, how each other smelled, being touched when they didn't want to be touched. It was everything and nothing. Each of them wanted Sybil or Freida to fix the mess they were in, and neither of them could.

It was amazing just how isolated she felt, even crammed in the small quarters with her cabin mates. She didn't know it was possible to be lonely around so many people. Yet, without her brother, without her rendezvous with Xavier, without the land to explore and be part of, and without Shiftwork—without shifting at all—she felt forsaken. Alone in a way she'd never experienced before. It was as if she were drifting with no hope and no strength to find a way back to shore.

Freida grew more frail as time went on, and Sybil found herself stepping into the role of cabin leader more and more. The lack of food, fresh air, and the strain of the circumstances took their toll on her. She slept a lot, and, when she was awake, she had less to say than usual.

Nell and Paul practically demanded every ounce of affection and comfort Sybil could muster. She was tired of little hands grabbing at her and clinging to her clothes; she wasn't their mother. They were bored, hungry, and afraid; but so was she.

Sybil hadn't seen Xavier or any of the other Shifts that had been in the Hold that first night since they removed her, nor Art, who, to her knowledge, still hadn't returned. She feared the worst: that he'd been caught finishing Donald's kidnapping. Imprisoned. Sentenced to death. Killed in a fight with Thanes over Donald. She tried to hold herself in check and not let the worry consume her. She couldn't afford to lose it. Not right now.

She was a Shift. She was born for resilience. To survive. To stand firm and not let her emotions get the best of her, no matter the situation. No matter the cost.

So, she kept going. She continued getting out of bed. Dividing the food. Breaking up fights. And eventually, when she really thought she would lose it, night would roll in. They'd crawl in bed, and she'd have a respite for a few hours. And then the routine began again in the morning.

Before she knew it, January turned into February. February into March. Time was funny that way. It could move agonizingly slow and in a flash all at once.

The snow began to melt away, and in its place came the mud. It was always a strange combination of happiness that spring was on its way and frustration that muck arrived to replace the ice. Depending on the March, it could be slippery and sludgy for weeks. The sun was sorely needed to dry everyone out.

It was an early morning in mid-March when Sybil went outside to use the outhouse—with permission, of course. After only a few steps, her shoes were caked in the mud. She still wore Roxana's heeled boots—which were not practical for mountain life but her best option—but they were unrecognizable now. She picked up a foot and shook it hard in an attempt to kick off some of the mud, unsuccessfully. Three steps later, she slipped and landed on her hands and knees.

Laughter echoed behind her. *Curse you, Thanes*, Sybil thought as she picked herself back up and flicked her wrists to dislodge the mud. She traipsed the remainder of the way to the outhouse in a foul mood, the cackles and eyes of the guards following her. One hollered a lewd comment. Heat boiled in her belly, and it took everything in her to maintain self-control. Reacting would only get her into trouble, so she bit the inside of her cheek and disappeared into the tiny shack.

She'd barely exited the outhouse when a hand clamped over her mouth and dragged her away.

26.

Sybil kicked and flailed and was about to sink her teeth into whatever she could when a familiar voice said, "Shhh. It's me!" The strong grip relaxed and released her.

She whirled around to see Xavier standing before her. Relief and gratefulness overwhelmed her. But, despite her delight to see him, all she managed to say was, "What the heck do you think you're doing?"

To her surprise, he looked well. The last time they'd been together, he was bloodied and bruised from the guards and his fistfight with Glen. But now, his face was healed. His nose was a little crooked, but otherwise, no permanent damage. He'd acquired a more full, sandy beard, which made him look older and distinctly more manly. His hair was longer than she'd ever seen it. He wore his off-white undershirt, the sleeves pushed up.

The relief she felt seeing him so whole and well again unsettled her. She had the sudden urge to fling her arms around him and kiss the man. *Art hates him.* But Art wasn't here... She grabbed him and threw her arms around his neck.

"Woah, woah," Xavier grinned. "What on earth did I do to deserve this?" He tightened his arms around her and lifted her slightly from the ground. She pressed her face to his shoulder and relished the feeling of his taut back against her palms.

She loosened her grip, and he set her down, his hands lingering at her waist for a moment before falling away. "I'm just... *really* glad to see someone other than my cabin mates."

"You sure know how to sweet talk a man."

Sybil laughed. Oh, it felt so good to laugh!

"Well, now that you got that out of your system, how 'bout a walk?" Xavier suggested brightly.

"A walk? I'm sorry, but have you not been living in the same place as me these last months? What about the guards? Oh, shoot, the guards..." Panic swelled inside her, and she whipped around to look for them, certain they'd be caught. Any moment a guard would appear from behind a tree with a gun drawn. She'd be taken back to the Hold. They both would!

"Relax, relax." Xavier caught her hand. "Calm down. Don't worry about the guards. I'll tell you everything. C'mon."

He led her away before she could protest further. She kept glancing over her shoulder, afraid someone was after them, but Xavier appeared entirely unperturbed.

They walked into the woods, the trees thick with the new growth of spring. The air rang with singing birds, scurrying squirrels, snapping twigs, and wind rushing through the foliage. It was a haven, and it breathed life into Sybil's weary bones.

Xavier guided her to a smooth rock by the stream, warm from baking in the sun. It was swollen from the melted snow and ice cold to the touch, but the water was clear and bubbling cheerfully. Undisturbed. On the opposite bank, the air held a ripple signifying another wall of the beorg boundary.

"I don't know if I can take your silence much longer, Xavier," Sybil said as they settled onto the rock.

"You lasted far longer than I expected." She swatted at his arm. "Okay, I'm done tormenting you. But hey, it's all good news! Gable is gone. And his replacement is sympathetic to the Shifts. We still have curfew, but he is givin' us a lot more freedom to function as normal.

Even gonna let us hunt and trap again, though guards have to go with us." He rattled this off like he was telling her about the weather.

"Hold up. Actually, go back. Gable is *gone*?" Sybil repeated, dumbfounded.

"Sure is."

"Where'd he go? A new assignment? Or do we not know?" Xavier's silence told her everything she needed to know then. "Oh, no. You didn't."

"It had to be done."

"B-but how? When?"

"Looked like an animal attack—a catamount. No one suspects a thing."

"How many of you?"

"There were three of us."

"How long did you plan it?"

"Couple of weeks. Had to stay on good behavior long enough for us to get out of the Hold and back to our cabins. And then we struck."

"I don't know what to say."

"You could say 'thank you, Xavier.'" He mimicked her, using a high-pitched voice.

She ignored his jesting. "Who else?"

"Susan and Penn. Sue delivered the final blow. She was terrific. And Penn's cover-up job was off the charts. I could hardly believe it myself when I saw the aftermath." He paused, "Why do you look upset?"

"I'm not upset."

"That is an upset face." Xavier aimed a forefinger at her. She frowned. He began his defense, his hands splaying out before him. "Look, we did our kin a service. Sybil, it *had* to happen. We have someone else in charge now; his name is Conrad. He's a good guy.

Things are gonna look up from now on."

"Yeah, well what if he wasn't a 'good' guy? What if someone worse than Gable took over? Did you think of that?" Sybil chucked a stone into the stream. "And what if they *did* get suspicious? What if things got worse around here? And, God forbid, what if someone *saw* you? You could be in jail. Off the mountain, facing a severe penalty for conspiring to kill a Thane. Facing death!"

"None of that happened, Sybil. Or is going to happen."

"But you didn't know that. Did you even stop to think about how this could impact the entire beorg?"

"We did this for the beorg!" He insisted.

"Why are you yelling?"

"I'm not yelling!"

"Yes, you are!"

Xavier jumped to his feet, angry. He paced for a moment, a vein twitching in his neck, before turning back to her. "Listen. I didn't act on my own. The whole group in that hall... after you left... We knew we had to take drastic measures. We knew we had to fight, even if it's one small battle at a time, or else who knows what would happen to us. We took a vote. We made a plan. You weren't there; you weren't part of it." This stung more than she wanted it to.

"But it's over now," he said. "Be mad at me if you want to, but it won't change anything. You're gonna have to deal with it. I don't think you can pretend you don't understand this. That you wouldn't have done the same thing."

The butler Regis entered her mind's eye, and a wave of nausea rolled through her. She completely understood it. And she hated that.

Sybil bit the inside of her cheek hard and threw another rock. After a painfully pregnant silence, with her eyes locked on the rippling water, she asked, "Were you hurt at all? Or Susan or Penn?"

She added.

"No."

"Was it quick?"

"Yes." He softened. "I know your brother and I have our differences. I don't know what he's said about me, but I'm not cruel. I thought you knew that."

"I… I do. I do know that. I'm sorry." She finally met his eyes. He lowered his lanky frame beside her once more.

"It had to be done," he repeated. "Gable… He was nasty, Sybil. His guards were unchecked. They've done some really bad stuff. I'm glad you were safe in your cabin, but we had rotating sources every time another Shift got sent to the Hold. The information we accumulated couldn't be ignored."

She both did and didn't want to know what he meant. "What kinds of things?"

"They withheld food and water from the troublemakers. When Penn begged for a drink, they actually doused him with water—in the middle of February—for so long he couldn't breathe. He lost a finger from frostbite. I think he had a particular axe to grind with Gable for that."

"You're kiddin' me."

"Wish I was. Marnie had an… uncomfortable encounter with some of the guards too." His expression darkened, and Sybil's stomach dropped. "It didn't escalate. Some of her cabin mates caught them. But Gable didn't do *anything* about it. I worried about that happening to someone else. To the kids… To you."

"Is Marnie okay?"

"She's tough. You see, we did it for all of us."

"I believe you," Sybil sighed.

Xavier stretched out. "I didn't realize you were so concerned about my welfare. If I'd known, I would've done somethin' dangerous a long time ago."

Sybil glanced at him from the corner of her eye, the corner of her mouth turning upward against her will. Xavier spotted her fighting the smile and grinned broadly.

"So, this new guy... Conrad? I haven't seen him," Sybil said.

"He arrived last night. He's calling a meeting to update everyone on how he'll be runnin' things moving forward."

"I sure hope you're right about him. It's been some long weeks. I thought I was going to lose my mind cooped up there with the kids. Not knowin' what's going on."

Xavier breathed out a bitter laugh. "I know what you mean."

"Freida's not doing so well."

"I'm sorry to hear that."

"How many more fights did you get in?"

"Have you no faith?"

"How many?"

"Two."

"Figures."

"Hey, look, we got plenty of time to mull over everything that's happened. Plenty of time to argue too, if you want to do that. I don't expect anyone is goin' anywhere in the near future. But right now... if you haven't noticed," Xavier whispered, "*We* are alone. Outside. In peace and quiet. Can you remember the last time any of us had that?"

Sybil inhaled deeply, tilting her face towards the sun and letting its warmth bathe her. The air was still crisp, but the sun was heavenly. "Before I left for Washington."

"That seems like a lifetime ago," Xavier said. Sybil couldn't agree with him more. His words hung in the air as they each considered the previous weeks. After a moment, he shifted onto his knees, cupped his hands in the frigid water, and brought it to his lips.

Sybil did the same. The fresh water was so cold it almost hurt as it ran down her throat, but she hadn't realized how thirsty she was. She continued to slurp from her hands, as Xavier splashed it over his face and rubbed the back of his neck.

Eventually, she sat back on her heels and wiped her mouth with the back of her hand. Sitting there, in this beautiful spot in the woods, with spring around the corner, she allowed herself to finally hope. Just a little.

Maybe things were looking up. There were still many unknowns she and her people were facing. But this momentary reprieve—this moment with Xavier—lifted her spirits.

She pulled off her old, slouchy sweater and rolled the sleeves up of her dress. She lay back against the rock and stretched out as Xavier peeled his shirt off and began to scrub dirt and sweat from his torso and arms. She casually watched him, unable to conceal her interest.

When he noticed her, he made a show of it, striking poses and flexing his muscles and grinning in between. Eventually, he ended his game to stick his head in the water and give his hair a good rinse. When he straightened, his long hair clung to his neck, and he smiled roguishly at her. Good grief, he was attractive; and he certainly knew it—the way he performed for her.

"You should probably clean up some too, Syb. No offense, but you don't smell much better than I do."

As much as she didn't want that to be true, she knew it was. She couldn't even be offended by the remark. She glanced at the icy water.

"What—after Washington, is bathing in the stream not good enough for ya?" Xavier flicked water at her.

Sybil laughed, "Hey, they had hot water! It's pretty hard to top that. Geez, it's hard to even remember that at this point." She unbuttoned the top part of her gray dress and let it hang at her waist. She hadn't taken off Roxana's travel dress since arriving home, as it was the warmest thing she had. She had since layered an undershirt underneath and sweaters over the top to get through the winter.

While they washed up, Sybil told Xavier more about her trip. She told him about the Alistaire Beck Hotel and Washington. They got a good laugh over Sybil's memories of Richard Worth. He commiserated with her about how polite and formal everything and everyone was off the mountain.

She told him about Calloway's children, Donald and Lenora. About her trepidation using them to get to him. Her guilt over Roxana. She glossed over Killian James, describing him as weird, bold, and always appearing at the worst of times. Constantly in her way.

Sybil wasn't sure what possessed her to share all these thoughts, but something about Xavier made her feel relaxed. Like she didn't need to have any pretense. And unlike Art, he never made her feel stupid or inexperienced. In fact, he exchanged his own stories from his first ops and how he felt the same way. He made her feel seen. Understood.

She even told him about Regis. He listened intently as she revealed her remorse before assuring her with a gentle touch to her cheek that she did what she had to.

When he told her he wished he could've seen her all dressed up at the gala and how beautiful she must have looked, goosebumps sprang on her skin for a different reason than before.

"Hey, we should head back," Xavier said after a while. "We don't want to miss the meeting when Conrad calls it."

"I suppose so."

They redressed in their layers and made their way through the woods back to the clearing. When they broke through the trees, they saw Shifts streaming out of their cabins towards the meeting hall. The expressions of the group varied from wary and nervous to exhausted and hungry to happy to be outdoors.

Sybil smiled as she watched a number of them tilt their faces to the sun, inhale deeply, and exhale. Their beautiful mountain restored their spirits yet again.

"Smart call," Sybil said as she and Xavier merged into line.

Inside the meeting hall, the benches had been put back in their usual spots, but there were dried bloodstains on the floorboards that weren't there before. Xavier grimaced, and Sybil frowned, thinking of what he and the others faced in here.

They found a spot next to her young cabin mates in the back. Little Nell immediately left Freida and climbed into Sybil's lap. Joan exchanged places with Dean to sit on the other side of Xavier and blinked at him admiringly. Sybil fought a smile at Xavier's obvious discomfort at the attention.

"Where have you been?" Roger asked. "I thought you were just going to the outhouse."

Before Sybil could answer, a middle-aged Thane entered the room. Sybil blinked twice before she realized the guard was female.

She was tall for a woman with a straight build. She had a long, crooked nose and a narrow face. Her eyes were a clear blue, and it looked like a permanent crease had formed between her eyebrows. Despite these features, she was pretty. Her hair was fiery red and pulled into a bun at the nape of her long neck. She took in the room as she strode to the front with a purposeful step.

"Good afternoon. My name is Corporal Delilah Conrad. I am Sergeant Peter Gable's replacement."

Sybil whispered in Xavier's ear, "You didn't mention Conrad was a woman."

Xavier shrugged and mouthed, "I had no idea."

"Two nights ago, Sergeant Gable was found dead—a victim of an apparent wild animal attack," said Conrad. Murmurs went through the crowd. "I am sorry to step in under such circumstances, but we must move forward. It is my understanding Sergeant Gable ran a tight ship. While I'm sure he had his reasons, I have my own. While I'm in charge here, we'll do things a little differently."

Oh, thank God. Xavier was right, Sybil thought gratefully.

"Curfew will continue at nightfall. Otherwise, you are free to move around within your beorg boundary. It will continue to be closely monitored, and the extra restrictive layer on shapeshifting will persist. I recommend being respectful of that decision. It should give you the freedom to scavenge, trap, and access the river once more. Select groups will be allowed to hunt at varying times, but a guard must be present with you.

"You will be free to move about, but please ensure you are back in your registered cabin before curfew and night checks. Because I am giving you more freedom, we will be checking each night to ensure everyone is where they are supposed to be. Should my rules not be followed and respected, I will be more than happy to restrict things once more. Are we clear?" Conrad spoke firmly and clearly but not condescendingly.

She continued, "The guards will be out of the cabins they… borrowed… by the end of the day and will be in tents we're setting up beside the meeting hall. I apologize for that prior inconvenience."

She let out a breath, and her shoulders drooped slightly. "Look, Shifts. Let me be candid here for a second. You don't want me here; I don't want to be here. I know you have a lot of questions. I'm afraid I don't have the answers. I can't tell you how long I'll be here, and I can't tell you how long you'll be under guard. However, I personally don't have any reason to take my frustrations with society out on you. So, you can get rid of me if you want, but Washington will only send someone else to take my place. I'm willing to work with you and make life more bearable for all of us. You can take me, or you can have someone else like Peter Gable. I assure you, there are many more where he came from.

"I want to give you more space. I want to make life more reasonable for you and for my guards. But if you give me a reason to, I'll take that freedom away in an instant. Don't make me make that call, okay?"

The room was silent. Shifts stared at the woman and at each other, unsure how to take this news. Then, a figure toward the front emerged from the crowd. It was Virgil, looking much older than the last time she saw him in the Hold. Stooped and weary, he shuffled from his seat to stand in front of Conrad, and he extended his hand.

Conrad gave him a hard look, probably trying to determine if he was messing with her. After a moment, she placed her hand in his wrinkled, bony one and gave it a firm shake.

Virgil gave a small crooked smile. "You got yourself a deal, Conrad."

27.

Delilah Conrad remained true to her word, and Virgil ensured the Shifts stayed true to theirs. A new routine quickly took hold and began to wash away the bad memories of life under Peter Gable, just as the warm weather took over for winter.

Being out in the sunshine and active once more brought color and strength back to the Shifts, both young and old. The children were free to run and play, and the adults permitted to mingle and provide for the group again. Hunting parties went out regularly and brought back deer, squirrel, and rabbit to supplement the rations that the government sent the guards. Conrad distributed the food fairly to the Shifts, and it felt like a bounty every day compared to how Gable managed it. Buckets of fresh water were brought back to the cabins for washing up and drinking.

Conrad ordered her guards to stay out of the way of the Shifts as much as possible and to intervene only if necessary. Breaking her expanded perimeter and picking fights with her guards warranted involvement; other than that, she remained hands-off. Outside of the strictly supervised hunts, she kept all weapons locked up as Gable had. She never budged on that rule.

Conrad herself steered clear of directly interacting with the Shifts, but she was always present. Watching. Waiting. For what, Sybil had no idea. It didn't unnerve her the way it had under Gable's eye and command. In fact, she was growing accustomed to it. Conrad's presence was commanding but not intimidating. She was an interesting woman.

Even the guards appeared less tense under Conrad. Following her arrival, most of them relaxed and grew almost friendly with the Shifts. One afternoon, Xavier came back from a hunt and told Sybil that their supervisors actually participated in taking down the buck. Sybil was able to return that a guard asked her how she was able to tell the difference between the edible and non-edible plants on their way back from the stream. Every change was welcomed and embraced.

All the while, Sybil kept an ear out for any conspiracy-type conversations, especially amongst the group that voted and planned to take out Gable. She never wanted to lose her freedom again. While she related to her fellow Shifts' fears over the unknown, she didn't want to act in haste and risk impacting their current set-up with Conrad.

Life was going smoothly.

And then it hiccuped once more.

Sybil was crouched at the stream, filling two buckets with water. Joan and Nell came with her but had since disappeared, claiming they found berries to pick. Sweat beaded on her forehead and rolled down her neck. She wiped at her forehead with her sleeve and tucked several strands of hair back underneath her faded bandana.

April proved to be a warm and sunny month, and Sybil was thrilled to put away the layers of patched clothing in favor of a light blouse and trousers to work in. Her trousers were tied with old rope at her waist and were rolled up around her ankles, and the baggy button-down billowed in the breeze.

The cool water splashed over her bare feet. She dipped her hand in and splattered some against her neck, washing away the sweat. Carrying water buckets to and from the cabin was not the most entertaining task, but Sybil cherished the solitude it brought when she was down by the stream. She tilted her face to the trees and watched the birds dance in the air and sing to each other.

"Sybil!" called Xavier.

She turned to look at him, shielding her eyes. "You have a knack for disturbing my peaceful alone time. Did you come for a wash or to help or both?"

His face was solemn, his lips pressed in a grim line. He had such beautiful eyes. They were such a clear, bright gray; but they gave away his emotions instantly. She watched as they darkened, and her pulse quickened.

"I think you should get back," he said.

"What? Why?" She hoisted a bucket onto a rock for him to collect and reached for another to fill with river water. "I need to wait for Joan and Nell. They went off to pick berr—"

"Art's back."

With those two words, her heart stopped, and her hands slipped on the bucket. She barely caught it from traveling downstream. She wobbled and mechanically shifted to sit on her bottom. She swallowed and wrapped her hands around the bucket's handle so tightly, her knuckles went white.

"Did you hear me?" Xavier asked softly.

"What?"

"The others too. The ones who went missing. Everyone came back at the same time."

"What are you implying?" Her voice faltered.

Xavier shrugged. "Nothing. Honestly. I just thought you'd... want to know. I'll wait for Nell and Joan. And I'll bring the buckets back, if you want to, y'know, go see him."

Sybil twisted to look up at him. She opened her mouth to say something but closed it again when she realized she didn't know what to say.

Sensing her distress, Xavier approached and knelt down beside her. "Aren't you relieved?"

"I think so… They're all back?"

"I think so."

"Where'd they go?"

"No one's talking, at least from what I've heard."

"Wait for Nell and Joan," she agreed to his prior suggestion. She stood and brushed off the back of her pants with her hands and steeled herself with a deep breath. "Wish me luck."

"Luck?"

"Because I kind of want to beat the crap out of him and I have no idea why," she said honestly.

"You've got my permission," he muttered.

Sybil stood in the open doorway of her cabin, glaring at her brother. He was framed by Paul and Dean, peppering him with questions. Their faces held excitement and relief, but Roger wore bitterness and suspicion plain on his face. He stood to the side, scowling. When he saw Sybil, he visibly relaxed at her presence, like he was more than ready to turn this situation over to her. She wasn't sure where Freida was, but she silently communicated to him that she had it in control with a slight nod in his direction and purse of her lips.

She turned her attention to her brother. Art looked about the same as he had last she saw him. Large and broad. His brown hair was closely shaved to his head. His clothes were the same—faded brown trousers and a thin blue button-down. Dried mud coated his worn boots, and she caught sight of the old denim jacket he had been wearing for years discarded on the bed. Just like always. Her heart thumped strangely.

There was something new about him too though. His eyes

usually had a seriousness to them. He was notoriously pensive and solemn. Today, they almost twinkled. He was smiling an actual smile—teeth and all—instead of the awkward close-lipped one he typically pulled out on rare occasions.

He's... happy, Sybil realized. Her hands began to tremble at her sides, and heat flooded her face.

"Kids, get out," she grit out from the threshold.

Dean launched into protests. They wanted to hear about Art's trip, where he'd been, and then, for good measure, Paul added it was lunchtime.

"Out!" Sybil snapped, not taking her eyes from Art's. As soon as the sharp exclamation left her mouth, his face fell, and the stoic mask with which she was so acquainted returned.

"C'mon, guys," Roger ushered the boys out. Paul went to jam his elbow into Sybil's arm, but she snatched his arm, immobilizing him before he could. Glowering, she slowly released Paul, and the young boy shrank under her warning eyes and scurried out into the yard. Roger, with one final look of solidarity at Sybil, closed the door behind him, leaving the siblings alone.

There was a long pause as the two stood on opposite sides of the small cabin. Sybil's jaw ached from clenching her teeth.

"Hey, Sis," Art said finally, breaking the silence.

Without any further hesitation, she marched over, her hands fisted at her side, and punched him in the jaw.

Art staggered backwards, his palms flying instinctively to where she had left her mark. "W-what is the *matter* with you? What was that for?"

"Are you seriously asking what is the matter with *me*?" Sybil screeched, advancing again. Her knuckles throbbed, but she was more than ready to strike a second time. When Art straightened, she slammed him against the cabin wall, her arm against his neck, pinning him in place. "Where have you been? Why didn't you show up at the Alistaire? And why haven't you come back?" She pressed tighter with every exclamation.

Art stayed still and silent until she was forced to take a breath. Then he took advantage, quickly locking his hand around her wrist, twisting it around, and pinning her arm to her middle back. Pain shot through her shoulder, and she cried out. Art pushed her against the wall, the roughly hewn log sides digging into her cheek. His grip on her wrist was crushing. He kept his legs clear of hers, so she couldn't kick him. They both panted as she writhed and struggled.

He spoke evenly into her ear, "I am more than happy to fight if that's what you want. I know you're angry."

"Angry? Try furious!"

"But I can explain," Art continued. "Give me a chance to explain everything, and then, if you still want to beat me up, I'll let you."

"You'll let me!?" She hissed. The coarse wood cut into her face as she jerked, and a warm trickle of blood rolled over the curve of her cheekbone and down her chin. Art's grip was firm as he held her still. Sybil let out a cry of rage.

Finally, she paused to catch her breath, her chest heaving. She was drained, and Art's nearness—his steadiness even in her fury—overwhelmed her. She could feel his heartbeat through his chest against her back. His breath was on her neck, and his familiar scent reached her. Tears pricked her eyes.

Over the past months, Sybil had tried to block out her feelings about Art. She alternated between confusion, hurt, and fear. She was angry over his long absence. At a complete loss as to why he'd stay away for so long. The only explanation she could come up with was that something had happened to him, and that terrified her.

She tried not to dwell on it. On him. No matter how hard she tried, she couldn't shake the thought that he was never coming back and that she'd never know what happened to him.

He was her only true family, a link to a past neither of them remembered. He had never been particularly affectionate, but he was the one who picked her up when she fell down. He taught her how to aim a gun, how to hunt, how to forage. He was the one who challenged her on her shapeshifting and pointed out the flaws in her appearance when she practiced. It was only because of him Vox hired her. Even on their op with his criticisms and bossiness, he helped her.

Now he was back. With her, in this twisted form of an embrace. For the first time in longer than she could remember, Sybil began to cry. Her shoulders slumped and began to shake.

Art loosened his grip. She fell into the wall, and he tenderly but somewhat awkwardly caught and turned her around, enveloping her in his arms.

"I'm sorry, Sybil. I'm sorry." His apology was barely audible, but she heard it. And it made her weep harder into his shoulder.

She didn't know how long she cried. It was as though she couldn't get her emotions back in check once she let them out. This humiliated her, so she cried more.

Before long, her tears were spent. She peeled herself off her brother and dried her face with the hem of her blouse. She couldn't meet his gaze.

"Well, that was embarrassing," she mumbled, studying the blood drops on her shirt. She touched her cheek gingerly.

Art laughed—a rare, rumbling chuckle she had once wondered if she'd ever hear again. "Ah, I missed you, Syb."

"You have *so much* explaining to do," she said, readjusting her bandana over her hair and swiping under her eyes. Trying to regain her dignity.

"I plan to. At least, I'll explain what I can."

"Let me guess. Classified?"

He grimaced. "Sort of."

She scowled. "Mhm."

"I'll tell you everything I can. I promise. At least I'm alive, right?"

"That's right; I was afraid you were *dead* this whole time! Or in jail! Art, what *happened?* I wasn't able to get to the alley, but you never showed and the news made it sound like Donald was not returned when you said he'd be..."

"I know... It didn't go according to plan," he said, lowering himself onto the bed. It creaked underneath his bulk. She crossed her arms, waiting for the account.

Art explained, "I went to drop Donald off at the drop point I had set up with Calloway, but his Thanes came. I couldn't make it there without giving myself up. So I basically had to start from scratch. I didn't do any ransom calls, didn't reach out to Calloway at all. I just waited one more day and then dropped Donald off near the White House in the middle of the night. According to the news, he found his way back, and they were reunited shortly after. But, by that point, you were long gone." He lifted his gaze to her. "I'm sorry we got separated, I really am, Sybil. Shiftwork is unpredictable. From the news reports, it seemed like you handled yourself well. I'm impressed."

Sybil took a moment to register what he had told her. He was only delayed by twenty-four hours or so. Why on earth had it taken him months to return to the beorg?

"What took you so long getting back?" She asked, unable to keep the sudden chill from her voice.

"Getting back? To the beorg, you mean?"

"Obviously."

He hesitated. "It's… classified."

"Classified," she repeated. The anger in her stomach began to heat again.

"Yeah."

"Does it have something to do with the other Shifts that disappeared after we left?" Art stared at his hands and did not respond. "Does it have to do with Vox? *Does it?"* Sybil cried.

"It's a long story," Art said carefully. "What all has happened here?"

"It's a long story," she returned.

"The guards… Have they been here since—"

"Since we left for Washington." She raised her eyebrows pointedly. "Stop deflecting. This isn't about me; it's about you. I want to know everything. *Now.*"

His mouth twisted, like he was trying to stifle a laugh.

"What is so funny?" Sybil asked impatiently.

"When did you become so bossy and controlling? Little Syb is all grown up! That op did wonders for your confidence." How could he say that? They had not seen each other for *weeks.*

She ignored his attempt at levity and clenched her hands at her sides. "I'm going to let the kids back inside now. And check on Freida. But we're still gonna talk about this."

"Of course." Even as he said it, Sybil couldn't help but have her doubts. She turned to open the cabin door, but before her hand reached the knob, it swung violently open. She fell to the ground, and pain exploded through her head. She made out raving, thunderous voices before everything faded into darkness.

28.

Sybil stirred. Her head throbbed something awful. She pressed a palm to her temple. She blinked, and little black spots dotted her vision.

"Syb?" Xavier was on her right, lightly shaking her shoulder. "Hey, are you all right?"

"Ugh," she groaned and tried to sit up. Dirt and sand clung to her face and burned in the scrape across her cheek. His gray eyes grazed her face.

"Did you and Art get in a fight? Did he do this to you?" His voice shook as he fought to keep his temper in check.

"No... I mean, sort of. We did fight... But I think... I think I got hit by the door," she said, working her fingers into the welt on the side of her head.

Unprepared for that response, Xavier sat back on his heels and stifled a laugh. "What?"

"Shut up. Someone busted in as I went to open it."

"We need to work on your reflexes."

"Funny. Help me up," she replied.

"All right, easy does it." He put his hands under her armpits and got her to her feet. "Take a second," he said, stabilizing her when she wavered. "Okay?"

"Yep, I think so." She felt a little woozy, but the dizziness passed after a moment. She rolled her neck to the right and then to the left before opening her eyes and looking at him. Xavier's face held the same grimness it had when he told her Art was home. Was he still upset over Art's return, or had something else happened?

"It was an accident?" he asked before she could press him.

"It must've been."

"Then why did they leave you?"

"I don't know." Sybil closed her eyes wearily. They felt tender and swollen after her meltdown with Art. Her face flushed thinking about it. How could she be so weak? Crying like that... She should be ashamed. "Wait... Art was here with me. Where'd he go?" She asked, suddenly alert.

Xavier frowned. "That's why I'm here. I brought the girls up and came to get you; and you were just lying on the floor. You kinda looked dead. I almost freaked out." He rubbed at the back of his neck. Sybil noticed he did that a lot, and she fought a smile.

"So concerned you are for my wellbeing," she returned coyly, reaching out to toy with a button on his shirt. "I guess you really do like me."

Xavier looked split between remaining sour and wanting to flirt back. His hesitation quickly planted unease back in Sybil's mind. She dropped her hand from his shirt, but Xavier caught it in his. He rubbed his thumb over her skin. "I think... I think you know I do, Sybil. That's why I'm here. And why I have to tell you that..."

"That what? What's wrong?"

"Art's on Stand, Syb."

"What?" she exclaimed. A Stand was *never* good news. It was the mark of serious trouble. "They didn't waste any time!" She made a break for the door, but Xavier reached out to slow her down.

"Hey, easy now. You just hit your head!"

"I'm fine, I'm fine. I should've known this would happen." She sprinted from the cabin, Xavier reluctantly but quickly catching her stride with his long legs. The courtyard was empty, but she could hear loud, furious voices pouring from the meeting house. As she went to grab the door, Xavier's arm shot out, and he blocked the knob.

"Wait, Syb. *Wait!*"

"What? I have to see what's going on!"

"I know you do. But we both know you... And, well, you can't get involved. This isn't about you. I know you're loyal to him—I'll never understand why—but you are. But you can't fight this battle for him."

"I... always let him fight his own battles," she said lamely. Xavier was totally correct, which was rather annoying.

"That's a lie; we both know you don't. You take it personally because you love him or you feel you owe him one. I'm not sure which it is... But Sybil... Whatever happens in there... Don't give them a reason to turn on you too. For me." She dumbly nodded.

Xavier's hand left the knob to gently brush her chin and to squeeze her shoulder reassuringly. They exchanged a dark but meaningful look before Sybil braced herself and wrenched the door open.

It was as she suspected and yet, somehow much worse. The absent Shifts now returned—Art, Ethel, Bo, Dan, Tanner, and Laurel—stood side by side on one of the narrow benches, elevated on display for the group to see. Their hands and feet were bound by old rope, and blindfolds covered their eyes. Each face was solemn, their mouths in stern lines.

They had been stripped to base layers, their jackets discarded on the floor. Their shirts and trousers were slightly skewed, and Sybil knew they had been searched for anything that could've been slipped past the guards upon getting home—weapons, documents, or valuables. Anything telling from their time away. Despite their humiliating state, they displayed no shame. No trepidation or fear. They stood straight and tall. For now.

Shifts from all across the room aggressively hurled questions and accusations at the six. They pointed their fingers and gestured wildly. They were riled up. If things continued this direction, it'd be a bloodbath. There were only a few instances in Sybil's lifetime where a Stand had taken place. None had ended well.

Stands only occurred when the worst of the worst happened—betrayal was *high* on that list—and they were nearly always a violent, crazed frenzy. There were no rules or procedure to be followed. It guaranteed public humiliation and made clear to whoever involved that they wouldn't get out unscathed. Only once had Sybil witnessed the accused even have an opportunity to defend herself; but it hadn't mattered, hadn't affected her case. Once the mob came to a conclusion, your best arguments and hard evidence were nothingness, blown away like smoke in the wind. The mob always won out.

Memories of her first Stand came unbidden to her, more vivid in her mind than ever before. An older Shift had preyed on a young girl in the beorg—a girl Sybil's own age at the time. The situation caused such outrage that the man was shot before he could open his mouth to begin the first sentence of his defense. There had been no warning.

She could still remember the way his body collapsed, the mess on the back of the wall, the gun smoke filling the room, and the ringing in her ears. To this day, she wasn't sure who had fired the shot. She had been eight. It was the first time she'd witnessed death. The first time she'd seen her kin for what they were.

She had run outside and thrown up violently. Tears poured down her face, and she couldn't breathe. Freida had followed her. She wrapped her wiry arms around her and soothed her. When her tears were spent, the older Shift cleaned her up and took the time to explain why things happened the way they did. Justice had to be served, even within the beorg:

"It may not happen the way we want it to. But we accept it, and it reminds us of the consequence of betraying our people. Our kin," she had said.

Sybil had hiccuped and wailed, "I don't want to be in this family! How can I love murderers?"

Freida gripped Sybil's chin and forced her to meet her eyes. "Child, it has nothing to do with love. It has to do with *loyalty*. With respect. Respect for our kin, this beorg, for our way of life. With keeping ourselves together and alive."

"What if I don't want to?"

"Don't want to do what? You don't get a choice, child. You were brought here because of who you are. You'll be hired. You'll be taught and excel in what the fyrnship calls 'crime.' That's our livelihood. *Your* livelihood. It's what we are here for. You can't deny who you are, Sybil. We do what we do to survive, to keep our place in the world. There's nothing wrong with that, do ya hear me?" Freida shook her shoulders a little. "One day, to protect your kin, you'll do the same things they did in there today. We're not murderers. We're Shifts."

Sybil remembered nodding, not wanting Freida to doubt her commitment to her kin, even as her young brain reeled at her words and replayed the execution over and over again. Burned it in her memory.

Now she faced her brother on the bench, bound and silent, accused of betraying their people. Of disloyalty. How could this be? She sagged against the doorframe, the knot on the back of her head pulsing.

"This isn't happening," she whispered to the air. She barely felt it when Xavier wrapped his arm around her waist to help support her. "This can't be happening."

The shouts and screams of the different members in the hall entered her ears as one voice. She couldn't differentiate tones, identify speakers, or make out the words. She could smell the sweat, the overpowering scent of earth from the mud tracked in, the spray of spittle with each hostile word. Then, she heard Art, and everything snapped into perfect clarity.

"We were hired for confidential missions by Director Lowell Vox."

"When did he hire you?" Virgil asked. He spoke faster than he usually did, which meant he was dangerous. He stood at the front of the crowd, unmoving and unreactive, while those behind him threw up fists and stomped their feet and yelled.

"Several months before he arrived for registration in January," Art said. Another uproar rolled through the room. Sybil pressed a trembling hand to her forehead. Art had told her about his prior arrangement with Vox when they left the beorg. Had he known about these others the whole time too?

"All of you at the same time?" Virgil pressed. Art only shrugged. "Don't mess with me, boy. Answer the question!"

"Different times."

"What were the ops?"

"Confidential."

Virgil swore loudly, reached over, and smacked the bench they stood on. "This is not a game, Arthur! Sybil told us about your op. *She* came back when it was finished. Why didn't you?" Art remained silent.

Say something, Art. Say something.

"Give us the truth NOW, or you will pay for it. All of you!" No response. "Gag him," Virgil ordered.

Glen was the first to move and quickly stuffed a stained cloth into Art's mouth.

"You. Laurel," Virgil began, directing his attention to the female Shift on Art's left. Laurel was swift and strong. She was an excellent fighter. Quick on her feet and quick-witted to match. She always intimidated Sybil, despite only having a few years on her. "What was the op?"

"Confidential," she answered steadily. The crowd hurled insults and curses.

"Do you not realize what is at stake here?" Virgil shouted, practically quaking in fury. "I can only keep this crowd at bay for so long. If you choose not to defend yourselves, then we'll move forward and punish you as willful betrayers to your kin!"

"We've betrayed no one," Laurel said.

"I AM SPEAKING!" Virgil roared, spit flying. Sybil winced, but those on Stand didn't even flinch.

Bo, who stood next to Laurel, hollered, "We haven't betrayed any of you!" Sybil had always considered Bo to be dim-witted. How did someone like him get hired by someone like Vox for special ops?

"Then stop lying to us! Tell us the truth! Where *have* you been? Why have you been gone so long?" Glen said over the crowd.

"Don't give us more reason to distrust you by keeping secrets," Marnie added. "Out with it. What did Vox want from you?"

Ethel, standing between Laurel and Bo, spoke next, her voice instantly grating on Sybil, "Confidential! When will you get that through your noggins?" *She could've stayed away longer,* Sybil thought.

"When will you get it through *yours* that we take betrayal of this beorg very seriously?" Marnie retorted.

Art suddenly gestured, vigorously enough that he caught Virgil's attention, who signaled Glen to remove the gag. He coughed loudly before saying, "We tell the truth. Vox hired each of us. Individually.

Months ago. There has been no disloyalty. It had nothing to do with what has been occurring here with the Thanes."

"Were you all on the same op?" Virgil asked. His voice held more control, but his face was a purple-ish shade of red.

"No," replied Art and Laurel in unison. She pressed her lips into a line, while Art forged ahead, "I didn't know—don't know—what they were doing. It was between us personally and Director Vox. One on one."

"All of you but Art left around the same time. But all of you arrived back at the same time," Virgil said.

"We did."

"And you expect us to believe you were on separate missions?"

"Yes."

Virgil aggressively scrubbed at his head before hissing out, "Someone else take over this friggin' mess. I need a smoke."

Marnie stepped forward and crossed her arms over her chest. She was a small figure to command such a crowd, but she did so with authority and confidence. Sybil couldn't fathom standing where Marnie was, all eyes on her.

Marnie fixated on the six in front of her, as if she had tuned out the mayhem surrounding her. "Art, when were you first hired? Give me the month."

"April. That's when I met Vox first."

"Laurel?" Marnie went down the line. All the answers were different. Laurel had been hired in July, Bo in May, Ethel in September, and Dan in November—still over two months before Vox publicly showed up on the mountain to lead Calloway's registration.

"Was it Vox who contacted you?" Again, Marnie went down the line. Virgil puffed on his cigarette in the corner, filling the room with its putrid smell. These answers also varied. Art, Laurel, and Dan had been directly met by Vox. Bo and Ethel had dealt with an employee of his.

"Were any of these ops contracted on a Career Day?" Marnie asked.

The answers matched. "No."

"They knew who you were?" Sybil asked. The words fell from her lips before she could stop them, ringing clearly from the back of the room, causing more than one Shift to turn and glare at her.

"*I'm* asking the questions right now, Sybil," Marnie said, irritated.

"Answer it," Sybil ordered, not taking her eyes from her brother's face. "It wasn't on Career Day. Somehow, Vox knew not only who each of you was but also *where* you were on individual, unrelated ops you were working over a six month time span. Right?"

"Yeah. Yeah, I guess that's true," Laurel replied.

Marnie caught onto Sybil's drift. "They'd been watchin' you," she said, almost to herself in shock.

"They've been watchin' *all* of us," Freida corrected. It was the first time she'd spoken all Stand. Murmurs went through the crowd.

"What does this mean?" Xavier asked. "That Vox had contacts within the Guild of Eorls? Is that really so surprising?"

"What was the point of the registration then?" Glen piped up.

"That was just the government verifying what the Guild already had. And expounding on it," Sybil said. "But Vox has known all along."

Marnie raised her voice above the crowd and directed her attention back to Art. "We need to know everything you know. Everything you did. What did Vox want you to do? What required the six of you to be working simultaneously?"

The six were silent. Maybe they didn't know? More likely, they weren't ready to tell.

Marnie cried out, "You had information, contacts, and reasons to be suspicious *months* ago. You didn't think we'd want to know? Vox aside, we could've been ready for those Thanes when they got here in January! We could've protected ourselves. You have put *all of us* at risk with your secrecy. Our entire way of life in jeopardy. Our freedom! And you don't even have the decency to admit it," she fumed.

"I think we're done here." Virgil threw his cigarette to the ground and stomped on it. He walked over slowly, the skin under his unkempt beard now dark red. "If that's how it'll be, how you want it... If you are going to choose to protect an outsider over your own people, perhaps we should treat you like outsiders. Show you what we do to traitors to our kin. Gag 'em all."

Sybil watched in frozen resignation as the six were pulled and pushed off the bench, landing hard on the ground, unable to break their falls with their hands and feet bound.

Virgil loomed over Art. "You were always too good for us, weren't you, boy?"

When the kicking started, Sybil's hands cupped her mouth, but she couldn't move and couldn't look away. She couldn't get involved in this. *They did this to themselves*, she repeated to herself. They deserved this. They'd been warned.

But each blow felt like it was crushing her as much as them.

"Stop this instant!" Conrad bellowed. The corporal flew through the doorway, knocking Sybil sideways into Xavier. Her guards sprinted into the room after her and began to break apart the mob. As soon as the six were separated from the Shifts, three guards began to yank, cut, and untie their bindings and assess their conditions.

"Turn around! Hands up against the wall!" Four armed Thanes pinned the remaining Shifts against a wall.

A guard noticed Xavier and Sybil in the back. He grabbed them by the necks and shoved them into the wood. "Arms up," he ordered. Sybil couldn't see him but felt his presence behind them acutely. She slid her arms over her head.

"Explain this," Conrad demanded. "NOW!"

"This is Shift business, Corporal," Virgil said from the wall.

"It is *my* business so long as I'm here," Conrad snapped.

Glen volunteered, "The six of them there have been missing for months, Corporal. They've broken every rule set by you and Peter Gable. They kept secrets from us and haven't followed protocol. They deserve punishment."

"Hear, hear!" went up amongst the Shifts. They began lowering their arms and turning around, but the guards quickly jostled them back into place and aimed their guns.

"This is your punishment? Beatings? What's next? *Stoning*? You are as primal as people think," Conrad hissed. The jab caught Sybil off guard. She had started to believe Conrad was on their side for some reason.

A fool, she was. No one was on their side.

"They've had their Stand. There's no more to be done." Virgil shook his head decisively.

"Their *Stand*? What does that mean?" She shouted.

"Their trial," Virgil said. "They've had the chance to speak."

"There will be no more trials. There will be no more beatings. I have done everything in my power to grant you a degree of autonomy despite my presence here, but this is crossing the line. If I, or any of my guards, see *any* of you lay one finger on another Shift, *you* will be the one punished. Learn some *control*. Where is your decency?"

"We are not the ones who abandoned our kin!" Glen screamed. "They have been on secret missions, Corporal!"

"I am fully aware of where you say they've been, and, at the moment, I don't care," Conrad replied sharply. "This is *over*. All of you—back to your cabins. *Now.*"

"And them?" Xavier asked.

Conrad turned her keen eyes on him. "They are not your concern. Guards, get these people back to their cabins. No one is going anywhere tonight."

Her guards jumped to action, bodily escorting all but the six out of the meeting house and into the yard toward their cabins. Before Sybil was pushed past the threshold, she caught a glimpse of Art and the others, barricaded by guards. Blood splattered their clothes, and Art held his side tenderly. She clenched her teeth and looked away as the butt of a gun pressed her back into the sun.

29.

Three full days passed before Sybil dared to approach the meeting hall again. Conrad had decided the six Shifts would remain there for their own safety, rather than returning to their respective cabins. She was so determined to prevent any manner of bloodshed that she posted a twenty-four-hour guard as well.

Sybil didn't want to give the wrong idea by showing up too soon after the disastrous Stand. The heat needed to cool before she attempted to manipulate her way into contact with her brother.

In the interim, she did damage control with the kids' confusion and frustration that Art had come and, in their minds, gone again. Joan, in particular, was enraged she never got to talk to him. The kids were a distraction, but Art never left her weary mind.

She waited and watched those three days. Watched the guards' bodies and faces relax once more. Waited to see if Conrad made any long-lasting decisions—or declared any punishments—for the beorg after the Stand. Three days of nearly status quo seemed plenty long enough, and Sybil knew she had to get out and see what she could do. For her brother, for her kin, for herself... Even she wasn't entirely certain of her motivation.

Slipping out of her cabin early, Sybil crossed the courtyard. Fog rolled through in wispy tendrils, and dew glistened on the grass under the morning sun. She wrapped her arms around herself as she encountered the guard in front of the meeting hall door.

"Hey there, Jim," she addressed the young man with a friendly tone.

"Mornin', Sybil. You're out and about early. Going to the woods today?" Jim couldn't be much older than Sybil. He was clean-shaven and soft-spoken with a sharp jaw, prominent Adam's apple, and deep dimple on his left cheek when he smiled.

"Actually," she stepped near and tried to appear as non-threatening as possible, "I was wondering if I could see my brother today? Art?"

Jim nudged a clod of dirt with his boot. "Gee, I don't know, Sybil. Conrad really doesn't want any more altercations. That Stand thing you all do was... pretty intense."

"An unfortunate practice," she waved dismissively. "But, Jim, you know *I* wouldn't do that. Art's my brother—my *actual* flesh and blood. I just want to speak with him. No one else. Please?"

Jim shrugged. "Yeah, but what about when everyone else 'just wants to speak' with someone? It could get out of hand again right quick."

"Our little secret? Cross my heart?" She made the gesture and looked through her lashes at him sweetly.

Jim scratched his chin as he hesitated. He looked right and left and whispered, "You promise to stay out of sight?"

"Promise."

"Won't tell anyone?"

"Not a soul."

"I'm going to regret this," he mumbled. "Fine. But be back in twenty. Got it?"

"Crystal clear. Thank you, Jim!" Sybil gave him a swift kiss on the cheek, and he flushed.

"I'll get him."

Sybil barely had a chance to congratulate herself on persuading

Jim to cooperate before he returned with Art.

"Off you go. Ten minutes," Jim said, nudging her toward the woods behind the meeting hall. Art stalked off briskly and silently, not giving her a glance.

"You said twenty!" Sybil protested.

"Fifteen."

"Thanks, Jim!" She tossed over her shoulder, hurrying to catch up with Art.

He was limping, and his arms were stiff at his sides instead of swinging with his gait. She reached him quickly. His eyes were swollen, his lip split. Bruising colored most of his jawline, and blood was crusted around his left ear. He wore clean clothing—she assumed from Conrad's resources—but she wondered what injuries hid underneath.

"Art," she breathed. "I'm so sorry." She timidly reached out to touch his shoulder, but he jerked away with a wince.

"Don't."

"None of this would've happened if you had just been straightforward," she said sorrowfully.

Art wouldn't look at her. "Did you tell the entire beorg every detail of your op for Vox? They realize you worked for him too, right?"

"Woah, woah, you want me to get beat up too? That would make you feel better right now?" She could sense her temper building, and they'd barely exchanged two sentences. She took a steadying breath. "For your information, I *did* tell people about the op, which you would've known if you had been here. I know there are many jobs that have been confidential over the years, and I think we've always respected that as a whole. But *I* didn't disappear for months. I didn't *hide* it for months! How could you and the others think we'd be so stupid as to overlook that?"

Art glared venomously at her.

Sybil paused and tried to regroup. Switching to a gentler tone, she added, "Look—we're not stupid, okay? But right now, it's just us. Me and you. You don't have to tell the whole beorg, but... Can't you tell me? Can't you work with me? We worked together so well in Washington!" She reached for his hand again and wouldn't let go as he tried to tug away. She held tighter, pleading with him, "Art, I'm your sister. We don't do secrets. This isn't who we are! Just *talk* to me."

He stared at her for a long moment. She watched his internal struggle play out in his eyes, in the twitching of his mouth, and the strain of his neck, but then he said, "I can't," and looked away again.

"You won't," she corrected.

"It's the same thing."

"It isn't. Not by a long shot. Who are you protecting? Vox? Yourself? Do you think you're protecting *us*? Because it sure doesn't feel that way. It feels like you're trading us in for him."

Art tensed at her accusation but said nothing. The brother who held her in his arms as she sobbed in relief that he wasn't dead was very far away. This man was a stranger. And he wanted to be.

Sybil dragged a hand over her face with a ragged breath and slumped against the side of an oak tree. "I don't want to argue, Art. I don't have a lot of time here with you, and I don't want to spend it all fighting. Is there anything you trust me enough to talk about?"

Art shrugged in acquiescence.

Searching for words, Sybil asked, "Are you healing up okay?"

"I'm all right."

"Everyone else?"

"Everyone else is fine."

Sybil ached at the tension between the two of them. She despised this. Did he? Did he care at all? She bit the inside of her cheek and reached for a pebble in the dirt. She turned it over in her hands absentmindedly.

"Sounds like things were pretty bad here for a while," Art said, avoiding eye contact with her.

"You could say that."

"How'd you hold up?"

"We made it through. That's all that matters. It was scary—not knowing what was happening, how long it would last, y'know? But Conrad turned things around. I respect her for that."

"She seems decent." More silence.

Sybil swore under her breath and threw her hands up. "This is a waste of time. I don't know what I thought I was going to get out of you. I thought you trusted me of all people, but it's pretty clear you don't. I'm going back to my cabin." She pivoted on her heel and strode back the direction they came.

She yearned to hear him call her name, to hear his heavy footfalls as he ran to catch her, to stop her. But there was nothing. No shouts asking her to wait. Nothing but the crunch of twigs under her feet, the birds chirping in the trees without a care in the world.

When she was out of Art's sight, Sybil took a turn left and made her way down to the stream instead of back to the cabins. She wasn't ready to talk to anyone. To explain where she went so early and how she had failed so miserably to accomplish anything.

She sat on her rock and pouted, watching the water lap the bank. She attempted to wipe her tears away as quickly as they fell but, despite her efforts, found herself watching her surroundings through a watery lens again. She was sick of crying. Some tough Shift, she was.

All she wanted was answers. The truth. How did Vox find Art and the others on their ops, unless he had unrestricted access to the Guild of Eorls? Were they all being tracked? How long would they live under guard? What did Calloway really want with their registration?

Sybil groaned and buried the heels of her hands into her eyes. Her life had always been straightforward. She remembered nothing from before her arrival in the beorg. This mountain was her world. She knew how to survive. She knew how to work. She knew how to transform herself into anyone else, how to lose herself in the process.

It wasn't an easy life. There were few comforts. The work could be painful and exhausting, especially at first. It was humiliating to be unwanted and despised but empowering to be such a disturbance to the outside world. To be feared by them.

Her week of luxury on her op was a daydream—the glamor, the food, the clothes, the manners. She could barely remember the magical aura of the Alistaire. The enchanting pull of Calloway. She hadn't even touched the gold, beaded ring she had swiped from her op. What good was something beautiful like that in a place like this?

This was reality. The fresh air, the animals scurrying to and fro, dirt in her fingernails, juice-stained fingers from picking berries. Dusty, calloused bare feet. Suntanned, sweaty faces. Loud discussions. Passionate relationships.

No matter how aggressive the weather was or how empty her belly felt at times, nothing took that away. Life went on in smooth monotony until Career Days, when the energy in the room was tangible—a shadow, she knew now, of the pure electricity of magic off the mountain. Career Days reminded her just how dangerous they were to the world around them. How vital they were, though the fyrnship was loathe to admit it.

She remembered the utter thrill of transforming to Roxana. Of manipulating the people around her. And the intoxicating pride and satisfaction when she saw the photos of her and Calloway in the newspaper. Would she ever feel that way again?

Sybil picked up a stone the size of her fist and, with a yell, hurled it as hard as she could. It bounced off a tree and tumbled out of sight. Her chest heaved with the exertion, and sweat beaded at her temples.

"What did that rock ever do to you?" Freida asked from behind her.

"Go away, Freida. I don't want to talk."

Freida hobbled over and lowered to the ground with some effort. She was getting thinner and more bent, her face more lined. "It's not all bad, child."

"Oh, it isn't? You mean, the months with guards watching our every move? Not working? Can you even remember the last time you shifted, Freida? And the fighting?"

Freida took Sybil's face in her hands. "Child, get control of yourself. I know it's been scary. I know Art's hurt you. But those kids need you; I won't be here forever. Your kin needs you. You're the only one who has an in with those six Shifts because you're Art's sister. You're the only other one who has had a job recently—one with Vox and the good president himself, no less. You must stay strong. You're an important part of this."

Sybil's shoulders drooped, and she mumbled, "I'm confused."

"We all are."

"Art won't talk to me, Freida. I've already tried."

Freida sighed. "Your brother is proud. His arrogance may be his downfall. But we ain't there yet. I believe he'll come clean eventually. Perhaps they all will. One day, they'll see that they need to protect their own, not a politician. Not even the op."

Sybil bent over and set her elbows on her legs. "I really thought something had gone horribly wrong with his op, Freida. I was so scared."

"Me too, Sybil. Don't look so surprised now. I raised you both." Freida's brown eyes stared out at the stream. "You can't control what's happening, my child. I've lived enough life to know that nothing is fully within your control. All you can control is how you respond to it. You may never find answers to your questions. And none of it is your responsibility to solve. We need to keep doing what we do: survive. When the time is right, you'll take action. Just like that trio did with Gable. For now, we're safe."

"For now."

"Such a downer," Freida scoffed. She tossed her thick braid over her shoulder. "I should be proud; I know you get it from me. But it's awful annoying when someone else does it."

Sybil laughed.

"Now help me up before I turn into a fossil." As Sybil assisted Freida to her feet—grimacing at how frail she felt under her hands—the elderly woman added, "You know, I kinda like that Xavier of yours. He's much more agreeable company than your brother has ever been."

Together, the two women trekked back up the hill to the clearing. When they emerged from the woods, Jim flagged Sybil down from the meeting house. "You were gone *way* longer than ten minutes."

"It was fifteen."

"Art came back without you. What gives?"

"Lost track of time," she replied.

"You could've gotten me in some serious trouble."

"I'm sorry, Jim. Won't happen again."

"Every time you Shifts make a promise like that, it happens again," he growled.

"We're flexible," she replied.

"You're unreliable." Jim harrumphed again, "Conrad has called another meeting. Noon. Be there."

"What's it for?" Freida asked, squinting, her grip on Sybil's arm tightening.

"Special guest. Get going, and stay out of trouble."

Freida and Sybil did as he said and strode back toward their cabin, arm in arm.

Sybil mused, "I wonder who it could be. Think it's Vox again? I can't decide if that would clear some things up or mess it up more."

"I don't know what he'd come back for. He's caused his damage," Freida said.

Voices filled the air, and they turned to see a group of well-dressed men enter the boundary. Men she recognized... Her stomach violently lurched.

"Oh no." The blood drained from her head, and her knees nearly buckled.

"What now? Sybil, child, you've gone white."

Her hand flew to her chest as she reminded herself she needed to breathe, but her breaths came out in short puffs.

"Sybil?" Freida shook her elbow, her voice sharper.

But Sybil couldn't speak. She couldn't move. She could only watch with horror as Branson Calloway stepped into the beorg.

30.

"It's Calloway."

"Calloway?" Freida repeated, squinting at the figures arriving at the clearing.

"How are two of my favorite ladies this fine mornin'?" Xavier asked, suddenly by their side, slinging an arm over Freida's shoulders. "Howdy, Freida. What's happening?"

"That's the president right over there," Freida said, pointing a crooked finger. "He's a handsome thing. Sybil seems a little nervous."

"Are you joking?"

"Freida never jokes," Sybil said, feeling dead inside.

Xavier stepped back, his eyes darting between the two of them and then over Freida's pointed finger. "Calloway-the President-Calloway? You're serious?"

"Yes," said Freida.

"Of Eastward Americana? *That* Calloway?"

"Yes, *that* Calloway. How many other Calloways do you know of, boy?" Freida snapped.

"Well, what d'you know?" Xavier crossed his arms, looking mildly amused and interested. "He's not *that* handsome, Freida. He lacks my rugged manliness, don't you think, Sybil?"

Branson Calloway stood with a Thane on either side of him, taking in his surroundings. He wore a tan suit with a crisp white shirt underneath and a navy blue tie. His hair was styled perfectly, his face smooth shaven and unreadable. His eyes absorbed the sights before him: the cabins, the woods, Conrad's guards, the Shift children playing in the courtyard. He was as perfect as Sybil remembered. And as intimidating.

She started to relax, remembering Calloway wouldn't know her as *her*, when she recognized one of the Thanes beside him—Killian James. "Oh, *shoot*." She darted behind Xavier.

"What?" Xavier asked. "What's the matter with you?"

"I gotta get out of here."

"Why? He doesn't know what you look like. Chill out."

"Not Calloway," she said quickly. "I have to go."

"Then who? Sybil!" Xavier called after her as she fled toward a cabin. "Sybil!" Xavier raced after her and grabbed her hand. She pulled him along until they were shielded by a cabin.

"It's Killian."

"Who the heck is Killian?"

She wanted to blend into the wall. She pressed her shoulder blades against it and tried to steady her breathing. "He's the Thane. Geez, I just can't get rid of him," she gasped.

"What are you talking about?"

"I met him in Washington."

"As Roxana."

"No, as Sybil!" she shrieked. She slammed her hand against her forehead. "I *knew* that was a bad idea. I knew it, I knew it. And I did it anyway. I am such an idiot."

"He met you as you?"

"Yes! And also kind of as Roxana."

Xavier cursed and banged his palm against the cabin. "Why would you do something so *dumb*?"

"Well, I wasn't exactly expecting him to show up *here*!"

Xavier pinched the bridge of his nose. "Okay, okay, um, do you think he'll recognize you?"

"Oh, definitely." She thought of Killian's friendly attention when they met in Washington.

Xavier swore again.

"What do I do, Xavier? I can't run and hide. Conrad will notice if one of us is missing. Nothing gets by that woman. By now, Calloway has to know he was targeted by a Shift, and now he'll know it's me! He'll take me back and put me on trial. I'm going to go to jail!" Her voice rose in desperation. "Xavier, help me!"

"Shut up for a second, and let me think."

"We don't have time to think. They're here! He'll be glued to Calloway's side. Oh, what I would give to be able to shift right now," she groaned.

"All right, I got it. It's not foolproof, but it's gonna have to do. Come with me."

Xavier snuck her into his cabin and told his cabin mates to scram and not ask questions. He had her change into a pair of men's trousers and one of his frayed flannel shirts. Together, they rolled up the sleeves and cuffs. Xavier moved around her to tie rope around her waist to keep the oversized pants from falling down.

"Throw this over your hair too," he said as he chucked a blue kerchief at her. She snatched it from the air, piled her hair up, and tied the faded fabric over it. He threw a wide-brimmed hat at her, and she positioned it over the bandana. They smudged soot from the fireplace into her skin and neck.

Xavier stepped back to look at her, cocking his head critically. He handed her another kerchief to tie around her neck.

"I mean, I didn't see you in Washington, but I certainly wouldn't expect Killian to see anything but a slight resemblance now. And even for that, he'd have to look at you for longer than a second. You look quite, er, rustic and sort of male."

"Thanks."

"Can't guarantee no one *else* will break your cover though. I can just hear Art asking why you're dressed like that."

"Well, Art's not talking to me, so," she said bitterly. "This'll have to do for now."

Sybil peeked through a crack in the wall. Conrad, Calloway, and several guards were standing in the courtyard. The children no longer played, and a number of Shifts stood outside their cabins watching with skeptical—even hostile—expressions. It was as if the thought going through everyone's heads was, "What *now*?"

Calloway did not seem particularly fazed by the eyes on him. Perhaps he was distracted by whatever Conrad was saying to him. He listened to her intently and then said something to her, to which she nodded.

And Killian. Tall, handsome, irritating Killian. His nose scrunched ever so slightly, no doubt in disgust over the Shifts and the beorg. She watched as he subtly repositioned his feet to avoid a mud puddle with his slick black boots.

Sybil wanted to scream.

"What do you think they're doing here?" Xavier asked, relaxing on his bed.

"I can't imagine. But presidents don't show up for nothing. Calloway was consumed with us when I was there in January… I just can't get my mind around why anyone cares about us after all this time. Especially a man like him."

"You sound as though he put a spell on you." He lifted a sandy brow.

"Ha!" she scoffed. "I put the spell on him. Didn't you see the papers?" Xavier laughed, but her stomach twisted. "Have you ever heard of a president showing up here? Or someone of a similar pay grade?"

Xavier shook his head as he retied a strip of fabric around his long hair. "Beats me. Seems like a lot of new stuff's happening here." He finished and flopped back again, looking at the ceiling. "You have to wonder though."

"Wonder what?"

"I just can't help but be surprised this didn't happen a long time ago."

"What?"

"Yeah—I mean, why have they left us alone for so long?"

"Because the arrangement was working. Everyone was happy. Everyone benefited." *Right?* She continued, "I mean, crime immediately plummeted... If you wanted to hire a Shift, you had to know about the Guild and how to find it. And you had to have the funds to pay them."

Xavier added, "Plus, the government's approval rating didn't go down, nor did they get a bad rap with the rest of Americana by trying to wipe us out or do away with us."

"Which would've been impossible to do anyways because we would've assumed the identities of legal citizens and hidden in plain sight. At least for a time... That'd get old quickly," Sybil reasoned, recalling how sore she was from full-body shifting for days on end.

"I'm just wondering if there's been more going on all along, and we've just had no idea," Xavier mused. "First Vox hiring those six traitors; then the under-the-radar acquisition of the Guild by the government; then Vox going behind Calloway's back, and now Calloway here... I think it's more than Calloway just wanting a change in policy. Things are getting complicated."

"Xav, I can't do this now. I am a nervous wreck with Calloway and Killian here. Can we stop talking about this?" Her voice squeaked at the end.

"Hey, hey. Sybil, it's gonna be fine!" Xavier sat up. He extended a lanky arm. "C'mon over here."

Reluctantly, Sybil dragged herself from her peephole in the wall. When she was within arm's reach, Xavier grasped her fingers with his and pulled her to him. He hooked her legs under his arm and swiftly settled her onto his lap. She looked at him, a touch surprised, but at his crooked grin, she leaned her cheek against his chest, finding solace in the steady beat of his heart.

"There's nothing you can do about this right now, Syb," he said, his hand resting atop her leg. "It's not on you to fix."

"That's what Freida said."

"Freida's right."

"I feel... responsible. Vox only hired me for the Calloway op because of Art. I didn't know what it all meant." *I still don't.*

"You're not responsible for any of this. You did what you were hired to do, what you agreed to. You're responsible for *that*." He knocked the wide-brimmed hat off, and she felt his chin press into her bandana. "Art, Laurel, Bo, and the rest of 'em, they're responsible for... for whatever they signed up for with Vox. That happened long before your op. Long before Calloway. That's on them. On Art. Don't carry his mistakes on your shoulders, Syb. You can't."

"I should've been going to you for pep talks a long time ago," Sybil murmured.

"I wish you had. I'm pretty good at 'em."

"You're good at a lot of things. No wonder Art hates you so much."

"Let's not talk about Art. Let's talk about all the things I'm real good at," Xavier said lowly. His voice had changed. It was thicker. Huskier. Her heartbeat quickened, matching his own.

"I wouldn't want you to get the wrong idea," she breathed. When his fingers came around to lift her chin, she was ready.

He kissed her slowly at first and then more passionately. He held her face in his hands, and she wrapped her arms around his back, pressing herself closer into him.

She should've kissed him a *long* time ago.

He pulled back, studying her face with those clear gray eyes. At her flushed cheeks, his trademark, confident smile returned to his face. Sybil touched his scruffy beard, grinning back, before kissing him again.

It's possible they could've stayed there, entwined with each other forever, but they wouldn't find out. Two hard knocks at the cabin door rudely interrupted them. Three more knocks sounded, and the gravity of their present situation settled back over them like a storm cloud. Xavier rested his forehead against Sybil's for a long moment as they caught their breath.

Before either of them made a move to answer it, the door swung open, and two Thanes strode in.

"Meeting. Now," the first said, his eyebrow cocking as he studied Sybil atop Xavier, his hands on her waist. He heaved a sigh. "Hop to it, you two."

Xavier reluctantly slid Sybil off him. He grabbed the discarded hat from the dusty cabin floor and settled it back on top of her bandana with a sly grin. For a moment, Sybil thought he'd kiss her again, right in front of the Thanes, but he didn't.

And she was glad because she wanted to hold on to that moment, to their kiss. To memorize it and cherish it, no matter what was to come. And she didn't want the guards to be part of it.

31.

Sybil and Xavier did as the Thanes commanded and silently made the short walk from his cabin to the meeting house.

The sun was hot overhead. Whether from nerves or heat, Sybil began to sweat, feeling beads form on her temples. The extra fabric and hat on her head and around her neck didn't help. She felt the aggravating sensation of a slow trickle of sweat traveling between her breasts. She resisted the urge to wipe at it with the front of her shirt as they entered the meeting house.

Her heart was still pounding from making out with Xavier only minutes ago, but now it beat faster and more erratically for a very different reason.

Calloway stood at the front of the room with one of his smooth, pleasant, imperceptible expressions. Staring at him, Sybil was struck by the differences between him and Vox, who stood in this exact spot four months ago.

Vox, with his steely eyes, strong chin, and rusty hair, had an intensity about him. Looking back, Sybil realized his commanding presence was composed of control and cleverness. Contrarily, Calloway had an ease, perhaps even a gentleness to his face and his body language. A way of making you want to trust him. While both were Sages and both held high-ranking political positions, they drew their audience in differently.

Vox drew you to him in a way that made you want to submit to him, but Calloway drew you to him in a way that made you want to befriend him.

Sybil wasn't sure which was worse. Despite the way Vox had started his meeting those many weeks ago, he had been straightforward. Candid. Calloway came across warmer, but Sybil questioned if that made him any more trustworthy. She wondered once more if Calloway was far more dangerous than he appeared.

She thought back to the moment she clung to him, kissed him, and when he kissed her back. A shudder rippled through her, and she swallowed nervously. She forced herself to follow Xavier to a seat and breathed slowly and deeply to steady herself.

Conrad was next to Calloway, feet planted and hands on her hips. Art and the other five traitorous Shifts sat on a bench with a guard next to them. Nasty looks were exchanged between them as the rest of their kin filed in. Art blinked in Sybil's direction before quickly looking away. Sybil's younger cabin mates wormed their way to sit near her, Freida hobbling slowly behind. Xavier stood up to make space for Freida on the bench.

"What's this about?" asked Roger, running a hand through his greasy hair, which fell back over his eyes.

"Who can know?" Sybil answered tiredly.

"Why are you dressed like that? What's on your face?" Paul asked.

"Shut up, Paul."

Conrad's commanding voice rang out, "Good afternoon. We have a visitor to speak with you today: President Branson Calloway. I expect you to give him your full attention and respect."

Sybil noticed the tension in Conrad's face, and her words sounded more clipped than usual. Was *she* nervous? She hadn't thought it was possible for Delilah Conrad to be nervous about anything.

"Thank you, Corporal Conrad," Calloway began. "Greetings!

It is a pleasure for me to be here today. I do not wish to take up an unnecessary amount of your time, so I won't beat around the bush. I understand Shifts are not involved in politics and government, so you may not be very aware of what has been going on over the last few years." *Years?*

"Three years ago, a journalist named Grayson Dalton wrote a rather scandalous piece titled 'The Shift Dilemma' in which he laid out the dangers and threats your race poses to Americana, but specifically Eastward and the Eastward magi. He pointed out the Shifts' role in history since long before Independence Days, when your kin was extremely loyal to Westward." Everyone stared rather blankly. Sybil had no idea what he was talking about.

Conrad hesitated before breaking in, "President Calloway? Forgive me, but I don't think Eastward's history is very well-known to the Shifts here."

Calloway looked around. "Ah, my mistake. Allow me to clarify. In most simplistic terms, hundreds of years ago, all the magi in Americana lived in Westward under Elfen rule." *Elfen?* The word was foreign to Sybil. But if they weren't magi like the rest of them, that explained why the Westward ambassador looked so… other than.

"Eventually, the majority of magi rose up against that subjugation. The Striders of Southward stood against them first and were banished, which is what resulted in them settling the desert plains of Southward. The rest of us—Sage, Sylvaar, Thane, and, yes, Shift—braved the Midgeard to settle here. To settle Eastward. Do you follow me?"

No one said a word. The painting in the White House of the four men in a battlefield flickered into Sybil's head. Four, not three. Sage, Sylvaar, Thane, and *Shift*.

Calloway plunged ahead. "Well, anyway, Grayson Dalton based his argument on the inherent nature of the Shifts, drawing on your history of loyalty to the Elfen and how quickly your kin grew unsettled here in Eastward, which led to the Inweard Conflicts in 1708 and eventually, your banishment from society." He gestured around. "Mr. Gray highlighted your 'elusive' behavior, labeling you as historically 'suspicious characters' with an intrinsic desire for evil and cruelty. He talked about the issue of deep-rooted group mentality paired with a primal 'survivor' mindset."

Sybil's mouth twisted. This Grayson Dalton, a man who had never set foot in the beorg, was surprisingly accurate with his assessment.

"Dalton highlighted the rarity of your race and how that leads to an elitist mentality—a view that one is superior over others. He went into the dangers of this group mentality and compared the Shifts to a cult, suggesting your danger not only to others but also to each other. He argued that Shifts are, by nature, wild—like an untamable animal, keen on doing nothing but hunting others, like a pack of wolves searching for prey. Strategically attacking unsuspecting civilians. And yet, when push comes to shove, Dalton claimed individual survival and success would always come first, which makes you unpredictable."

Calloway paused, rubbing a hand over his mouth, and then asked, "Can I sit here?" He gestured to a table that was pressed into the wall behind him. When no one responded, he hoisted himself onto the table and leaned his elbows onto his thighs in a relaxed position, like he was holding this conversation friend-to-friend.

"All that to say, Mr. Dalton's 'The Shift Dilemma' garnered excessive attention. Most notably, it shook up the public magi's conventional attitude towards Shifts. Conventional being, well, just avoiding thinking about them—about you. Right or wrong as that may have been, our current generation held the idea that if they simply don't think about the problem, it'll go away or, rather, won't affect them. Mr. Dalton thoroughly challenged this and demanded a call to action, to change, or else the country would suffer. Families would suffer. The future would be at risk for our children."

Calloway chuckled softly, "I'm not sure about all that personally. Seems like a lot of bold statements for a man who has never encountered a Shift. But nonetheless, the seeds were planted. 'The Shift Dilemma' became a great subject for debate leading up to this current election. It was surprisingly divisive. On the one hand, we had people not wanting to shake the status quo. Saying that, if we changed the system with the Shifts, someone else would take your place in... less-than-law-abiding activities. Others argued that, if I can be blunt, there are so few of you as a whole, we should just eliminate you and the issue entirely."

Calloway waved a hand casually through the air. "And then there were others saying that, before we could make any decision, we needed more information. That's the side of the issue I admit I fell on. We began auditing the Guild of Eorls and ultimately acquired your management from them. Then, several months back, Director Lowell Vox was sent to introduce himself to you and begin the process of registering each of you. The purpose of that was not to lock you in cages but to obtain the necessary data to make a well-informed decision for the benefit of all." He sighed and scratched his neck.

"Folks, I'm going to lay it out here for you. Congress doesn't know I'm here. No one does, except my right-hand aides. I have heard all about the conclusions pulled from the data. I've heard the myriad of experts' conclusions on how to move forward and terminate this issue. But I didn't want to just hear what was provided to me. I wanted to come here and talk to you. Meet you. Draw my own conclusions." *Like Roxana told him to.*

Freida stiffened beside her, and when Sybil looked over, she was slowly shaking her head and staring at the ground. Doubt rolled off her in waves.

Calloway said, "I recognize you have no reason to trust me. And I want to be quite clear: I have nothing to gain from talking to you. I've been told I'm not taking this situation seriously, that I'm seeing it all through rose-colored glasses. I've been called a Shift-lover. It's affected my family. I've received threats. I've even been impacted by a Shift directly."

Sweat trailed from Sybil's temple to her chin.

"But I put my personal feelings aside because I swore an oath to do what is best for this country. To be a leader for the good of the people. And as of now, whether we like it or not, you are a part of this country. In your own way. Regardless of what happened in the past, your kin sacrificed just as much as the rest of us in Independence Days. I believe that's worth remembering."

Calloway jerked up his chin and squared his shoulders, connecting his body language to his speech. Physically demonstrating intent, passion, and sincerity as the words rolled off his tongue. "So, here I am. I would like to speak with each and every one of you, but only if you are willing. I won't force you to engage. I want to know what *you* want. What concerns you, recognizing your livelihoods could likely be at stake.

"If I could be perfectly frank, the public attitude towards the Shifts right now is... not great. There's been a lot of inexplicable happenings recently, and it all points back to you." Sybil looked at Art and the others on their bench.

"I advise you to think very carefully before you write me or my words off as unimportant. This may very well be your only chance to speak up for yourselves and have someone actually listen. I can't guarantee the outcome, but I'll do my best to do what is right and fair for everyone. Thank you. Corporal?"

Conrad looked a little like someone had hit her over the head as she came forward again. Her brows were furrowed, as she processed his words along with the rest of the room. "Er, yes. There will be no hunting parties today. While President Calloway is here, please stay in or near your cabins. If you wish to speak to President Calloway, wait outside in an orderly fashion. You're dismissed," she said, glancing over at Calloway as though to confirm this was what he had intended when he turned the room back to her.

Slowly, Shifts rose to their feet and shuffled out of the meeting house, whispering to each other and stealing looks over their shoulders at Calloway. His posture was easy-going, but his eyes absorbed everything as the meeting hall emptied.

As soon as she stepped outside, Sybil heard a clear, bass laugh to her right. Killian stood chatting with some of Conrad's stationed guards at the threshold to the meeting house, facing her. Their eyes met. *Shoot.*

She ducked her head and wove into the crowd, but she was sure he saw her face. She could only hope he didn't get a good enough look and her attire would throw him off. Surely he wouldn't be expecting to see her here either.

Roger and Dean walked ahead of Sybil, helping Freida shuffle along. Paul and Joan raced ahead, and Nell clung to Sybil's hand.

Xavier followed her, walking back towards Sybil's cabin instead of his. "So that's him, huh? Calloway?"

"Yep."

"I can't get a read on him."

"Nope."

"That's how he was when you were with him?"

"Absolutely."

"He's probably a lousy kisser too. Right?"

"Lousy," she replied, yanking off the stupid hat and fanning herself with it. As they reached their cabin, Sybil saw Art coming up behind them. Freida ignored him entirely and went inside to lie down.

"Art," Sybil said, surprised. "You're here."

Roger blocked the open doorway of their cabin and growled, "What are you doing back?"

"I live here."

"I don't think so. You don't belong here anymore. If Conrad hadn't stepped in, you'd be long gone," Roger said. Sybil clenched her jaw.

"I'm surprised you're not first in line to get chummy with Calloway," Xavier contributed. "You've had enough practice."

Art glared. "It's not what you think."

"But it's classified, right?"

"Stop it," Freida ordered from inside. "I am an old, tired woman, and I don't want to deal with this right now. If you boys cannot coexist for more than two seconds, then at least close the blasted door!"

Roger muttered, "Sorry, Freida."

"Sorry, Freida," Xavier echoed.

"Sorry, Freida..." Art didn't sound very sorry.

Sybil closed the door and told the children to go play. Joan, Dean, Paul, and Nell looked cranky at being excluded but did as they were told.

Sybil plopped down on the front step, and Roger sat next to her. Art and Xavier both peered down at them.

"You okay?" Xavier asked.

"Fine," she mumbled, twisting the hat in her hands.

Art said, "It's not all that bad, Sybil. Maybe you should be one of the ones to talk to Calloway."

"They made it clear we don't have to if we don't want to," said Roger defensively.

"I was talking to Sybil," Art said. "It could help clear the air. He doesn't know you were the Shift. He may have suspicions, and you could turn him off the trail if you talked to him. I think if we all met with him, we could maybe turn this thing around some."

"What thing? We don't even know what the 'thing' is," Xavier said. "For all his talk, it doesn't seem like Calloway does either. Are they putting us in jail? Do they want to exterminate us? Are they integrating us into society? Shippin' us off to another country? Turning us into the circus? Are we people or property? I mean, how the hell are we supposed to keep anything they want to have happen from happening? It's just a game. Him being here is just a publicity stunt for Calloway to look all the more compassionate and personable as a leader."

"I disagr—"

"I thought you were Vox's man. Why the sudden change to being pro-Calloway?"

"I'm not pro-Calloway or pro-Vox," Art declared. "I'm pro-Shift and what's best for us here."

"Could've fooled me."

"*Stop*!" Sybil shrieked in frustration, cutting them both off. She weakly repeated, "Just... stop. I need a minute. Roger, watch the kids." She hopped off the step before they could stop her, slapping Art's hand away as she passed him. She crossed the courtyard to the tree line and rested her head against the bark of an old oak that cast a wide shadow. She squeezed her eyes shut, feeling drained.

Sybil knew how to look out for herself. She knew how to gather food, how to mend clothes, chop wood, how to start fires. She could take out a deer and trap rabbits and squirrels. She could block a punch and get a few good ones in too. She could shoot straight. She cut her own hair; she bandaged her own knees. And that was okay with her. She liked her independence. Her strength.

She could morph into whoever she needed to. She could shift her dialect to match what she heard. She only had to hear it once, and she'd never forget it. She picked up people's tics—tics they often didn't know they had. Biting their nails, chewing their lips, blinking too much.

She could read a room. Manipulate people to accomplish her purposes. *Like a Sage*, she thought. Defend herself like a Thane. But she certainly lacked the compassion and easy way of living of the Sylvaar. Sybil had never once envied a Sylvaar. She had always viewed them as lesser because they seemed so ordinary. But in this moment, she looked toward the courtyard she had lived in for most of her life, filled with the only people she knew, and wished for the inherent peace the Sylvaar seemed to have.

Instead of peace, she felt disoriented. She didn't know who she could trust anymore. Art not only betrayed their kin, but he also lied to her. She was starting to believe he never intended to come home with her after Washington.

Then there was Vox and Calloway. Everything started with those two politicians. It was their fault they were in this mess now. Were either of them actually on the side of the Shifts? Could either be trusted? Vox worked for Calloway but also against him. Calloway with his obsession over the Shifts seemed dangerous. Unhinged. She recalled the way he badgered Roxana with questions that night in his study. And coming here in secret...

Or, was Xavier right and it wasn't a secret at all? Was he manipulating them? Were they both just playing the entire beorg for personal gain?

And, on top of it all, not a single Shift could come to an agreement on what they should do. In the midst of the mess, Virgil called a Stand. They could've killed their own people while their livelihood was at stake. *What a stupid thing to do.* We *are stupid.*

She opened her eyes to see some of the younger Shift children, including Joan and Paul, kicking an old battered ball around the courtyard. She sighed. Maybe they'd exterminate themselves before Congress decided what to do with them. It'd save them a lot of paperwork.

After all this time—all the years Shifts had lived here, doing their jobs and nothing more—why did it have to change? Could it truly be because of a scathing exposé by one journalist?

Surely the fyrnship knew if the Shifts stopped their criminal work, someone would take their place. Evil always found its way. The world was never—and would never be—good enough for the perfect harmony Eastward magi desired. Shifts were just the only ones willing to acknowledge it.

Sybil dropped to the ground and pulled her knees up. Her fingers skimmed the soft grass. She absentmindedly pulled at a clump of dirt, dissolving it between her thumb and pointer finger. Her hands were red and dry. She looked to her bare feet, tanned and dusty, and thought back to January. To the glitter of Washington with its golden lights at night, its paved streets, and rumbling motorcars. Its order, beauty, and peacefulness.

If it was truly his aim, then what was Calloway thinking, wanting to bring the Shifts into *that* world? They didn't fit. They were rough, sleazy, violent people. Their magic didn't fit.

Sage, Thane, Sylvaar, Shift…

It may have started that way hundreds of years ago, but it wasn't that way anymore. Sybil didn't know the history of her kin, and something definitely went wrong after they settled in Eastward. It clearly didn't work for them to live amidst the rest of the magi then, and it wouldn't now.

Sage, Thane, Sylvaar.

Shifts were somewhere far down the list. Where they belonged.

32.

Her heart was racing before she stepped foot inside the meeting hall. From the threshold, Sybil saw Calloway relaxing on the same rickety table he had given his speech from, one knee pulled up, his arms draped over it. His eyes never left Sybil's as she stepped in and Conrad closed the door behind her. With a quick glance at the woman, Sybil noted her taut, straight face. She wondered just how on edge Delilah Conrad was with Calloway's impromptu visit.

Move, Sybil. Take a step. Sybil forced herself to approach Calloway and tried to mask her nerves. Calloway, at first, looked remarkably indifferent; but when she neared him and came face to face with him, she saw the familiar sincerity and kindness in his eyes. He flashed a smile.

"Ah, so, women live here too. I've been visited by man after man today and could use a change of scenery," he joked. "What's your name?"

"Sybil."

"A lovely name. Tell me, Sybil, why are you here?"

It was a simple question, but Sybil didn't know how to answer. She wasn't sure what possessed her to meet with Calloway. After her tantrum in front of Art, Roger, and Xavier, she stayed in the tree line around the beorg for a couple of hours, watching various Shifts go in and talk to Calloway. She replayed everything she could remember from before that fateful January Career Day and after it. She thought through her interaction with Vox and her time with Calloway in Washington. Her brain reached and stretched for connections and explanations.

Everything she knew had been filtered through somebody else—Vox, Calloway, Gable, Conrad, Art. Even Xavier. That's when she decided she wanted to make her own conclusions as best she could. The only way she knew to attempt that was to show up and hear what he had to say.

Conrad cleared her throat, and Sybil realized with horror she'd been standing there with her mouth hanging open, unable to get any words out. She closed her jaw with a snap and sat on a bench.

Calloway thoughtfully asked, "What would you say—how would you react—if you were taken off your mountain? If you had an opportunity to attend school or work in a real, paying job? Live in your own home. Be in charge of your own future."

"I'd say it wouldn't work," Sybil answered truthfully.

"Why is that?" Calloway leaned forward. She could smell his cologne. It was the same scent he wore when she was with him in January. What would he do if he knew she'd been the one to target him?

"Why do you think? You can't control us or our magic. It'd be like letting loose a pack of wolves in a pasture of lambs with no shepherds."

"You seem to think that you're required to be a wolf. Have you ever thought about how you could use your magical capabilities for something other than illegal activity, as all other magi have managed to do?"

"Why would I? It's all we're good for."

"It's all you've been *told* you're good for," Calloway countered. "It's true the Shifts don't fit perfectly into a pre-existing branch of magic. Eastward magi are scared of what they don't understand,

and we've never truly understood you. But we've also not tried. It was wrong of our country and our leaders at the time, decades and decades ago, to choose your path for you. To take away your options. You have lived a life you've been told you deserve. All of you. But what about the life you want? If you had the choice, what would you choose?"

Sybil internalized this. She had no idea how to answer him. She'd never given it a thought. Never had reason to.

Calloway said, "I want to give you an option once more. I'm offering the opportunity for you to make a decision about *your* future for yourself. Not to work for another person. Not to be forced to become someone else."

"It's foolishness..."

"With all due respect, Sybil, if anyone should be called a fool, it'd be you. You who think you are worth nothing because you've been told you are. Told by some group of policymakers long dead. You all of you—could have so much more than this life on the mountain waiting for the next Career Day to come around. Only a fool would decline that opportunity."

"A life doing *what*, Mr. President? We can't read or write. We can't operate machinery and technology we've never even seen. For land's sake, we don't raise families. We don't marry. What do you expect us to do in your neat little society of magi?" Her chest heaved with her outburst, and she could feel the heat in her cheeks. Her voice dropped wearily. "We don't *fit*, Mr. President, and I don't believe we ever will."

Calloway stared intently at her. There was no pity in his eyes, but there was also no offense or anger. "You have been taught to think very little of yourself."

Biting back a sneer, Sybil said, "Fine—I'll bite. Since *you* clearly think quite highly of us, how would you do it? How would you mold us to fit into your world?"

Calloway sat back. "Thank you for asking. You're the first, surprisingly, to show an interest in the rehabilitation plan."

Rehabilitation? She frowned.

"I have some experts working to fine tune this, but the initial thought is something along these lines: We'd bring you all to a facility where we can provide medical care you've never received; we can interview you and assess what interests you may have or skills you possess; we begin the fundamentals of reading and writing and, I think, also a lifestyle class to help you best understand things like finances, home ownership, and the like.

"Ideally, once we've spent some time with you individually and collectively to assess your capabilities, we would then set you up on your own. Like a starter package—an apartment, an initial quantity of cash, and an education and work schedule—a six month to a year plan, perhaps. I'd also like to set up a program for the Shifts to work through to gain official citizenship, including identification and voting rights."

Sybil interrupted, "How are the fyrnship magi going to feel about sharing the streets with us?"

"Fyrnship?" Calloway asked, cocking his head, puzzled.

"It's what we Shifts call your society... We have our beorg. You have the fyrnship with all your customs, routines, and expectations."

"Interesting," said Calloway pensively.

"Do you have people willing to teach a bunch of Shifts these things? Is your kind really gonna be okay with that effort? Oh, there's also the question of how you'll keep track of us. You won't be able to restrict our shapeshifting. And what skills will we have outside of our one magical ability? Manual labor? Factory work?" She sighed. "We'll be nothing but nuisances. At least, if we are left alone here, we're only nuisances to one another."

Calloway smiled faintly. "You ask a lot of questions."

"I have a lot of questions. I think... I think this is a terrible plan," Sybil mimicked his body language by sitting back and crossing her legs.

"Well, that is what I want to know, so I appreciate your candor."

"Can you answer my questions?"

Calloway lifted his hands in mock submission. "As you wish, Sybil. You asked about the magi in the *fyrnship.*" He tested out the word. It sounded funny coming from him. "I think if we can present a foolproof plan of rehabilitation that they can feel confident in, most magi will come around. There are always those who resist change. But I do not intend to let my country be held back from progress by fear."

"Spoken like a true politician."

"Oh, hardly. Nothing political about that. In fact, you can consider it my personal drive and ambition. I don't mean to diminish your views, Sybil, but I've been in politics longer than you've been alive. The one thing that I have seen time and time again is pandering to those who just want what is comfortable. I want what is *best*... which makes me a progressive at best and a radical at worst."

Sybil stiffened. She wanted to hate everything coming out of Calloway's mouth, but he was making points with which she didn't know how to argue. She didn't want to live under restrictions, but learning... going to school... seeing the world... If he could persuade the magi and they accepted it... Was that really wrong? Dangerous?

And what was the alternative if it didn't happen? Now that they were registered with the government, their work would surely not continue as it had. That already proved to be true, what with Thanes crawling all over the beorg.

"So," she finally said. "The plan is rehab?"

"You can call it boot-camp, if you'd prefer."

"And my other questions? Are you going to put trackers on us to make sure there's no shifting and funny business going on?"

Calloway laughed. "No trackers. But it does pose an interesting dilemma. To me, it also opens the question to how many Shifts are already *off* the mountain without anyone knowing."

"Excuse me?" Sybil found herself checking over her shoulder to look at Conrad by the door, as if Conrad would be on her side. They met eyes before the Thane woman turned her face away. Sybil wished she could read her mind, but Conrad remained as inscrutable as ever.

"Correct me if I'm wrong: Shifts are born to anyone, correct?"

Sybil mumbled an affirmative.

"And usually by their first birthday, they have displayed some level of shapeshifting capabilities, though it could be as late as their third. Correct?" Sybil pursed her lips.

"And typically, the family contacts the Guild, who arranges for their deposit here. Correct?"

"Correct," she bit out.

"It begs the question: what if a family did not turn their child in?"

Sybil faltered. "Why wouldn't they?"

"I'm not suggesting there would be much benefit for them to keep them. Quite the opposite, in fact. I cannot imagine there would be a way for them to permanently hide their child's shapeshifting or their lack of expected magical abilities, depending on who they were born to, of course. You see my point?"

"What does this have to do with anything?"

"Sybil, it has to do with tracking you off the mountain, like you asked. We know there are about sixty to seventy of you on your beorg at any given time. There have been up to twenty away on ops—as I believe you call them—nearly one hundred percent of the time." Sybil wondered how they determined those numbers. "There are an estimated ninety in a Georgia commune, thirty in Pennsylvania, and over one hundred more in Rhode Island."

Sybil couldn't conceal her shock. *There are more of us.* Over a hundred more, if he was right. How come she never knew this? She swallowed hard and pressed her shaking hands into her lap. Not one of them had any idea of reality, not really, for all these years.

"Are you well?" Calloway asked. "Oh. You didn't know," he stated.

She shook her head.

"Interesting. Well, not to mention, there could be tens or hundreds of you off the mountain living amongst us already." Her surprise abating, disbelief took hold of her, and Sybil started laughing.

"I'm sorry—is this funny to you?" Calloway asked, tilting his head to the side.

"Why, yes, it really is. This is outrageous."

"I hardly think it is far-fetched," Calloway disagreed politely. "We wouldn't have any documentation of a child being a Shift if the guardians did not volunteer the information. How would anyone know?"

Sybil pressed the heel of her hand to her head. Calloway was insane. Wasn't he? Who would choose to raise a failure like a Shift in their family? How would they hide their inability to do magic like everyone else? And how did she know if Calloway was telling the truth about the other Shifts? Communities of shapeshifters in three different states.

Calloway proceeded, voicing his carefully formulated plan. "We have already begun the process of registering all of you; you know this. Director Vox has done a stupendous job on this involved effort. I believe, if we show the public there is nothing to fear and that there'd be no repercussions to being a Shift, that any others in the country may feel they can come out of the woodwork, so to speak."

He paused a moment. "I really don't want to track any of you. I want you to live freely, like any other citizen. I want my country to be truly united. To embrace what other countries in the world fear and avoid. I want us to *advance* and work together to be the *best*, Sybil."

Uncertain how to feel at this point, Sybil stuttered out another question for him, "So, you'd be okay if we shapeshifted? Took another person's identity? There'd be no consequences to that?"

Calloway closed his eyes, gave a tight-lipped smile, and shook his head slightly before answering. "I never said there'd be no consequences. We would certainly put laws in place to prevent the Shifts from taking advantage of other magi. Just like now, if you are caught in crime, you face the penalty."

"But we'll be able to continue shapeshifting?" Sybil pressed.

"I want to say yes, but I don't hold all the power here. *If* I get my way and Congress votes Integration & Rehabilitation versus... the alternative, then hopefully, we could work through some of those nitty-gritty details and come to a conclusion that pleases everyone."

"What's the alternative, Mr. President?" Sybil studied his face.

Calloway winced ever so slightly. "A true shame, if it came to pass."

Sybil dropped her eyes to her feet. "You seem to have a lot of good ideas. Plans. Hopes. But no proof you can deliver on them." She looked back up at him and propped her chin in her hand.

"I suppose, in a way, that's true. But you have my word that I am trying. And I would like very much to work *with* you and not against you."

"You claim you've been a target of a Shift. And you still want to bring us into your world. Why do you care so?"

Calloway stilled. After a long uncomfortable silence, he said slowly, "I find that we are more comfortable accepting what has always been rather than what should be. There was a day when the Shifts were like any other magi in Americana, in Eastward. It only took a few ambitious, if not misguided, leaders to change the direction for your kin. I want to be one of the leaders to change it back."

"But *why?* Why you? It seems personal."

Conrad's voice rang from the door, "It's been fifteen minutes, Mr. President. There is another waiting to speak with you."

"Thank you, Corporal." Calloway rose to his feet, straightening his suit. "I'm really sorry you feel the way you do about so many things, Sybil. It must be exhausting to view the world as such, but I understand why you might have the feelings you do. I hope our conversation has given you, at the least, some clarity on what you may want for your future and the future of those around you."

Sybil held his stare as she stood. "Mr. President," she started, as calmly as she could manage. "I may not believe there's hope in what you want for the country… but I appreciate your coming here and speaking with us." She extended a hand to him.

A tingle ran up her arm when he put his warm hand in hers and firmly shook it. It was as though she was right back in his library. Right back to his gardens. It caught her off guard enough to trigger one more question as she quickly pulled her hand back: "What makes you think you were targeted by a Shift?"

Calloway's dark eyebrows lifted. He pursed his lips and thought for a long moment, his brows furrowing. "I have no hard evidence, only one woman's word against mine."

"What happened?" she asked. Her heartbeat quickened.

"A perceived love affair. Looking back, it felt very… intentional. All the right places, the right times. I know my critics mocked me for many of my family values, arguing I couldn't possibly uphold them. I always figured it'd be what they'd want to destroy if they were to do anything. And that's exactly what happened. Not to mention it hit the papers so quickly; I couldn't help but think it was planned. And then..." He swallowed, and grief flooded his features. "My son. Someone took my son."

"I'm sorry."

"Thank you," he said quietly.

"Who do you think would target you? Who are your so-called critics?"

"I can think of a few names. But I don't think that's really any of your business now, is it?" Calloway stared at her. "Why, do you know something, Sybil?"

"Not in the slightest. But if you are so sure it was a Shift, well, someone didn't do their job right," she bluffed.

"Thank you for your time and your honesty this afternoon, Sybil. You asked some smart questions. Perhaps we'll meet again some day."

33.

Rap, rap, rap.

Sybil stirred.

Rap, rap, rap.

"What the...?" she murmured groggily, lifting her head from her pad on the floor. It couldn't possibly be morning. She'd lain awake for so long, her head spinning from her talk with Calloway; it felt like she had just fallen asleep.

The knocking continued, increasing in intensity.

"Ugh, make it stop," Roger moaned.

Sybil glanced his direction and noticed Freida and Art were both sound asleep, which meant it fell on her to deal with. With a heavy sigh, she dragged herself from her pallet, stumbled in the dark to the door, and yanked it open.

"What?" She barked.

Two Thane guards stood before her with big, metal flashlights. She recognized Jim and then... Killian. He was studying her intensely, and then his full lips parted with recognition. Recognition she'd been dreading.

Jim said, "Sorry to wake you, Sybil. We need you to come with us."

"I didn't do anything," she protested quickly, gripping the door frame tightly.

"I-it's important," Jim stuttered, and he looked embarrassed for rousing her in the middle of the night. "Please."

There was no use fighting. Sybil sighed defeatedly. "Oh, all right."

"I'd get dressed first," Killian interjected, looking her up and down with his black eyes. She self-consciously crossed her arms over the baggy, rumpled shirt she slept in. Goosebumps ran up her bare legs. "We'll wait here."

She shut the door as quietly as she could and made her way back through the cabin to find a pair of trousers. She tucked the oversized shirt into the waistband and rummaged for Roxana's coat on the floor. It wasn't cold outside, but she couldn't find her underclothes in the darkness. Wrapping the coat around her made her feel less naked.

She could barely see her cabin mates' figures, but the silence was loud. If anyone had awakened, they'd fallen back asleep already. She fingered through her hair in an attempt to tame it before slipping out the front door into the night where Jim and Killian waited with their flashlights. They pointed straight at her, blinding her, and she felt eerily like she was getting arrested.

"What is this about, Jim?" Sybil whispered, as the young guard inclined his head towards the meeting hall to wordlessly get her moving. She purposefully turned away from Killian, fruitlessly hoping he hadn't put two and two together and recognized her from Washington, though she knew he had. The way he looked at her... He knew.

"I can't," he replied, pressing his lips together sympathetically.

Sybil sighed and marched forward alongside him. The air was hot and thick with moisture. It was silent except for the bullfrogs and crickets singing deep in the woods. The Thanes' boots made a hard thud in the dirt with each step, but Sybil's bare feet pressed into the ground without hardly a sound. Her stomach twisted, and her heart pounded bruises into her chest. She pulled the coat's sleeves over her hands nervously but resisted wrapping her arms around her. She didn't want to look weak or afraid. She *wasn't* afraid.

"Here we go," Jim said as he reached for the meeting hall door and pulled it open, nudging Sybil inside. Killian followed her, but Jim stayed outside. He shut the door behind them. There were no other guards present in the room except Conrad.

Sybil did a double take when she saw the corporal. It appeared Conrad had been rudely awakened as well. The woman, always buttoned up and neatly dressed in her smart uniforms, wore a long robe over a thin nightgown that brushed the tops of her feet. Her red hair was plaited loosely, and the long braid hung over her shoulder to the small of her back. She was clearly uncomfortable to be seen like this by anyone. She looked much younger than Sybil had initially pegged her. In her soft green robe with wisps of hair framing her face, Sybil wondered if she was even over thirty.

The only other individual in the room was Calloway. And she knew instantly. Something had gone very wrong.

Unlike Sybil and Conrad, Calloway definitely did not look like he had been sleeping this night. He wore the same suit, though it was more wrinkled than it had been earlier in the day. His hair, which had been perfectly coifed before, had relaxed. His expression was grim. Hostile.

"Sorry to have woken you, Sybil," he said, his words terse. "We need to have another conversation. Have a seat."

When she didn't move, a hand was placed between her shoulder blades and propelled her forwards. She didn't have to look behind her to know it was Killian.

Conrad cautiously spoke up, "Surely this can wait until morning, Mr. President."

"I'm afraid I disagree with you, Corporal. It cannot wait. And

I think we could use the privacy." A chill ran up Sybil's spine. Why did Calloway suddenly sound so frightening? She checked over her shoulder at Conrad, who stared at the wall in stoic defeat, her mouth in a tight line.

Calloway folded his hands together and rocked forward. "Roxana Bloodknight." He drew the two words out and emphasized the 't' in her last name. Sybil paled. "Oh, so you know her?" The sarcasm dripped from his lips as they curled into a sneer.

"I..."

"Spare me your lies! Do you realize how much trouble you have caused me?" Calloway exploded. He dug his hand into his coat and pulled out a pile of crumpled papers. He aggressively shook them out and held them up to her. She didn't know what they said, but their pictures were front and center in each one. "Look. Take a *look*," he seethed.

He began to read the headlines. "*President of Eastward Takes a Lover. Calloway: Family Man or Assailant? First Lady: 'I'm Leaving My Husband!' Calloway's Affair Exposed: A Timeline.* Hm, let's see. Oh, this one was one of my personal favorites: *Calloway's Family Values Include Mystery Lover.* Let's see, let's see..." He flipped a few pages. "Ah, here is another good one: *Calloway to Seek Professional Help for Insatiable Sexual Appetite.* I must admit, that headline got to me."

Sybil clenched her teeth but forced herself to keep her eyes on him.

Breathing heavily, Calloway haphazardly put his newspapers back in order. His hands shook badly. He let out a loud curse, the papers falling to the floor in a heap. A line of blood formed in the space between his pointer finger and thumb from the paper cut. He visibly wrestled to compose himself as he pulled out a handkerchief and pressed it to his hand. His chest heaved with ragged breaths, his jaw twitched, and his brows drew together.

After a long moment of strained silence, he said, "Show me."

"Show you what?" Sybil was embarrassed at the tremble in her voice when she answered.

"I want to see her. I want to see Roxana."

Sybil resisted glancing back at Conrad for support. "I… there's a boundary since Vox first arrived. No magic for anyone inside."

Calloway's nostrils flared. "It has been temporarily lifted," he growled. "Do it."

Sybil exhaled shakily. With him staring at her, so full of wrath, she felt like she couldn't focus. Like she couldn't breathe. It took her three tries before that familiar warm buzz started at her scalp. Out of practice and under pressure—a bad combination.

Her eyelids fluttered shut as the warmth spread into her fingers, down into her toes. If only the circumstances were different, she could've relished the sensations. *It's been so long.* Foreign and so familiar at the same time.

Calloway's audible gasp broke her stupor.

"Unbelievable," he murmured. He dropped the handkerchief and stepped forward to touch Sybil's cheek. His hand was still bleeding, and she felt the warmth of his blood seep into her skin. His thumb closed around her chin, and he tilted her head to one side and then the other. His hand trailed up to finger the blonde hair.

"Stand up," he said. She obliged, pink filling her cheeks as he analyzed her.

"Amazing. Inches taller… The legs…" Calloway mumbled under his breath. His finger brushed across Roxana's full bottom lip. "So beautiful." He spoke so softly Sybil wasn't sure if she heard him correctly. He pushed off her overcoat which fell to a heap on the bench. Goosebumps broke out along her arms despite the humidity.

"Mr. President..." Sybil heard Conrad protest, but it felt distant. She was completely consumed by Calloway's attention. She felt trapped by it. Was he staying her mind? Was this what it was to be mentally frozen, unable to respond?

Calloway jerked his hand back as if Roxana had burned him, and the spell cast between them was shattered. Clearing his throat, he said, "It doesn't cease to impress me—Shiftwork."

"May I sit back down?"

Calloway nodded once. "And while you're at it, get back to yourself. It's unnerving to see Roxana Bloodknight here of all places." He spread his arms wide.

The buzzing dissipated from her body, leaving her cold and shaky. Her dark hair spread back over her shoulders. She pulled the overcoat back on, and this time, she couldn't fight the temptation to wrap her arms around her body. She pinned her eyes to the ground.

Calloway paced before her. "So, here we are. I don't even know where to begin with you." His tone held a combination of disgust and disappointment. He stopped abruptly in front of her. "Who ordered the op?"

"Classified," she forced out.

An almost maniacal laugh escaped Calloway. "I know it was Vox. I was just testing you to see if you'd be truthful or not."

"How do you know that?" Sybil gasped, taken aback.

"You Shifts are more than happy to stab each other in the back if it gets you a pay day." One of her own told Calloway about her. Betrayed her. There's no other way he could've known.

"Who did you get under your thumb?" Sybil demanded.

"It's classified," he hissed. "Why did he do it? Vox?"

After a moment's hesitation, Sybil said, "I suppose because he is one of the people who doesn't agree with your plan for us. He wanted us to live in peace, on our own, as we always have. He said he wanted to discredit you to help sway the public in favor of alternative plans for us."

"So, you decided to help a man who wants nothing to do with you?"

"Haven't you been listening? We don't want anything to do with *you*! We *want* to be left alone. We have freedom and purpose both."

"Left alone? Is that what Vox suggested? I don't know if *you've* been listening, Sybil—" Calloway said her name with a surprising amount of spite, "—but I don't think 'leaving you alone' is on the table. It never has been."

"Y-you said it was."

"I said there were some who felt we should leave things status quo. I never suggested that was actually a viable option. And I can assure you, it is not one Director Vox supports. He may work in the White House, but he's been very vocal of his opposition to my ideas. He's played you, woman."

"And you're not?"

"Not what? Playing you?" Calloway shook his head and ran a hand through his mussed hair. "How have I led you astray? Manipulated you?"

"You're a Sage. Every word out of your mouth could be a lie, and I-I don't know how I would know."

"You must've heard wild tales about Sages, Sybil," Calloway said with a shake of his head. His voice took on a demeaning tone, and humiliation caused Sybil to drop her gaze again. She felt like a child under his cruel stare. "If I wanted to tell you a lie as a truth, I'd have to beguile you. Did you feel a change in the room? A cloudiness in your head?"

Sybil thought back to when Calloway attempted to read her mind at the White House. "No."

Calloway jutted his chin out and paced again, "It's a conscious choice to read a mind, to speak a lie and make all who hear it believe it's true, just as it is for you to morph into another. Magic may be nonverbal, but you would see its effects—whether a gust of wind, a sheen to a room, a dimness to your mind. Have you noticed any of those things since you've been here?"

"No," she repeated.

"Precisely."

From the back of the room, Conrad firmly said, "Mr. President, I don't think we're making much progress here. We should consider picking this conversation up in the morning."

"I don't think so, Corporal."

"Mr. President, respectfully, what are you seeking to accomplish? I think we all know that whatever Director Vox had in mind, he wouldn't have revealed it all to a Shift, nor would a Shift ask for a blueprint of the long game. They do their job, and that's the end of it. Sybil did her part, just like the other six he hired."

"Other six?"

Conrad froze, her mistake dawning on her. Her eyes closed tiredly.

"What other six, Corporal? I demand an answer!" Calloway shouted, a vein in his forehead popping. The cords of his reddening neck were tight.

Sybil timidly volunteered, "Five Shifts went missing not long after I arrived in Washington for your job. When they came back only a few days ago, they claimed they were each hired by Director Vox. Months before he arrived here to introduce the registration procedures. They won't say anything else to anyone."

"Five? Or six?"

Sybil paused. "There was a sixth. He was already working for Vox when the rest left, but he was part of it as well."

Calloway rested a hand against the table and leaned heavily into it.

Sybil bit her lip. "It sounds to me like Vox has fairly grand plans against you and that he's been workin' on them for a long while now. He mentioned what you had in mind, and I thought he was on our side. It was a job, yes, but, at least for me, I thought I was doin' something to help my kin."

Calloway studied her critically.

"I think that's how the others may have felt too. Whatever Vox told them about you or your administration and plans... He made it very clear it was for our demise. How could we know any differently?" Sybil wasn't sure when she had changed communication tactics and become an open book, but she was desperate.

Perhaps he'd think they're not that unalike—she and he. They both wanted what they thought was best for the Shifts and for themselves.

"Do you know who took my son?" He asked quietly. Sybil was silent.

A bead of sweat dripped down Calloway's forehead. "Names," he said, his voice barely above a whisper now.

"I... I can't do that."

"I need the name," he repeated. "I need to know who took my son."

"No." Sybil violently shook her head, backpedaling. The open book strategy was on the table, but betrayal was not. She was going to be better than her brother. "I may have been sold out by someone, but we're not all the same, President Calloway. I won't give you their names."

"Corporal?" Calloway gestured aggressively to her.

Conrad stepped closer and stood next to the bench Sybil was seated on. Her presence—simultaneously imposing and comforting—relaxed Sybil's nerves a tiny bit. "I think this is something we should discuss in private, Mr. President."

"I disagree."

"Mr. President, it is the *middle of the night*. You haven't slept. You've had a shock. Even a few hours and some time to clear your head—all our heads—would do wonders for us."

Calloway stared at the ceiling for a long moment. Conrad, in a steady tone, said, "Branson. Let the girl go back to her cabin. We will talk more in the morning."

"*No*."

"What more do you want from her? You cannot force her to speak."

"Can't I?" He mumbled. When Calloway lowered his gaze and locked it on Sybil, his pupils were huge. The rage in his eyes frightened her. She immediately felt him attempting to break into her mind. It went cloudy, thick, monochrome.

Fight it. Fight, Sybil. Don't let him in. The clouds vaporized.

This seemed to enrage him further. "I don't understand. Why doesn't it work on you?"

"Mr. President, please," Conrad appealed.

"No. I want to take her back with me."

"What?!" Sybil cried, as Conrad deadpanned: "You cannot be serious."

"Corporal Conrad, you have done an excellent job here, but I now ask that you stay within your bounds. This does not involve you."

"Sir, my job here is to not only supervise the Shifts and keep them from trouble in this interim but also to protect them—from each other and from others. I cannot send a minor away. And with the president, for goodness' sakes. What would people say?"

"She's not a minor. She's a working professional, right, Sybil?"

Calloway squinted pointedly at her.

"It's *highly* inappropriate! And for what purpose would you have her come?" Conrad demanded.

"I have hatched a rather excellent plan, actually, Delilah. Sybil here is going to come back with me to Washington and become the poster child for my Shift rehabilitation campaign."

Sybil jumped to her feet. "Absolutely not!"

Calloway grabbed her arm in a bruising grip, yanking her toward him and out of Conrad's reach. "Then you will leave me no choice but to put you in prison and bring charges against you." His face was inches from hers. "Don't forget—Regis's blood is on *your* hands."

The air was painfully sucked from her lungs, and her mouth dropped open.

A wicked grin spread across Calloway's face. His head bobbed rapidly. "Oh yes, *yes,* I know all about Regis. I was at his funeral. I watched his elderly aunt and his two sisters mourn for him. How much of a struggle did he put up, Sybil?"

Sybil couldn't think, couldn't breathe. Her body shook, as fearful tears trailed down her cheeks. "It was an accident."

"An accident," Calloway repeated. His hold on her arm tightened as his gaze bore down on her. "Was taking my son an accident?" He held her now with both hands, pinning her arms into her sides. "Let me be perfectly clear: if you do not come with me and do exactly as I say *when I say it,* I will make absolutely certain that you will be locked away not because of the false stories against me but for murder in the first-degree. You will never see the sun again, and I will *personally* authorize whatever means are necessary to get you to tell me who kidnapped my son."

"Mr. President, that is *enough.* Back away!" Conrad ordered sternly.

Calloway loosened his grip, and Sybil broke free, stumbling

backwards. Conrad steadied her and then protectively positioned herself between Sybil and the president. Sybil was embarrassed at how she willingly hid behind the corporal but didn't have it in her to do anything about it. She folded her fingers over the tender spots on her arms.

The president smoothed back his hair and straightened his suit jacket with a quick jerk. "It's the best we can do, Delilah. I have every right to prosecute Sybil for her crimes against me and in the death of my butler. You are a Thane; I know you know this. Don't forget your commitment to justice, Corporal, in favor of these people."

"I know my commitment," Conrad replied coolly.

"However, I am a reasonable man," continued Calloway. "I am more than happy to overlook a few things, but it will cost her. I want to know who took my son; I want every bit of information on those six Shifts; and she works for me and my administration, no questions asked."

"What would you have her do?" Conrad asked.

"If she comes back with me, we'll make her the perfect example of what someone can become with the right teaching. The country will see it's entirely possible to integrate the Shifts back into our society. She'll be tutored. She'll learn to read and write. She'll have lessons in homemaking and social skills. Finances. Photo ops, interviews. She could be the best tool in our arsenal to prove the doubters wrong. It'd be for the good of everyone."

"Even after all that's been done," Conrad stated rather than asked.

"As I said, I'm willing to let that go. My oath to my country surpasses my personal grievances. For once, we'll make a Shift truly useful."

"You'll make her into a slave."

"She's always been a slave," Calloway said cruelly. "She could have a far worse master than me. In fact, I can think of a few correctional facilities with temperamental orderlies that would love a crack at her."

A muscle in Conrad's neck twitched. She pivoted and looked down at Sybil. "It's up to you."

"I… I want to think about it," Sybil stuttered.

"You don't get to *think* about it," Calloway fumed. "It's a very simple choice. Either come back with me and live an entitled life in the spotlight—doing what *I* tell *you*," he clarified, "or spend the rest of your days in prison while I seek the death penalty for you."

Sybil felt nauseous. Vox had been right to go after this man. Too strong and manipulative for his own good. She knew the risks when she accepted the op, and now she faced them. Alone.

On the one hand, if she merely accepted her punishment and went to prison, she'd never be accused by her people of being a sellout. A betrayer, like they labeled Art and the others. She would stand firm and unashamed as a Shift. Unless they tortured it out of her. Could she withstand that?

On the other hand, she'd get to experience life outside the beorg again; she'd miss home desperately, but she'd potentially have another role in the bigger picture for her people's future. She'd maybe find chances to influence those around her. Except, she'd be forced into sharing all information with *him*.

"I'm waiting!" Calloway barked.

Sybil didn't have time to weigh her options or to run through every possible scenario. She had to make a decision quickly before the opportunity was lost on her forever. She swallowed the lump in her throat. "I'll go with you."

Conrad's shoulders dropped at her words. Calloway smiled wryly. "Wise choice. Corporal, we'll leave first thing in the morning. I trust you can ensure Sybil is in the car."

"What do I say to the others, sir?" Conrad asked. "They notice when their own are missing."

"Tell them the truth. She is coming to work for me."

"Yes, sir."

"Take her back now. I'd like to get some rest before we leave in a few hours," Calloway ordered.

"Yes, sir. Killian, get Jim from outside and have him return Sybil to her cabin. He is to remain posted outside her door until daylight. She is not to leave that cabin under any circumstances."

Sybil had forgotten about Killian. He'd been in the back the entire conversation; she wanted to bury her face in her hands. To disappear from this humiliating nightmare.

As Killian went to open the meeting hall door, a distinct odor caught Sybil's attention. Distant but growing stronger by the moment.

"Corporal," Sybil began. "That smells like..."

"FIRE!" exploded from Jim as he fell into the meeting hall, colliding straight into Killian who had just turned the doorknob. A hazy light flooded the darkened building.

"Corporal," Jim gasped. "The cabins are all on fire!"

34.

Conrad snapped into action at an impressive speed. She was outside ordering her soldiers around before Sybil had fully processed Jim's message. Killian grabbed her and Calloway by their arms and dragged them from the meeting hall. A horrifying, unbelievable sight greeted them.

Flames engulfed the beorg one cabin at a time with a fire glowing more blue than red. It crawled up and down the cabins like fiery spiders.

"That's no ordinary fire," Calloway said, pressing his fist to his mouth, his eyes wide on the scene before him.

"What was that, sir?" Killian panted.

"This is a Sylvaar fire. I've never seen one in person before. This is a unique type of fire, unique only to them. You can't make it with physical resources; only they can conjure it. This was intentiona—" Calloway's voice drifted.

"James, get the president through the boundary, to his car, and off the mountain this instant. Don't come back here for anything. Your one and only priority is his safety," Conrad instructed, and Killian immediately manhandled Calloway towards the woods. The president sputtered only a minor protest before willingly subjecting himself to his guard and fleeing.

Sybil didn't wait to see what Conrad did or said next. She ducked in front of Jim and sprinted through the chaos to her cabin.

“Sybil! Sybil, come back here! Get to the stream!” Jim shouted after her.

“Don’t worry about her right now,” Conrad reprimanded Jim. “Get the others to safety and keep them there. Evans, you go with him. The rest of you, start fighting these flames. We’ve got to get this out before it spreads. Set up a perimeter; don’t let it reach the trees.”

Sybil couldn’t focus on anything but her path to her cabin. It was complete chaos. Panicked Shifts—young and old—blocked her path in their haste to get clear of the flames. Thanes pushed them towards the river. She elbowed her way through, coughing on the black smoke filling the air.

When she reached her cabin, her heart shattered. The front of the cabin had collapsed into itself, the charred wood melting into a smoking heap.

She fell to her knees, screaming, “Freida! Art! Joan! Roger!” She rotated through her cabin mates’ names as she attempted to dig her way in.

Wood cut into her hands, and her fingers bled; but she didn’t register pain in her frenzy. The smoke choked her, and her coughing grew uncontrollable. Her chest tightened and clenched as it became harder to breathe. Her head swiveled, checking over her shoulder to see if they were already out before returning to her task. It was nearly impossible to see anything in the darkness of night and smoke. The firelight cast strange shadows all around her.

“Kids!” She tried to shout, but her voice came out strangled and weak. She coughed again.

“We’re here! We’re here!” *Dean*.

Tears of relief welled in her eyes. She groped around in the rubble until her hand finally connected with his. “Oh, thank God, Dean!” They worked together to widen the space, and she made out his stricken face.

"Are you all right?" She choked out.

Dean fumbled, "Uh… I… Art! Art—it's Sybil. Help me here!" A sliver of Art's face appeared in the crack. *He's okay! They're okay.*

"Let's get you out. Quickly now!" Sybil said.

Between Dean, Art, and Sybil, they managed to widen the gap. She began pulling the younger ones out—Paul first, then Joan, and finally Nell. Dean began clambering through. Art passed Freida to them before following.

Sybil crushed them to her, weeping, "When I saw the cabin… I thought…"

"It's okay, we're okay," Art mumbled. They broke apart, and Sybil turned to the younger ones. Soot coated their young faces. They couldn't stop coughing. Tears and sweat streaked down their cheeks like angry rivers. All but Nell… Her tiny face was devoid of any emotion. She looked like a corpse. When Sybil reached for her, she went without a word to her. Her hot little body fastened so tightly to her, Sybil could feel her rapid heartbeat against her own.

Dean swiped at a cut above his eyebrow to stay the blood before it could drip into his eye and bent over, trying to gasp in fresh air before realizing it was all thick with smoke.

"We gotta get to the water," Sybil coughed, pointing towards the break in the trees. "Everybody, quickly now. Stay together!"

Art lifted Freida into his arms. Sybil grabbed Paul's hand, and Dean took Joan's. They weaved through the mayhem of the beorg—or what was left of it. Knowing her cabin mates were safe, Sybil dared to slow long enough to take a look. Conrad and her Thanes were still aggressively working to get the fires out. They looked exhausted but in serious focus. But their focus suddenly collapsed when a new fire broke out in the meeting hall, somehow beginning inside and moving outwards like a bomb. The roar was deafening, and the blast knocked the nearby Thanes to the ground.

As quickly as they fell, more took their place to try and get the explosion under control.

She couldn't believe what was happening, but she forced herself to pick up speed and get to safety. The seven of them ran through the woods, soon meeting up with the rest of the Shifts who had gathered at the stream.

Judging by the size of the group gathered, it looked as if Sybil's cabin was one of the last to make it. The Shifts huddled together on the riverbank in various states of undress, covered in soot and ash. Coughs and cries filled the air. Several Thanes stayed alert, whispering to each other quietly and carefully monitoring the group.

Dean, Paul, and Joan collapsed on the river's edge and cupped their hands in the water, drinking, sputtering, and trying again. Art set Freida down and splashed his face and scrubbed at the soot that had sunk into his pores. Sybil couldn't detach Nell from her, but she attempted to lower herself by the water and bring some of it to her lips with one hand.

"Nell. Drink some water," she murmured, tucking her chin to her shoulder as more coughs racked her body before trying again to bring a handful of water to the little girl's mouth. Nell's only response was to bury her face into Sybil's chest and shudder.

Art tried to bring some water to Freida, who lay silently on the bank. Then he fell back onto his heels, then to his bottom, his big shoulder bumping into Sybil. "That was horrifying."

"What even happened?" Sybil rasped.

He hacked into his elbow. "It happened so fast, Syb. We were all asleep and suddenly, it was like a fireball exploded right on the roof. It was like fire rained down from nowhere. By the time I put together what was happening, the beams at the front door had already collapsed. It was pitch black and the smoke... I couldn't begin to figure out how to get out. The kids were panicked and screaming, and… Wait. Where were you?"

"I'll tell you later." Thankfully, Art was too drained to push her. He covered his face with his hand and exhaled slowly.

An orange glow rose into the sky in the direction of the beorg, giving off enough light for Sybil to make out the faces around her. She started taking inventory as best she could. Some of the younger kids had fallen asleep, exhausted. It appeared most of the adults were awake, speaking to one another in hushed voices. Confusion, anger, and fright filled their soot-coated faces.

Sybil couldn't make out anyone with severe injuries, but she knew the Thanes had probably tended to—or were tending to—those individuals. Still, the golden haze illuminated a number of cuts and gashes. Blood-soaked garments. She realized for the first time her own hands were bleeding, shredded from splinters. The pain set in with her awareness, and her stomach rolled. She tried to think of something else immediately.

It wasn't until then, as they settled in from the mayhem up the trail, that she realized Roger wasn't with them.

"Art, where's Roger?"

Art, hunched over and heaving in breaths, didn't move.

"Art?"

He slowly shook his head but couldn't meet her eyes.

Roger didn't make it.

Sybil didn't know how she was supposed to feel or how to react. She felt simultaneously unsurprised and stunned. In many ways, she barely knew Roger. They didn't talk; they didn't play together. She couldn't say what he cared about, who he spent time with outside of the cabin, or what he wanted to do as a shapeshifter. Did he have a girlfriend? Had he ever kissed anyone?

Yet, she felt like a big sister in every sense of the word. She helped him understand what his body could do and watched him shapeshift for the first time; his freckles had disappeared, and he had been ecstatic. She remembered the pride and excitement she felt sharing in that moment with him. They ate their meals together. She knew he was deadly accurate with a knife. That he loved dirty jokes and fishing.

Art cleared his throat. "There was nothin' I could do." His voice quivered.

Sybil swallowed and sniffled, gaining composure. She reached out a throbbing hand to touch his shoulder, pressing a blood stain into his thin t-shirt. "I know. Don't blame yourself. It was an accident."

"It happened so quickly," he repeated. "I couldn't hardly see him, y'know? He didn't make any noise. Something must have knocked him out. He just... He didn't move again."

Sybil didn't want to hear this. It made her feel sick. "It's okay, Art. There's nothin' you could've done."

Art nodded, but it was obvious he didn't believe her. He covered her hand on his shoulder with his and squeezed. She sucked in a breath at the pain, and he pulled back, noticing her raw fingers. "Syb," he breathed. "That doesn't look good at all."

"It's just a few cuts. It could be worse." She could be *dead*. The unspoken thought fell over them. *Dead like Roger.* Her throat constricted.

"Here, let me." Art peeled off the t-shirt he had slept in and put a tear in it with his teeth. He tore it and dipped some of the rags in the water. He rang them out over her hands to try to clean them. She bit down on her lip to keep from reacting. He sloppily wove the cloth around them and shrugged. "I'm no medic, but it'll hopefully protect from something gettin' in there. Infection and stuff."

"Thanks," Sybil said, wrapping her arms once more around Nell, who could have been mistaken for dead if not for her rattling breaths.

A horrible rasping sound caught her attention. Sybil and Art simultaneously twisted to see Freida, laboring to breathe.

Art rushed over. "Freida? Freida?" She was unresponsive. He pressed two fingers to her wrist. "Her pulse is weak."

"Freida?" Sybil murmured fearfully, holding Nell a little bit more tightly.

"I'm going to take her to the Thanes. Stay with the kids."

"Yeah. Go."

"I'm coming!" Dean declared, stumbling to his feet. Art didn't argue. He lifted Freida's skeletal frame and stumbled toward one of the supervising Thanes, Dean close behind. Ash, dust, and splinters coated their hair and faces. With his shirt off, even in the dim firelight, she could see bruising across Art's well-built back. She wondered if it was a new injury or an old one. It dawned on her the Stand was barely a few days ago.

Another cough wracked her body, dislodging Nell who whimpered.

"Nell? Nell, you're okay," Sybil said, craning her neck, trying to get a look at the girl's face. "Are you hurt?" No response. "I know that was scary, but you're safe now. We're all safe." *All but Roger.*

Nell pressed her forehead against Sybil's sternum. She knew it wasn't because of the child, but Sybil suddenly felt like she was suffocating. Like someone was pressing into her neck and not letting up.

She had to get some space.

She needed air.

Roughly, Sybil tried to push Nell off her. "Nell, just let go for a second. Just a second. I need a drink. You do too. We'll settle in until the corporal comes and tells us what to do." Nothing. "Nell, come on. I..." Exhaustion, grief, and pain closed in on her, and she erupted. "Damn it, Nell! *Get off!*"

Immediately, Sybil regretted her outburst. The child jerked her head to look her in the eyes, her waist-length caramel hair falling back and brushing Sybil's legs. Nell stared at her, unblinking, her dry lips parted.

Tears filled her round eyes, her face crumpled, and Nell began to wail. Gut-wrenching, heaving sobs.

Relieved that Nell was still in the realm of the living, Sybil embarrassedly gathered her back to her, letting her rest her head against her chest. Nell's tears quickly soaked into Sybil's nightshirt and into her skin. She shrugged off her overcoat to drape it over them both and softly stroked Nell's hair.

"I'm sorry, Nell. I shouldn't have said that..."

"What's wrong with her, Sybil?" Little Paul stood in front of her, the front of his shirt wet from the water he had been bringing to his lips. Joan stood behind him, positively alarmed.

Comfort them. They're as scared and confused as you are. Sybil awkwardly cleared her throat and said, "She's just tired." *So comforting.*

She gestured for them to come sit by her, and Paul and Joan quietly obliged.

Joan asked softly, "What's going to happen now? We don't have a home anymore." Sybil bit back her initial retort, which was, "At least it wasn't much of a home."

Although it was far from perfect, it *was* the only home any of them knew, and she couldn't deny that. She was in only one other cabin for a short amount of time after arriving in the beorg, and she didn't remember much about it. All of her memories took place in Cabin Thirteen with Art and Freida and, before long, Roger, Dean, Paul, and Joan also. The same went for all of the kids.

Their life was always centered around that cabin and the beorg with the life purpose of using their shapeshifting in whatever jobs they could get. All of that was being stripped away, layer by layer.

Ops, shapeshifting, and now their beorg.

"I really don't know, Joan," Sybil eventually answered. "We'll stick together, and I… I'm sure we'll be okay. We're survivors, you know that?"

Dean returned then, and he settled down next to Paul. He draped his elbows on his knobby knees and rested his chin on them.

"Did you learn anything?" Sybil asked.

"Nah." He shrugged his shoulders slightly. "Art's trying to find out more. I was hoping someone had some food. Oh, but I saw Xavier. He looked okay. Thought you'd want to know."

Guilt shot through Sybil. She'd been so consumed with finding her cabin mates and getting to safety and then the realization of losing Roger that she hadn't even thought of Xavier. "Thanks. And Freida?"

"She's with the Thanes. She can't seem to breathe. I don't know what they're doing to her." *She can't breathe. Not Freida too.*

"Sybil, I'm hungry," said Paul.

"We're just going to have to wait. Doesn't look like the Thanes are letting anyone out of sight right now. Probably for good reason. I'm sure we'll find out something soon, and then we'll be able to hopefully find something to eat. Try to get some sleep."

"Yeah, okay," the kids mumbled in agreement. Nell's body stilled once more, but Sybil could hear and feel her hiccups and sniffles against her chest. She focused on rubbing Nell's back rhythmically. Soon, her own eyes, dry from smoke and grit, grew heavy, and she fell asleep against the old tree with the kids curled up close by.

35.

The loud snap of a branch jerked Sybil out of her fitful sleep. Heart pounding, her eyes anxiously darted around the trees until she remembered where she was and what had happened.

Fire. Roger. Woods. Guards. Calloway. Fire. Roger. Woods. Guards. Calloway. *Freida.*

Her head ached. Her neck was stiff, and she couldn't turn it to the left. Her bandaged hands pulsed with a burning pain, like she was repeatedly being stabbed in the fingers. Her eyes felt gritty, her vision blurry. Sybil rubbed at them with the back of her hand.

At some point while they slept, Nell had slid down and lay with her head in Sybil's lap. Joan slept on her side with her back pressed into Sybil's leg. Dean and Paul lay on her other side. The four kids were fast asleep, despite the hard ground they lay on. Art was nowhere to be found. Maybe he was still with Freida. She wondered how long she'd even been asleep.

Sybil stretched and rolled her neck to one side and then the other. She breathed in shakily and exhaled slowly. *Everything is going to be fine. Everything is going to be fine.*

Several twigs broke from behind. Someone was coming toward her. She couldn't turn to see who it was.

"Who's there?" Her voice came out scratchy and deep and triggered a raspy cough.

"It's me, Sybil." Xavier's tall frame came into view.

"Oh, Xavier, thank God." Sybil collapsed back against her tree with some level of relief. Xavier came around and knelt in front of her. The soft light from the rising sun revealed he was unharmed. He was as dirty and sooty as everyone else, and his sleeveless undershirt had some holes in it, though whether that was from the fire or from wear was up for debate. His hair was knotted against his neck. His face was full of concern without a trace of its usual jocularity.

"I'm sorry I didn't come to see you sooner. Everything has been crazy," he said. "Are you okay?"

"I am. It's been quite the night," she said with a humorless laugh. "You?"

"Yeah, yeah. I'm so glad you're safe," he said softly. His eyes darkened, and he placed a hand on her leg. "I heard about Roger."

"Pretty messed up, isn't it?

"I'm really sorry, Sybil." He was so sincere Sybil wanted to joke about not recognizing him, but she couldn't.

"We'll be okay. It was an accident. Have you heard if anyone else..." Her voice drifted off. "Freida? Have you seen Freida?"

Xavier dropped his eyes, just like Art had when he told her about Roger.

"No," she wheezed.

"The Thanes said she inhaled too much smoke. She's so old, and her lungs were already weakened. I'm sorry, Sybil. Art was with her last I saw."

"I... I need to see her."

"Yeah, okay." Xavier reached for her but paused when he caught sight of her haphazardly bandaged hands. His fingers curled around her wrist. "Hey, have you had your hands looked at?"

"I washed 'em out. They're fine."

"Washed them out, or touched some water and called it a day?"

"The latter," replied Art from above. Xavier and Sybil looked up to find him standing over them. He was still shirtless, and in the morning light, his bruising looked much worse than it had in the dark. "She can't argue because I'm the one who did it. Xavier, why don't you take Sybil to the water and help her out with that? I'll stay here with the kids."

"Good idea," Xavier said.

Did it really take their entire beorg burning down for the two men in her life to have a civil conversation? *That's just stupid,* she thought incredulously, feeling a little like she was in some alternate universe. Or a dream. *Yeah—a dream! Maybe all of this has been some really, really bad dream.* Her hands hurt enough to remind her she wasn't dreaming and to stop being foolish.

"But... Freida. Art, where's Freida?"

"They took her already, Sybil," Art said sadly. "She's gone."

"But... but I..." Sybil couldn't think, couldn't function.

"Xavier, take her to get a break," Art said, his eyes pained.

"But... Nell..." she protested.

"I'll be right here with Nell when she wakes. The kids are tougher than you think. Don't you remember how you were at their age? They'll be fine. Besides, if you don't get your hands properly checked out and bandaged, they could get infected."

"It's just some cuts and splinters. Please, I want to see Freida," she said again.

"She's gone, Sybil, you can't. I'm so sorry." Art's eyes were glassy with his own unshed tears. "Take her, Xavier." Art pulled Nell from Sybil's lap, and Xavier gently tugged her to her feet. He wrapped an arm around her waist. Her whole body felt sore.

"Wait!" She planted her feet. "Art, did you find anything out? Do they know who started it?" Xavier stilled beside her and looked expectantly at Art.

"Not that anyone knows of, guards included. Sounds like most of the buildings took a pretty good hit. The fire was some magical Sylvaar thing. It burns hotter and faster than a regular fire. No serious injuries. A few broken ribs and sprained ankles. A few people got burned pretty bad, but the Thanes took care of 'em nearly immediately. They'll be okay. The flames are out; Conrad is probably just figuring out what happens next. I'm sure we'll be allowed up from the stream before long."

"How could this have happened?" Sybil swayed on her feet.

Xavier shrugged. "We may never know. Just gotta pick up the pieces and move forward. What are Shifts good at if not that?"

"True words," Art replied. "Now go on, before everyone wakes and starts asking questions. This place is gonna be madness."

A warm breeze ruffled the dewy grass. The stream bubbled and splashed against its bank, so clear you could see the small fish as they went along with the current. Nothing had rocked their little world.

The sun wasn't quite high in the sky, but in the pockets where tree branches didn't create a canopy, it cast its warmth and brightness down into the woods below. It was a perfect picture of a spring morning.

Except it was so far from that.

Xavier and Sybil walked past dozens of Shifts sleeping anywhere they could find a space—on the bank of the water and up by the trees on the grass. The air smelled strongly of smoke and body odor. Thane guards moved about the crowd, making sure everyone was accounted for and checking on those who had been injured and tended to in the night. It was a pathetic sight. The Shifts had never looked more haggard, filthy, or desolate. She couldn't stop looking for a glimpse of Freida's body, unable to believe she was gone already.

Xavier led them away from the makeshift camp but still easily in view of the Thanes. They crouched on the bank of the river, and he gingerly began unwrapping her hands. She sucked in a breath sharply as it tugged and pulled at her skin. Blood had dried and caked on the cloths.

"Sorry." Xavier bit his lip, trying to figure out how to make it hurt less. "Maybe this is worse than I thought. I'll flag down one of the Thanes to fix you up."

"No!" Sybil exclaimed a little too loudly. "N-no. I'll just... soak them off."

"I don't know if that'll work..."

She thrust her bandaged hands into the water. "It'll be fine."

"Why are you being so stubborn?"

"I don't want their help!" She snapped.

Xavier sat back on his heels and lifted his hands in defeat. "Fine. Do it your way."

Sybil's lower back quickly grew sore from where she hunched over the water, her hands dangling uselessly in it. The damp ground of the bank soaked into the knees of her trousers. She tossed her head to get her hair out of her face. It quickly fell back in her eyes.

"This is ridiculous."

"Oh, I have a piece of twine. I'll tie it back for you."

"Not my hair, Xavier!" Sybil cried. "This! Everything!"

Xavier bit his lip and watched her.

"I... I'm sorry," she tried to laugh her overreaction off, but it came off far too maniacal to be settling for Xavier. "It's just, I mean... This has all been *pretty* crazy, don't you think?"

"Crazy. We've established that." Xavier arched an eyebrow.

"I mean, forget about the last few months of complete chaos. The president just showed up here and wants to take me back with him. And then our home burns down. It's almost comical, isn't it?"

"Calloway is taking you back to Washington?" Xavier asked

incredulously.

Sybil wilted. “He was going to. I don’t know what will happen now.”

“Why didn’t you say anything about Calloway before?” Xavier pulled her hands out of the water and tried again to unwind the bandages. They still tugged at her skin but started coming off more easily than before.

“I told you that would work,” Sybil said, nodding her head to the soggy pieces of Art’s shirt Xavier was piling up beside him.

He held her gaze. “Why didn’t you tell me about Calloway?”

She sighed. “I didn’t have a chance. It was in the middle of the night. I was in the meeting hall with him when the fires started. That’s why… That’s why I wasn’t there to help Art and get the kids out.”

Xavier’s fingers paused. “You did get them out though. These hands prove it.”

“If I had been there… If I hadn’t been spending my time arguing and haggling with Calloway… I could’ve helped. I could’ve saved Roger and…” Freida’s name died in her throat, and she dropped her head.

“You know that’s not true. It’s not your fault.” Xavier tilted her chin up. “C’mon, it’s not your fault. None of this is,” he repeated, his hand moving from her chin to cup her cheek. “You being there wouldn’t have changed anything.”

She couldn’t look at him. “I was going to leave them all.”

“Only because you felt you had to.”

Sybil couldn’t hold her tears back any longer. They poured down her cheeks—ugly, snotty, gasping tears. She tried to cover her face with her hands, but Xavier tugged her to him before she could. She cried into his shoulder. She cried for Roger. She cried for Freida. For her home. For the unknowns they all faced. She cried because her hands hurt, her eyes stung, and she was hungry.

Xavier said nothing but held her close. As her sobs lessened, she heard an occasional sniffle from him, and she knew she wasn't the only one struggling with the loss. With the chaos and the looming future. She looked up at him with watery eyes and brushed a tear from his cheek. His face reddened, but he didn't pull back. Instead, he rested his cheek against her palm, as though trying to tell her without words they could be weak together. At least for a little bit.

They held each other for a few more somber moments before Sybil knew it was time to toughen up again. She sniffed and reached out to unstick his tear-soaked shirt from his skin. "Sorry," she said with an embarrassed laugh.

"It's okay."

"No telling anyone about this, right?"

"Of course not. Our secret." She gratefully accepted the tender kiss he brushed on her lips. "Let me finish with your hands," he said. They were silent as he re-bandaged them neatly with strips from his shirt, his thick sandy brows pinched together in concentration.

"What are we going to do, Xavier?" she asked wearily when he finished and washed his hands off in the stream.

"Accept the fact that life isn't going to be the same again," he said with a small shrug.

"Hey!" A voice called from the line of trees. Sybil and Xavier jumped and looked around. An older Thane guard—Sybil couldn't recall his name—waved them over. They scrambled to their feet and approached cautiously. Sybil held her aching hands tight to her chest.

"Corporal Conrad is calling us back," the guard said. "You need to get going with the others." He gestured with his baton towards a line of Shifts forming and making their way up the hill. Xavier exchanged an uncertain glance with Sybil, and they wordlessly joined.

36.

The trek back to the beorg felt more arduous than ever. Sybil wasn't sure if it was from smoke inhalation, fatigue, or dread that made it feel so much longer and steeper to her. She felt like she couldn't get a deep breath, and every time she did, she began coughing. She and everyone else, it seemed. Sweat formed on her forehead. Her thin nightshirt clung to her back, and her hair stuck to her neck.

The Shifts walked in solemn silence—a state she wasn't used to anyone being in, much less all at the same time. Trepidation and doom was evident on each dirty face. Nothing but the sound of coughing and leaves and sticks crunching underfoot filled the air.

News of Freida and Roger's deaths had spread throughout the night, and Shifts kept glancing at the residents of Cabin Thirteen pityingly.

Though Sybil braced herself, she wasn't prepared to see the charred remains of the beorg when they broke through the woods to the clearing. Audible gasps went through the displaced Shifts as they processed the ruins of what had been their home for generations.

Sybil brought a shaking hand to her mouth as a pile of rocks settled in her stomach. Xavier beside her hung his head and sucked in a sharp breath. A few Shifts began to weep. Terrible, desperate, completely depleted cries.

The usually lush, dewy grass was scorched. Of the thirteen cabins, only four remained intact and standing, though some of the external walls looked as though they had been painted with charcoal. Smoke rose in graceful tendrils from piles of burned logs and planks. Broken wooden tables, chairs, and shelves from the interior cabins had been thrown into piles.

The stone fireplace was the only standing feature from the meeting hall the Shifts had worked so hard to assemble. They had been so proud of it, and now it was ash and debris. Firewood.

Conrad stood before them amidst the rubble, no longer in her nightdress but in her orderly uniform, flanked by her Thanes. Compassion shone in her eyes. She opened and closed her mouth twice before speaking:

"I—uh..." She cleared her throat and tilted her chin up. "I'm sorry to each of you for what has happened to your home. I'm sorry for the loss of two of your kin. I know you are each experiencing grief and shock in your own ways, and I wish more than anything I could give you time to process those feelings, as well as rebuild your lives here..."

Sybil watched as Conrad fixated on something above their faces, obviously trying to appear as though she was meeting their eyes while being unable to.

"Unfortunately, I cannot allow you to do that." The woman took a steadying breath. "As you may have suspected, the fire that occurred here was not accidental, nor was it natural fire. It, in fact, was fire that only Sylvaar magi conjure and control. We are entering into an investigation to figure out who conjured it and why. President Calloway managed to escape the danger unharmed and has been taken back to the capital."

Was Sybil off the hook now? Their verbal agreement burned up in the fire as well?

"As for each of you, you are..." Conrad bit her lip. "You are immediately being escorted to an off-premises facility. There are five vehicles waiting at the end of the road outside the boundary to… transport you."

"What?!" roared several Shifts, outrage replacing sorrow.

"Where are they taking us?" Laurel cried.

"We didn't do nothin' wrong!" Bo exclaimed.

Conrad's resolve faltered. "I hear what you're saying, I do. But you have to understand how this is being perceived. The president came here for off-the-record talks with you, and while here, his life was put in jeopardy. This is being taken very seriously. It has to be."

"What, they think we burned down our own home to kill the president? That's absurd!" Art shouted. Sybil looked around and found him at the front with the kids, Nell in his arms.

"Yeah, if we were gonna kill him, we'd do it without killin' our own at the same time!" Dean contributed harshly. His pubescent voice cracked on the last words.

"I didn't say you conspired to kill him. But a full investigation has to be conducted, and, in the meantime, you can't stay here. Not until conclusions are drawn from facts."

"Who is runnin' this investigation?" Virgil demanded, painstakingly moving his way toward the front of the crowd.

"I'm not at liberty to say. It is an outside party."

"Why aren't you doing it? You know we wouldn't have done something like this, Conrad!" Marnie said.

"It doesn't matter what I believe." Conrad slowly shook her head. "It happened under my watch. My entire operation—including every one of my guards who put themselves in danger to extinguish this fire and, don't forget, care for your wounded—is also under examination. I'm sorry, but this is out of my hands now." She took several steps back and nodded towards her guards. "Escort them to the trucks, please."

An uproar followed Delilah Conrad as she turned her back on

them and disappeared into her tent.

"Conrad, let us bury our dead first! Please!" Laurel cried after her. Conrad did not look back.

The Thane guards surrounded the crowd of Shifts. It was clear on their faces they felt disconcerted as they herded the group away from their home.

Sybil didn't detect compassion in their eyes as much as she did doubt, as though they didn't quite believe in what they were doing anymore than Conrad did. They were fairly understanding and considerate at first, guiding them without force. But as some of the Shifts tried to protest and fight back, the guards stood their ground and whipped out their batons. Bo assaulted the guard nearest him, but it only led to him being cuffed and taken to the front with his nose bleeding.

They jostled the weary group through the beorg boundary and down the old trail. The same trail she and Art had used to get to Miltown. A lifetime ago.

Sybil noticed Xavier's body tense as Dan and Glen tried to make a break for it. It took four guards to wrestle them down and handcuff them as they had Bo. "I know what you're thinking," she whispered. "Don't join that fight."

"I wasn't going to."

"Don't lie. I could see it written all over your face. You think this is totally unfair and unjustified. You're always one of the first to jump in with guns blazing."

"Not this time," he mumbled.

"What's that supposed to mean?" she asked as they walked side by side at the back of the procession.

"Nothing."

"Xavier, do you know something?"

"No."

"What did you do? You did something, didn't you?"

"Shut up, Sybil. You don't know what you're talkin' about." He looked around anxiously.

"Like hell, I don't!" She dug her nails in his arm, trying to slow his pace. "I am going to call a guard over here if you don't fess up. Tell me *now*—before we're separated. Please." *Don't lie to me too.*

"This isn't the time. There are people all around," he said.

"There may not be another time!" Sybil argued urgently. "You know something, and I want to know what it is."

"It's nothing," he deferred.

"Then why hide it?"

Xavier swore and raked a hand over his face, frustrated. His eyes darted back and forth, and he snuck a glance over his shoulder.

"Stop making a big deal out of it. Just talk, like we're having a normal conversation, and they won't think twice about it," Sybil said, feigning outward calm as a storm raged inside her.

"And if they do come over here and ask?"

"I don't know. Just profess your love for me or something dramatic. Now tell me!"

Xavier groaned but slowed to walk in step with her. He kept his eyes forward, his shoulders hunched, as though trying to make his tall frame as small as possible. He spoke softly, to the point that even Sybil had to strain to hear his words, barely moving his mouth.

"He contacted Dan and Ethel first. And they looped in Bo and Tanner..."

"Who did?"

Xavier looked around again before whispering from the side of his mouth, "Vox."

Sybil stopped in her tracks. "What?"

"You heard me the first time. Walk. Before someone sees."

Xavier tugged her forward.

"Vox?" She repeated, tripping over a tree root in the ground.

"Well, not personally," he amended hastily. "He sent someone in his place. I didn't meet him. Dan and Ethel said Vox had another job that would help protect us from Calloway's plans. All of us. If not protect, then at least delay them. He told them to start a few fires, and he'd take care of the rest. He said no one would get hurt, but it would ideally change Calloway's mind about removing us from the beorg."

"Why didn't Art say anything?" Sybil whispered, looking in the direction of her cabin mates.

"Art didn't know." At Sybil's surprise, he explained, "Dan, Ethel, Bo, and Tanner didn't feel like they could trust Laurel and Art. Thought they'd squeal to Conrad. They didn't involve them, kept it secret."

"Then how do *you* know this?" she asked the question, but she knew the answer already. Her heart sank.

"They asked me. They needed more bodies," he replied. She wasn't sure if it was shame or regret she heard in his voice.

"Xavier, what have you done?" Her growing mortification was overwhelming. Suffocating.

"It wasn't supposed to turn out like it did!" Xavier defended. "It was natural fire, I swear. We even picked Ethel and Bo's cabins; they promised both would be completely empty. I was just keeping watch for the guards. That's it, I swear, Sybil!" His voice broke. "Then all of a sudden, as soon as we got that one fire going... It was like someone threw dynamite on it. It exploded. Everything went haywire. Fire started raining down. Eruptin' from nothing. You saw it yourself!"

Sybil couldn't speak. She stared at him, her eyes tracing the sweat trailing down from his damp hairline.

"I had no idea, Sybil. No idea. I don't know if the others did or not, but no one told me. They just needed eyes. An extra body if someone spotted them and they needed help defending themselves. That's all."

The pleading desperation in his voice—to convince her or to convince himself—brought tears to her eyes. She blinked them away. She shouldn't have pushed him. Not right now, not here. Surrounded by their kin, shuffling along as prisoners to God knows where.

He'd been right. This wasn't a conversation they could have here. It wasn't the conversation she thought they'd be having at all. She had needed to know, but now she wanted her ignorance back. But that wasn't an option. She couldn't look at him.

"Sybil, please. Look, it had to be Vox's man he sent. He was Sylvaar. He's the one who cast that fire; I'm sure of it. Sylvaar are the only ones who conjure. I think Vox did it to frame all of us. It's the only explanation! I think we've been wrong about him!" Xavier pulled up short and placed his hands on either side of her face. "Believe me, Sybil. I didn't know. I never would've... No one was supposed to get hurt," his voice broke. She knew he was referring to Roger and Freida.

She steeled herself. "I'm going to go be with my kin."

"No, Sybil, I'm sorry! I can explain... Please, Sybil. I don't know what's about to happen, where we're gonna go."

Sybil avoided his gaze. "Let me go."

"Syb..."

"Let me go, Xavier!" She cried.

"What's going on here?" A guard demanded, appearing and breaking them apart. "Come on now. Keep moving!"

Sybil used the opportunity to dart into the crowd and toward Art and the kids. She swiped at her cheeks with her sleeve and tried to subtly clear her throat before she made it to them.

"Oh, there you are," said Art. He carried Nell in his arms. Joan, Paul, and Dean walked next to him. Small Paul seemed ready to drop. "I was starting to worry."

"I got held up in the back," she lied. This appeased everyone. She reached out and took Nell from him. Art nudged Paul and swung him up to his back to give him a break.

"They'll probably load us by age or by cabin, so just stay nearby for now," Art said matter-of-factly, as if this was just the next step of an op. He was preparing himself. Preparing them.

"Of course," she replied, shifting Nell around. She resisted checking back over her shoulder to see Xavier. She couldn't get his broken face out of her mind. Or Freida's soot-covered one. Or Roger's.

37.

Waiting at the end of the road, in nearly the exact spot where Sybil had ditched the Bloodknights' chauffeur at the conclusion of her op, were five bulky pickup trucks. Underneath dust and dried, caked mud, the front cabs were a faded shade of red. The beds were made up of old wooden planks, like rickety chicken coops on wheels. She had to assume they were commissioned from some civilians in a small town nearby—maybe even Miltown—because they were definitely not military or commercial vehicles. She almost expected old farmers to step out of the driver's seat, but they were Thanes—uniformed, armed, and serious.

Their uniforms didn't resemble what the army guards wore back at the beorg. They were of a paler green, more like the herbs found in the woods. They had pistols strapped to their sides and batons, but none of the larger weapons the guards of the beorg carried. A different branch perhaps? Sybil had no way of knowing.

"All right, you lot. Split up. Women over here, men over there," a Thane ordered from behind her. He was a beefy fellow who had arrived with Conrad when she succeeded Peter Gable. Harry Sterns, she thought his name was. "Start loading those trucks."

Verbal protests broke out, but, to Sybil's surprise, no one lifted a fist or tried to make a run for it this time. Did everyone feel as resigned to their fate as she did?

She was done fighting. For months, she tried to have hope for their future. She did her part, going to Washington. Even agreeing to go back with Calloway was for her kin more so than for herself. It seemed everything she did ultimately failed, and she wasn't sure she had anything more to give at this point. She was tired, confused, and betrayed. *First Art, now Xavier.*

Sybil took Joan's hand and, without making eye contact with Art, Paul, or Dean, was the first to break from the group and approach a truck. Joan resisted her, squirming and trying to wrench her wrist free.

"I don't want to go! I don't want to go!" She let out a few high-pitched, frustrated squeals and then shouted, "I'm not going!"

Sybil, aware others were watching them, yanked Joan toward her and bent at the waist so they were eye-to-eye. In a low, cold voice, she snapped, "No one cares what you want! We're leaving whether you like it or not. Now get on the damn truck."

At first, Joan's almond-shaped eyes rounded, startled by Sybil's harshness; but then they narrowed as resentment filled them. She jerked her chin up angrily and snatched her hand free. Flipping her stringy straight hair over her shoulder, Joan marched the opposite direction to the truck furthest away from where Sybil and Nell stood and climbed in the back without a word.

Several Thanes snickered to each other. Sybil could feel the heat in her face and the eyes on her back. Anger boiled in her stomach. If Joan didn't want to try and stick together as part of their makeshift Cabin Thirteen family, that was fine by her. Sybil wasn't going to waste her energy on Joan.

She set her jaw as she lifted Nell into the truck bed and followed her in. They settled in the back, closest to the cab. Sybil situated Nell on the bench next to her, even as she tried to crawl back into her lap. The kid had to toughen up, but she couldn't resist putting an arm around Nell's bony shoulders.

With her weight off her feet, she realized how sore they were. She, and most of the others, were barefoot, having been so rudely roused from sleep. Sybil could feel tiny pieces of rock lodged into her feet but resisted picking them out, not with the others watching her. Her feet throbbed alongside her bandaged fingers.

Harry's loud, oily voice broke in, "Glad someone did as I asked. Get on it now before I split you up."

Dragging their feet and casting loathing glances at the guards, the rest of the Shifts merged into two groups and, as directed by the Thanes, clambered onto the truck beds. A few exchanged hugs with one another or squeezed hands as they passed, the unknown of the future hitting hard.

Sybil kept her gaze straight ahead, her back erect, hoping her face was unreadable. She knew there was a high probability that she'd never see those men again. Perhaps not even the women in the other trucks.

Art, Dean, Paul

Virgil, Bo, Glen, Dan, Tanner, Penn.

Xavier.

And so many others she couldn't remember even speaking to. She didn't know their ages, couldn't remember their names, had no idea what their skills were or what ops they had been on in their careers; and now she never would. She had never cared before. *What good would it do to care now? It's over.*

For a brief moment, she wondered if she was about to have a heart attack the way her heart seized up. Would it only be her and Nell from now on? It may not even matter; they could all get the death penalty considering how unhinged Calloway actually was.

Or how unhinged Vox was.

There was no way they'd get out of this.

Perhaps she should've forgiven Xavier. Reconciled, so at the very least her parting moment and memory of him wasn't throwing Roger's death at him. But how could she ever forget something like that? Roger burned to death. Freida suffocated. They'd never have a chance to lay his bones to rest, if they hadn't been turned to ash before Conrad extinguished the flames, and the Thanes stole Freida's body away before the Shifts could bury her properly and give her the honor she was due. She deserved better.

The sun was hot overhead. Between her dry throat from inhaling smoke and the long walk down the mountain with Nell in her arms, thirst set in with a vengeance, and sweat poured off her. Nell's body heat was stifling, and Sybil was relieved her overcoat had been shed and left by the stream.

The truck bed rocked under new weight as women boarded. They were recognizable to Sybil. She wasn't sure if she was glad for this or not. Part of her wanted to be alone, to suffer whatever was coming in private shame. The other part of her felt a sliver of comfort that, whatever came, she wouldn't be entirely on her own.

Marnie, Laurel, and a woman Sybil rarely interacted with named Ingrid sat across from her. They were the closest to her in age out of the group. She was dismayed that Ethel squeezed in next to her, pinning her against the back window of the truck. There were two children in addition to Nell. One girl seemed quite independent and sat proudly in her seat, much like Joan would. The other kept close to an older woman who likely cared for her.

It was cramped on the two wooden benches. Four would've fit comfortably on each, but there were seven on one and eight on the other. The truck bed was not wide, and their blistered, dirty feet bumped together.

Although it was open-aired, the breeze only circulated the stench of their bodies. They were sweaty and reeked of smoke.

Nell shuddered next to her, and that's when Sybil noticed the warm liquid seeping into her trousers. Nell had wet herself.

Ethel jumped to her feet, bumping several women into each other and kicking Ingrid across from her. A string of foul words streamed from her mouth, and she raged, "You disgusting little brat! You pissed all over me!" She gestured wildly to a small, damp spot against her upper thigh.

Nell began crying, her fragile frame shaking, her head hung low in embarrassment. Sybil immediately stood her up and tugged her away from Ethel's flailing limbs. Nell's nightgown was wet between her legs, and a dark wet spot had indeed formed on the wooden bench.

When none of the other women did anything but stare and try to avoid being spat on by Ethel, Sybil clenched her teeth and took Nell in her arms, pulling her onto her lap. The stale, bitter smell of urine settled in quickly, but she made herself not care. She adjusted Nell so her head was resting on her chest and stroked her hair.

"It's okay," she whispered to her. Sybil supposed she wasn't quite finished trying to comfort and care for this child.

All the while, Ethel ranted and begged a Thane to let her off the truck. Shifts in other trucks were watching them, and a surge of anger flooded Sybil.

"Good grief, woman, would you sit down!" She cried at Ethel, tightening her hold on Nell.

"What did you just say to me?" Ethel turned slowly to face her.

Sybil bit out, "Sit down. And *shut up.*"

"How dare you! Do you wanna go? Because I'll go with you." Sybil forced herself to stay seated and straightened her posture as Ethel loomed over her and Nell. She could smell her stale breath and see her little yellow teeth.

"Break it up," said the supervising guard finally, climbing into the truck bed and sticking his baton between the two of them. "You—"

he addressed Ethel, "Sit yourself down and stop with the trouble."

"I want on a different truck!" Ethel insisted, turning her red-rimmed eyes to the guard.

He laughed and poked her with his baton, "You're in no position to make demands, missy."

"Don't you 'missy' me!" Ethel shrieked, her great chest heaving as she batted the baton away. She nearly snatched it, but the guard was quick.

With a lazy wave of his arm, he hollered, "Any of you ladies going to take one for the team?" There was a long silence. "There you have it," he raised his eyebrows at Ethel.

"Wait!" interjected a young voice. Sybil arched to see around the guard. Joan was standing up in her truck bed, her face pale. "I'll switch with her."

"I was just joking, kid," the guard said.

Harry Sterns, from his post surveying the scene at the start of the trail, threw his cigarette to the ground, stomped on it, and ordered, "Let them switch, Officer Byron. Then move out!"

Byron pursed his lips together in surprise before shrugging, hopping off the truck, and dragging Ethel with him. He returned with Joan, who clambered up and took Ethel's spot. She said nothing to Sybil and didn't look at her or Nell.

Sybil wet her bottom lip and took a deep breath. She removed one hand from Nell's back and, without glancing in her direction, took Joan's hand and squeezed it. Joan squeezed it back.

Officer Byron pushed up the tailgate and fastened it with several latches. He tapped on it hard with his baton, and, with a loud roar and a jolt, the trucks promptly started up, nearly in unison with each other. Exhaust filled the air as they lurched forward and took off down the winding road.

Last to leave, Sybil was forced to watch the other pickups pass by, one by one. She spotted Paul and Dean with Art. She didn't manage to make eye contact with Xavier when his truck rolled by, but she stared at the back of his head until she couldn't see him anymore.

Their truck drove about four car lengths behind the others. One Thane officer drove; another sat in the front, armed. Sybil briefly ran an escape scenario through her head, but she knew it was pointless. She knew she didn't truly have it in her to do it, and a half-hearted attempt would undoubtedly be disastrous. The trucks moved at a fast pace as soon as the roads evened out at the foot of the mountain. No way would the Thanes not notice, and they'd be on them before she would be able to find a spot to hide.

Besides, she knew she couldn't leap *with* Nell and Joan, and she had grown resolute to not abandon them. She didn't want to be their mother, but she couldn't live with herself if she left them to face their fate alone. They lost Freida; they didn't deserve to lose her too.

38.

The women rode in silence for nearly two hours. The trucks moved at a fast pace, and it was impossible to hear one another over the engines. Their hair whipped violently in their faces. All too frequently, a rock or stick was kicked up by the tires and grazed their bare arms and legs. The wind was harsh, and the sun bore down on them. Sybil tried to shelter Nell as much as possible with her body, and, before long, Joan pressed up against her and bent her head down too.

Eventually, they approached a town, and the pace of the trucks slowed, their engines quieting. Sybil's ears rang.

It was Laurel who took advantage of the decreased noise and spoke first, "May not hurt to know each other's names." Her voice was scratchy and triggered a cough from deep in her chest. "Who knows how long we'll be together."

Her face was fairly expressionless, but the corner of her mouth quirked upwards. Laurel was not quite twenty and had been one of the strongest and quickest Shifts when she came of age to work. Lately, Sybil had regarded her with a great deal of skepticism as one of the six under Vox's thumb. But now she watched her curiously, finding her level-headed despite their situation. So far, at least.

Marnie, sitting next to Laurel, nodded. "Yeah—all right. I'm Marnie. I've been living in Cabin Two. Been working for about six years."

After Marnie and Laurel was Ingrid. She had lived in Cabin Four with Ethel and Glen and seemed more comfortable staying silent and blending in. Sybil could only imagine the dysfunction living with Ethel. She'd probably try to disappear too.

Then there was Rosie—nearly fifty and an old lover of Virgil's. She didn't volunteer this, but everyone knew it. She was very thin, and her tanned skin sagged against her bones. Her coarse black hair was streaked with gray and hung in a thick braid down her back. She reminded Sybil of Freida at a younger age.

Molly and Daisy came from Cabin Eleven. Daisy was the girl Sybil estimated to be about Nell's age. She had the same gaunt face Nell had from the lack of consistent nutrition but was much more gangly, with long skinny legs and arms.

The last two women on the bench across from Sybil were Olive and Gemma—probably in their low to mid-thirties. They were unrelated but uncannily resembled each other with pale blonde hair and brown eyes.

Laurel looked expectantly at Sybil to speak next, as the first in line on their row. She cleared her throat and mumbled, "Sybil. From Cabin Thirteen. And this is Nell. She's seven, and Joan."

Joan offered, "I'm twelve."

"They're both from Cabin Thirteen as well," Sybil said.

"You're the one who went working right after Vox came, aren't you?" Gemma asked, her eyes narrowing.

Sybil couldn't hold in her scoff. "Yeah, you could say that. Sent me to Calloway." Several eyebrows went up in either surprise or disbelief.

Molly laughed. "He sent you? What are you, fourteen?"

Sybil tilted her chin up. "Seventeen, actually. Hope that's okay with you."

Laurel quickly asked the woman next to Joan her name. It

was Sophie. Her voice was clear and confident and held a level of authority and experience. Mabel introduced herself next. She was easily the oldest woman in the group. Her silver hair was cropped close to her head, and her back was hunched.

"I don't know most of you. Don't recognize your voices," Mabel said. "It's probably important for you to know I'm blind as a bat. My years of working were long over before any of this crap got started. But I can still hold my own, so don't try anything on me." Her voice was low for a woman's, and, when she lifted her head, Sybil noticed a creaminess to her eyes, like a film pulled over the irises.

Mabel patted the child sitting next to her on the shoulder. "This here next to me is Annie. She's nine and mute," she explained. "Unwanted even amongst our kin. We stick together."

"Thank you, Mabel," Laurel said. "That just leaves..."

"Me," the last woman spoke. "Shauna." And that was all she offered.

"Okay then." Laurel lifted her hands. "There we have it then. Thanks, ladies."

"You aren't expectin' us to start some kinda quilt sewing circle, are ya?" asked Rosie.

"Absolutely not," Laurel said. "That's not who we are. Just thought we could try to have each other's backs some..."

"You aren't the leader here, child," Mabel said, her face tilted towards the sun. "I, for one, haven't forgotten your dealings with the devil." *Vox.*

"I'm not trying to be a leader," Laurel said. "I just... I thought it was somewhat sensible to know each other. If we're going to be cooped up together for God knows how long. I'd consider us allies more than friends, but y'all can make that decision for yourselves." Laurel fell silent, crossing her arms over her chest and looking past Sybil at the passing landscape.

The truck's speed soon increased again as they reached the end of the town limits, and the wind and engine drowned out any further discussion by the group. Sybil wasn't sure how much time went by, but before long, Nell fell asleep, her head drooping onto Sybil's breast.

Joan whispered in Sybil's ear, "I have to pee."

"You're going to have to hold it," Sybil whispered back.

"I can't."

"You have to."

"My head hurts," Joan said.

"Mine does too." The hot sun and the constant whipping of the wind in their ears had Sybil's temples pounding and her neck aching. "Close your eyes and try to rest."

"I can't."

"Try."

Just when Sybil thought she may join Nell in the blissful ignorance of sleep, Joan poked her rib. "Sybil?"

Her eyes snapped back open. "What?"

"I couldn't hold it." The burning embarrassment in Joan's voice told Sybil all she needed to know.

"It's okay," Sybil replied in her ear. "You couldn't help it."

"My clothes are wet."

"I know."

"What do I do?"

"Nothing. Just have to wait." Joan scooted closer to Sybil and leaned her head on her arm, her eyelids drooping. Sybil took her hand in hers. When Joan moved, it revealed the urine spot on the bench. Sophie glanced at it beside her and then to Sybil. Sybil couldn't keep the blush from her cheeks and turned her face away. She wasn't going to apologize for the children. Not for something like this. But it *was* embarrassing.

The swaying of the truck soon lulled Laurel, Marnie, Mabel, and the other two young girls to sleep. Ingrid stared at her feet as if she was in a trance. Molly, Gemma, and Olive spoke lowly to each other over Daisy's still form.

Sybil wished she could doze off too, but every time she closed her eyes, her mind whirled, her thoughts bouncing off each other chaotically. She thought of Roger, reduced to charred remains in their cabin. Freida buried in an unmarked grave in their woods.

She pictured Xavier striking a match behind Cabin Four. It was so vivid she could see his long hair hanging over his shoulder and the sandy beard across his cheeks and chin in the firelight. She could see his fingers deftly maneuvering the kindling and his thin lips blowing onto the sparks. Physical pain shot through her heart, as though someone had taken it and driven a knife through it.

Could she judge him though, she wondered? She rested her right temple against the truck window. Xavier did what he thought was best for his people. He listened to Vox, just as Art had. And Laurel, Ethel, Bo, and the others. And herself. She worked with Vox. She killed a man for his op.

Sybil couldn't begin to imagine what the future would be for them. She hated the thought of that being her last goodbye to her brother and the boys. That she hadn't kissed Xavier goodbye. If it was found out he participated in the fires, would he face a different sentence? Would he be taken elsewhere or sentenced to death?

Regret settled deep inside her, and she tightened her hold on Nell. Why was it she always jumped to conclusions, assumed the worst, and reacted hotly? Why didn't she just accept what Xavier had told her? Given him a second chance the way she tried to with Art when he returned to the beorg.

But Art hadn't murdered Roger; Xavier had, a small voice in her brain whispered. *Although, had it really been Xavier... or Vox?*

She mentally countered. After all, he only did it because Vox hired them to.

It certainly seemed like everywhere Vox went, some kind of trouble followed. How could she have been so wrong to place her trust in him all along, to think he would defend them and their way of life? Had it been Calloway from the beginning she should've believed in, instead of trying to ruin him?

Maybe you should just stop believing in people, Sybil. Her mind retorted. *Why would anyone* really *want to help a Shift? It was only a matter of time before they took control. Be grateful for the freedom you had while you had it. Don't expect it again.*

The truck suddenly hit a pothole so hard and fast it sent the women careening into each other. Everyone woke in a startle, curses flying and hands groping for anything to steady themselves. Nell screamed. Joan landed hard against Sybil's hip, and she let out an exclamation at the pain.

"What happened? Where are we?" Nell whimpered.

"We're still on the road," Sybil answered. "Just hit a hole."

"Where are we going?" For the first time, Nell perked up and began looking around. It was her first time seeing anything outside of the beorg limits. Curiosity, at least for now, drowned out her fear. Her eyes were wide as they roamed the city before her.

"I'm not sure. We'll find out soon enough." Sybil was just as anxious to know where they'd end up as Nell was.

"Does anyone recognize where we are?" asked Marnie. "Anyone work here before?"

"Describe it to me," responded Mabel. "I've been a lot o' places in my lifetime."

"Well, let's see," said Laurel. "We just went through a smallish town. Lots of brick and white paint. Neat little storefronts. Sidewalks."

"That does narrow it down," Mabel said wryly. "Any peculiar signs or things on the way in that stood out to you?"

"Er... I've been asleep," Laurel said.

"A lot of us dozed off," Marnie confessed.

"Well, aren't you lot a bunch of keen observers. Someone close to the window, give it a rap and ask."

"I don't think they'll be wanting to clue us in," Molly snorted.

"One way to find out. Knock."

With a shrug, Marnie obliged. She knocked once and then twice, with no response. On the third rap, the officer looked over his shoulder with an aggravated expression. He threw his hands up as though he was asking, "What could be so important?"

Marnie gestured for him to open a window and, with animation, mouthed, "I have a question!"

He brushed her off, said a few words to the officer driving, and manually rolled down the window. "What?" He yelled over the noise of the truck.

"Where are we?" Marnie shouted back.

"About to hit Roanoke."

"Where's that?"

"Virginia. Roanoke, Virginia!"

"How much further?"

"Couple hours!" The officer rolled up the window before she could ask anything further.

Marnie twisted in her seat to face the other women again. "Roanoke, Virginia," she repeated, even though they all heard the officer.

"Does that mean anything to you, Mabel?" Laurel asked.

"I can't remember."

Exasperation flashed on Laurel's face, and she rolled her eyes. "Anyone? What's only a couple of hours from here?"

Molly piped up, "My guess is they're taking us to Richmond."

"Richmond?"

"Yeah. It's the capital of Virginia. Big city. Not far from Washington. If they're transporting us this far from the beorg, then it's probably for press. Richmond would be a good place for that," Molly reasoned.

Surely enough, that's exactly what happened. Just as Sybil thought she couldn't take it any longer—her rear long gone numb on the wood bench, her bladder screaming, her stomach cramping, her head hurting—the procession of trucks rolled into a large, historic city. Then, they began to slow.

The air grew thick, heavy with smells ranging from fuel and chimney smoke to the sweet scent of flowers in bloom. As they moved into the bowels of the city from the outskirts, people stopped what they were doing to stare. They hovered at the entrances of shops, craning their necks, whispering to each other, and pointing. If Molly was correct, the news of them being taken here had certainly been publicized. If she had been waiting for an infamous people group to show up in her hometown, she'd stare too.

Sybil was sure they looked like hell. Compared to the magi on the streets in their pastel spring dresses, shiny shoes, and linen suits, the Shifts were practically aliens. Another species entirely. She glanced around her truck again.

Their unwashed hair had been blown into tangles and knots. None of them wore their brassieres, which hadn't embarrassed her until now. Under the scrutiny of the crowds, she felt the need to hide herself. It appeared the other women felt similarly, and many of them crossed their arms and hunched their shoulders. Sybil lifted Nell higher, letting her rest her head on Sybil's shoulder, which protected her from the leering of men on the sidewalks.

Both Daisy and Joan turned and crouched in their spots to

peer through the slats of the truck until Molly snapped at them to sit straight, look ahead, and not give the crowds any attention.

"If they're gonna make a dog n' pony show out of us, you don't have to be such a willing participant," she hissed.

"There's no proof they're doin' anything like that," Laurel said evenly.

Molly scoffed, "If you were them, what would you do? Shifts are so unnatural to them I wouldn't be surprised if they put us in a damn circus."

"Okay, c'mon, ladies." Marnie held up a hand. "Let's not get worked up. We're sticking together through whatever happens next, right?"

Sybil nodded in agreement, but no one else did.

Marnie shrugged in indifference. "Pick your side soon. I think we're here."

The trucks rumbled to a stop in front of a large building made up of white-washed stone with towering pillars and innumerable steps to the entrance. At the base of the wide stone steps was an ivory-painted podium, a man standing behind it. He had a neatly trimmed red beard and sharp, dark brown eyes, creased at the corners. He looked vaguely familiar, down to the formal Thane uniform he wore, but Sybil couldn't imagine how.

Before him was an impressive crowd, a blend of reporters and citizens of Richmond. The reporters scrambled to look past one another and prop their cameras up to capture the arrival of the Shifts. Some held pens and paper pads; others, cameras; and even more, equipment she didn't recognize. She watched as mothers found their children in the mix and pulled them back into their arms or altogether left the proceedings.

Officers swarmed the trucks and instructed everyone to get down and queue up in an orderly fashion. They were efficient, merging them into rows and directing them towards the big building. In short time, the Shifts were lined up in six rows, side by side, flanked by armed guards. As much as Sybil wanted to appear unbothered and above the chaos, her curiosity won out. Her head swiveled, rotating from the crowd to the officers to the historic buildings surrounding them. They reminded her of Washington.

The officers marched them near the impressive stone building but stopped them shy of the steps and the podium. Sybil was somewhat dismayed to be on the outside of the lineup, right where the cameras could pick up everything about her. Her natural state for the world to see, from her hair to the color of her eyes to the shape of her face. She would no longer have any of it to herself. She was so disheartened by this that she imagined the Shift magic draining from her very soul.

The lights were blinding. Turning her face away, her eyes sought Art, Paul, and Dean but couldn't locate them. She spotted Xavier—always standing taller than anyone else in a crowd. He looked miserable, dejection distorting his features.

The man at the podium spoke, drawing her attention, his voice booming loud through a microphone. "Good afternoon," he said. "I am Richmond's Chief of Police Abel D. Conrad."

Conrad? Was this man related to Delilah Conrad? He had to be. That's why he looked so familiar at first glance.

Chief Conrad continued, clearly and confidently, just like Delilah. "Thank you all for joining us today. We appreciate your patience through this difficult time and complicated investigation. I am pleased to report—thanks to the quick and effective work of our local Thane forces—that we have not only identified the individuals responsible for the attempted murder of President Branson

Calloway that occurred this morning—April the twenty-second at approximately one a.m.—but we have each and every one of them in custody.

"To my right, you will see seventy-one Shifts, who have lived in the Appalachian Highlands for generations. There is overwhelming evidence that these crime-for-hires conspired together to assassinate President Calloway during a goodwill visit he made to their compound.

"We will continue to work with the District Attorney's office to ensure that these responsible parties are held accountable for their actions. Thank you all for your attention. The department will provide any relevant updates as they occur in this investigation and leading into trial."

Chief Conrad planted a hand on the podium and lifted his eyes from the press release he'd been reading, looking over his audience before slowly eyeing the line-up of Shifts.

Then he delivered the sentence: "As of this moment, you are each under arrest for conspiracy to commit murder and for the attempted homicide of President Branson Calloway of Eastward Americana."

Exclamations, questions, and demands poured forth from the press, and murmurs went up amongst the Shifts around her. It was a complete onslaught of sound, but everything felt muffled and distorted to Sybil, as if her ears were plugged. Her breathing grew rapid; her heart hammered. She'd been bracing for this for hours, but now she knew for sure.

She, and everyone she knew, would go to prison. Or to their graves.

Acknowledgments

Thank you to the team at Apprentice House Press for taking a chance on me and this story. Thank you for your diligent work and feedback. You were a pleasure to work with, and I am forever grateful for the opportunity you've given me.

Thank you to my beta readers for the time you each took to read and review *Shift* and help me make it the best it could be. Special thanks to Camber for reading it twice, catching typos and inconsistencies, and asking such good questions.

Thank you to my parents who have encouraged my love of reading and writing from the very beginning. Thank you, Mom, for instilling in me a passion for correct punctuation and grammar and for helping me proofread! Dad, thank you for making me laugh throughout this whole process, especially when I felt discouraged.

To my sister: thank you for sharing my love of reading, for four fun years reviewing books together as the Literature Ladies, and for an entire childhood of crafting stories together through play. Thank you for being one of the first readers of *Shift* and making it through that very rough first draft.

I am thankful to the three of you for your unwavering support, excitement, love, and laughter not only in this process but throughout my entire life.

Thank you to my husband. Without you, this book would not exist. Thank you for encouraging me out of my comfort zone and holding my hand all along the way. Thank you for the long walks and car trips where you listened to me brainstorm and tested my ideas with your unfailing logic and your own creativity. Thank you for reading the manuscript repeatedly. Thank you for helping me pursue this lifelong dream and for the many ways you sacrificed to make it happen. And thank you for telling everyone around you that your wife is an author. You are the best cheerleader and my greatest friend. I love you.

Thank you to my little boy for being who you are. You inspire me daily, and I am so proud of you. May you never lose your creativity, animation, and imagination. Never stop telling your stories. It is my hope that watching Mama pursue her dream will help you realize that you can always pursue yours, even when it's scary. I love you more than you can imagine.

More than anything, thank You to my Lord and Savior Jesus Christ, apart from Whom I am nothing. Everything I am and do and have is because of You and Your great mercy, grace, and faithfulness in my life. May all glory and praise be given to You now and always.

About the Author

J.P. Lee has been storytelling since childhood, writing her first story

at the age of eight in a notebook. She completed a full-length fantasy novel during her high school years. A Durham, North Carolina native, she received her degree in English Language, Writing, and Rhetoric from North Carolina State University. Lee loves immersive books into which she can escape, and that is what she desires for her readers. She resides in Tennessee with her husband, son, and two beloved cats. When not writing or reading, she enjoys cooking and taking long walks with her family. *Shift* is her debut novel.

Apprentice House is the country's only campus-based, student-staffed book publishing company. Directed by professors and industry professionals, it is a nonprofit activity of the Communication Department at Loyola University Maryland.

Using state-of-the-art technology and an experiential learning model of education, Apprentice House publishes books in untraditional ways. This dual responsibility as publishers and educators creates an unprecedented collaborative environment among faculty and students, while teaching tomorrow's editors, designers, and marketers.

Eclectic and provocative, Apprentice House titles intend to entertain as well as spark dialogue on a variety of topics. Financial contributions to sustain the press's work are welcomed. Contributions are tax deductible to the fullest extent allowed by the IRS.

To learn more about Apprentice House books or to obtain submission guidelines, please visit www.apprenticehouse.com.

Apprentice House Press
Communication Department
Loyola University Maryland
4501 N. Charles Street
Baltimore, MD 21210
Ph: 410-617-5265
info@apprenticehouse.com • www.apprenticehouse.com

www.ingramcontent.com/pod-product-compliance
Lightning Source LLC
LaVergne TN
LVHW010557100826
845148LV00014B/2744

* 9 7 8 1 6 2 7 2 0 6 5 7 0 *